SUNSET RISING

BY

S.M. MCEACHERN

Sunset Rising is thrilling; there is no better word for it. Romance, intrigue, and action all come together beautifully here to create an experience that will leave anyone asking for more.

— Molly Burkemper for <u>Readers Favorite</u>.

Apr. 21 2017
Comox BC

I am shocked this is this author's first book... I would rank this book up among some of my other favorites, such as... Suzanne Collins *The Hunger Games*... and Neal Shusterman's *Unwind*. This page turner is a must read!

As a Young Adult dystopian novel, this has got to be one of the best I've read and now I can't wait to read more. (Sunset Rising) will definitely be read time and time again.

Summary:
In a post-apocalyptic world, seventeen-year-old Sunny O'Donnell
unwittingly starts a rebellion when she marries Jack Kenner.
Young Adult (16+) Science Fiction/Dystopian

Cover Art and Design: Nathália Suellen
Edited by: Laura Koons, Red Adept Editing
Proofreader: Christina Galvez

Author's blog site: http://smmceachern.wordpress.com
Twitter: https://twitter.com/smmceachern
Goodreads: http://www.goodreads.com/book/
show/17312777-sunset-rising

ISBN 13: 9780991733033
ISBN: 0991733037
(eBook ASIN: B009G321O0)
Revised Kindle Edition September 2013

Dedicated to my husband, Michael, currently overseas serving his Country… and for all those who serve with him.

PROLOGUE

Date: February 16, 2024

Benjamin Reyes wasn't the kind of man to tell people *I told you so*, but everything he'd predicted was coming true. No one in the Valley had ever liked him. The kids made fun of him and called him "the hermit." The adults talked about him, too, but never to his face. They all thought he was crazy. So when he told the town a global nuclear war was imminent, they all laughed at him.

Their ignorance dumbfounded him. Didn't they watch the news? All they had to do was connect the dots. People were suffering the effects of climate change all over the world. In some countries, people were being killed daily by massive flooding; and in others, scores of people were dying because of drought. Countries with abundant water were reluctant to share because they feared that one day they too would face a drought. People all around the world were dying from the famine and disease brought on by the misery of human suffering. Instead of helping each other, countries all around the world strengthened their military defenses and threatened war.

News reports that one country or another was threatening to launch a nuclear attack had become commonplace. No one paid much attention to it anymore. Except Benjamin Reyes. He always paid attention. He paid attention to all the military vehicles and aircraft coming through the Valley and up into the mountain. No one else found that suspicious. Military vehicles had been coming up and down the mountain for as long as anyone could remember. Everyone knew the government had some kind of secret base up there, and no one questioned it. Why would they? The people trusted their leaders.

However, during the past week, Benjamin had noted that the vehicles were going up the mountain but weren't coming back down. So he started warning everyone in the Valley, but they just laughed at him... until they turned on their televisions and saw a tearful President Taylor giving the news that bombs were falling. She urged everyone to take cover then asked God to bless them all.

Benjamin knew where they could find cover, and people were finally listening to him.

The entire Valley population followed the path that the military vehicles had taken and walked up the mountain for hours. Mothers and fathers shared the load of carrying babies. Older children helped smaller ones. The elderly had to try to keep up on their own. No one brought any personal belongings; there was no time.

Eventually, the road ended at a hangar that appeared to have been carved out of the side of the mountain.

Military personnel were busily trying to fit helicopters and large trucks into an already cramped space. The civilians surprised them. The soldiers weren't sure what to do until they were given the order to force the civilians back. The refugees would not be granted entry.

The civilians continued to push forward, desperate to get to safety with their children. Someone shouted the order to fire on them. Reluctantly, soldiers armed themselves and sent a hail of bullets into the oncoming crowd.

Benjamin Reyes grabbed as many children as he could and hid them behind vehicles still parked on the tarmac. He shouted for the people still coming up the mountain to turn back, but they kept coming. A rumble from the sky announced the arrival of the first of the nuclear missiles. Panic spread through the crowd, and the clash between military and civilian became more desperate.

Finally, the soldiers stopped firing, and Benjamin peeked out from behind the truck and saw people being let into the hangar. He took the smallest children by the hand and bid the rest to follow him. Bodies lay where they'd fallen all along the tarmac, and he had to pick his way through them to get the children safely inside the Dome.

"Three more minutes, and those doors are shut. I don't care what the president says," a well-decorated general said to a group of soldiers.

Benjamin realized that not everyone would be saved. Thousands were still coming up the mountain. Three minutes later, he watched helplessly as the soldiers shut the doors, drowning out the screams of the people left on the tarmac. He thought he would be sick.

"I am General Edward Holt," a voice boomed over a loudspeaker. The refugees quieted, anxious to hear what the general had to say. "Nuclear bombs have begun to reach our country's major cities. You are very lucky to have found refuge here, for which you can thank President Julia Taylor. This is a bio-dome capable of supporting life for as long as we need it. Forget about your homes and whatever family you've left behind. These doors must remain sealed for at least the next thousand years."

Sobs among the crowd turned to panic as the severity of their situation dawned on the civilians. The world as they knew it was ending.

"However!" the general yelled over the cries of the people. He only continued when the room became silent and he had their attention. "Your arrival was unexpected, and we'll have to make room for you. Until we can work that out, you'll have to stay here in the hangar."

Their stay in the hangar lasted days, but they were given food, water, and bedrolls. Children found ways to entertain themselves, and the adults comforted each other. Everyone thanked Benjamin Reyes for leading them to the Dome. So when General Holt returned and asked to speak with their leader, Benjamin was unanimously elected. Reluctantly, Benjamin accepted the position and met with General Holt in private.

"I am sorry to say that President Taylor is dead," the general said. "Although I suspect you already knew that."

"The president is dead?" Benjamin asked, shocked. "I thought she was here, inside the Dome."

"She was safe inside the Dome, or at least we thought she was, until she let in a bunch of civilians. Don't try to deny that it was all of you who killed her. You're trying to take over the Dome."

The accusation hung in the air between the two men while Benjamin collected his thoughts. "General, that isn't true! No one has even left the hangar. We're under constant guard."

"I am 'President' Holt now. You may address me as 'Mr. President.'"

Benjamin was getting an uneasy feeling about this man. He knew that no one in the hangar could have harmed President Taylor. However, General Holt had an entire army behind him and plenty of opportunity to kill her. And why had the general advanced to the presidency instead of Vice President Kenner? The whole situation put him on edge.

"Now that I'm president, I simply won't tolerate your mutiny. But I'm not coldhearted enough to send you all out into a world toxic with radiation. So I've drawn up a treaty, which clearly defines how you will live inside this Dome. It's not negotiable. Take it or get out."

The president produced the document and a pen.

"May I at least read it?" Benjamin asked.

Holt nodded his consent.

The terms of the treaty designated a place called the Pit for the civilians to live in. Living quarters would be constructed immediately, and everyone would be given food and water rations. In return, they would mine the Pit for coal. The crude resource would be fed into gasifiers and turned into a liquid gas, which was needed for the replicators. It would also serve as the main source of fuel until the nuclear winter was over and solar energy could be harvested.

The last part of the treaty outlined a Cull. The treaty stated that the elderly, defined as anyone who had reached the age of fifty, were considered a drain on resources and a liability rather than an asset. Therefore an annual Cull would be held in order to maintain sustainable use of resources and control population growth.

Benjamin's eyes widened with shock as the realization of what the general was proposing sank into his numbed mind. "You can't possibly think we would agree to being killed at fifty?"

"With your arrival, there are now two hundred sixty-seven people we didn't count on living inside this Dome. When the Dome was built, great care was taken to ensure that it could sustain a growing population. Population models were based on the initial three hundred people who were approved to be here. Now we have a population of five hundred sixty-seven, and we're only in our first week. You see the problem, I'm sure."

He wondered if the rules in the Pit would apply to those living in the Dome as well as in the Pit. "So *everyone* in the Dome agrees to be Culled?"

"You needn't concern yourself with how I run the Dome. Your only concern right now is signing that treaty. If you don't, you'll all be out today."

Benjamin knew Holt wasn't joking. They were already under constant guard by his soldiers — the same soldiers who willingly opened fire on them when the general gave the command. As president, he would have even more power. But how could Benjamin sign? He tried to think of how many people he had seen who looked to be fifty or older, but all he could remember was the children. Even in the face of global doom, they were adapting to their new environment, playing the games that children play, somehow immune to the misery going on around them. It was for them that he had to sign. So he did. Benjamin himself was sixty-five. He was signing his own death warrant.

After he signed, he was told that the first Cull would take place the next day. Holt was generous enough to give him time to break the news to the people and let them say their goodbyes. They were all shown to the Pit, their new living quarters. They were marched through the massive main floor of the Dome, with its modern architecture, all open and airy with lights bright enough to mimic the sun's rays. Comfortable furniture was scattered about the large room, which was dominated by a fireplace with a simulated fire burning in it. But the room was still under construction.

"What are they building?" Benjamin asked one of the soldiers.

"A barrier to keep you urchins out," the soldier said.

"So we return to the feudal system of the bourgeoisie," Benjamin mused.

The civilians were marched past the construction, down a narrow hall, and through a door. It was as though they entered a different world, one which was dark, cold, and damp. The Pit was nothing more than the first two levels of a hollowed-out mine. There was no place to sleep, except on the cold, damp stone.

"President Holt promised us living quarters," Benjamin said.

"And you'll get them as soon as they can be replicated. So you had better get mining. The replicators can't work without coal," the soldier said, then laughed.

Benjamin covered his eyes with his hands, overwhelmed by these inhumane conditions. He shook his head, wondering what in God's name he had done to these people. Maybe it would have been kinder not to have signed the treaty. Maybe it would have been better to let them take their chances outside.

With growing dread, he realized he was one of the lucky ones. Suddenly, the Cull didn't seem so bad after all.

CHAPTER ONE

Date: May 15, 2307

R ed.
    I lived in a dark world of rock and artificial light, surrounded by dark-haired people. My red hair shone like a beacon in the Pit. And I hated it.

I picked up a lock of hair and rubbed it between my thumb and finger in a futile attempt to erase the color. Of course it didn't work. It never did. So I ran a piece of coal along the strands just like my mother taught me. It didn't completely hide the red, but it helped me blend in down there.

Even though my mother knew the red drew attention, she loved my hair so much she'd named me for it: Sunset O'Donnell. I'm not sure why she went with "Sunset" because she never saw one for real. If the sun was still rising and setting, then it was doing it outside the Dome.

I guess she must have seen a picture of a sunset in a book or maybe in one of the movies they showed in the common room. But whenever anyone asked my name, I always said it was Sunny.

Sometimes I missed my mother so much I could hardly breathe. It had been two months since she was Culled, and I still felt as if nothing in my life would ever be right again. I knew my emotions were irrational because the Cull was something we'd lived with all our lives. My ancestors signed a treaty almost three hundred years ago that condemned us to it. Not that I blamed them. It was either agree to strict population control or take their chances in a world toxic with radiation. I guess they thought that having a short life was better than not having one at all.

When they signed the treaty, they never could have envisioned how much it would change over the centuries. Under the original terms, a person living in the Pit wasn't obligated to join the Cull until the age of fifty. But as our population grew, the bourgeoisie, or "bourge," as we called them, lowered our death sentence to thirty-five. The Pit didn't just readily accept the change, but the bourge had all the power, and we had none.

The bourge reminded us daily that we were uninvited guests inside the Dome, and in order for us to remain welcome, we had to pull our weight. Ever since we first arrived in the Pit, we mined their coal, processed their sewage, cleaned the Dome, and did anything else they tasked us with. In exchange, they gave us credits, which we used to pay for our housing and basic needs. Without enough credits, we ended up homeless. And homeless people disappeared after the lights went out. The credit system was just another way the bourge ensured that every person in the Pit remained useful. Freeloaders were not tolerated.

The thought of losing my job urged me to move faster this morning. I finished running the coal through my hair and reached up to put it away. As I did, there was a dull twinge of pain in my left side. I lifted my t-shirt and examined the bruise. Although it was still a bit tender, it was healing nicely. I blamed my own stupidity for the injury. My supervisor had warned me plenty of times about being slow at my job, but I was just so sad about losing my mom. Thankfully, my supervisor knew that, so instead of firing me, she ordered a guard to give me some incentive to move faster. The cracked ribs didn't hurt nearly as much as the humiliation I felt at being beaten in front of my coworkers. My job performance was now greatly improved.

For my father's sake, I was grateful I hadn't been fired. He had almost completely stopped eating, and his already skeletal frame grew thinner every day. I encouraged him to stay strong, but my attempts were halfhearted. Painting a bright future for him was difficult when all he had to look forward to was joining the Cull next spring.

Yesterday, he lost his job because he was too weak to get out of bed. That made me the only one earning credits. I thought watching my mother leave us the morning of her Cull was the hardest thing I would ever endure. But watching my father die of grief was every bit as painful, only slower and more drawn out.

I was supposed to marry Reyes Crowe in a month from now, but I told him last night that I couldn't abandon my father. The law prevented a married couple from taking in their parents. It was just one more way the bourge identified those who had outlived their usefulness. I had assumed Reyes would be sympathetic to my dilemma, so his anger surprised me. It wasn't as if I was calling off our union. I was only postponing it so I could support my father until the next Cull. Spring was only ten months away, which didn't seem that long at all.

Peeking into the bedroom at my father, I saw he was still asleep. Since I didn't have time to take him to the common room for breakfast anyway, I decided it was best to leave him alone. I would just have to make sure he made it to supper tonight.

Leaving our apartment, I joined the throng of people heading toward the stairs. Some people descended almost two miles down into the mines, and others, like me, climbed a mile up to the Dome. I worked in the kitchen on the main floor with my best friend, Summer Nazeem. Kitchen duty was a coveted job, and we were lucky to get such good positions. And if I didn't get moving, I was going to be late. After my recent less-than-stellar performance, I didn't need to add tardiness to the list.

I walked to where Summer and I always met to go to work together but was surprised not to find her there. I took a step backward, preparing to wait for her, and accidently tromped on someone's foot.

"*Get off!*" the woman yelled, and pushed me into the stone wall.

"Sorry," I mumbled and peered into the crowd.

Someone said, "Sunny, what are you doing?"

I turned in the direction of the voice and saw Bron.

"You're going to be late," she said.

Bron was one of the guards in our sector. All the guards in the Pit wore white uniforms so they stood out in the darkness. Their stark presence was a constant reminder that our every move was being watched. Some guards were meaner than others. Bron was one of the good ones. She and my mother had been pretty good friends. Well, as good friends as two people could be when one was a bourge from the Dome and the other an urchin from the Pit.

"Have you seen Summer?" I asked.

Bron shook her head. She shifted her rifle onto her other shoulder and placed a comforting hand on my back. "Most likely on her way to work, which is exactly what you should be doing."

I saw the concern on her face. She was trying to speak with my mother's voice, and it wasn't that I didn't appreciate it, but so much had changed over the past two months and Summer had been my only source of strength. I didn't want to go to work without her. I didn't want anything else in my life to change.

I moved further along, away from Bron, and flattened myself against the cold stone wall to let people pass. When I went to school, my history teacher taught me that life in the Pit hadn't always been so crowded. Our ancestors only numbered around two hundred when they took up residence in the Pit, and almost three hundred years later our population was around five thousand. In the past, we accommodated our growing numbers by constantly mining farther down into the earth. Now, at almost three miles deep, the mine could stand no more, or so the bourge engineers told us. We were on the verge of collapse. A few of the mines had already closed, resulting in miners getting fired. And the ones who continued to work in the mines were scared.

As people brushed past me in the crowded hall, I caught snippets of excited chatter about the upcoming royal wedding. In two days the president's daughter, Leisel Holt, would marry Jack Kenner. The wedding was going to be televised, and rumour had it that a big table of food would be set up by each television in the common rooms. And from what I overheard, people were already making plans to stake out a good spot.

Maybe Summer and I would try to get a good spot too. If there really was going to be a feast, the food would go fast. I just hated the thought of having to sit through the wedding. All presidential events began with President Holt giving a speech, reminding us of all we had to be thankful for. He'd remind everyone in the Pit how generous the bourge were when they gave us shelter from the bombs, maybe even flash some pictures of our ancestors signing the treaty, and then give a quick rundown of how we have all thrived living in the safety of the Dome. But like most people living in the Pit, I couldn't care less about the wedding or about giving thanks. I was only interested in the food.

"Sunny!" Summer called.

I turned to look for her. "Summer! I'm by the stairs!"

"I know." Suddenly, she was right beside me. "I couldn't believe it when I saw you standing here. Why didn't you go ahead without me?"

"We always go to work together. Where were you? We'll be lucky if we're not late."

"Oh, we're going to be late. We'll be lucky if we don't get *caught*."

"We'll get caught when we scan in." I thought hard for a solution but only came up with a weak one. "Unless we take our alternate route." We hadn't used the old mine shaft in months, because the last time we did we got in trouble for showing up to work dirty. But it only cost us half a day's credits, and we didn't even get a beating.

Summer thought about it for a second and then nodded. She knew as well as I did that losing a few credits was better than losing our jobs. We ducked around the stairs and headed for the end of the hallway, which meant we were moving against traffic instead of with it. That slowed us down, but once we reached the shaft, it would be a lot faster. I mumbled apologies as I squeezed past people and endured their rude looks and even ruder comments.

"Have you come looking for me to break my heart some more?" Reyes whispered in my ear. From behind me, his arms slid around my waist, and I turned within the circle of his embrace to face him. Even though I was taller than most girls, I still needed to tilt my head back to meet his gaze.

"You two really do make a nice couple," Summer said.

"She's right." Reyes said, ignoring my attempts to loosen his grip. He wound his finger around a lock of hair that had escaped my ponytail. "So when are you going to marry me, Sunset?"

"Can we talk about this some other time?" I hated it when he used my full name, and he knew it. He was saying it deliberately to provoke an argument.

"We talked about it last night. I was hoping you'd have changed your mind this morning. I told you I don't want to wait ten more months."

"And I was hoping you would understand my situation, but you don't. We need to talk about this later, Reyes. Summer and I are late." I tried again to squirm out of his embrace.

"Don't put me off, Sunny. I barely got any sleep last night."

"I'm really late, Reyes." Panic rose in my voice.

I tried to pry his arms off me, but he spun me around and lifted me up off the floor. As our eyes became level, he kissed me roughly on the lips.

"Tonight we talk again. Promise me."

"I promise." Although I knew I wouldn't change my mind.

He kissed me again and then passed me along to his friend, Raine, who was standing next to him. Raine passed me to Mica, and Mica passed me to the next boy. They all knew we were headed to the old mineshaft. Lots of people took the shaft as a shortcut when they were desperate to get to work on time. I looked back and saw Summer being passed along behind me. In no time, we were deposited in front of the door to the shaft.

"Thank you!" I called to Reyes, but I wasn't sure he heard me. He was probably already descending the stairs to go work in the mines.

I opened the door, and we slipped inside. The shaft was almost pitch black, but my eyes quickly adjusted. We had come that way so many times before that our hands and feet had memories of their own anyway. The climb up to the main level was one mile, and without thousands of people crowding our way, taking the shaft was faster than the stairs.

"So you haven't told me why you're late," I said.

"I stopped to talk to Adam." Summer was breathing hard with the exertion of the climb, and it took her a minute to continue. "I think he might ask me to marry him."

"Are you kidding me?" I wasn't sure whether to laugh or yell at her. "We're late because you were flirting? I mean, do you even like him? You just met him a week ago."

"What does that have to do with anything? It's fine for you, Sunny. You already have Reyes, but when my parents are Culled next year, I'll have no one. I need to find a partner, and most boys our age are already married."

She was right. Partnerships in the Pit were every bit as important as having a job. A single person wasn't eligible to be assigned an apartment because that was considered a waste of space. The need for housing was the driving force behind most marriages in the Pit. Although, in my case, it was the reason I couldn't leave my father.

"Oh, Summer. If you weren't so picky, you could have been married by now. But whenever a boy is interested in you, you're suddenly not interested in him. I think you like flirting more than actually having a boyfriend."

"That's not true. I just haven't met the right one yet."

"Though you do bring up a good point. You're running out of time."

Summer could have had her pick of any boy in the Pit. A full head shorter than me, her small stature and delicate limbs gave her an elegant, feminine quality. I always felt large and clumsy next to her.

"You know, we're always talking about me," Summer said. "How are you? How's your dad?"

She might regret asking that question, but I gave her an honest answer. "Dad lost his job yesterday because he didn't show up for work."

"Oh, Sunny. What are you going to do?"

I heard sympathy in her voice, and exasperation, too. My father had always been a little self-destructive. My mother had done a fairly good job of protecting me from it, but without her, I was on my own with him. "I told Reyes last night I couldn't marry him until after the next Cull."

"You're postponing? Again?" she asked. "That's a bit drastic. I'm sure your father can get another job. He's had a lot of experience in the mines."

"He's barely been eating since Mom left, and now he's too weak to get out of bed."

"But you've put your marriage on hold once before, and I can't imagine Reyes is happy with postponing again. And you're not getting any younger, Sunny. You're almost eighteen. Aren't you afraid Reyes is going to get fed up with waiting and move on to someone else?"

I had never thought about Reyes being with someone else. We had been together forever. And at our age, it was getting kind of late to go looking for a new partner. Of course he would wait for me. If I gave him enough time, he would eventually understand that my father needed me right now, and I couldn't leave him.

But there was wisdom in her words. At seventeen, I was middle-aged, and that didn't bode well for getting approval to have a child. Population control in the Pit was getting stricter all the time. Reyes really wanted a child, but if I was being honest with myself, I didn't. I guessed that was why I didn't feel an urgent need to get married right away.

I finally reached the top of the shaft and crawled onto the platform.

"We *will* finish this conversation, Sunny. You have to talk about it," Summer said as she scrambled up behind me.

I slowly opened the door to make sure there weren't any guards in the hall to catch us. The light on the main floor was so bright that I had to struggle to keep my eyes open until they adjusted. When I was able, I focused in on the clock.

"We're two minutes late."

Summer gave an exasperated sigh. "And after all that climbing."

"Let's see if the back door is unlocked and sneak in."

"We still have to scan in. They'll know we're late."

"Yes, but *forgetting* to scan in won't get us fired. We'll probably just have to go without lunch or something."

Summer moaned and gripped her stomach. We had both missed breakfast.

When we were sure no one was around, we stepped out of the shaft and quietly made our way down the hall until we reached the back entrance to the kitchen. I breathed a sigh of relief when I turned the knob, and the door opened. All kitchen staff had to wear clean uniforms, so we took off running toward the changing room. I pulled up short at the sight of our supervisor, and Summer slammed into my back.

"So you thought you could put one over on me?" Bailey asked.

"No, ma'am. Traffic in the stairwell was heavier than usual, and it made us late. We were running to make up for lost time," Summer said.

Bailey snorted. "It makes no difference why you're late. I should fire you, O'Donnell. You've been nothing but trouble lately."

Maybe it was just from the long climb, but my limbs suddenly felt weak and shaky. She couldn't possibly fire us after we'd tried so hard to make it here on time. Summer caught her breath, and I knew she was trying to hold back tears. Then I realized that my own eyes had started to sting.

"I can offer you an alternative to being fired," Bailey said with a sly glint in her eyes. "The president is hosting the bachelor party tonight, and they've requested servers to entertain the gentlemen guests."

Her meaning was clear. Prostitute ourselves, and we could keep our jobs. That kind of request wasn't unusual in the Pit. The supervisors who sent the prettiest girls were usually rewarded. She had been in the changing room, waiting for us. The fact that we were late only gave her the leverage she needed to force us into accepting.

"No," Summer said resolutely.

"I'll do it," I said.

"Sunny, no." Summer grabbed my shoulders and turned me to face her. "*No!*"

"I don't think I have choice," I said in a low voice, hoping that Bailey couldn't hear me.

Summer stood up taller and squared her shoulders. "I'll do it, too."

"Summer, you don't have to do this. If you're fired, it's okay. Your parents are still earning credits."

"I'm not going to let you do this alone."

Bailey cut in. "I don't know why you're arguing. Being asked to serve at a presidential party is a great honor. I'd do it myself if I was allowed." She walked toward us and waved her scanner over our hands. "There. You're both signed up. Be there or you'll be punished."

She started to walk away but stopped before she left the room. "This is the second time you've both shown up for work filthy. You're really starting to make me look bad. No lunch today and you both lose half a day's credit. Now get to work."

CHAPTER TWO

A t the end of the day, I stripped off my kitchen uniform, taking great care not to tear or damage it because I would have to pay for any repairs. I placed it in the big hamper. The laundry staff would clean and fold it, and have it waiting for me in the morning.

I tried to ignore the cramps in my stomach, but they were terrible after a full day of work without food. I wished I had time to eat supper before the party, but Bailey told us we needed a bath more than food.

Summer moaned beside me. "I'm so hungry."

"Me, too."

"I heard that if you're a good *server*, they give you a plateful of food." Summer's voice dripped with sarcasm.

My mouth watered at the mere mention of food. It had taken every bit of my will power not to eat the carrots I peeled at work. But if I had been caught eating even the peelings, I would have been beaten. Vegetable scraps were meant for the compost, which was far more important than a hungry urchin. In the Pit, our food was whatever was left over after the bourge and livestock had eaten their fill.

"Maybe they'll even give us dessert," I said. I had never had dessert, but I'd heard it was heavenly.

Summer licked her lips dreamily. "Mmmmm... I can only imagine how it will taste." She sobered after a moment. "Come on. We better hurry up in case there's a line at the bath. We don't have a lot of time."

I laughed at the thought of a line at the bath. No self-respecting urchin went to the communal baths unless ordered. Next to oxygen, water was the most important resource in the entire Dome, and, like the food, we only got the leftovers. The bulk of the water supply went to the bourge and the agricultural sector. The Pit received the least, and what we did get was rationed for both drinking and bathing. We wouldn't waste it on bathing at all if the bourge hadn't made weekly bathing mandatory in order to prevent disease.

The traffic on the stairs was always faster going down than climbing up, so Summer and I made good time getting back to the sixth level. We parted ways to go to our respective homes and collect our towels and soap. My father hadn't moved much since I left him this morning, but, at my arrival, he turned over to look at me.

"How was work?" he asked, but his expression was vacant.

"Still there." I sat on the side of his bed and placed my hand on his back. He felt frightfully thin. "I got a job tonight, too, so I won't be home until later."

"What kind of job?"

"Just some extra kitchen duties." He didn't need to know what I would be doing. I couldn't bear the thought of adding to his pain.

"Probably to do with that wedding."

"Probably. Since I have to get back upstairs, I can't take you to get dinner tonight. You'll have to go by yourself."

"That's okay, dear. I'm not hungry." He rolled over, turning his back to me.

I sighed. "Dad, promise me you'll get up and eat."

"Okay, Sunny. I promise I will."

I was almost certain he wasn't going to get out of bed, but there was nothing I could do about it. If only Mom were here. I kissed his cheek and left him to get a bar of soap, a piece of coal, and the one towel assigned to me. I made my way to the bathroom and, as I suspected would be the case, there was no line. Summer was already waiting for me.

"I'll wet my towel," I said.

The trick to taking a bath in the Pit was never to set foot in the bathtub. The cold stone tub was fairly large and deep, so if the water was allowed to sit undisturbed, the dirt and sediment fell to the bottom. By bathing in pairs, we could soak one person's towel to use as a washcloth and then dry off with the other. But a completely soaked towel down here in the Pit took forever to dry.

"No, let me," Summer said. "It's my fault we were late this morning. I got us into this mess."

"You didn't have to say yes to tonight, Summer. I wish you hadn't."

I stripped and let her clean my back. The water was freezing, and I shivered.

"And you didn't have to wait for me this morning. Best friends do things for each other."

I snorted. Going with me tonight went well beyond friendship. "You know what you signed up for, right?"

"I know," she snapped.

Her anger took me aback but made me realize that she was feeling every bit as apprehensive about tonight as I was.

"I know," she said again, a little more calmly. "But we don't have to make it all about *that*. I mean, it's just sex, right? How bad can it be? We've never seen inside the main part of the Dome, and they might share the food. I *hope* they share the food!" She handed me the soaked towel so I could sponge the rest of my body clean.

Summer could always see the silver lining in every situation, a talent I wished I could learn. But I couldn't even squelch the anxiety that was growing inside me. I had never had sex. I always thought my first time would be with Reyes after we were married, although

I hadn't spent much time thinking about it. Now I was terrified.

I finished bathing and handed her the wet towel. Picking up the dry one, I wrapped it around me. I used my piece of coal to touch up my hair. "One of the things I love most about you is that you can take a bad situation and see the good in it." I took the wet towel out of her hand and started washing her back. "But I worry that your love of life is going to get you into trouble."

"Which brings us back to our conversation this morning. Reyes."

"No it doesn't!" Although her back was to me, I drew my brows together and made a face. "I'm not sure how that brings us back to Reyes, but for the record, I don't want to talk about it."

"Why? I need to understand why you keep putting him off."

"My dad is useless on his own, and I miss my mother horribly." Tears stung my eyes. I didn't want to cry. Crying was such a weak thing to do. "Things are changing so fast, and I don't want them to. I need to be me for a little longer. You know, before I become Reyes's wife. Before I become someone's mother."

I wasn't sure where the words were coming from, but it felt like a weight lifted off my shoulders. When my tears began to spill, there was no way I could stop them. I handed her the towel and busied myself getting dressed. Summer wrapped the towel around her and turned to look at me. Her expression was sad.

"You should never have postponed your marriage in the first place. I really think your mom wanted you out on your own before she went."

I was pretty sure my mom wanted me married off before she left too, but how could I abandon my own father? Maybe he hadn't been the best dad in the Pit, but he was *my* dad.

Summer put her hand on my shoulder, but I shrugged it away. I regretted that immediately. She was my best friend. We met on the very first day of school and had been inseparable ever since. No matter what happened in my life, she was my support.

"I don't mean to upset you, but you need to accept that things will never be the same again," she said. "Reyes loves you, and that's the greatest gift any of us can ever hope to get."

I wanted to tell her that she was right as usual, but I couldn't speak past the lump in my throat. I nodded. I was a fool to keep Reyes waiting and yet powerless to leave my father.

Suddenly Reyes yelled my name from the other side of the locked bathroom door. By the sound of his voice, he knew I was being sent upstairs. I quickly dried my eyes.

Summer dressed hurriedly. "Meet me by the stairs, and don't be late." She picked up our towels and opened the door to leave.

Reyes bolted through the door and almost threw Summer out of his way to get to me. "Is it true?!"

"Is what true?" I hoped to downplay the importance of my serving that night. I could see by the wild look in his eyes that he was ready to explode.

"Are you serving at that bachelor party tonight?" He grabbed me by the shoulders.

"Yeah, but it's no big deal." I couldn't even look him in the eyes.

"You can't. You have to back out."

Now I did look him in the eyes. "We both know I can't do that." I would be beaten, quite possibly to death, if I didn't report to work for such an important event.

"How did this happen? How did you get picked?"

"We were late, Reyes. Bailey was going to fire me if I didn't agree. Dad has already lost his job. I can't lose mine too."

"You should have let her fire you and come to me. We could have gotten married and been assigned our own apartment. You know that!" He was losing his composure. I had never seen him this upset before.

"Reyes, I can't just leave him," I said softly. I laid my head against his chest.

He shifted his arms to encircle my waist and pulled me tightly against him. "Sunset. Do you know why your mother named you that?"

"Because of the color of my hair."

"Did you ever wonder how she knew what a sunset looked like?" he asked as he pulled away from me and tilted my chin up to look at him. "I know you don't want to hear this, but your mother was sent upstairs when she was young, too. If the stories are true, she was requested for dinner parties a lot."

The empathy I'd had for Reyes suddenly turned to anger. I pushed against him, trying to break out of the circle of his arms. "Who told you these lies?"

"Maybe I shouldn't have told you."

"No, you shouldn't have! Why do you always have to find some way to hurt me when you're mad?" I pounded my fist on his chest. Finally, he released me. "I can't be late," I said with disdain and headed toward the door.

"Wait!" Reyes stepped in front of me to block my exit. "I'm sorry."

He reached out to take me back into his arms. I pulled away from him for a moment but relented even though I was still angry. I didn't want to face what was waiting for me upstairs knowing we were in a fight. It would be better to put things right between us before I went.

"If anything happens…" He paused, a grimace of pain crossing his features. "I want to protect you. I'll always be here for you. I'm not going anywhere."

I understood what he was trying to say. Regardless of how the bourge used me tonight, he still wanted to marry me. Requests for young girls to entertain the bourge weren't unusual in the Pit, but marriage prospects were frequently poor for those girls who went.

He studied me for a moment, and I smiled, hoping to convince him that everything would be okay. I brushed a dark curl away from his brow, and he pulled me toward him roughly. He lowered his head to mine and captured my lips with his own. His arms wrapped tighter around me. I had never felt this kind of desperation in his kiss before. Slowly, he pulled away from me and cupped my face in his hands.

"You can't be late," he said sadly.

"I'll see you tomorrow." I spoke it like a promise.

I couldn't stand to see the pain in his eyes, and my own tears threatened again. I left him and caught up with Summer by the stairs.

"Are you okay?" she asked.

I didn't respond. I needed a moment to compose myself.

"I'm sorry," she said. "This really is all my fault for making us late this morning."

"We have to stop blaming ourselves, Summer. We didn't ask to be playthings for the bourge. It was forced on us. We had no choice."

"Don't talk like that, they'll hear you," she whispered. We all knew the stone walls had ears, and my ranting was only going to get us into more trouble.

My limbs felt like dead weights as I made my way up the stairs. I shouldn't complain about the climb. The people who lived the furthest down the Pit had a two-mile climb up. Then there were the miners who had to descend three miles down into the mine every day and then back up again. One mile wasn't much, but I hadn't eaten all day, and it felt like a lot.

Finally, we reached the main level and stepped into the lobby. Usually we would make a right turn toward the kitchen to go to work, but tonight we walked straight to the reception area in front of the big steel doors that led inside the Dome. My mother took this same walk when she was Culled. I tried not to think about how she must have felt, but it was impossible not to. I was petrified to go through those doors myself.

But before we could pass through those imposing doors, we had to get through reception. There were a lot of guards, most of them wearing the white uniform of the Pit and some the khaki uniform of the Dome. While the guards in the Pit stood out in white, the bourge preferred their guards to look less conspicuous. We called them Domers.

"Scan in," a guard dressed in white directed me as we approached reception.

I turned the back of my hand above the scanner, and it beeped. Summer had been sent to a different scanner, and I waited for her.

"Move on," the guard instructed me. I started to tell that him I was waiting for Summer, but he cut me off. "Move on."

Since I had no choice, I joined the queue and walked through one of the large steel doors. Of the two doors, only one had been opened, so we had to file through in pairs. No one was really talking, and I kept to myself as well. I was unprepared for the sight of the Dome when I passed through those doors, and I gasped.

"Let me guess. It's your first time here," the girl beside me said. She looked younger than me.

"I've never seen anything like it."

"Well if they *really* like you, you'll get to see it *all* the time."

"You've been here before."

"Too many times," she said glumly. "But I guess it's not so bad. The food is good. If he decides to share it."

"Oh." I wasn't sure what to say to her. Suddenly I had the urge to turn and run.

Summer came to stand beside me. "Isn't it beautiful?"

"Another newbie," the girl said with feigned surprise and walked away.

"What's her problem?" Summer asked.

I thought about telling her but decided it was best if I didn't. "Nothing. Just promise me that you won't be your usual happy self tonight. Try not to smile too much. Okay?" I didn't want anyone upstairs to *really* like Summer, but she was so pretty that I didn't know how she would avoid it.

"I promise. I'll be miserable."

As we stood waiting with the others, we took in all the colors of the Dome. It was almost impossible to believe that this beauty existed right above our dark world of rock, concrete, and steel. All the walls were smooth and painted in shades of yellow. Colorful framed pictures hung on the walls, so much richer in detail than the charcoal sketches and carvings we made in the Pit. Even the floor came alive with richly patterned rugs resting under overstuffed sofas and chairs.

"Line up!" a matronly looking woman shouted.

Summer and I took our place in line, but this time I clasped Summer's hand firmly in mine so we wouldn't get separated again.

"Is that a real plant?" she whispered.

I looked in the direction she was staring and saw a large green thing sitting in some kind of pot.

"I think it is!" I could hear the excitement in my own voice. I'd never seen a live plant before, just fruits and vegetables in the kitchen.

"There will be no talking!" the woman said, glaring at Summer and me. We quickly fell silent. "I'm your supervisor for the evening. Do everything I say, go everywhere I tell you, and we'll get along just fine. Follow me."

She led us across the big reception room to another set of doors that were much smaller than the main doors behind us. We filed through in a single line and walked down a short narrow hall that ended in another doorway. The doors were made of frosted glass and "Gym" was written across them. The room was smaller than the last one and full of weird equipment.

"For all you newbies, this is the gym. It's where people come to stay in good physical condition," our supervisor said.

Summer gave me a questioning look, but I didn't know how they used the equipment to stay in good physical condition either. We continued through another set of doors, and the air was suddenly very humid. We stepped inside, and I saw the biggest pool of water I had ever seen in my life.

"Wow!" Summer exclaimed, a little too loudly. "What is it?"

"Who said that?" our supervisor demanded.

Everyone pointed at Summer.

She gave Summer a look of disgust. "It's a swimming pool, you dumb girl. Although I shouldn't be surprised that an urchin wouldn't know that. Unfortunately, it's the only area large enough to bathe all of you. We can't have you serving at a presidential dinner as filthy as you are. But, not to worry, when you're done, the pool will be drained and fresh water added."

I thought of our own dirty stone tubs in the Pit and wondered where they found enough water to fill such an enormous pool. I looked over at Summer to see if she was just as shocked as I was, but she had her hand in the air trying to get the supervisor's attention. I made a grab for her arm to pull it down, but it was too late.

"Yes?" our supervisor asked in an exasperated voice.

"We had a bath before we came," Summer said, proudly pointing at the two of us. I wanted to hide my face in my hands.

"Really." She looked us up and down, not convinced. "If you don't get into that pool yourself, I'll assign someone to strip you and scrub that dirt off your filthy body. Am I clear?"

"Yes, ma'am," Summer said quickly.

I didn't want to strip in front of the other girls and the supervisor. My mother taught me to bind my breasts with tightly tied fabric, and I wore baggy clothes to hide them. She never wanted me chosen for this kind of work, and, as much as she loved the color of my hair, she was the one who taught me to use the coal to cover it up.

I stripped reluctantly, ignoring the glances from the other girls, and eased myself into the pool. I was relieved that the water was chest high and my ponytail only grazed the surface—the bath shouldn't disturb the coal in my hair. I relaxed a bit and enjoyed the warmth of the water. I wondered how this enormous pool stayed so warm.

Our supervisor gave us a bar of soap and a nailbrush to pass around and then shampoo. My heart sank. I wasn't afraid of anyone seeing my true hair color, but it would draw attention to me, and, tonight of all nights, I wanted to blend in. Figuring the guard's threat about getting someone to scrub me if I didn't scrub myself applied to hair as well, I decided it was best just to get on with it. I pulled the elastic out of my ponytail and slipped it around my wrist. I wet my hair and began to work in the shampoo.

"Sunny," Summer whispered. "The suds are black. The coal is washing out."

Black suds were dripping into the pool, darkening the water all around me. I pulled a few strands of my long hair down in front of my face and studied the bright red shining through the suds. Then I realized that most of the girls were staring at me. Our supervisor tutted. My face burned, and I sank down under the water to rinse the shampoo out of my hair. As I resurfaced, we were ordered out of the pool.

We were each given a crisp white uniform to put on, and I sighed. How could we keep these clean while serving food? What if someone bumped us, or spilled something on us? Would we be getting any extra credits for tonight's work so we could cover the cost of the uniforms if we had to? I was already strapped for credits since I was docked half a day today.

"Well, my, my," the supervisor said, stopping to look me up and down. I didn't like her expression. She took a lock of my hair between her fingers and thumb and rubbed it, almost as if she were testing to see if the color would come away. She smiled. "You are going to be very popular."

I wondered what she meant by that then realized I probably didn't want to know.

CHAPTER THREE

I n silence, I donned the crisp white uniform and tried to gather my hair into a tight bun, but a few wisps always escaped the elastic. Frustrated, I took a deep breath and smoothed my palms over each side of my head, willing the errant strands into place.

Summer gave me a sympathetic look. "She's just trying to scare you."

Maybe Summer was right. After all, people in the Pit noticed my hair because it was a spot of color in an otherwise monochrome world. But up here in the Dome, the bourge were used to seeing a lot of colors. The walls, the floors, the furniture, the plants — everywhere I looked color shone out. My hair would blend in.

Our supervisor told us to line up for the elevator. She explained that the kitchen was six floors up, which was too far for us to walk. Since I walked a mile of stairs to work every day, six floors didn't sound like a very long climb at all, but I was happy to take the elevator. I had never been in one before.

When our turn came, Summer grabbed my arm as the doors closed. The elevator began its ascent, and a rolling sensation gripped my stomach. For a moment, I thought I might be sick. Then the elevator came to a stop, and the doors opened again. I'm not sure I enjoyed the ride. Summer looked a little green, too.

The kitchen was a short walk from the elevator, and we were shown through the servants' entrance. This kitchen was different from the one Summer and I worked in on the main floor. There was polished steel everywhere, huge refrigerators, and twice as many stoves as in our kitchen. The floors gleamed white despite the many people rushing around preparing food.

"Go over there," said a busy cook, pointing to where a group of girls dressed exactly as we were stood waiting patiently.

We joined the queue and waited for the rest of our group. Once we were all present and accounted for, our supervisor marched us into the dining room. It was positively breathtaking. Real wood floors shone with a glossy polish. Round tables scattered about the dimly lit room were draped in heavy white tablecloths and adorned with crystal glasses and silver cutlery. What looked like actual candles stood in the centre of the tables—but I was sure they couldn't be real because the law prohibited open flames inside the Dome. Any open flame would be too much of a fire hazard. But the flickering glow from the candles was still real enough to make sparkles of light dance on the crystal and silver.

A camera crew was set up to broadcast the president's arrival. Some of the dinner guests were already seated at the tables while others still shuffled in. Our supervisor told us to stand along the back wall with our backs straight and our arms at our sides. The president would be the last to enter the room, and we, along with the rest of the guests, would have to salute him.

It took forever, but finally everyone was seated. The national anthem began to play, heralding the president's arrival. The sound of chairs scraping across the floor filled the room as everyone stood to attention for the arrival of President Damien Holt.

The whole thing was all so pompous, yet I was excited by the thought of seeing him for real. I glanced over at Summer, and I could tell she was excited too.

The front of the room was hard to see with so many people in the way, but I was tall and standing on my tiptoes gave me a partial view. I saw the president enter and was struck by how short he was. The patches of grey at his temples stood out in stark contrast to his otherwise dark hair. He took his position at the head table and waited for the music to end. When it did, everyone in the room snapped their right arm straight up in a salute then quickly placed it over their heart—a gesture meant to show support and demonstrate obedience. The room was silent until the president cleared his throat.

"We are here tonight to toast this young man, Jack Kenner." Damien Holt patted the back of the man standing beside him. I recognized the bridegroom from the interviews I had seen on the television in our common room. It was hard to tell from this distance if he was as handsome in person.

"In two days he will be joined with my most prized possession—my daughter, Leisel. This will mark the first time in the history of the Dome that the Holt and Kenner families will be united by marriage. And one day, Jack, you will occupy the Presidential Office with my daughter at your side. Together you will lead our people into the next century."

The crowd clapped, and a cheer went up.

"I won't lie to you, Jack. It won't be an easy task for you and my daughter. These are turbulent times. It has been almost three hundred years since the enemy dropped nuclear bombs across our lands. Almost three hundred years since our people were forced into the bio-dome to seek refuge from the fallout of those bombs. And almost three hundred years later, here we all stand." He paused to look around the room, giving an air of drama to his words. "A testament to our strength and power. Despite our enemy's best efforts to annihilate us, we continue to survive!"

All the guests were clapping again, shouting
"President Damien Holt" at the top of their lungs. The
bridegroom was no exception. They all seemed a little
crazy. Then the president raised his hand, and the crowd
immediately fell silent again.

"I know there have been rumours, my friends.
Rumours that our food is running out and that it's
time we moved out of the Dome and back onto our
lands." He paused again, this time pointedly looking
at some individuals in the room. A few men shifted
uncomfortably. "Who here thinks that I would let my
people starve? Who here thinks that I do not know
whether our land is arable yet?" Another uncomfortable
pause as he waited for anyone fool enough to answer
him. No one did. "I have always been honest with you.
And I have always been open about the samples the
drones bring back to us, and they are still *radioactive!*
Going out there is not an option!"

The president was yelling so loud that it hurt my
ears. The bridegroom continued to stand beside his
future father-in-law, vigorously nodding his head in
agreement. Holt straightened his tie and then smoothed
back his hair in what looked like an attempt to regain his
composure. He took a few deep breaths.

"These vicious rumours are causing unnecessary
apprehension, and they must cease before hysteria
results. Already there has been unrest in the Pit because

these falsehoods are leading our friends down there to believe they are being treated unfairly!" The president drew his lips into a tight line and balled his hands into fists. "Did we not open our doors to all those civilians who came to us seeking shelter from the bombs?"

The crowd nodded their heads and a few yelled, "*Yes!*"

"And do we not continue to provide shelter, despite their growing population and despite their growing demands on our food and water supplies? The Dome is capable of providing enough for everyone if we continue to live sustainably. So I say to our neighbours in the Pit that we must *all* do our part to maintain harmony and balance within the confines of our refuge!" As he spoke, his voice became steadily louder until he was yelling again. The guests shouted their agreement, giving the president their full support. He held up his hand to silence them once more.

"We can continue to grow strong, but it is up to each and every one of us to make that happen. And the marriage of my daughter to this man, Jack Kenner" — he patted the bridegroom on the back — "demonstrates that our life here can be every bit as good and beautiful as human existence was before the bombs. I can't think of anything more inspiring than to see two young people in love joined in holy matrimony with all the possibilities the future holds before them. They are the embodiment of hope. And it is with these sentiments that I invite all of my people to take a day off from work and celebrate

Leisel's day. I have authorized the wedding to be televised. And for all those who think we are on the brink of starvation, I give a feast. It will be a day of celebration! A day to rejoice in all that we have to be thankful for!"

He reached for Jack Kenner's hand and held it high in the air. The guests were going crazy. Shouts of "Long live President Holt!" went up. I heard a few people giving their praises and congratulations to the groom. I could only imagine the reaction in the Pit now that the rumour of a feast was confirmed.

It seemed like an eternity before the two men finished patting each other on the back and the president took his seat. Everyone else followed suit. The camera crew packed up and left. Our supervisor ushered us back to the kitchen and ordered us to start taking the food out to the guests.

The girl in front of us turned to look at Summer and me. "Since you're new, I'll help you out." She was the same girl I'd spoken with downstairs. "You'll be assigned a number when they give you a tray. Go out through those doors and find the table with your number on it. When you serve, you put the plates down *gently* between the cutlery in front of the person at the table. Usually you serve ladies first, but this is a bachelor party for the groom so there are no ladies here tonight. When everyone at the table is finished eating, clear the plates away. Then you can serve the next course."

"Thank you," I said. I had no idea it would be so complicated. "I'm Sunny, and this is Summer."

"I'm Wynd," she said, and gave us a halfhearted smile.

We were each given a tray holding four plates. We had to balance the tray on one hand so the other was free to set plates down. I was afraid I would drop it, but when I focused on just putting one foot in front of the other, I made it to the dining room with no trouble. I'd been assigned table nine. I searched out that table and headed toward it.

There were twelve men sitting there, all oblivious to my arrival. I set the plates down at each place setting just as Wynd had told me. No one complained, so I assumed I was doing it right. I expected them to start eating right away. I would. The food looked and smelled delicious. But they just continued talking among themselves, ignoring both the food and their server. My tray empty, I made my way back to the kitchen for more. My tray was refilled with four more plates, and I returned to table nine. Still no one had eaten. How could they ignore all that food? It was taking every bit of my will power not to eat it myself. I delivered the plates and went back for more. When I'd served all the plates, the men finally began to eat. I joined the other servers standing at the back of the room as we waited for our tables to finish.

While I was waiting, Wynd told Summer and me that the bourge ate their meals in courses. Tonight the first course was salad, the second soup, the third a plate of meat and vegetables, and the fourth—and final— dessert. It was going to be a very long night.

With each course I served, it became harder and harder to ignore the smells wafting up from the food. I was practically drooling. I was certain that the sound of my stomach growling was loud enough to be heard over the din of conversation and music. But on and on they ate. I delivered a full plate and took it away only half empty. Finally I served the last course—dessert. It looked scrumptious.

"Listen up girls!" our supervisor called out. "After you finish cleaning off your assigned table, wait by those doors for further instructions." She pointed to the doors we'd come in through earlier. "Once you've been given something more appropriate to wear for the evening, you'll be brought back to the dining room. Under no circumstances should you approach any of the men. If someone wants your company, he'll let you know."

Nausea rose up inside me. I'd been hoping this part of the evening would never arrive. Summer looked worried too, although she tried to hide it when she caught me looking at her. Glumly we picked up our trays and went back into the dining room to clear tables. This time I kept a close eye on Summer. I didn't want us separated again, so I matched my speed to hers. When we were finished clearing, I walked just fast enough to get behind her.

Summer walked through the doors, stopping to place her tray on the racks provided for dirty dishes. The small alcove leading to the kitchen gave us a precious moment of privacy.

"Don't leave my side tonight, Summer."

She turned to look at me. "I'll try, Sunny. But I'm scared."

"So am I."

She stepped aside to allow me to set my tray down, and as I did she plucked a tidbit of leftover dessert from one of the plates.

"Summer, what are you doing?" Stealing food was never tolerated. She knew that. I almost dropped my tray onto the rack.

She opened her mouth to say something, but a muffled noise signalled that we were not alone. A jolt of panic went through me. Without thinking, I snatched the food out of Summer's hand and popped it into my mouth.

"Hungry?" a woman asked from the shadows.

She pushed away from the wall where she'd been leaning and approached us. She looked vaguely familiar, but I couldn't quite place her. She and I were about the same height, but that's where any similarities ended. Her hair was blonde and her eyes looked blue, but all the makeup she was wearing made it hard to tell.

"Yes, ma'am. I'm hungry. But I know I shouldn't have taken the food. I apologize," I said. Summer bowed her head and turned her eyes to the floor like any good urchin did in the presence of the bourge. I did the same.

"*You* took the food?" she asked. "I saw everything. Your friend took the food and you're covering for her. I think that's sweet. What's your name?"

I risked glancing at her and saw she was staring at me. "Sunny O'Donnell."

"I didn't mean to spy. Well, not on you anyway." She laughed. "I was peeking through the door to see if my fiancé is behaving himself tonight. Sometimes he drinks a little too much wine."

Did she say fiancé? I realized she must be Leisel Holt, the president's daughter. My heart sank and panic rose up to take its place. Of all the people to catch us stealing food!

"He has behaved himself tonight, hasn't he?"

"Yes, ma'am," I said.

"Really, there's no need to be afraid of me. I won't hurt you. Please, call me Leisel." She sounded overly friendly. Summer and I gave each other a nervous glance. We were confused. "I mean, it might even be nice to make some friends. I don't have many... being the president's daughter and all." She studied me, but I didn't know what to say to her, so I remained silent.

"Most people think it must be the most wonderful thing in the world to be the president's daughter, but it isn't. It's absolutely horrible! I don't have any friends. I have to live my life in the public eye—always behaving myself and looking my best. And as if constantly having people look at me weren't enough, there are rumours that someone wants to kill me. Can you believe it? Someone actually wants to assassinate me." Tears welled up in her eyes. She looked pathetic.

I surprised myself by reaching out to take her hand. "That's awful." I wasn't really sure what I was doing, but I thought if we showed her a little sympathy, she might return the favor and not tell on Summer for taking the food.

"I'm sorry, I don't mean to cry." She grabbed my hand as if it were a lifeline and held it tight. "I'm really trying to be brave. But it's so scary thinking someone could kill me at any time."

"I can't believe anyone would want to hurt you," Summer said. I wasn't sure if Summer knew what I was trying to do or if she was just being her genuine, loving self.

Leisel considered her for a moment, but turned her attention back to me. "You're both so very sweet." She took a tissue out of her pocket and dabbed the corners of her eyes, careful not to smudge her makeup. "Oh, I must look awful. But I feel so much better. Thank you for listening."

Seeing that she had stopped crying, I began to relax my hold on her hand, but she tightened her grip and refused to let me go. "We are friends, aren't we?"

Her eyes seared into mine, waiting for my answer. "Of course." I was confused by her strange behaviour.

The last of the girls carrying trays walked past us into the kitchen and gave us puzzled looks.

"I have an idea! We should hang out tonight," she said, clearly meaning only me. "I like talking to you, and

I really do think it was very noble of you to cover up for her." Leisel looked at Summer but with no kindness in her expression. I got the feeling we were being threatened.

"I have to work tonight," I said awkwardly.

"I thought you were almost done?"

"No, ma'am. There's a party this evening."

Understanding came over her features. "Oh right, it's a bachelor party." She seemed to ponder the dilemma for a moment. "I know. I'll get Jack to make a request for you. He can take you back to his apartment, and I'll meet you there."

She looked pleased with her plan, but alarms were going off in my head. I had a really uneasy feeling about her, but I knew that if she wanted me to do something I would have to do it. There was no way I could refuse the president's daughter.

"If you're worried about your friend, I'll see what I can do about getting her off duty for the night."

I looked at Summer. She seemed worried.

"Okay," I said. I had little choice. I was grateful that Leisel offered to send Summer home. It made the situation a little more tolerable.

"It's all settled then. I'll just go out and tell Jack, and he'll come and get you when the time is right. We're going to have so much fun!"

"Her name is Summer. Summer Nazeem," I said pointedly, wanting to be sure she excused the right girl from work.

"Summer. I'm sure I'll remember."

She gave my hand a final squeeze before she walked out into the dining room. I heard a volley of clapping from the guests as she entered, then laughter.

"Sunny, what are you doing?" Summer asked in a terrified voice. "Why did you say you'd go with her? She's a wackadoodle!"

"Ssshhh! Someone might hear." I looked around to see if anyone else was lurking in the shadows. "We just got caught stealing food. You know we could be beaten to death for that. And didn't you hear her say she'd get you off duty tonight? Not only are you not going to be punished, but you get to go home!"

"And you get left behind with *her*."

"Do you really think I have a choice?" Her look of resignation told me she knew I didn't. "Look, I'd rather sit around holding her hand tonight than being entertainment for one of those old men out there. *And* you get to go home. So something good is coming from all of this, right?"

"I don't know about that, Sunny. I have a bad feeling."

Summer didn't often have a bad feeling about anything. I took her seriously, even though there was nothing I could do about it. "I'll be fine, I promise," I said with more conviction than I felt. "We should get back before we get into any more trouble."

As we entered the main part of the kitchen, we came face to face with our angry supervisor.

"It's about time!" she yelled. "Where have you been?"

"We were stopped by the president's daughter," I said. An idea was forming in my mind. I could still hear the crowd shouting out comments to Leisel, asking why she was at a bachelor party. There could be no question that she was indeed here.

"Is that so? And why on earth would the president's daughter want to talk to you two?"

"She asked about her fiancé and whether or not he was drinking a lot of wine. She wanted to know if he was behaving himself. That's all."

She stared at us for a moment.

"You can ask her yourself."

"Hurry up and get in line. You need to be back in that room in twenty minutes."

Relieved, Summer and I hurried to join the lineup of girls by the door. We were the last to arrive. Our supervisor led us to a room where the rest of the girls were in various states of dress. Some were getting their hair done up, others having makeup applied.

A young woman took me by the arm as soon as I walked in. "I have just the dress for that hair."

Someone else led Summer away in the opposite direction.

The woman with me picked up a floor-length emerald strapless dress. She motioned for me to get undressed. Once I had, she slipped the silky gown over my head. The bodice was too big for me, so she pinned it and then made a few quick alterations. I could tell it had been altered several times before.

She laughed. "At least I won't need to hem it."

I looked down. The hem of the dress hovered above my ankles.

She tapped her teeth with one fingernail as she stared at my feet. "With the right shoes…"

She left me for a few moments and then came back with a pair of sparkly high heels.

"They're not too high—we don't want you towering over all the men! But it will make the dress look like it's been shortened deliberately to show off the shoes."

I strapped the shoes on my feet and tried to stand up. I had seen women in the movies wear heels, and I tried to walk like they did. Satisfied with my outfit, the woman told me to go to the hairdressing station. I practiced walking in my high heels on my way there and almost twisted my ankle.

"Your hair is absolutely gorgeous!" the hairdresser said as she took the elastic out and let my hair fall down my back. "I'm tempted to leave it just the way is." She pulled it this way and that. "Just a few curls to frame your face, I think."

She took a hot curling iron from a holder and twirled locks of my hair around it. "There. You're going to have a lot of suitors tonight."

She sent me on my way to makeup.

The makeup artist examined my face carefully. "Let's see." She picked up a pair of tweezers and began plucking my eyebrows. It hurt. A lot.

"Sorry, hon. Normally I'd do this with wax all at once, but it would leave welts that wouldn't have time to heal."

Once she'd applied my makeup, I hardly recognized myself in the mirror.

Dressed and painted, I was ready to go back to the dining room. I didn't see Summer anywhere, and I was relieved. I hoped she was on her way home.

I joined a small group of girls gathered at the door. None of them looked very excited to be there, although I could easily tell the newbies from the girls who had been there before. I wondered if the fear I was feeling was written all over my face, too. Although Leisel frightened me, I held out hope that she hadn't changed her mind. An evening with her seemed less frightening right now than what else might be in store for me.

Someone led us back to the dining room, and it looked just as we'd left it. The tables were clear and the candles still flickering. A few girls, still in white uniforms, circulated with a bottle of wine in each hand. I looked around, wondering if Leisel was still there. Maybe she would come and get me herself.

But it wasn't Leisel I saw. All dressed up in pink with an old man falling all over her, was Summer. She looked absolutely terrified.

CHAPTER FOUR

An old man stumbled toward me. "Now you, my dear, are worth the cost of a drink."

The little hair he had left on his head had gone completely grey, and he had a big round tummy. This was the closest I had ever been to an old person since there were none in the Pit. His breath stank of food and wine. He handed me a glass of wine, and I accepted because I didn't know what else to do. I was pretty sure I wasn't supposed to tell anyone I was waiting for Jack Kenner.

"Haven't seen you here before. Where've you been hiding? Down there in that Pit? No place for a beautiful woman." He slurred his words.

He snaked one of his flabby hands out toward me and unsteadily pulled me closer to him. It took all of my will power not to scream. I was taller than him, and he leaned his head against my neck. His hot, putrid breath tickled me. He slid his head lower, trying to lay his cheek on my breasts.

A young man walked up to us. I prayed it was Jack Kenner, here to take me away from this. "Wilson, old man. What are you doing?" he asked jovially.

"Jack, you little devil." Wilson released his hold on me.

Relief flooded through me at the mention of his name.

Wilson grabbed onto Jack's arm to steady himself. "Don't worry, son. You'll be married soon enough, and then you'll know what I'm doing with this young lady." He tried to wink at Jack, but it looked more like a blink.

"I think this young lady might be too much woman for you, Wilson. You couldn't kiss her if you stood on your tiptoes." Jack laughed.

"It's not kissing I'm hoping for tonight!" Wilson said, elbowing Jack in the side.

Jack looked at me for the first time and appraised me from top to bottom and back up again. "You have good taste, old man, I'll give you that. She's the prettiest girl here. In fact, I think I'll take her off your hands."

"Wait a minute!" Wilson waved an unsteady finger at Jack. "I found her first."

"Yeah, but I'm the guest of honor. So I get first pick."

Wilson tried to straighten himself up, but he was still unsteady on his feet. "'Course you are, Jack. She's all yours."

Wilson took back the glass of wine he had given me and stumbled away in search of another girl. Jack watched him go and then stepped so close to me that we were only a few inches apart. My high heels made us about the same height. His tilted his head toward mine, and I wasn't sure what to expect. I thought he was here to save me from all of this.

"You're Sunny O'Donnell?" he whispered.

He stared at me with those intense blue eyes that I had seen so many times on television over the past few months. He was about to marry the president's daughter. He would be president himself one day. That made him a very important person. I felt so intimidated, but I managed to nod.

"Leisel asked me to come find you. I'll take you back to my apartment."

I was relieved and anxious all at the same time. Leisel was going through with her plan after all.

But I was still worried about Summer. I tried to look over Jack's shoulder discreetly to see where she was. I didn't want to leave her alone.

"Unless you didn't want to go back to my apartment? Maybe there's someone who caught your eye?"

"Your fiancée said my friend could go home for the night, but I saw her here," I said, risking the possibility of being punished. Would he think I was out of line?

"I forgot. She told me to put in a request for... Spring, is it?"

"Summer."

"Yeah, Summer. Leisel told me to put her with old Forbes. He's drunk and harmless. He'll fall asleep at a table, and she'll be sent home. Until then, she can stay and enjoy the party."

I finally spotted Summer. Wilson was competing for her now. By the look on her face, she wasn't enjoying the party at all.

"The president has already left and everyone is waiting for me to clear out," Jack said as he extended his elbow toward me. "Come on. No one can leave until the guest of honor does."

"Okay."

What choice did I have? I wanted to catch Summer's eye before I left, but Wilson was blocking my view. Jack was still holding his elbow out toward me, and I wasn't sure why. Finally he picked up my hand and tucked it under his elbow. I was surprised he had expected me to do that—to touch him. My shock must have shown on my face because he gave me a questioning look. I realized my mouth was hanging open, and I closed it.

I could feel his muscles under my hand, caught where it was in the crook of his arm. He stood up straighter as he walked across the room and steered me toward the main doors. He had the confident swagger of someone who knew he was the most important person in the room. I heard a few men shouting out "Good for you Jack!" and "She's a looker!" They all clapped as we left the room. I had never felt so humiliated in all my life.

Jack remained silent as he escorted me to the elevator and pressed the "Up" button. The doors opened, and we stepped in. He pressed the button for the eighth floor. The small elevator seemed awkwardly quiet and intimate after the bustle of the party. I was very aware that my hand was still trapped in the crook of his arm. I stared at the floor. Although I wanted to break the contact, he hadn't given me permission.

The elevator doors opened, and we stepped out into an opulent hall. The floor was covered with a plush carpet, which I found difficult to walk on in high heels. The walls were off-white except for one long wall that was painted deep red. A few large flowering plants stood against the red wall with a long mirror in between. My reflection shocked me, dressed as I was in a silk gown and on the arm of Jack Kenner.

He noticed me looking in the mirror. "You're really pretty." He didn't say it like a compliment, more like a fact.

I looked away from my reflection when Jack straightened his arm and pressed his hand against the small of my back, urging me to keep walking. I was grateful not to have to hold his arm anymore.

As we left the elevator lobby, we passed a picture hanging on the wall. Bold strokes of red and yellow sometimes blended together to make gold. The colors were set against a dark background, making them appear even more striking.

"What is it?" I asked, staring, fascinated.

"It's an abstract of a sunset."

I looked at a lock of my own hair and compared its color to the painting. Where the red and yellow mixed, I could see the resemblance to my hair. Reyes's words came back to me: *Did you ever wonder how she knew what a sunset looked like?* Was this the picture my mother was thinking of when she named me? Had she been here on this same floor, chosen by some drunken bourge to entertain him? It was a sickening thought.

"Was it something I said?" Jack asked.

I shook my head. "No. Not you. Something someone else said."

Jack looked around. "There's no one else here."

"Sorry. I meant a different conversation." My cheeks flushed red.

"Well, don't let me interrupt."

I felt so stupid.

Four different hallways led away from the elevator lobby, and he turned right. We walked for quite a distance before he stopped in front of a door at the end of the hall and passed his hand over the scanner. I heard a click, and he opened the door.

"Oh, Jack! You did it!" Leisel said. She threw her arms around him and hugged him close. I felt awkward and out of place standing there witnessing their intimacy.

"You know I'd do anything for you, darling," he said.

I turned my head away when I realized he was going to kiss her, but not before I saw some of the kiss. Something about the way he was holding her, about the way he kissed her, didn't seem right. They were almost stiff and polite with each other, but maybe that was just the way of the bourge.

After a moment, Leisel turned to me. "Look at you, Sunny! You are positively breathtaking! Isn't she, Jack?"

"Not as breathtaking as you, my love." He kissed her again. "I'm going to go read. You girls have a nice evening." Jack headed toward another room and closed the door behind him.

"He's probably had too much wine. He'll go and sleep it off. I ordered us some food. I assumed you would be starving after working all night."

I was starving. My last meal had been over twenty-four hours ago.

"Can I take off my shoes?" I asked. I really didn't think I could take another step in them.

"Yes, of course. You poor thing, working in those all night, your feet must be killing you."

They were. I gladly slipped them off. The carpet was thick and cushiony against my aching feet.

I followed Leisel into the living room. A large sofa and two smaller chairs were grouped around a low table. Plates of food sat out, and my mouth watered at the sight and smell. I prayed my stomach wouldn't start making noises again. It was so quiet in there.

Leisel picked up a small remote and pointed it at a television hanging on the wall. Soft music began to play. I hadn't seen the television at first, and I was surprised by it. No one in the Pit owned a television.

They were only in the common rooms. But I guessed I shouldn't have been surprised. Jack and Leisel were privileged.

"Please make yourself comfortable," she said, waving me toward the sofa. She walked over to a small table and poured two drinks. She sniffed the contents of one glass while handing me the other. "Blackberry wine—my favourite! Why should the men get to have all the fun tonight? No one threw me a big party, and I'm getting married, too. Cheers!" She clinked her glass against mine and then raised it to her lips, so I did the same. I had never tasted wine before, and it burned going down my throat. I almost choked.

Leisel made an appreciative noise as she savoured the taste of the wine. "Blackberries grow best in the Dome. They respond well to our artificial light. There are other berries too, but blackberries grow big and juicy and make the best wine."

I nodded. I had no idea what to say or even why I was there for that matter.

The food looked so good, and my stomach was so empty.

"Oh, I'm being rude. Please help yourself." Leisel gestured toward the food. She'd either read my mind, or my hunger was obvious.

There was no fork, so I assumed it was okay to pick it up with my fingers. I had never eaten food like this before. The only things on the plate I recognized were the vegetables because I've peeled so many working in the kitchen. I chose an orange wedge of something and popped it in my mouth. It was delicious.

"I wasn't sure what you like to eat so I just ordered some things that pair well with the wine."

"Thank you. It's delicious." I wasn't sure what she meant about pairing food with wine. Food was food.

I followed the orange wedge with a bite of bread and then picked up something that looked like meat. I didn't like it as much. Leisel clinked my glass again, and I took another sip of the wine. It didn't burn as much this time, and a warm relaxing sensation came over me. I set my glass back down on the table to free both hands to eat.

Leisel watched me for a moment. "Thanks for hanging out with me tonight. I know it's not much of a party with just the two of us, but I really don't have good friends to share my special day with. Isn't that pathetic?"

Tears formed in her eyes, and she quickly brushed them away. I was still wondering what role I was supposed to play tonight. Did she want me to hold her hand? I was relieved when she reached for a decadent-looking cake instead.

"Like you said before—you're the president's daughter. You're a very important person and it's difficult for people to get past that." I hoped this was what she wanted to hear.

"Do you really think that's why no one wants to be my friend?" Her self-deprecating look told me the conversation was going in the right direction.

"I'm positive. You're very kind and generous." I tried not to choke on the words. The Holts had been anything but kind and generous to the Pit. "Letting my friend Summer go home tonight proves it."

"You know the boys mean well — they think they're doing you girls a favour by letting you into their little parties. But I think most of you don't want to be there, do you?"

Most of the girls didn't want to be there? Try *none* of the girls wanted to be there. I popped another piece of food into my mouth to keep from saying anything. I was afraid of how I might answer her question, so I just shook my head.

"Sunny, we're friends. I'll never betray you. You can talk to me."

Leisel picked up my glass and handed it back to me. She clinked it again with her own glass, and we drank. I didn't really want any more wine. It was making me sleepy. I set my glass back down and concentrated on the food.

"Jack didn't behave inappropriately with you, did he?" Her question sounded more curious than suspicious. Was she testing me?

"No, not at all! In fact, he rescued me from an older man who was very drunk. Mr. Kenner is very kind."

"And handsome! Don't you think he's just gorgeous? That dirty blonde hair and those blue eyes! I mean there aren't many men in the Dome who look like that! I'm so lucky he chose me to marry him."

"He *is* very handsome. And you're very beautiful. You make a nice couple."

"Do you have a handsome someone in your life?" Leisel asked.

I thought of Reyes. He wasn't handsome in the rich, clean-cut aristocratic way that Jack was. Reyes had the dark hair and black eyes of most people who lived in the Pit, but his chiselled features and six-foot-four frame set him apart. Lots of girls were attracted to Reyes, but I was the one he wanted.

"Yes, I do."

"Well, what's he like?"

I found the question odd. She was the president's daughter—why did she care who I was involved with? I thought I was there to talk about her.

"He's tall and handsome and strong. He works in the mines," I bragged.

I picked up more food and realized the plate I had been eating from was half empty. Leisel had only sampled a cake. I leaned back against the sofa and silently scolded myself for eating so much. I relished my last bite.

"Are you going to marry him?" Leisel picked up my wine and handed it to me.

I took a sip. The warm feeling from the wine intensified. "One day."

"You don't sound sure."

"It's complicated."

I didn't want to meet her gaze. My world was so different from hers. I needed to support my father until he met his fate in the Cull next year. Did she really not understand life in the Pit?

"I'm a good listener, and we have all night."

She seemed to want me to be a true friend and share secrets with her. I wasn't convinced that was a good idea, so I tried to tell her as little as I could. "My mother's gone now, and my father just lost his job. I need to look after him, so marriage will have to wait for... well, until I'm available."

"Then you and I have something in common. I lost my mother, too." She leaned forward to hug me, and I tried not to recoil. I stiffly hugged her back. "She died shortly after I was born. She had a heart defect. How did your mother die?"

I shifted uncomfortably. How could she ask me that question? "She was thirty-five."

"Oh, she was Culled," Leisel said. She took both my hands in hers and looked into my face, her eyes bright with unshed tears. "I promise you that things will be different under Jack and me. We'll change things." She hugged me again, tighter this time. "That is, if I manage to live long enough to get married."

"You mean someone is really trying to kill you?" I slapped a hand over my mouth, mortified by my outburst, but Leisel didn't seem to notice.

"Yes. My guards tell me they've stumbled upon an assassination plot. Someone wants me dead! Someone doesn't want me to marry Jack."

"It doesn't make any sense, though." My voice sounded slurred. I tried to sort it all out, but my thoughts were getting confused. It must have been from the wine. I put my glass down.

"It makes perfect sense, Sunny. Jack and I don't want to live with things the way they are now. We want change. But there's someone out there who doesn't agree with us, so they're trying to stop the marriage by murdering me."

Questions were trying to make their way into my muddled thoughts. Like why not kill Jack? He would be an easier target. She refilled my wine glass and handed it back to me. Dutifully, I took a sip.

"It's all so hopeless. My guards think the assassins will wait until my wedding day, when I'm in public. Daddy's holding the wedding in the main reception hall of the Dome so that everyone can come and watch. I'll have no protection."

"You'll be defenseless!" I cried.

"I knew you would understand."

"There must be something you can do. Tell your father. He'll change the wedding plans." It was as if someone else was talking on my behalf. I could hear myself saying the words, but I wasn't in control of them.

"No he won't. There's been a lot of unrest in the Dome lately and our wedding is a political statement to show everyone things are still good. There's no way he'll change the plans."

"I wish I could help." Somewhere inside my head a little voice told me that was the very opposite of what I wanted to do.

"Perhaps you can help, Sunny," Leisel said, her expression brightening. "Maybe you can take my place in the wedding."

CHAPTER FIVE

I don't know what I was expecting, but it wasn't that. Take her place? As in *be the bride*? I shook my head. It would never work.

"Just listen for a minute," Leisel said, her tone suddenly serious.

I couldn't really get up and leave, so I stayed and listened.

"We're the same height, but I'm a little... well, healthier than you are," she said of her figure. I had to stifle a smile. In the Pit, we called her plump. "My wedding dress is big enough for you to put a bulletproof vest on under it. We can cover up your hair with a wig, and I have a veil that will go over your face. No one will ever know it's you and not me."

"Your fiancé will know!" And the entire Dome would be watching the wedding. Someone was bound to notice.

"Jack!" Leisel called. "Can you come in here for a minute?"

A tired-looking Jack came into the room. His tie was gone, his shirt unbuttoned and wrinkled. It looked like he had been sleeping.

"Sunny and I have an idea," Leisel said. I opened my mouth to correct her, but closed it when I remembered whom I was about to correct. "We were thinking that she could pose as me during the wedding. Now I know what you're thinking—it's a crazy idea. But she's thin enough to get bulletproof clothing under the dress, and we'll keep her face covered. No one will suspect a thing."

"Is this about the assassination plot again?" Jack asked. He seemed irritated.

I was surprised that he would be so callous about his fiancée's life being in danger. If my life were in danger, Reyes would do anything to protect me. I took another sip of wine.

"What else would it be about?"

"I think the guards have been filling your head with nonsense. I had some people check into the possibility of a plot and nothing's been uncovered."

"Are you accusing me of *lying*?"

"No. I'm saying someone's trying to scare you." He was beginning to look worried.

"My guards wouldn't lie to me. And I can't believe how easily you just dismiss it. Maybe you don't love me,

Jack. Maybe this whole wedding is a big mistake!" She burst into tears.

"Leisel!" Jack crossed the room and pulled her off the sofa and into his arms. "You know that's not true. I want more than anything to be your husband."

Not for the first time that night, I felt that I really shouldn't be there witnessing their intimacy. Although I believed Leisel did have a point. Jack hadn't exactly declared his love yet. I busied myself with my wine.

"If that's true, then you'll want to protect me. Do this for me."

"But if she's the bride, then I won't be marrying you, will I?" Jack said gently. Leisel refused to look at him. He lifted her chin to meet his gaze. "Will I?"

"It will be me, just by proxy, that's all. She can walk down the aisle and exchange vows with you — that doesn't legally make you married to each other. We have to scan in and register to make it legal. So I'll just meet you in the Registry room and exchange places with her. It will work."

"It's a crazy idea. Of course it won't work. There will be other people in the Registry room with us during our scan-in."

"Not if I tell my father I don't want anyone else in the room. He knows I'm not happy about how public he's making everything. If I ask for just this one single private moment, he'll give it to me."

Jack dropped his arms from her waist and took a step back. He raked a hand through his hair. He clearly didn't like her plan.

"I don't want to die, Jack, and I'm really scared!" Leisel threw her arms around him. "We have such a bright future planned together. I don't want anything to take that away."

I stared back down at my wine. They obviously had some issues to work out, and I wanted to be anywhere but there.

"I honestly don't see how it's going to work."

"Will you agree if I promise to tell my father? He's worried about the assassination plot too, but he doesn't want to call off the wedding. After all, he's using it to show everyone that life is still good in the Dome, so he can't very well cancel it because someone is trying to kill me."

"If your father approves, then I'll agree to your plan."

"Then I'll tell him. I know he'll approve." Leisel looked victorious. Jack smiled, pulled her close, and kissed her lightly on the lips. "Oh, Jack, I knew you'd understand. I knew you'd want to protect me."

I cleared my throat.

"Oh, Sunny! Sorry, we got a little carried away," Leisel said. She let go of Jack and came back to sit on the sofa beside me. Her tears were gone, replaced with a smile. I hoped the lovebirds wanted to be alone now and would send me home. "It looks like we'll go through with our little plan."

I didn't recall agreeing, although I had the impression I didn't have a choice in the matter. "I'm not sure I'm comfortable with this plan," I said. I knew she could order me to do it. "I mean, there will be a lot of people watching."

"I thought you agreed with this. You understand how important our marriage is, don't you? You want to support us?"

"I do! I just think if it doesn't work... if I'm caught..."

"I know it's a big favor I'm asking of you. It's a risk for me too, even with my father's approval. But if the risks are worth it in the end..." Her voice trailed off and her expression became serious. "You know, when I saw your friend Summer stealing food, I was obligated to report her to the authorities. But I didn't." Leisel's hand came up to caress my hair. "You know, I'm still obligated to tell the truth about her. If anyone asks me if I saw anything, I'd have to say yes. I could get into a lot of trouble for lying. But sometimes friends do things for each other."

Although my head was swimming from the wine, I understood her implication. Do this for her or Summer was doomed.

"I'll do it," I whispered. "It's very late. Can I go home now? I have to work in the morning."

"No, silly, you can't go home! You'll have to stay here. We have a lot of work to do before the wedding." A smile lit up her face, and she hugged me.

I just wanted to go home. I wanted to be with my father. I wanted to make sure Summer was home safe and sound. I wanted to tell Reyes everything was fine. I missed them. It felt like it had been forever since I saw them.

"You can stay here in Jack's room. He can take the sofa and you can have the bed."

"What?" Jack said.

"Well, you requested her from the party. No one will question it if she spends the night here."

"I requested her for you, not me."

"Jack, be reasonable. She can't go home. I need to fit her with the wedding dress, teach her how to walk down the aisle, how to act, and, well, everything! There's so much to do and not much time left before the wedding."

"But I need to go to work in the morning. I'll lose my job if I don't show up," I said. Was it the wine that was making me so brazen? I had never even spoken to a guard like that before.

"Don't worry about your job. When this is all over, I'm going to hire you to be my personal maid. We're always going to be good friends." She stood then and went to Jack. "I'm going to go get some sleep, and I suggest you two do the same. We have a big day ahead of us tomorrow."

She kissed her fiancé and then skipped out the door.

The apartment suddenly became very quiet except for the soft music playing in the background. Jack stood in the middle of the room looking at me. I remained on the sofa, looking at him. My head was starting to pound, and the food I'd eaten sat heavy in my stomach. I really didn't feel good. I just wanted to go home.

"You can have the bed," Jack said.

"If I could just go home…"

"You heard her, you can't!" he snapped. He dragged a hand through his hair. He was obviously angry, and I didn't want to upset him any more. He could do whatever he wanted to me and no one would ever question it. "You take the bed."

"Yes, sir." I set my half-empty wine glass on the table and stood up. Suddenly the room was spinning around and I tried to grab something to steady myself, but there was nothing to grab.

"Whoa! How much wine did you have?" He was standing next to me, holding my arm in case I fell. I didn't remember him even moving.

"I didn't think..." I put my hand to my head.

"You've never had wine before, have you?"

"No." My stomach roiled. "I don't feel good."

In an instant Jack picked me up and carried me into his bathroom, where I promptly vomited.

CHAPTER SIX

The pounding in my head wouldn't let me sleep anymore. The room was hot, and I threw a big fluffy blanket off of me. I was wearing nothing but my underclothes, and the bed I'd been sleeping in wasn't familiar. It was big, soft, and very uncomfortable. I tried to sit up, but it only made the pounding in my head worse.

I was dying of thirst.

A glass of water stood next to the bed, and I sat up to drink it. The movement didn't help my head at all, but the cool liquid sliding down my throat felt heavenly. I fell back on the bed, exhausted with my exertion, and tried to recall the night's events.

The last thing I remembered was getting sick. I looked across the room and confirmed there was a bathroom adjoining this room. If I wasn't feeling so awful, I'd probably be astonished that he had his own private bath, but all I could do was wonder if there was more water in there. I swung my legs off the bed and stood up. It felt like my head was going to blow right off my shoulders. I stumbled in and found a tap. I turned it on, ducked my head under, and drank.

My thoughts suddenly turned to my father, and anxiety gripped me. I wondered if he had at least managed to get up from his sick bed to drink. He wouldn't go to the common room unless I was there to make him, of that I was sure. How long were they going to keep me here?

I went back to the room and lay down on the bed, but it was so uncomfortable and the room was so hot. The temperature in the Dome was much warmer than in the Pit. I rolled off the bed and onto the floor. The carpet was about the same thickness as my own bed, and it was a little cooler down there. I managed to drift back to sleep.

"Sunny? Spring? Summer?" A frantic voice disturbed my sleep. "What's-your-name, where are you?"

The voice was demanding now. It sounded angry. I pushed up onto my elbow and was relieved that my head didn't hurt as much as it had last night. Then I remembered I wasn't dressed, so I pulled the blanket off the bed to cover myself.

Suddenly, Jack Kenner's face peered over the side of the bed.

"What are you doing down there? Did you fall out of bed?"

Would he understand that I preferred the floor to his soft bed? Probably not. "Yeah."

"Are you okay?"

"Fine, thank you." My head hurt, I had an unquenchable thirst, and my stomach was growling again. All I wanted to do was go home.

"You scared me. I thought maybe you found a way to get out of here. Leisel would've killed me."

"I'm still here."

"Come on. They delivered a protein drink to me this morning in case I had a hangover. You have it." He rolled off the bed and threw a bathrobe at me. "Wear this. Your dress needs to be washed."

Tentatively, I stood up. Not as bad as last night, but I was still a little shaky. I slipped into the bathrobe, grateful to have something to wear.

Jack was sitting on the sofa reading something on a computer tablet when I came into the living room. He looked up at me and held out a glass. Hesitantly, I accepted it. I was suspicious of why he and Leisel were being so good to me. Despite her threat to turn in Summer, Leisel didn't have to feed me or share her wine last night. And Jack had been kind to help me when I was sick and he was sharing his food. It was all so confusing.

I sat down on one of the chairs across from the sofa and took a sip of the thick liquid. It tasted like the food in the Pit. I gulped it down.

"Slowly or you're going to get sick again," Jack said. "Do you remember everything from last night?"

I thought for a moment. "I think so. You and Leisel want me to pose as the bride because you're afraid someone is trying to kill her."

"Well, you're almost right. It's what Leisel wants, not me."

"Right."

"I'm going to marry Leisel no matter what. I just prefer she's the one standing beside me at the altar. So how are you and I going to make that happen?" He took his blue eyes off his tablet to give me a piercing look.

"What can I do? I'm powerless."

"I disagree. She seems to really like you. You might be able to influence her."

I laughed. "Me? Have influence over *Leisel Holt?*" Even the thought was absurd.

"Just convince her that no one is trying to assassinate her!"

My eyes opened a little wider at his angry tone. For a moment I'd forgotten exactly who I was addressing. My situation was impossible. I was caught between two of the most powerful people under the Dome. And I was no one. If I didn't help Leisel, she would report Summer to the authorities and have her punished for stealing food. If I did help Leisel, then I could only imagine what Jack would do to me. Either way, I was in trouble.

I wished Summer were there to show me the bright side of the situation. I tried to think like my friend, to see what good I could find in all of this. Maybe I could find my answer in Leisel and Jack. Perhaps it wasn't too far-fetched to believe that they were good people who did want to change things in the Pit for the better. If that was true, then I would be helping my own people by ensuring these two came into power one day.

"I might get myself in trouble with you for saying this," I said, "but she told me about your plans together. She told me that you both want to... change the way things are." I paused for a moment to gauge his reaction, but his expression hadn't changed. "I know this is completely unimportant and doesn't have anything to do with your wedding, but recently my mom was Culled and my dad lost his job. I know it was his own fault, but he's just so sad right now, and I am, too. I miss my mom so much. But if I don't keep my job, my dad and I are going to lose our home. Do you know what that means where I come from? To lose your source of credit?"

"Look, I know you probably have issues in your life, and I'm really sorry for you. But I can't change anything. I don't have that kind of power."

"I know you don't have that kind of power *yet*. And I know my situation isn't important to you. But what is important to me is that *when* you become president, you can change things."

He studied me silently for what seemed an eternity. No longer able to meet his gaze, I looked at the floor. With growing apprehension, I wondered if I had just pushed him too far.

"I don't know what my fiancée has discussed with you, but any plans she and I make for our future together are private. And if our private plans were ever made public, well, let's just say I would never be given the leadership role." He glared at me, and his lips were drawn into a tight line.

It took a moment before I realized he thought I was trying to blackmail him, which was the furthest thing from my mind. Who would listen to an urchin anyway?

"Please don't misunderstand me. All I'm trying to say is that if you and Leisel want to make life better for us in the Pit, then I owe it to everyone I love to make sure you become president one day. So if someone is really trying to kill her, then I'll do whatever it takes to protect her." For a moment I wondered if I was being brave or just plain stupid. I decided to go with brave. It sounded better.

Something in his expression changed when I said that. His intense blue eyes narrowed. He seemed to want to look inside me, see right into my soul. Maybe he thought I was lying.

"So you're saying you'll pose as the bride and risk taking a bullet for her in order to save your people?"

"Yes."

What I was saying could be considered treason. Jack could call in the guards and have me arrested right now. But I was going on the hope that what Leisel had told me was true—that they really did have plans together to change the Dome.

"So, you're not going to talk her out of this?"

"Look, I don't want to be the bride any more than you want me to be, but I think we both know I really don't have a choice."

The doorbell rang, and Jack set his computer down to go answer it. Leisel swept into the room wearing a big smile and carrying a large garment bag.

She kissed him. "Good morning, Jack."

"Darling."

"Look what I brought you, Sunny." Leisel held out the garment bag for me to see, then laid it carefully across the sofa and unzipped it. "Isn't it beautiful?"

"Leisel, I'm not supposed to see it!" Jack said, suddenly turning into the playful bridegroom.

"Then go away." She watched as he went into the bedroom. "He behaved himself with you last night, right?"

"He was very nice. He slept on the sofa and gave me his bed. He loves you very much. I don't think you should worry." I suddenly felt very self-conscious in his robe.

"You need some clothes, don't you?" It was almost as if Leisel read my mind again. "I'll bring some later. But right now, maybe you wouldn't mind trying this on."

She produced her wedding dress with a dramatic flourish. I knew I should feel honored. There were thousands of people excitedly anticipating seeing her wedding dress the next day, and here I was about to try it on. But I was all too aware of what it would mean for me to wear this dress and walk down the aisle. I could be caught. I could be shot.

The dress was beyond beautiful. The top was silk with a high collar. The bodice was form fitting to mid-hip, and then the silk seamlessly dropped away into a waterfall of chiffon. The back of the dress was just as stunning with a row of diamond buttons ending at the small of the back in a cluster of silk and chiffon roses. From there the dress cascaded away into a long train.

"It's beautiful, Leisel."

"Isn't it? I had it replicated from a picture in an old magazine. I saw it years ago and thought if I ever got married, this would be my dress."

"I can see why. You'll look beautiful in it."

"No, *you'll* look beautiful in it. Try it on, but first this." She produced a thick vest. "You'll be bulletproof."

I took off the robe and pulled the vest over my head. It felt heavy and hung from my slight frame, but Leisel adjusted the Velcro fasteners and pulled the vest snug to fit my form. Then she slipped the dress over my head. Even with the bulletproof vest, the dress was too big. It looked horrible. I tried to hide my relief.

"I don't think it's going to work," I said, a little too happily. I bit my lip.

"Don't despair. I've brought pins."

My tiny spark of hope fizzled out quickly as she shook a box of pins. She set to work taking it in on either side, pulling it this way, tucking it that way. At least we were the same height so it didn't need to be hemmed.

"There," she said when she was finished.

She guided me to a mirror on the back of a closet door. I couldn't believe it was me in the reflection. "This dress makes me look beautiful." I wasn't being modest. The dress was truly spectacular. As I admired how perfectly it fit, all hope of getting out of this plan faded.

"No, you make the dress beautiful. It never looked this good on me."

"I'm sure that's not true, Leisel. It was made for you and —"

She held her hand up to cut me off. "No argument. You look beautiful in it. In fact, when you get married — I mean for *real* — you can wear this dress, and I want to be there to see it!"

"What?"

Leisel laughed at my confusion. "I think it's a shame that no one will actually get to see you in this dress. Everyone will think you're me. You're helping me out so much, Sunny, the least I can do is let you borrow it for when you marry that handsome man you were telling me about last night." She smoothed my hair back into a ponytail. "And I hope you'll let me be part of your special day, too."

I had to think about what she was proposing: me in a big white wedding dress, down in the Pit, marrying Reyes, with bourge as guests. And not just any bourge, but the president's daughter. Somehow, I just couldn't see it happening, though the image was nice. I managed to stifle my laughter, but I still broke into a huge smile.

"See, I knew that would make you happy."

"It's not the dress that makes me happy. It's the thought of living in a world where I could have a wedding with you there as my friend." I spoke the truth, even though I knew it was a fantasy.

"That's the world I want to live in, too. I've never had a best friend before, Sunny. I don't ever want to lose our friendship."

Our eyes met in the mirror, and I searched her face for a hint of sincerity. With all my heart, I wanted to believe her.

"Well, don't make me cry! My makeup is going to run, and Jack and I have a televised interview this morning. Do you believe people want to know about us?" Leisel shook her head in disbelief. "Why? We're so boring."

Too swept up in our plans, I had forgotten all about the excitement rippling through the Dome about the upcoming nuptials. They had been showing the young couple on television as often as possible, getting everyone excited. Although, down in the Pit, people were more excited about being treated to a feast than they were about watching the wedding. But that wasn't something I would ever tell Leisel.

"I don't think you're boring. I think sharing your wedding day with everyone makes you closer to them."

Leisel hugged me. "You're so sweet. But speaking of the interview, I need to finish getting ready. I'll just slip you out of the dress—careful of the pins. They need to stay exactly as they are. When we switch in the Registry room, I can just remove them and the dress will fit me again."

I put Jack's robe back on while she carefully tucked the dress away into the garment bag.

"I probably won't see you again until tonight. But you look like you should get some sleep anyway. I didn't want to say anything, Sunny, but you look exhausted."

And then she was gone.

Jack peeked around the corner.

"All clear?"

I nodded. "Leisel's gone to get ready for the interview."

"About that," Jack said, coming into the living room. "I'm not going to be here most of the day, so you'll be on your own. Once I lock the door, I'm the only one who can unlock it, so you won't be able to leave. Which is for the best, because if you're caught walking around up here unescorted, it won't be good for you. Do you understand?"

"Can't I just go home, please? I promise to come right back. You don't need to hold me prisoner." I really needed to check on my dad.

"I'm sorry, but that's just not possible. I want you to know that your loyalty to my fiancée won't go unrewarded. Once we're married, I'll make sure you and your family are taken care of — it's the least we can do."

I was sickened when I realized he thought I was doing this for my own personal gain. I wanted to say something, but the doorbell rang again. Jack motioned for me to go into the bedroom. A few seconds later, he told me I could come back.

"Here's your breakfast," he said, setting a tray on the table.

There was a time when the Dome used replicators for meals, but someone discovered that processing the food that way resulted in lost vitamins and enzymes. Now the kitchens produced food the old-fashioned way and served it in cafeterias throughout the Dome. I shouldn't be surprised that Jack Kenner had his meals delivered, though. He came from an important family and would one day be the most important person in the Dome. The evidence that he had personal servants reminded me of just who I was dealing with.

"I can trust you alone here today, can't I?"

Heat crept up from my neck to cover my cheeks.

"Yes, sir." I looked at the floor. I was too humiliated to look him in the eyes. I heard the door open and close.

I was alone.

CHAPTER SEVEN

My feet seemed rooted to the spot where I was standing. I listened and waited. Waited for what, I wasn't sure. A hand turning the doorknob? Guards to come crashing through and arrest me? But the only sound in the apartment was of my own breathing. I took a tentative step forward, heard the whisper of my foot sinking back into the carpet, and froze. Was anyone in the hallway? Could they have heard it too? I waited and listened again. No one was coming. I was being paranoid. Why would anyone come barging into Jack Kenner's apartment without permission?

My focus turned to the tray of food sitting on the table, and my stomach growled. I put my hand over my tummy to muffle the sound. I was pretty sure they heard it all the way down in the Pit. I grabbed the tray, ran on my tiptoes into the bedroom, and sat down on the floor where I'd slept the night before. I felt safer here. If someone did come into the apartment, I could roll under the bed and hide.

I took the lid off the tray and savoured the smell of breakfast. Two eggs, a piece of ham, bread, and fruit. It was more food than I was given in the Pit in an entire day. I ate one egg and some of the bread, then replaced the lid and tucked the leftovers under the bed for later. Then I sat there on the floor with absolutely nothing to do.

After a moment, I tiptoed back out into the living room. I wanted to turn on the television to watch the interview when it aired, but I was afraid it would make too much noise. I had never been interested in the royal couple before, but now that they wanted me to dress up as a decoy bride for any would-be assassins, my interest in them had been piqued. Sure, I had seen them on television before, but they were just images on a screen then. Now I knew them personally.

Did they really want to change the Dome for the better?

Maybe I could find out more about Jack Kenner. I was alone in his apartment, after all. I knew I shouldn't snoop in his personal things. In fact, I had told him that he could trust me. But if I was going to risk my life for him so he could one day hold the office of president, then I owed it to myself to make sure he was worthy of it.

I opened the cabinet doors on either side of the television and was pleasantly surprised to discover shelves full of old books and magazines. Some of the magazines dated as far back as the 1990s. They looked original, not like the stiff and glossy replicated ones. A pair of white gloves sat on one shelf, and I assumed they were required before touching the antique paper.

I closed the cabinets and continued my search. I went back into Jack's bedroom, but all I found in his closet and dresser drawers were clothes. There didn't seem to be anything personal in the apartment at all. No diaries, letters, or photographs. Only the library of old books.

I went back to the cabinet and put on the gloves. I recognized many classics I had learned about in school but never read, like *Pride and Prejudice* and *Paradise Lost*. Although I would've loved to read them, I was still hoping I wouldn't be there long enough to finish them. Instead, I turned my attention to the magazines. They ranged in topic from news to nature, from architecture to computers. I took one out and looked at the front cover; it was dated April 2012, and the headline read "US and NATO Plan Defence Project." The next one was dated May 2012: "Russia Vows Pre-Emptive Strike Against US and NATO." I jumped ahead to the most recent magazine, and the headline read "Korea Not Happy with Vice President Kenner's Visit." The name Kenner caught my attention.

The article was a short commentary on Vice President Theodore Kenner's meeting with North Korea's leader about working together to solve the current nuclear crisis. The meeting didn't go well because the North Korean leader expected President Taylor herself, not the vice president. The article went on to say that instead of repairing relations between the two countries, the rift had grown larger. It was dated January 2024. The nuclear holocaust happened February 2024. Was the Kenner family somehow implicated in the start of World War Three?

That the Holts and Kenners had never gotten along was no secret. Not that we followed that kind of gossip in the Pit—it was just common knowledge. The engagement of Leisel and Jack had come as a surprise to everyone. Maybe that's why they were making such a big deal of the wedding. The Holts were finally forgiving the Kenners for their past mistakes.

I thumbed through the rest of the magazines but didn't find anything more about the Kenners. One headline dated early February 2024 read, "Are We on the Brink of World War Three?" I wondered why our ancestors were smart enough to ask that question but not smart enough to avoid a war. Reading about nuclear war was depressing. I already knew how we all ended up living in the Dome. What I wanted to know was when we could get out.

I abandoned the depressing news magazines for the ones on nature. Seeing images of the outside world always lifted my spirits. I selected a few and shut the cabinet doors. As quietly as I could, I returned to my spot in the bedroom and curled up to read. I still felt safer tucked away in the corner with my food tray close at hand.

But reading about nature turned out to be no more uplifting than the news magazines. Most of the featured articles were about global warming and how extreme droughts and vicious storms had wiped out more than a third of the earth's population. Food production had become a global issue since the countries that received most of the rain were the northern countries that didn't receive enough sun to grow the food. The world had become unbalanced. Even if there hadn't been a nuclear war, the human race had seemed doomed anyway.

Feeling hungry again, I took off the gloves and ate some of my leftover food. Then I replaced the lid and got up and washed my hands. As soon as I turned on the faucet, I shut it off, alarmed at how loud it sounded in the silent apartment. I held my breath for a moment, straining to hear if someone was coming. But when no one rushed in to arrest me, I felt more confident and turned the water on again to take a good long drink. Then I returned to my spot and fell asleep.

The pressure of a hand on my shoulder jerked me awake. At first I thought I'd been caught in Jack Kenner's apartment, and my heart jumped into my throat.

But it was Jack. "Fall off the bed again?" he asked with a sarcastic grin.

I placed a hand over my chest. "You scared me."

"It's time to get up. Leisel wants you in her apartment to get ready for the wedding."

"The wedding? How long have I been sleeping?"

"You were asleep when I got in last night. I decided to leave you that way."

The magazines were gone. I felt ashamed at being caught with his personal things. He had asked me if he could trust me, and I had said yes.

"I thought you and Leisel were both coming back last night. I thought we would all get the chance to talk again." I was still looking for a way out of the plan.

"Leisel decided to go straight back to her apartment last night. I think she was angry with me for trying to talk her out of this little farce."

"And did you? Talk her out of it, I mean."

"No. But she promised me that she told her father. We should be safe."

What did he mean by "we?" I was the one not only taking the risk of being caught impersonating the bride but also of playing decoy for an assassin. "Did you ask the president? You know, just to make sure she really did tell him?" I had no right to question him, but I was desperate.

"If Leisel said she talked to her father, then I believe her." His tone brooked no argument. "Now we really are running out of time."

"I have nothing to wear." I was still in his bathrobe.

He hardly looked at me. "That will have to do. You're ready then?"

"I guess so." I didn't have any more excuses.

"Just give me a minute." He picked up his computer tablet and tapped away on the screen. "Okay, that should give us enough time. Let's go."

Jack tentatively checked up and down the hall before he opened the door wide enough for me to exit. Putting his finger to his lips, he gave me the "ssshhh" sign, and we quietly walked down the hall and into the elevator. Leisel lived on the tenth floor, the highest floor in the Dome. The ride was short, and within seconds we were exiting onto the tenth level. I expected Domers to be guarding this level, but the hall was empty.

The layout of this floor was a little different than the eighth floor where Jack lived. Instead of hallways feeding off the elevator lobby, there were four large ornate doors, and above each door four family names stood out—Holt, West, Powell and Forbes—the four most powerful families in the Dome. No one should be on this floor without a formal invitation.

Jack led me to the door with the name "Holt" above the entrance. He waved his hand over the scanner, and a click sounded as it unlocked. He opened it hesitantly and made sure the hall was clear and then waved me through. I was so scared of being caught that my stomach was in a tight knot.

We made our way down the hall, hurrying as much as we could without making noise. Then we heard a door opening. We stopped dead in our tracks. There was nowhere to hide. A figure stepped out into the hall, and I held my breath for a second. Then I saw it was Leisel. She motioned for us to hurry up, and we rushed inside her apartment.

"I'm so relieved you're here, Sunny! I kept torturing myself with thoughts that you went back home—that you decided not to help me and I'd have to make that walk myself. Thank you so much for staying."

"I'd better go," Jack said. "The guards will be back soon." I wondered where the guards had gone, but thought it best not to ask. They seemed to have it all worked out.

"I'll see you soon, my love," Leisel said, wrapping her arms around him. "Everything will turn out just fine. I can't wait for us to be married." She gave him a long, passionate kiss, and I busied myself staring at the wall.

"I'm still worried, but I trust you, Leisel." He gave her one more kiss and then slipped out the door.

Leisel laughed when she took in my appearance. "I see you're still wearing that bathrobe. Let's get you into the shower. We have a lot of work to do to get you ready for the wedding of the century."

CHAPTER EIGHT

L eisel's apartment was luxurious, and I had never
felt more out of place. She led me through to her
bathroom and gave me a warm, plush towel. When she
left, I disrobed and stepped into the shower. The set
water temperature felt hot, but its warmth helped to
relax my tense muscles. I scrubbed myself from head to
toe then reluctantly turned the water off.

I put on the clean bathrobe Leisel had laid out for me.
Its silky softness felt light against my skin after wearing
Jack's rough terry-towel robe.

Leisel sighed when I emerged from the bathroom.
"You look much better. How are you feeling?"

"Scared to death. But I know I'm doing the right
thing helping you, so I'll get over it."

"You're so brave, Sunny. What you're doing for me is huge." She walked over to me and took both my hands in hers. "I'll never forget it. Now, let's get to work! I've told everyone I'd rather get ready alone, so no one is going to disturb us. And I've already ordered up food. We only have a few hours."

The morning passed more quickly than I would have liked. Leisel started by combing my wet hair into a tight bun at the base of my neck and then fitting a wig — an exact replica of her own hair — over my head. She tweezed my eyebrows to make them look more like her own. Then she applied makeup on my face in exactly the way she wore it. When she finished, she turned me around so I could look in the mirror. I was amazed at what she had achieved. My face was thinner than hers and my eyes had the large, black pupils so common among people from the Pit, but we would look the same from a distance.

"With a veil over your face, no one will know it's not me." Leisel looked pleased with herself. "Only an hour left before my entourage picks me up to escort me down to the wedding. Get a bite to eat, and then I'll dress you."

"I couldn't eat a thing." I was sick with fear.

"Okay, then let's do a rundown. My entourage will come and get you, which will consist of my father flanked by his guards and another set of guards for me. You won't have to talk to my father, so don't worry. You'll follow him — and never get ahead of him. The president is always first. He'll take the elevator with his guards, and you'll wait for the next. The elevator will come back for you. The only time you'll be in my father's company is in the downstairs elevator lobby. That's where the first set of cameras will be. My father and I are supposed to pose for the cameras at that point and then he'll be taken away to his seat by the guards. Once he's seated, the bride will begin her walk to the altar. You'll be on the second floor and will have to walk down the grand staircase. Once you reach the bottom of the stairs, just follow the white carpet all the way up to the altar. Jack will be there waiting for you. Once you're there, our spiritual leader will bless the bride and groom and then ask you to commit to each other. The answer is *yes*" — Leisel smiled at me — "but say it low. The leader won't be suspicious of a nervous bride. When you're done, you'll be taken into the back room to register the marriage. That's when I'll meet you and change back into my wedding dress."

It all sounded easy enough, but I still wasn't feeling very confident. Anything could go wrong. My only safety net was that the president was in on the plan. Still, if someone noticed I wasn't Leisel, what then? Would the president come to the aid of an urchin in front of the entire Dome? Somehow I doubted it. I had to keep myself focused on why I was doing this: to save Summer from being punished for stealing food. To give everyone in the Pit hope for a better future. I tried to take some comfort from that knowledge and managed to calm down a little.

Leisel chatted away happily to me as she fitted the bulletproof vest to my skinny frame. It was flexible enough to show my small bosom, but she decided to make me bigger by stuffing socks down my front. She pushed the mounds this way and that until she was satisfied. Then she eased the dress over my head. The pins were still there, but she was careful not to stick me, and the vest protected me as well. It seemed to take forever for her to do up the diamond buttons in the back and then put on the veil. She fixed it to my wig and pulled a layer of tulle down over my face.

"There!" she said.

She spun me around so I faced the full-length mirror. I looked like I had just walked off the pages of a bridal magazine.

"I don't look anything like myself," I said, relieved.

"No one will know it's not me. I can't even tell."

Someone knocked on the door, and my heart lurched. It was time.

"Don't be afraid. I love you for this," Leisel said. She gave me one last hug and hurried into her bedroom to get out of sight.

I took a deep breath and walked to the door on shaking legs. Two guards stood there waiting for me, one of them with flowers in his hand. He held the flowers out to me, and I accepted them, trembling. Leisel had never mentioned the flowers. I didn't know I would have to hold anything.

I stepped out into the hall. The large door I had come through with Jack just a few hours ago stood wide open now, and I could see the president and his men waiting by the elevator. I began my walk, the walk that would eventually take me all the way to the altar. One of my guards was ahead of me, one behind. Before I could reach the end of the hall, I heard the elevator doors open and the president disappeared into it. I was relieved to see him go.

We stepped into the elevator lobby and waited for the elevator to return. I felt like a criminal standing there with the guards. Couldn't they tell I wasn't Leisel? Hadn't they noticed how much my bouquet was shaking? I was glad when the elevator doors opened, and I could move again. One guard went in first and I followed. The train on the dress was long and cumbersome, but the second guard picked it up and carried it into the elevator with him. He pressed the button for level two, and the doors closed.

I felt trapped in such a small space with guards on either side of me. I could hear my own laboured breathing and tried to steady it, but only made it worse. Now I was afraid of hyperventilating. The sensation of the elevator descending wasn't helping my stomach either. I kept my eyes fixed on the seam of the doors and tried to will my body to relax. It didn't work. Then the doors opened on a scene of pandemonium.

Bright lights were pointed directly in my face, and I felt my eyes rolling into the back of my head. My eyes were sensitive enough to the brighter light in the Dome without having lights aimed directly at me. People were shouting questions at me. A few members of the media were clapping at my arrival. Everyone wanted to know about my dress.

The president came to stand beside me and placed his hand on the small of my back. It took every bit of my will power not to jump or scream at his touch. I tried to remember that he knew about the plan and trust that he wouldn't deliberately expose me. So mutely I stood next to him with the cameras pointed at us. He answered a few questions. Somewhere in the distance, I heard music begin to play, and his guards stepped forward to escort him to his seat. Some of the cameras followed the president, but most stayed focused on me.

Then it was time to make my way to the altar. My guards escorted me from the safety of the elevator lobby to the top of the grand staircase but left my side before I came into view of the public. I was on my own from there. As I came to stand at the top of the staircase, the music changed and the guests all stood. I began my descent, and a few people clapped. Others gasped. The cameras were everywhere. I expected someone to yell out that I was an imposter at any moment. And then I remembered why Leisel wanted me to take her place. An assassin might have me in his sights.

I reached the bottom of the stairs without falling, being shot, or getting recognized. The white carpet Leisel mentioned stretched all the way to the altar. Red flower petals were scattered on it—I didn't remember Leisel mentioning these. Was I supposed to avoid stepping on them? I hoped not. I had enough on my mind.

As I walked down the aisle, a few people softly called Leisel's name, but I refused to make eye contact with them. Instead, I turned my gaze toward the altar to see how far I had left to go. A huge television screen behind the altar showed live coverage of the bride walking down the aisle. I was so shocked to see myself on television that I almost stumbled, but I also realized with some relief that it was impossible to tell it wasn't Leisel under all that white fabric and tulle.

I looked for Jack just as Leisel told me to but could only find an official looking military officer standing by the altar. I wondered why he was there. Leisel hadn't said anything about the military being present. Had I been discovered? My legs weakened at the thought. But then, all at once, I realized that the man in uniform was Jack Kenner. He looked so official that it scared me. My body began to recover from the shock of thinking I had been caught. I stayed focused on closing the distance between the altar and me. It seemed to take an eternity, but then I was finally standing beside Jack with my back to the crowd.

The music stopped, and the room became utterly quiet. My breathing was still laboured, and I was sure everyone could hear me.

"Who here gives permission for this young couple to be joined?" the spiritual leader asked the congregation.

President Holt stood up. "I do."

"We do," another couple said as well. I assumed they were Jack's parents.

With permission granted, the spiritual leader began his blessing. I wished I could focus on what he was saying. I wished I had the presence of mind to understand every word. But I couldn't. I was too busy trying to stop my hands from shaking. My legs were beginning to feel weak again, too.

"Leisel, my darling," Jack said gently. Someone was standing beside me with her hand out. "The flowers," he whispered.

I handed the flowers to the woman. I was afraid of dropping them anyway. Jack took my left hand, and the spiritual leader began to speak again. Jack gave me an almost imperceptible nod, and for a moment I stared blankly at him. Then I remembered Leisel had told me to say yes.

"Yes," I said.

The crowd gave a collective sigh. I must have done it right. The leader droned on.

"Yes," Jack said in a loud and clear voice.

More sighs from the crowd.

The spiritual leader went to stand behind the altar. He held a small shiny object up in the air and began another blessing. He placed the object on an open book and made the sign of a cross above it, then returned to us and handed the object to Jack. It turned out to be a ring with a large diamond in the centre. Leisel hadn't mentioned a ring.

Jack took it from him and placed the ring just on the tip of my finger. I could tell it was going to be too big. The leader began to read from a book, and Jack repeated everything he said word for word. Now I was worried there was a ring for Jack, too, and I was going to have to repeat everything the leader said. I would be caught for sure. Jack slipped the ring onto my finger, and as I thought, it was far too big. I curled my finger under to hold it in place.

Jack continued to hold my hand and then the leader wrapped some kind of holy cloth around our joined hands. I tried to keep my hands steady and my eyes downcast. The leader was so close to us that I was sure he must be able to see I wasn't Leisel.

Then it was done. The cloth was taken away. The crowd was clapping for us. Jack held his elbow out toward me. This time I understood to take it, so I wrapped my hand around his arm, and we began the walk to the registry room.

I was almost home!

The cameras followed our slow progression to the registry room, and I expected them to stop when we walked through the door, but they kept coming in. Someone had made a mistake. I was sure they would be asked to leave. I glanced at Jack. He looked confused, too, but he remained calm. He just kept walking toward the table where an ordinary scanner had been set up and decorated with flowers.

I almost fainted when I saw President Holt and his guards come in behind us; and then Jack's parents, followed by the spiritual leader. How could Leisel and I switch with all these people here? Did she forget to tell them this was supposed to be a private moment? Jack's arm tightened under my grip. Sweat was forming on his upper lip. He raked his free hand through his hair. He always seemed to do that when he was frustrated.

"Ladies first." The spiritual leader held out his hand for mine.

I knew the minute my hand was passed over the scanner, the machine would turn red and sound an alarm. I was not Leisel. I looked desperately around the room, hoping to see Leisel, but there was no sign of her.

"Miss Holt... er, excuse me, *Mrs. Kenner.*" The leader smiled. A few people chuckled. "Your hand, please."

This time he didn't wait for me to give him my hand. He picked it up and waved it in front of the scanner.

It beeped, and lit up green.

It took a few moments for the realization to penetrate my numbed brain that a green light came on.

The leader held out his hand toward Jack. "Mr. Kenner."

All the color had drained out of Jack's face. His jaw was tightly clenched, but he gave the leader his hand. The scanner beeped, and the green light went on. The small group in the room was elated. Everyone clapped and seemed to surge toward us to offer their congratulations.

"You haven't kissed the bride yet," said Jack's mother.

Jack looked down at me, his eyes wide. He would have to remove my veil to kiss me. I wanted the floor to open up and suck me back down into the Pit. But somewhere in the distance, voices were raised in alarm. Something was happening.

Before I could make sense of anything, Leisel burst into the room—bruised and with torn clothes. Tears streamed down her face.

"Daddy, *help* me!" she screamed through tears. She clutched at her father's arm then crumpled to the floor. "You have to arrest them!"

She pointed directly at us.

CHAPTER NINE

I stared dumbfounded at Leisel's crumpled figure on the floor. Her hands covered her face, and she appeared to be inconsolable. Her face was bruised, and I wondered what had happened. Did the assassin find out about the switch? Did he find her?

"Leisel!" Jack said. "What are you doing?" He looked stunned.

President Holt shot Jack a deadly look. The threat was obvious. Jack said nothing more.

Everyone in the room was looking from Leisel to me. Guards grabbed Jack and me, twisted our arms behind our backs, and cuffed us. Jack's mother walked up to me and ripped off my veil, taking the wig with it. I was exposed.

The anger on her face transformed into an expression of shocked disgust when she saw my urchin eyes. "Who the hell is this?"

I was too frightened to speak. Would Leisel stand up for me? Would the president?

Leisel wailed, and lowered her hands to point at us again. "Daddy! They hurt me! Jack decided that he doesn't love me anymore, and that he wants *her*. So he hit me and put me in a closet." She was sobbing so hard she couldn't go on. She buried her face in her hands once more. I was finally realizing that Leisel had said *they* hurt me. I certainly didn't give her the bruise, so why was she including me in the blame?

"Someone get a doctor!" The president yelled into the crowd. "My Leisel is hurt. Get a doctor!" He looked from one person to another with wild eyes. Finally, someone ran out of the room.

"Jack! What is going on?" his mother asked, her tone accusatory.

"It's not what it looks like, Mom. *She* planned this whole thing!" He gestured toward Leisel.

"He's *lying*!" Leisel said. "He's been hiding that... that... *urchin* in his room for days — ever since his bachelor party. Remember, Daddy, I went to the party? Jack and I made plans that night to be together even though I knew it was wrong. I shouldn't have planned to meet him when we weren't even married. But when I went to his apartment that night, he sent me away. I thought he was up to something, and then… this morning…" Leisel broke down sobbing again.

"Take a deep breath, my baby, and tell me what he did."

"He hit me! He told me he didn't love me and never has. He said he loved that urchin girl. So he hit me and… I don't remember much after that. I woke up in the closet and couldn't get out. He'd put a chair up against the door, but I just kept jiggling the door until it finally opened and then I came straight here." Leisel choked, sobbed, and gasped throughout her little speech.

"*Leisel, you lying little b—*" Jack began, but his mother slapped him across his face, cutting off the rest of his words.

His mouth gaped open and his eyes grew wide. He stared at his mother as an angry red welt began to appear along his cheek.

"How could you, Jack? How could you do this to *us*? To *her*!"

"Mom, I swear to you! I'm the one being betrayed." Anyone could hear the passionate sincerity in Jack's words. They came from somewhere deep inside him. "It wasn't my idea. She gave me no choice."

Tears were welling up in his eyes as he looked at his parents. I was stunned to see this side of Jack Kenner. He no longer resembled the powerful man who would one day become president. Now he looked like a boy appealing to his parents for help.

"I thought you loved me, but you were just using me," Leisel said through her sobs. Then she turned to her father and grabbed him by the lapels of his jacket. "Daddy, he told me he planned on making changes in the Dome once he becomes president. He said he wanted to change everything! He even wants to break the treaty with the urchins and stop the Cull. I told him it would never work!"

I tried to make sense of what she was saying. She'd told me she wanted those changes, too. She'd told me she wanted to make the Dome a better place to live. I understood then that she'd manipulated me into doing what she wanted. I'd played her game unknowingly.

"Treason!" the president said, his lips tight. "You're telling me he spoke *treason* to you?"

"Yes, Daddy. I don't think he ever loved me. I think he just wanted to be president."

Holt slowly got up and walked toward Jack, his eyes never leaving Jack's face. I was afraid that this might be it for us, or at least for Jack. The president looked mad enough to kill. I wished I could move my terrified limbs. I wished I were brave enough to turn to the cameras and tell my dad I loved him. Tell Reyes I was sorry. Tell Summer to take care of them both for me. But all I could do was watch the president come closer.

"The fabric of our nation was founded on democracy and freedom for all, and you would seek to destroy that and replace it with *communism*?" His face was red and his eyes looked wild. "*Who do you think destroyed our nation and sent us into this Dome? Who do you think sent the bombs? Communists!"* His entire body was shaking with anger. Spittle flew out of his mouth and ran down his chin. His face was completely red. He looked insane. Then he glanced at one of the cameras out of the corner of his eye, and his disposition changed slightly. He smoothed back his hair and straightened his well-decorated military tunic.

"Apparently, I have been so busy worrying about unseen enemies *outside* the Dome that I didn't notice the enemies we have *inside*. You, Jack Kenner, will be put on trial for treason. If you are found guilty, you will be executed according to our laws. And if you are found guilty, I fully intend to hunt down all of your supporters." The president gave Jack's parents a threatening look.

Three armed Domers rushed into the room, adding even more chaos to the already dramatic scene. The media people had to scramble to get out of their way.

"Mr. President, we need to get you out of here, sir. There's a riot starting in the Pit," said one of the Domers.

At this news, the president dragged his eyes away from Jack and looked at me for the first time. His look was still murderous, but there was something else, too. Something in the way he was clenching his jaw and drawing his lips into a sneer made me think he hated me the most.

"Get Leisel to safety," the president said to the guards. Then he turned his attention to the camera and looked directly into it. "Mobilize the guards and lock down the

Pit. If the urchins persist in their little demonstration,
shut off their ventilation system until they comply." The
president turned back to us. "This is not the first time
I've regretted the fact that we don't have a prison inside
the Dome. Remand them to Jack's apartment and call the
council for an emergency meeting." With that he strode out
of the room with his security entourage surrounding him.

The Domer behind me tightened my cuffs and shoved
me back out into the main reception area. The guests
were going crazy. Everyone had seen what just went
on in the registry room on the giant television behind
the altar, and now we were being marched out in front
of them for real. The guard behind me kept shoving
me forward, but with every other step he trampled on
the train of the dress, impeding my progress. At one
point, I heard the dress rip and my first inclination was
to worry that I might be punished for damaging it. But
then I remembered I was doomed anyway. There was no
doubt in my mind that I would be killed for what I had
done. And somehow I found solace in the thought that
I would never have to worry about ruining a uniform
ever again.

Jack fought the guards every inch of the way. He was
obviously angry, and I didn't blame him. The woman he
thought loved him had just betrayed him, and if Leisel
was able to convince everyone of his treason, then he
was every bit as doomed as I was.

We were thrown into an elevator together with a
few guards, our hands still cuffed behind our backs. I

couldn't help but wonder why they were treating us so nicely. If we'd been in the Pit, we would have been beaten to death by now. But neither of us had been hit even once.

When the elevator doors opened, the guards shoved us out. The dress kept dragging me down. For something that looked as light as air, it was turning out to be a chain around my ankles.

At last, we arrived at Jack's apartment and the guards threw us inside roughly. One guard stepped in and unlocked our cuffs, and then left.

As soon as we were alone, Jack turned on me. "Did you know about this?"

His fists were clenched at his sides, and I could feel his anger rolling off him. As I stood under his accusing gaze, it occurred to me that this was the first time anyone had spoken to me since the whole fiasco began. All morning, people had been talking all around me, but no one had actually spoken to me. So far I had been an outsider—a participant in the event, but not actually a prominent player. I realized I liked the anonymity. It made my role less important. I didn't want Jack to take away that small shred of comfort. I didn't want him to talk to me. So I walked into his bedroom and returned to my safe little spot on the floor beside the bed.

He didn't follow me, for which I was grateful. The dress still felt like a dead weight wrapped around my legs, so I gathered it up and tucked the train behind my back. It made a nice cushion against the hard wall. I leaned back on it, smoothing out the front of the skirt. I wondered if they would give me something else to wear when they executed me or if I would have to die in this dress. I wished I had my own clothes. If I was going to die, I wanted it to be as me and not as some wannabe bourge.

I hadn't thought too much about Reyes until now. I wondered if he had seen the wedding. Of course he had. The entire Dome saw it. I tried to imagine what it must have looked like on television. Could he tell the wedding was a sham? Or did he think that I betrayed him? I tried to remember how much Summer knew before we were separated. She would have told Reyes that I went with Leisel, but then I never returned to the Pit. It must have been a shock to see me on television standing where Leisel should've been beside Jack Kenner.

I heard Jack get off the sofa and come into the bedroom. How long had we been in the apartment? An hour? More? I sank lower on the floor, hoping he wouldn't see me. No luck. He walked around the bed and sat on the floor next to me.

"We have about thirty minutes of privacy," he said.

"I don't understand. What happens in thirty minutes?" I asked.

Jack held up a pocket-sized computer tablet. "I was eight years old the first time I hacked into the mainframe. There are hidden cameras everywhere, even in this room. Usually they're not turned on in private homes, but I'm guessing they've turned on mine now. Anyway, I learned a long time ago how to super-impose a different feed over what the camera was supposed to be recording. That's how I got us to Leisel's apartment this morning without being caught. Right now, if anyone is watching or listening, they'll see us as we were thirty minutes ago, not as we are now. Privacy."

"Why do we need privacy?"

"Because I want to know if you're in on this with Leisel or not."

His clear blue eyes that I had once thought beautiful seemed cold and calculating. I had a sudden urge to lean forward and claw those eyes out. "The only reason I'm facing certain death is because I got caught between two crazy bourge bent on destroying each other. And you want to know if this is *my* fault?" My anger was so intense that I didn't care who he was or whether he had any power left.

"I'm sorry." He roughly pulled a hand through his hair. "If you weren't in on it with her, then you have every reason to be upset." He studied me with his blue eyes, and I leaned farther back against the wall, hoping to somehow evade them. I didn't trust him. "I want you to know that I've never lied to you. Your presence in all of this was... unexpected. I completely misread Leisel. I thought I had her under control."

"What? *Had her under control*? That's not exactly a declaration of love."

"I never loved Leisel," he said matter-of-factly.

"So she was right? You were just marrying her so you could become president?"

"Yeah, I was." Jack laughed. "But it sounds so seedy when you say it."

"Were you the one that gave her the bruise? Did you lock her in the closet after I left?" I'd been thinking it was Leisel who betrayed Jack, but now...

"No!" Jack shook his head. "I didn't touch her. I honestly don't know who did that to her. I just want you to know Leisel is the one who betrayed you, not me. I think she planned the whole thing out the moment she met you. You're both the same height."

"I'm confused. Why do you care if I believe you betrayed me or not? Why are you so intent on making sure I know Leisel is the guilty one? You're not exactly innocent in all of this."

"I don't know. Last confession? Unfortunately neither one of us has much longer to live." He finally dropped his gaze and looked at my hand resting in my lap. I still had on the ring. It looked shiny against the white dress. A sad look came over his face. "I'm guilty of a lot of things, but being a traitor isn't one of them. The true traitor is Damien Holt."

"What does President Holt have to do with this? I thought this was between you and Leisel." I instantly regretted my question. I really didn't care. Whatever issues there were between Jack and the president were for them to sort out. I was already dealing with the backlash of getting caught between two bourge. I had learned my lesson.

"When Leisel told you I wanted change in the Dome, she wasn't lying. I talked about it with her a little to see how she would react, but she doesn't know the entire story. You see, my family heads up a secret organization called Liberty. Our goal is to restore democracy to our government."

"Restore it? But we have a democratic government."

"No, we don't. Holt and his buddies have revised our history so much that most people don't know the truth. But the Kenners know the truth. We have evidence."

"What truth? What evidence?" My curiosity was aroused despite my desire to stay out of bourge politics. But if I was going to be executed because of a secret organization trying to take control of the Dome, I wanted to at least know who they were.

"Where do I begin? Well... probably at the beginning of the Dome's history." He gave me a roguish smile. The smile made him almost seem human, but I wished he would change out of his military uniform. He looked like someone I should fear. "My great, great, great, great, great, great grandfather — give or take a few greats — was Theodore Kenner, Vice President of the United States before the bombs. He entered the Dome as part of President Taylor's entourage when the bombs were launched. *General* Edward Holt was also part of that entourage." Jack looked at me closely when he said "general."

I couldn't remember ever hearing about a President Taylor, except for the article I had read in one of Jack's magazines. The Holts had always held the presidency in the Dome.

"So the Holt family wasn't in line for the presidency?"

Jack shifted, bringing one of his legs within touching distance of me. I bent my knees and hugged them close to my chest, steering clear of any contact. He didn't seem to notice.

"Actually, in a democratic government there's no such thing as being *in line* for the presidency. In a democracy, the people choose a leader through an election process and, once elected, the leader is expected to represent the people. But the Holts don't operate that way. What we have under the Holt regime is a dictatorship, which gets passed along from generation to generation through the males in that family."

"How did General Holt become president then? Was he elected?"

"No. My family has evidence that implicates Edward Holt in the murder of President Taylor and her husband." He smiled at my look of surprise. There had never been a female president in the Dome. "Vice President Kenner kept a written journal and video clips of his life in the Dome, which the Kenner family has kept all these years. Every Kenner has read the journal and watched the videos, and we continue to share them with others who want to know the truth. The video that made the most impact on me shows civilians from the valley climbing up the mountain to the open hangar doors where military vehicles were still coming into the Dome.

The civilians tried to fight their way in, but soldiers were pushing them back and used machine guns to stop them. General Holt ordered the soldiers to fire, but President Taylor called a stop to it. In the video, you can see bodies everywhere, rivers of blood flowing down the mountain, but still the people kept coming to the Dome. They were desperate to get to safety." Jack paused for a moment, his eyes bright with unshed tears. "No one with a soul could turn those people away, and President Taylor didn't. She told the guards to let them through.

"That caused a huge rift between President Taylor and General Holt. His callous behaviour bothered Taylor so much that she started looking into Holt's military career, and during her investigation she discovered that Holt had betrayed her. It's complicated, but I'll try to explain. In order to launch missiles, two people were required to enter secret codes into a computer that controlled the warheads. It was a safety precaution to make sure that a bomb was never launched accidentally. The two people who held those codes were President Taylor, the leader of our nation, and General Edward Holt, the leader of our military. President Taylor reluctantly agreed to launch the warheads after General Holt informed her that both Russia and Korea had launched theirs at us. But General Holt had lied to her. No one had launched. When she punched in her secret code and activated the missiles, she started World War Three. Countries sent their missiles in retaliation against us, not as an offensive strike. Our Allies launched in our defense, their enemies launched in their defense... and on and on it went until the earth was devastated by a global nuclear war.

"When Taylor discovered the betrayal, she was going to have Holt formally charged. She had already confided in Vice President Kenner about everything she had found out, which is why all this ended up in his journal. But from this point on, much of what Kenner wrote is hearsay. The president and her husband were murdered just hours after she made her discovery, and General Holt was the first one at the murder scene. He took complete control of the investigation and claimed to have found evidence that their murder was the result of a conspiracy by the civilians—the same civilians they had so generously given shelter from the bombs—to take over the Dome and throw everyone else out. As the head of the military, it seemed natural for Holt to be the one to step up as leader to get the civilians under control. That's when he made the famous treaty with them—the treaty that turned you into slaves."

What Jack was saying was a lot to take in—especially after the day I'd had. I was exhausted. How was I supposed to react to all of this information? He seemed so self-righteous in his confession, yet I saw another side to his story. If the Dome had been built right in our own valley, why hadn't the president and her entourage invited us in when the bombs were launched in the first place? Why did the civilians have to fight their way in at all? It sounded like there should have been more than enough room, if they were driving vehicles in...

"Considering the amount of time and effort the ruling class put into building a secret shelter to protect themselves from a nuclear holocaust, it seems to me they had damned us long before they launched the bombs," I said. Jack looked surprised at my words. I wondered if he was going to hit me, but I pressed on. "So the Kenners have known this all along and haven't exposed the Holts? Why? Why didn't anyone fight for us? Why didn't Vice President Kenner step up and have him arrested?"

Jack looked at me thoughtfully. I wasn't sure if he was mad or not. "I'll try to explain, if I can. By right, Vice President Kenner should have become president, but General Holt had control of the military and felt it was in the best interests of the Dome to retain a military government. And not only did he have the military behind him, but he was also in possession of both his own codes and President Taylor's codes for the warheads. Remember I told you that two people are needed to launch the missiles? There are warheads inside the Dome. It's part of the Dome's defense system.

"The codes get passed to each president when he's sworn in and only the Holts have held that office since the beginning of the Dome. There are a lot of people living here who would like to see a return to our democratic government, but the Holts still control the military and the warheads. Every Holt who has come to power has threatened to blow up the entire Dome if there's an uprising—and each Holt has been crazy enough to do it. They would rather see the end of civilization than relinquish their power. So we try to have a quiet revolution. We plan and plot and hope that one day we'll find the codes and usurp their control. I've searched the computer memory banks, but I can't find them," he said.

"I don't understand why General Holt wasn't exposed back then. I mean if he had the president's codes, then the only way he could've gotten them was from Taylor herself. But if he found her already murdered..." I shook my head. If I could see the flaws in Edward Holt's story, couldn't the people back then see them too? "Maybe he doesn't have the codes. Maybe the Holts have been lying all along in order to stay in control."

"That's a really astute observation, Mrs. Kenner," he said, giving me an appreciative look.

It annoyed me that he was surprised I had a brain, but he went right on talking, oblivious to my irritation.

"We have medical evidence that President Taylor's husband was badly tortured before he was killed; however, there are two different stories to explain this indisputable fact. Holt's explanation, which is in the official report, claims that the civilians tortured President Taylor's husband in front of her. This was supposed to be an attempt to manipulate her into giving the order for all officials to leave the Dome to the civilians. But VP Kenner wrote in his journal that he believes Holt tortured President Taylor's husband in order to get the codes out of her. Officially, Holt claims the president whispered them to him before she drew her last breath." He pulled his knees up and rested his arms on them. His anger seemed to have been replaced with melancholy.

"It doesn't change anything, though, does it?" I asked. "I mean, *knowing* the horrible history of how everything came to be doesn't change it. People in the Pit will continue to live as slaves, you and I will be executed as traitors, and the bourge will continue to win."

"That's not true. The Kenners know, and we've shared the information with as many people as we can trust. We do have supporters. We're trying to change things the only way we think we can without harming the entire Dome. Try to understand that our family was cast way down after Edward Holt became president. He didn't want any reminders of the old regime. We clawed our way back up, getting back into the good graces of the other influential families. My marriage to Leisel was the moment my family has been waiting for. Once I became president, we would have the codes. The Holts would lose their power."

"If the Holts dislike the Kenners so much, how did you become engaged to Leisel in the first place?"

"Because there is no one else. When Edward Holt claimed the presidency, he made it law that the title can't be passed to a woman. And they've been lucky because every generation has produced at least one son, except this generation. Usually the Holts choose their spouses from the West, Powell, or Forbes families, but right now there's a generation gap. The only boys in those families are under the age of twelve. It's the first time in the history of the Dome that this has happened. My mother noticed last year that Leisel was showing interest in me and told me to pursue her. When I asked the president if I could marry his daughter, I promised she would keep her last name and all our children would carry the name Holt as well. He liked that. It also helped that Leisel said I was what she wanted, and the president always gives his daughter what she wants."

"So you were prepared to spend the rest of your life with someone you didn't love in order to restore democracy?"

Jack nodded. "I just wanted to be honest with you. After all that's happened, you were owed an explanation. I am truly sorry you got caught up in all of this." He reached for my hand and held it in both of his. Slowly he brought it up to his lips and tenderly kissed it, then placed my hand back on my lap. "Time's up," he said.

And he went back out into the living room.

CHAPTER TEN

I kept my hand in my lap exactly where Jack had put it down. A tingling sensation lingered where he had pressed his lips against my skin. I stared at my hand, but it didn't look any different. I never expected kindness from a bourge, especially one so aristocratic. If he thought I had anything to do with Leisel's betrayal, why didn't he just beat me? Or kill me? No one would care. But instead of hurting me, he confided in me. In fact, his openness about his feelings toward President Holt and Leisel shocked me. Treasonous words were never heard in the Dome.

I didn't know what to think of Jack Kenner or his story. If his family really was intent on restoring democracy to the Dome, they had had almost three hundred years to do it. Yet there we all were, still at the mercy of the Holts. I wondered if life would be any different if Liberty succeeded. For all Jack's talk about wanting to get rid of the Holts, never once did he actually say life in the Pit would get any better.

He seemed kind enough, but he was definitely conscious that I came from the Pit. I felt it when he questioned if he could trust me to be alone in his apartment; I heard it when he congratulated me on pointing out some of the obvious flaws in his story. He thought of me as an inferior. I wanted to tell him that we *are* educated in the Pit. Maybe not in elaborate schools like the bourge attended, but our common rooms in the Pit served as classrooms during the day when the adults were working. Although in the Pit, the most valuable lesson was to learn to think on your feet. Every urchin needed a quick mind to get him or herself out of situations that might otherwise result in a beating or death.

Maybe that was the problem with the Kenners and Liberty. They were over-educated in the classroom and no longer had the ability to think for themselves. After all, they'd had almost three hundred years to confront the Holts with their evidence, and they were still in the planning stage. Perhaps they weren't as desperate for change as we were in the Pit.

My stomach growled, reminding me I hadn't eaten anything in more than a day. My last meal had been the breakfast Jack had given me before he left for his interview with Leisel. I looked under the bed, relieved to find the tray of food right where I had hidden it. There was an egg, one and a half pieces of bread, and almost a whole piece of ham left. I was about to take a bite of the bread when I remembered Jack. He had been kind to me, so maybe I should share it. I returned to the living room, the dress dragging behind me, rustling.

"Decided to join me?" he asked without looking up from his computer.

"What are you doing?"

"Writing my farewell letters." He put the computer down and raised his eyebrows at the sight of the tray. "You've been hoarding food?"

"It's what every good urchin learns from an early age. That or starve." I offered him some of the food.

A barely concealed look of disgust crossed his face. "Cold eggs and ham. No, thanks."

"Suit yourself." I guessed you had to be an urchin to appreciate that a meal was a meal no matter what temperature it was. I picked up the piece of bread and sat in the chair across from him. I almost choked on it when I heard the apartment door unlock. Leisel walked in, a Domer following closely behind her. Jack was instantly on his feet.

"Well, here's the happy couple!" Leisel said with a smile. "Oh, and look, you're sharing a meagre breakfast. What is that anyway? Cold ham?"

"What do you want, Leisel? Come to finish off the job yourself?"

"Well that's hardly the response I expected from my jilted fiancé. What, no mourning the loss of my love?" Leisel sneered. Jack just glared at her. "I thought not. I knew you never loved me, Jack, and as much as I would love to finish the job myself, I would never deprive my father of that pleasure. He's really mad at you. I mean, it took some convincing to get him to let me marry a Kenner in the first place and then you turn around and do this to me." Leisel pouted. "Your family's never going to recover from this."

"Leave them out of it, Leisel. They had nothing to do with it. This is between you and me."

"I think we both know *that's* not true. Your family has been trying to take mine down for hundreds of years, and now my father has a legitimate reason to destroy you all. Starting with you."

"Why? Why are you doing this to me?" Jack asked between clenched teeth.

His hands were balled into fists at his side, and every muscle in his body was tensed and ready to spring across the room at her. The guard standing behind Leisel tensed up too, his hand reaching for his weapon. Without really thinking about it, I jumped up and grabbed Jack's arm with both my hands. If he went for Leisel, there was no doubt in my mind that the guard would kill him, and I didn't want to be left here all alone. I didn't want to be executed alone. I hung on tight.

"Sunny, how touching. Oh, wait. I think I have a… a… *tear in my eye*," Leisel said, pretending to wipe a tear from the corner of her eye.

I wanted to slap the sarcastic expression off her face. "Shut up, Leisel," I snapped. My words shocked even me.

"So the urchin has a voice. Not that you need one. I mean no one is putting you on trial for anything. You're going to die simply for wearing that dress and marrying above your station. And, by the way, I lied to you — that dress looks way better on me."

Jack scoffed. "You wish!"

Leisel looked taken aback but she recovered quickly when her guard stepped forward to be at her side. "Keep your little insults to yourself. I only came to say thank you. Thank you so much for playing your roles in my little plan so *flawlessly*. I really do wish I had been there to see the look on your faces when Sunny's scan actually worked. I bet you were so surprised." She laughed. She was actually enjoying this. Her guard was smiling, too.

"So what's your plan, Leisel? You might as well tell us. We're going to die anyway," Jack said.

"Why not? My plan has always been to become president. I mean, who came up with the rule that a woman can't be president? You know, when I went to my father saying that a Kenner was the most eligible bachelor in the Dome, I had hoped he might consider changing the rules. I was absolutely flabbergasted when he said I could marry a Kenner! He'd rather have a male Kenner as president than see his own daughter inherit the title. So that little plan backfired, and I ended up engaged to *you*." Leisel shook her head. "It was frustrating, you know? So I had to come up with something else. That's when I saw Sunny. We're the same height, and I knew I could alter the dress. I couldn't believe my luck when you both agreed to go along with everything. I mean you both must've been so desperate. You to become president, Jack, and you, Sunny, to save your little friend."

Summer! All that time I had been thinking about how Leisel betrayed me and never thought that she probably went back on her word about Summer, too. A knot formed in the pit of my stomach. I did this all for nothing. Now I wanted to kill Leisel myself. I dropped Jack's arm and headed straight for her, but he grabbed me around the waist, preventing me from reaching my target.

"Let me go!"

"She's not worth it, Sunny! She'll just kill you."

"Listen to him, Sunny, because I will," Leisel said, all business now. Her guard drew his gun. "Desmond, put that away. Jack at least knows better."

Leisel placed her hand over the guard's, a familiar gesture that was hard to miss. She caught me staring at them.

"Desmond has been a huge source of support to me. Without him, my plan would never have succeeded. He's captain of the guard on this level." A smile played around her mouth. Now I knew how she was able to get rid of all the guards so I could come to her apartment this morning. "When I'm president, we'll live in a world where he and I can get married. You see, I do want change in the Dome."

"I still don't see how you're going to become president. Your father won't agree to that," Jack said.

"Are you kidding me? After the public betrayal I've gone through? The humiliation of being the jilted bride... the broken heart I'm suffering..." She pouted, shaking her head. "When I tell my father I never plan on marrying again, he'll understand completely. I mean, who's left for me to marry anyway? I'd have to start scraping the bottom of the barrel to come up with someone who's eligible, and Daddy would never stand for that. I'll convince him the only way to keep a Holt as president is to let me succeed him."

"I guess you have it all worked out then. Thanks for stopping by." Jack gestured like he was dismissing her.

"Oh, don't be like that, Jack. We did have a few good moments during our... relationship." Her voice was a purr.

"To be honest, Leisel, I detested the sight of you. So you can imagine what inner strength it took for me not to run every time you touched me. I guess I should thank you, too. Turns out the thought of getting a bullet in the head isn't nearly as bad as the stress I was under wondering how I was going to get through my wedding night with you."

By the look on Leisel's face, Jack's words hit home. She curled her lips into a snarl.

"Good bye, Jack. The next time I see you, you'll be with your executioner. Enjoy the rest of your short life." And with that, Leisel turned and left the room, her guard close on her heels.

I wanted to run after her — claw the door open and race down the hall to find her. A creature that evil should not be allowed to live, let alone have a chance to become president. Life in the Pit was already bad, but it would be intolerable under that monster. And I had unwittingly helped her. She had to be stopped. I tried again to get to the door, and then realized Jack's arms still had me in a vise-like grip. I tried to pry his arms off me. "Let me go!"

"She's gone, Sunny. She's gone."

"I'll get the door open. Let me go before she's gone." Why did he want to stop me? He must hate her, too.

"Sunny. Sunny." His lips were by my ear. "Relax. She's gone. I don't want you to hurt yourself."

My strength left me. He was right. The door was locked, and I couldn't get at her.

"How did she get in here? You said there are cameras everywhere, but she got in here and said all those things. She wasn't worried about being caught."

Jack grabbed his computer, did something on it, and then looked at me triumphantly. "You're a genius. She has the cameras jammed on this entire floor. And I just locked it in. She won't be able to unjam it for quite a while."

"Then I'm not going to waste it. I'm going home."

The determination I felt was stronger than anything I had ever felt before. I knew I wouldn't get far. The Dome was only so big. But if I could just get enough time to go home! I didn't want to die wondering if Reyes thought I betrayed him. I had to let my father know I wasn't long for this world and he needed to get out of bed and look after himself. I wanted to make sure Summer was okay and that she knew Leisel had betrayed us.

I marched into the bedroom to look for something less conspicuous to wear than the wedding dress. I opened Jack's closet doors. My green dress was still there. Nothing else would fit me.

"Um...what are you doing?" Jack asked, standing in the doorway watching me.

"Can you help me get out of this dress?" I remembered how long it took Leisel to do up the buttons this morning. It would take forever to undo them. "Just rip the buttons off."

"Where are you going?"

"You have your computer to say your farewells, but I have nothing. I need to go home and see everyone before I'm executed. Will you help me?"

He considered me for a moment. "Only if you take me with you."

"Then help me get out of this wedding dress. I might get noticed in it." I took the green dress out of the closet and put it on the bed.

"Trust me, you're going to get noticed in that dress, too."

"There is nothing else."

Jack went over to his bureau and took out pants and t-shirts and then came up behind me and ripped the back of my dress apart. "Have you thought about where we're going to go once we leave the apartment?"

"Home."

I let the dress fall to the floor in a heap and stepped out of it. I was still wearing the bulletproof vest. Jack took off his military uniform, and I could tell he was thinking about my plan.

"Keep the vest on," he said as he threw a shirt and pair of pants at me. "The Pit's on lockdown. There's no way for us to get down there."

He stripped down to his underwear. I was surprised by how muscular he was. He wasn't as muscle-bound as Reyes, but he was in good shape. And he needed to be physically fit to get down into the Pit the way I was going to take him.

"I can get us down there. Can you get us out of *here*?"

"I don't think my chip will unlock the apartment door anymore. In fact, we're going to have to dump our chips and get new ones. We'll have to make a quick stop along the way."

I pulled out all the stuffing Leisel had shoved down the vest to make me look bigger then yanked Jack's t-shirt over my head. He gave me a curious look, but didn't say anything. I put on his pants, but they were way too big. He got a belt out of his dresser and a knife from the drawer of the bedside table. He handed me the belt, and I pulled it through the loops on the pants. Then he pulled the belt together until it was the right size, punched in a new hole, cut off the excess leather at the end, and cinched it around my waist.

He studied me for a minute. "You better cover up that hair." He took two hats out of the closet and handed one to me. He put his hat on and pulled the visor down to cover his face. I did the same, glad my hair was still in a tight bun.

"Ready," I said. We walked out into the living room and stared at the door.

After a few moments, Jack said, "This is crazy, Sunny. We're never getting out of here, and if we do, they'll catch us and kill us right away."

"So you'd rather sit here waiting to die? If you want to stay, then stay, but I'm getting out of here. If I actually make it to the Pit, then at least I have the chance to say goodbye to my father and friends before I die."

"Okay. We need a plan to get out of here. I'm sure there are guards on the other side of the door. If we can create some kind of diversion to bring them in here, we can —"

I screamed at the top of my lungs.

The door opened and in rushed two Domers.

Jack grabbed the gun away from one guard, and his leg came up to snap the other guard in the face. Neither one was expecting the assault, so Jack had the advantage. He almost had the gun when the guard jerked back to wrestle him for it. The other guard was shaking off the pain Jack had inflicted and was reaching for his weapon. I ran forward to snatch the guard's gun to prevent him from using it, but he easily overpowered me. Jack swore under his breath. He brought his knee up and rammed it in between the legs of the guard he was fighting, seized his gun, and cracked him under the chin, knocking the guard's head backward. Then Jack had the gun. He turned on the guard who had me locked in a choke hold and whacked him over the head with it. The guard dropped to the floor. The door stood wide open.

"You want to give me a little warning next time?" Jack asked.

"Where'd you learn to fight like that?" I was truly impressed with his skills. After that display, I thought we actually stood a chance of reaching the Pit.

"Military training. Next time, stay out of the way." He went back to the table and retrieved his computer. "Come on."

We looked up and down the hall before exiting the apartment. It appeared the guards Desmond had sent away hadn't come back yet. The carpet in the hallway muffled the sound of our footsteps, so we were able to make fast progress. Jack led us to a door with an exit sign above it. He paused for a moment to look at his computer then tapped on the screen. "Go," he said, opening the door.

We entered the stairwell and looked up and down — no one but us. We headed down to the second floor and stopped in front of another door while he tapped away on his computer. I could hear movement and voices on the other side of the door. This was a busy part of the Dome.

"Through the door and to the right," Jack said. "Follow me. Keep your head down. Don't make eye contact with anyone."

Jack opened the door, and we joined the flow of traffic as if we had every right to be there. For the second time today, I found myself parading in front of people trying to be someone I was not. The first time didn't end so well. I was hoping this time I would be luckier.

As we walked along the hall, I overheard many conversations. It seemed everyone was talking about the wedding and how Jack ditched Leisel for an urchin girl. And everyone was wondering who that urchin girl was. I pulled my hat down just a little lower.

Jack found the room he was looking for and knocked on the door before walking in. I was shocked by his boldness, but I followed him, trying to act with the same confidence. We entered a large storage room with shelving units lining the walls. A few sealed bins stood off to one side.

"What are we looking for?" I whispered.

"We're looking to replace our chips. According to the map, the surplus chips are stored somewhere in here. I don't know exactly where, though."

I studied the shelves and quickly picked up on the pattern that organized them. The bins were grouped by size, and each group was in alphabetical order. I started with the smallest bins first, looking for the words "chip" or "scanning." Jack was looking in the sealed bins off to the side.

"I found a bin labelled 'microchips,'" I said. I pulled the bin out and looked inside. There were millions of tiny chips in a protective bag, a pair of tweezers, and an implantation device with the word "Spritze" written on the handle.

"Perfect!" He popped open a drive on his table and, using the tweezers, took one chip and placed it in the drive. He closed it. "Who do you want to be? Name?"

"What? You can't just change the chip?"

"No, I have to make us new ones. And we can't be Jack and Sunny anymore—that will get us killed. So what do you want your new name to be?"

"Well if we need new names, we might as well have new identities, too. You know, just in case we go unnoticed down there for a while. We'll need jobs." An idea was beginning to form in my mind. If I could get a new identity and job, then I would still be able to make enough credits to keep my father's apartment. It didn't matter if it was Sunny O'Donnell with him or someone else, as long as he had a partner to support him.

I could tell by Jack's wry expression that he doubted we would be down there long enough to need new identities. "You're making it more complicated." He tapped on his computer. "Laundry?"

"Fine."

"And for me…" He continued to tap on his computer. "Definitely not sewage… Mines. I can work in the mines. So we need names. I'll be Benjamin. According to the records, every other guy down there is Benjamin, so I'll blend right in. And for your name… lots of girls named after the seasons… Summer, Winter, Autumn… weird, there's no Spring."

"The Cull happens every spring. Who's going to name their daughter after that? Use Autumn."

"Okay... so Autumn and Benjamin Jones are now employed, and they need a place to live."

"*What*? We're going to pretend we're married?" I needed to live with my father. And it was bad enough Reyes saw me marry Jack on television without actually dragging a "husband" down to the Pit with me. How was I going to explain it was all a mistake while Jack was living with me?

"Well, technically we're not pretending. We actually are married," Jack said absentmindedly as he continued to tap away on his tablet. "And you're not leaving me on my own down there."

"Your presence will... complicate my life." I hoped to change his mind. I was sure I could find someone to take him in so we didn't have to live together.

"Boyfriend?"

I nodded.

"Don't worry. I'll stay out of your way." Somehow I wasn't reassured. "Okay, your chip is ready."

Jack took a Spritze out of the bin and felt the back of my right hand until he found my chip. He placed the device over my chip and extracted it. It was painless. He fitted the new chip into the Spritze and injected it into the back of my hand.

He placed a new chip into his computer and programmed it.

"My turn," he said, handing me the device. "Just press this button for extraction and this one to insert."

I did to his right hand what he had done to mine. Jack took our old chips and crushed them on the floor with the heel of his boot. "There go Jack Kenner and Sunny... I don't even know your last name, although now that we're married, I guess it's Kenner. Anyway, say goodbye to them."

"O'Donnell. My name is Sunset O'Donnell." I looked down where he had kicked our chips under the shelf and was struck by sadness. Why did it feel like a little death to see my chip destroyed?

Jack gave me a strange look. "Sunset?"

"My mother named me Sunset because of the color of my hair. I always hated it... until now. Now my name seems like a gift she gave me... something that was special to her... and it's all I had left." I needed to shake off the melancholy that suddenly gripped me. I was still Sunset O'Donnell. I didn't need a chip to tell me that.

"I remember that the night we met you were interested in a painting of a sunset. Why? Did the picture mean something?"

"Maybe. I don't know. I guess I was wondering how my mother knew what a sunset looked like." Why was I confiding in him? Why did I even bring this up? We were in the middle of an escape. "Forget it. We're running out of time."

"You lead the way." Jack held the door open for me. The hallway was still busy, and once again we joined the moving crowd.

I was halfway home.

CHAPTER ELEVEN

The big steel double doors were our only way out of the Dome and into the Pit, and to get to them we were going to have to walk through main reception. The whole area was still in a state of pandemonium after that morning's wedding debacle. Jack was hoping we could slip into a service elevator unnoticed to get to the main floor, but there were long queues at every elevator. We were going to have to go down the grand staircase in full view of everyone.

I followed the same path I'd taken that morning as a bride and approached the top of the staircase. I hesitated for a moment, the memory still fresh in my mind, but Jack didn't miss a beat. He wrapped an arm around my waist and swept me along with him.

Traffic on the staircase was thick, but Jack didn't let go of me until we reached the last step and began our trek across the busy room. Both steel doors were open for the servants wheeling carts back out to the kitchens. I noticed that none of them were wearing kitchen uniforms and then remembered the Pit was on lockdown. The bourge had to do their own work during lockdowns. I decided that we could easily act like we'd been sent to help. I led Jack over to the line-up of carts waiting to go and motioned for him to take one. I grabbed one and started wheeling it toward the door. I looked back and saw that he was following me.

I kept an even pace, resisting the urge to run through the doors. There was a line, and I realized with a sinking feeling that they were going to make us scan-in to pass through the doors. I stared down at my hand where Jack had inserted the new chip. I bit my lip, wondering if it would work. I was so close to being home. Just through those doors, then I could get back to the Pit. Beeps sounded up ahead as people passed the scanner before they filed out. Armed guards stood on the other side of the door. They were always there to keep the urchins out of the bourge's domain.

One more to go, and then it was my turn. The person ahead of me scanned and continued on his way. I began to sweat. I moved forward and waved my hand in front of the scanner. Nothing. I tried again. Nothing. My heart pounded harder. Out of the corner of my eye, I glanced at Jack. He looked nervous, too.

"Wait a minute," said one of the guards as he walked toward me. For just a second, there was no doubt in my mind that I had been caught, but I couldn't run. My legs were too weak and my feet felt like dead weights. "Scanner's been acting up all morning," he said, hitting the side of it a few times. "Try it again. I might have to find a new one."

The guard watched as I raised my hand to try again. My hand was trembling ever so slightly, and I focused on getting it under control. I passed my hand over the scanner. A beep, and then a green light flicked on. The guard waved me through and motioned for Jack to come forward. I heard the beep behind me.

It took all of my energy to walk on my weakened legs. I hung onto my cart tightly in case they gave out on me. Then I was through the steel doors and out into the lobby and the entrance to the Pit. The other people with carts were well ahead of me, but I knew my way to the kitchen. This was familiar territory. I walked down the hall and joined the line for the kitchen. I looked behind me and Jack was there. I gave him a worried look. Someone was bound to recognize me in the kitchen. In fact, I was sure I heard Supervisor Bailey instructing people on where to put their carts. She would know me for sure.

A few more carts pulled up behind Jack. I shuffled ahead as the queue moved, and my panic rose with each step. I cast Jack another look.

"Hey, buddy," Jack said to the guy behind him in line. "Can you do us a favour and take these carts in? We were told to get back ASAP to start tearing down that altar. I guess it's offending the president."

The guy rolled his eyes. "Can't imagine why. Although you can't blame Kenner. Leisel's not much of a looker even if she is the president's daughter. That urchin he married isn't hard on the eyes, though. What's her name?"

"Sunny O'Donnell." Jack grinned. "Hard to forget the pretty name that goes with the pretty face."

I couldn't believe how brazen Jack was being. He was going to get us both killed.

"Sunny O'Donnell," the man said. "That *is* a pretty name. Yeah, sure I'll take your carts for you. See you back in there."

"Thanks." Jack turned and walked away.

He didn't wait for me, so I walked quickly to catch up. The hall we needed to go down was coming up on the right, and I pulled Jack into it when we came upon it. We hurried down the hall and turned left, toward the old mine shaft. No one was back there, so I broke into a run. I could see the small door to the shaft. When I reached it, I took a deep breath and pulled it open. I was relieved. They usually forgot to lock the shaft doors when they did a lockdown, and I was glad this time was no different. We went in, and I shut the door. It was dark.

"Just give your eyes a minute to adjust," I said.

"It's pitch black in here. My eyes aren't going to adjust."

"They will. What about cameras? I assume there aren't any in the shafts?"

My eyes had already adjusted, but I was comfortable in the dark. I searched for the rope I knew was here. Years ago, the shafts were used to transport coal and mining debris up to the Dome. But the system was prone to breaking down, so they built a new one, closer to the place where debris was dumped.

"There aren't many cameras in the Pit—only in the common rooms. It was going to be a lot of work to put them in, and there didn't seem to be much need."

"We were always told that there were cameras everywhere. That the walls have ears."

"That's exactly why we didn't bother putting cameras in. Rumour seems to be working just as well. That, and there are armed guards everywhere. Any of you get out of line, and they can just shoot you," he said, in a joking tone.

"Oh, Jack. You'll soon find out that was no joke."

I found the rope and gave it a good tug to make sure it was secure. "Here. Use this to rappel down. I'll go first and guide you along as best I can." I scrambled over the side and began my descent.

"Wait! Aren't you going to use the rope too?" He sounded terrified.

"I don't need it. I've been doing this since I was five. And besides, I don't think that old rope is going to hold two of us."

I climbed down about ten feet and waited for him to start. I heard him double- checking the rope. "Come on," I said.

"I can't even see!"

He finally lowered himself over the side. Hanging onto the rope, he tentatively lowered one foot. I descended another ten feet and looked up. Jack hadn't made any progress. "Jack, you're taking too long. Trust the rope."

"You mean this *old* rope? Easy for you to say. You don't even need it. I can't see anything. How can you do this?!"

"Just lean out away from the rock, hang onto the rope, and start walking backwards. You have the rope — you don't need to find footholds." I heard him take a deep breath and watched him lean out. He lowered one foot, then the other, and again.

"Hey, I'm doing it!" he said excitedly.

He continued to rappel in a slow and steady rhythm. I descended another ten feet. I probably shouldn't be this close. If he fell, he would take us both down.

"How far do we have to go?" he asked.

"About a mile."

"Please tell me you're kidding."

"Nope. But we're almost there," I lied.

Down we went, me staying ten feet below Jack and encouraging him along. He was painfully slow, but I tried not to get frustrated. I remembered it was hard the first time I did it, too. Of course, I was only five.

Finally, I arrived at the sixth level. I reached over and pulled myself onto the landing.

"Almost there, Jack," I called up.

When his feet dangled just above my head, I gave them a little tug to help him along.

"Stop!" Jack's voice was edged with panic. "I'll do it myself."

I let go of him. I didn't need him screaming and bringing the guards in here. He lowered himself far enough to reach over to the landing. I grabbed him by the elbow and pulled him in. He hugged the side of the shaft, testing to make sure his feet were firmly on the ground.

"That was the scariest thing I've ever done in my life." His face was covered in a sheen of sweat.

I left him alone to collect himself and walked over to the door. I pressed my ear against it but didn't hear anything. There was usually traffic in the halls, but everything was quiet. Again, I had to remind myself that the Pit was on lockdown. Everyone would be in their homes.

"I keep forgetting about the lockdown. The only people in the halls right now are the guards."

"We can pretend we got lost or something. Took a wrong turn and we're trying to get back to our home. Make something up."

His naïveté surprised me. "The guards will shoot us on sight—they're not going to stop and *ask* us anything."

"They don't fool around down here, do they?"

"Nope."

Jack walked toward the shaft. "What if we climb back up and…"

"Stop!" I yelled.

He froze. He'd been about to walk over the edge. I went to him and gripped his arm. The toe of one of his shoes hung over the edge. "Back up," I said, pulling him back with me.

The door opened and a dim stream of light fell on us. We turned around slowly. The only escape was back into the shaft, and we would be nothing but target practice for the guard in there.

"Sunny? Is that you?" someone called from the doorway.

I squinted at the guard. "Bron?"

"It's me." She came in and shut the door. "Mr. Kenner, sir, it's an honor." She nodded at Jack. "What are you two doing here? I thought you were in the Dome waiting for your… trial."

"Are you going to turn us in?" I asked. I needed to know. I had come so close to getting home.

"I could get in a lot of trouble if I don't."

"I know. Which is why I won't ask you to help. I just wanted to get home and see my dad before… you know…"

"That was quite a wedding. Everyone is talking about it. Everyone's talking about you, Sunny." Bron smiled.

"The whole thing was an accident, Bron. Leisel betrayed us. It's a long story."

"Then keep your story to yourself. Right now you're a hero down here. You were sent upstairs to be a plaything at a bachelor party, but instead you married the groom and made the president's daughter a laughingstock. Don't tell them it was an accident."

"Don't tell them? Does that mean you'll let me go and see my father?"

"I can take you to him, but you can't stay there for very long. There'll be more guards down here soon for the check-in."

"Check-in?" Jack asked.

"When we're on lockdown, we have to return to our apartments and stay there. We can't visit anyone or go to the common rooms. The guards frequently carry out check-ins to make sure everyone is where they're supposed to be," I said.

"Divide and conquer," Jack said.

I gave him a confused look.

"Riots happen out of anger, so if you're left to stew together, you might just talk and come up with a plan to revolt. If you're separated, you can't talk."

"I always thought we were just being punished." It never occurred to me that the bourge would ever see us as a threat.

"You're correct, sir. We are under strict orders not to let them fraternize during a lockdown," Bron said. "What will you do after you see your father? Do you have a place to go to?"

"I secured an apartment for us. It's on the fourth level," Jack said.

"Well, come on then." She held the door open for us. "I'll take you to see your dad."

I hugged her. "Thank you, Bron."

"I'm doing this for your mother. I know she'd be very proud of you right now. And I'm doing this for the Kenners. I've been a loyal member of Liberty all of my life."

I was shocked to hear that Bron knew about Liberty.

"I appreciate it," Jack said. He held out his hand and they shook.

Bron looked pleased beyond words. I had no idea what was going on between them, so I said nothing.

Bron opened the door, and we walked out. I had walked these halls since the day I was able to take my first step. This was my home. When I was up in the Dome it felt like it had been an eternity since I had been here, but now it was like I had never left.

Luckily, we didn't pass any other guards on the way. My home was an exact replica of all the other homes down here: square box houses made from replicated wood and all attached to each other in a long row, backing onto the stone wall. Each box had a narrow door that led into a two-room apartment. I opened the door and turned on the light. My father was probably still in bed, right where I left him.

"Stay here," I told Jack.

My father lay under the thin blanket with his back to the door. I went in and sat down beside him on the bed. I placed my hand on his back, feeling for his heartbeat. It had been almost three days since I'd seen him, and he hadn't eaten that last day either. Four days.

"Dad?" I said softly. No answer. "Dad. *Dad.*" I was starting to panic, but then he stirred slightly. "Dad, it's me, Sunny. I'm back."

"Sunny?" He rolled over to look at me. I was shocked by how pale he was. "Is that you? Where have you been?"

"You scared me. I thought you were... Have you eaten since the last time I saw you?"

"I'm not hungry. I missed you, though. I wondered if you were coming back or if you had run off and married Reyes."

Obviously my father had not been out of bed that day or he would know that I did indeed get married, but not to Reyes. Jack came into the room with a glass of water. I was annoyed that he didn't stay out in the living room as I'd asked but thankful he brought the water.

"I wouldn't run off and leave you, Dad. I love you too much." I took the glass of water from Jack and put it to my father's lips. He drank.

"Who is this young man?"

"I'm Jack Kenner, sir. I'm pleased to meet you." Jack bent down and extended his hand. My father took it and gave it a weak shake. I watched Jack for a moment, surprised and confused by the respect he was showing.

"I've never met you before. Why are you here with my daughter?"

"I'll let your daughter explain that, sir. Sunny, I'll be out in the living room. Bron's gone to get some food."

"Sunny?" my father asked when we were alone again.

"Well... I guess maybe I did run off and get married, although I didn't mean to. It's complicated. Jack Kenner was supposed to marry the president's daughter today, but instead he and I got married. It was kind of an accident."

How could I explain all this to him without telling him I had been forced into going to Jack's bachelor party? I didn't want him to think badly of me.

"An accident? You got married by accident? To a bourge?" My father was smiling now, almost laughing. It had been a long time since I'd seen him look happy.

"It's not funny, Dad!" But I couldn't help but laugh, too. It all sounded so ridiculous. "Don't ask me how I got involved in this, but I met the president's daughter, Leisel, and she convinced me to take her place at her wedding today." I decided to leave out the part where Leisel thought she might be assassinated, so I played the role of decoy for her. "We were supposed to change places before the bride and groom were registered, but she didn't show up. So I had to scan in myself and, well, the scanner worked. It shouldn't have. It should only have worked for Leisel, but she betrayed us. Jack and I are in a lot of trouble."

"So President Holt didn't know it wasn't his daughter getting married?" He was still laughing.

"Not until Jack's mother ripped off my veil and wig."

My father was laughing so hard he started to cough. I realized laughing was using up what little energy he had left.

"I bet you caused quite a ruckus up there. The president must be red-in-the-face, spitting mad."

"He is. Spit was flying everywhere. I've never seen him that mad."

No one in the Pit liked the president. He was known for his rages. Whenever something went wrong in the Pit, or we didn't produce enough coal or diamonds, he would televise a lecture, and we would be forced to go into the common rooms and watch him. When we were all stuck there like that, what else could we do but make fun of him?

"Oh my daughter, you make me proud. But now you're in a lot of trouble. How much trouble?"

"How much trouble do you think an urchin would be in for humiliating the president's daughter and marrying her fiancé?" I tried to sound lighthearted. But our moment of humor was gone, and the reality of my situation hung in the air.

A tear trickled from the corner of my father's eye. "Are they going to make it a public execution?"

My breath caught on a sob. Was this our goodbye? "The only reason I'm here with you right now is that I escaped. I don't know if they've discovered we're gone yet or not, but when they do, they'll come looking for us. I don't intend to go back into the Dome alive. I won't give them the satisfaction of a public execution."

My father sat up and looked me in the eyes. "Then you *stay hidden*. Do you hear me? You don't let them find you."

"I'll do my best, Dad. Jack and I have new identities, so maybe we can live down here for a while."

"You do everything you can to stay alive, Sunny. Get more coal and cover up that hair of yours. Stay out of sight."

The front door of the apartment opened, and the smell of the food Bron had brought wafted through. She came into the bedroom and handed me the container.

"I promise to stay alive if you promise," I said to Dad. "Eat this." I opened the container of stew and started spooning it into his mouth. I could tell it was making him feel sick, but he swallowed it. I managed to get a few more mouthfuls into him before he collapsed back on the bed. I put the glass of water to his lips, and he drank.

"You're running out of time, Sunny. I need to get you upstairs," Bron said quietly.

"Can't I stay here with him? I don't want to leave him like this."

"I'll be fine, Sunny," Dad said. "I promise I'll eat and drink. You try and come to see me tomorrow."

"I'll check in on him," Bron said. "Right now, we have to go."

I kissed my father goodbye and went back out into the living room. I took the coal I always kept in my cupboard and put it in my pocket. Jack gave me a questioning look but didn't say anything.

"The place is filling up with guards now, so I want the two of you to march in front of me. It will look like I caught you out during curfew," Bron said.

"Let's go." It pained me to leave my father, but I risked everyone's safety if I stayed. If I were discovered here, my father would be in trouble for hiding a criminal. And if I sent Jack on to the apartment that Benjamin and Autumn were supposed to share and Autumn was absent during the check-in, then he would be questioned about my whereabouts, which would probably blow our cover. I had no choice but to go. I silently cursed Jack for giving me an identity that prevented me from looking after my father.

We marched toward the stairs, Bron behind us with her gun. We only had two levels to climb, so it would be a short walk. As we started up, two guards coming down stopped us.

"A couple of troublemakers?" one of them asked.

"Nothing I can't handle," Bron said. She motioned for us to keep moving.

"Why are you even bothering to take them upstairs? Just shoot them," the other guard said.

"That's against regulations." She prodded us with the barrel of her gun. "Keep moving."

"Since when do we worry about regulations down here?" The guard laughed and the other joined in. "Listen, if you want to get your exercise climbing up and down those stairs, be my guest. But I see anyone out, I'm shootin' them."

We made it to the fourth level then without further incident. Once we located our new apartment, I nervously passed my hand over the scanner. I was relieved when I heard the door unlock. My new chip worked.

"I have to go back down, so you're on your own. I'll keep an eye on your father," Bron said.

"Thank you for everything." I wanted to give her another hug to show how much I appreciated her help, but if a guard came around the corner and saw it, we would both be in a lot of trouble.

"Thanks," Jack said.

"It's been a real privilege, sir. I'll help out any way I can." She left to go back to the sixth level.

We went in and checked out our new home. The place looked tidy. I wondered about the previous occupants and where they might be now. Culled? Shot during the riot? How long had it been empty?

"Why was Bron acting that way with you?" I asked.

"I told you Liberty has supporters, and I guess she's one of them. Why did you take the coal?"

"My hair." I took off my cap and threw it on the table. My hair was still in the tight bun I'd worn under Leisel's wig. I took out the elastic and shook it loose. It felt good. I picked up the coal and rubbed it against a lock of hair.

"See? No more red. You should use it too. No one has light hair down here."

I finished rubbing the coal through my hair and handed it to him. He took it, looking at it dubiously. Then he took off his cap and started rubbing his head with it.

"Not like that. You're making a mess." I sat him in the chair and rubbed the coal just against his short strands, staying away from his scalp. "There." Dark hair didn't suit him at all, but I decided to keep that to myself.

I walked over to the sink and turned on the faucet, hoping the previous occupants hadn't used up all their water rations. The water flowed. I took a glass down from the cupboard and filled it.

"There won't be any food in here, but we have water," I said. I had almost drained the glass when there was a knock at the door.

"Is that the guard for the check-in?"

I nodded, went to the door, and opened it. A guard stood there with a scanner. We waved our hands over the scanner and received green lights. I realized too late that we didn't have our hats on, but at least we'd covered our hair with coal. The guard moved on to the next apartment.

"How can your father do the check-in if he can't get out of bed?" Jack's voice held a note of concern.

"Bron's been the guard in that section for as long as I can remember. She's probably checking him in."

"He looks really sick," Jack said softly.

"He is." He was sick with grief over the death of my mother; sick with despair knowing his own death was only months away. I should be with him, but I was trapped. "And thanks to you, he's on his own."

Jack held up both his hands as if to ward off a blow. "I didn't know."

"I told you! Before your wedding, I told you my dad was sick and I had to look after him. But you didn't listen because you didn't care."

"I'm sorry."

I saw the sincerity on his face, but the sentiment had come too late. My father was alone because Jack didn't want to be left on his own down here. I blamed him for my predicament.

"I need sleep." Without another word, I escaped into the bedroom and closed the door. I didn't care where he slept or even if he stayed. I just crawled onto the thin mattress and tried to blot out the last three days of my life.

I felt so hopeless.

CHAPTER TWELVE

I t wasn't the sound of the *bong bongs* going off that startled me awake but the reaction of the person in the next room. I sat up, eyes wide open.

"What the hell is *that*?" Jack asked, as he raced into the bedroom.

"What are you doing?"

"Aren't there any windows in here? What's going on out there?"

"Relax. It's just the morning call to work. The lockdown must be over. That's why no one came to check us in again during the night."

"Morning call to work?" He looked confused.

"Happens every morning down here in the Pit. We have about fifteen minutes to get to the common room for breakfast. Exactly one hour from now, we need to scan in at our place of work. And we can't be late or we'll lose our jobs, and Benjamin and Autumn will be homeless and no better off than Jack and Sunny."

I got out of bed. I realized I still had the bulletproof vest on, and it was beginning to feel like a dead weight. "I have to take this thing off."

"Leave it on if you can stand it. It makes you look heavier — less like Sunny."

He was probably right. Plus the added protection against bullets might come in handy if I was caught.

We went out into the living room. Jack donned his hat and threw mine at me. Hats weren't very popular in the Pit, but there were a few people who wore them, so we shouldn't look too out of place.

I decided to go to the sixth-floor common room for breakfast. There was already a lot of traffic on the stairs — early risers hoping to be first in line for breakfast. Technically we were supposed to stay on our own level for meals, but the guards never bothered to enforce that rule. Mealtimes were about the only time throughout the day when we could socialize, and the guards didn't mind, as long as we went about it peacefully.

We reached the sixth level, and I turned toward my home to get my dad to come to breakfast. I was hoping I could get him out of bed quickly, because I didn't want to miss out on the food. It had been more than twenty-four hours since I last ate and it appeared that I would have to go and work a full day in the laundry room. As I rounded the corner in the hall, I could see Bron standing not far from my father's apartment. She looked startled to see me and silently shook her head.

"Stop," Jack said, grabbing my arm to prevent me from going any further. "Something's wrong."

I gave Bron a questioning look, and she mouthed the word "guards." I didn't know if she meant someone was at my father's house right now or if they had been there. I wondered if my father was okay, or if the guards were there to kick him out of the apartment now that I was no longer there to support him.

"Turn around," Jack said. "Take us to the common room. There'll be a bigger crowd there to get lost in."

Since I had no choice, I did as he asked. I had to trust that Bron wouldn't let anything happen to my father. At least I'd been able to get food and water into him the night before.

There was a long line of people already waiting for the common room to open its door. Meals weren't served during a lockdown, so everyone was starving. I scanned the faces of the people in line hoping to see Summer or Reyes. I saw a lot of familiar faces, but not those two. I hoped no one would recognize me.

The doors to the common room opened, and everyone began to shuffle in to get their breakfast ration. Jack and I shuffled along with everyone else, keeping our heads down. When our turn came to enter the room, I saw the big television screen was lit up with the presidential seal, which could only mean that there was going to be an announcement. People were groaning at the sight, not wanting to sit through another lecture. So much of our day was spent working that meals were considered a special time to spend with friends and loved ones. No one liked being interrupted by President Holt.

"Again?" someone behind me complained loudly when he entered the room. "Does the president think we need more reminding of how lucky we are?"

"Yeah, we were all real lucky yesterday," someone else chimed in.

"Don't start another riot!" a third person said, his voice booming as he stepped out of line ahead of us. It was Reyes, his glare directed at the two in the back making all the complaints made even more impressive by his tall, muscular frame and crop of curly dark hair.

Even though I had been searching the crowd for him, his appearance was still a shock. All I could do was stand there and stare at him. Now that he was in front of me, what could I say to him? How could I explain everything that had happened? He scanned the line to see if anyone wanted to challenge him, and his eyes came to rest on me. I could tell by his shocked expression that he recognized me right away. I was afraid he might give me away, so I looked past him at the guard standing at the back of the room. His gaze followed mine, and he nodded in understanding. He made a slight motion with his head in the direction of the tables. He wanted me to join him.

"What are you doing, Autumn?" Jack asked when he noticed my exchange with Reyes.

"He's a friend. I need to talk to him."

"It's risky."

"Remember the only reason I came was to say goodbye to the people I love, and that's what I'm doing." There was no way I was going to let him cheat me out of saying goodbye.

"You're right. I lost sight of our goal here. So is that your boyfriend? The guy your father thought you ran off and married?"

"Does it matter?" I snapped. Reyes was none of his business.

"Yeah, it matters. Look at the size of that guy, and I just married his girlfriend!"

I studied Jack's expression for a moment to see if he was joking. I had seen him fight and knew Reyes wouldn't stand a chance against him.

It was our turn to get breakfast, and we were each handed a sealed container with a spoon and a glass of water. I saw Reyes sitting with his friends, Raine and Mica, and for a second, I hesitated. I trusted Reyes, but not always his friends. Would one of them shout out my identity? I didn't want to get caught so soon. My dad was probably in danger, and I hadn't seen Summer yet.

Seeing me hesitate, Reyes motioned for me to join him again. He probably already told everyone we were here anyway. I went to sit with him, and Jack mutely followed behind me.

"This is Benjamin and I'm Autumn," I said in a firm voice. I couldn't believe those were the first words out of my mouth, but I was afraid Reyes or someone else would use our real names.

I took the empty chair beside Reyes and Jack sat across from us. Reyes gave him a murderous glare before he turned his chair to face me. He put his head close to mine and talked in a low voice.

"What happened?" His voice cracked with emotion. "I waited and waited for you to come back from that bachelor party and you never did. The next thing I know you're on television in a wedding dress marrying that… bourge!"

"It was all a mistake." I didn't know where to begin. "I know what it looked like on television, but that's not the way it happened. Leisel lied to everyone."

"If you're not in love with him, then why did you bring him here?"

"He helped me escape. I owe him." I hadn't quite realized it until then, but strangely I did feel responsible for Jack. I knew I shouldn't. It was partly his fault that I was in this predicament. I glanced over at Jack. He was busy taking the lid off his container and sniffing the contents. His nose crinkled in distaste, but he tried it anyway. Then he put the bowl down and replaced the lid.

Raine and Mica were staring at him too, not sure what to say or how to treat him. We didn't tend to get a lot of bourge down here dining with us, particularly famous ones.

"What the hell happened, Sunny? Do you know what it did to me to see you up there on the screen with *him*? The president's daughter saying he jilted her because the two of you are in love? When the guards dragged you off, I thought they killed you."

The pain I had caused Reyes was clearly written on his face and a stab of guilt went through me. "I think the president wanted to kill me, but he couldn't because we were being televised. Then the guards came and took him to safety because of the riot down here." I was babbling, not answering his question.

"Why did you do it?" He grabbed me by both my arms. His fingers bit into my flesh, and I winced.

"Because the president's daughter conned me into it!" At my answer he finally released me. Even though I was used to Reyes being rough with me, I rubbed my arms to assess the damage. It wasn't bad. "Have you seen Summer? Did she tell you anything?"

"Summer told me about the president's daughter and how she invited you to his place, but then you never came back. I went nuts trying to find out what happened to you, and then I saw you on television marrying him." Reyes narrowed his eyes, casting an accusatory glare at Jack. I couldn't tell if he was angry or sad, so I didn't know what to say or how to make it right. "What the president's daughter said—about you and him falling in love and trying to get rid of her—made sense at that moment. What other reason could there be?"

"Leisel manipulated me into taking her place at the wedding. She caught Summer stealing food after the bachelor party and threatened to tell the authorities. She also gave me a story about an assassination plot planned against her for her wedding day and wanted me to take her place wearing a bulletproof vest. She convinced me that when she and Jack took control of the president's office, things in the Pit would get better. So I played the decoy bride. I did it to save Summer. I did it because I believed her when she said she wanted to make things better down here. But in the end, she used us. The whole thing was a plan to convince her father to let her succeed him as president."

"So you're not in love with him?"

I shook my head, sorry to be the cause of so much heartache.

His pained expression transformed into one of anger. "If you had just let me protect you in the first place, none of this would have happened. But you're always so worried about protecting everybody else!"

I pulled my chair away from his, putting a little distance between us. Reyes had a habit of being hurtful when he was angry. Not that I didn't deserve his anger, but having a conversation with him right then would be pointless. I turned to Raine and Mica. "So what happened here? Why was there a riot?"

"Everyone's bloody fed up with the bourge, that's why," Reyes said, staring at Jack. Jack glared back at him.

"He's not wrong," Mica said. "People started lining up for the so-called feast the night before the wedding. The guards didn't care because no one was making trouble and the night had kind of a festive feel to it. After waiting all night, you know what the feast turned out to be? Bread. They gave us bread with our stew. Do you believe that?" Mica was clearly getting upset, which made me nervous. I didn't want him to draw attention to our table. "So they're showing us the wedding on the screen and the well-dressed guests taking their seats, but all we can see are tables heaped with food *everywhere!*" Mica shot Jack a look of disgust. "Did they actually think we wanted to see your stinkin' wedding? We only came for the food!"

"Mica, keep it down," Reyes said. The guards in the room remained oblivious to us. "You'll start another riot, and yesterday's was bad enough. Three people were killed, including a little kid. We don't need to start killing each other too—there are enough bourge doing that for us."

"He's just saying what we all felt," Raine said. "Everyone was just so… *angry!* So you can only imagine how much we enjoyed seeing the president's daughter crying her fool head off. I mean we were confused at first because we thought she was the bride. But there she was, falling on the floor, crying and looking pathetic and humiliated. It was epic! We didn't think it could get any better than that, but then someone tears off your veil." Raine looked at me with a smile. "It was sweet, sweet revenge finding out that Leisel Holt was humiliated by one of us *and* you stole her husband! An urchin married the next president."

"It's true," said Mica. "The entire Pit went nuts. Everyone was laughing and clapping and cheering for Sunny O'Donnell... except maybe Reyes." He eyed his friend. Reyes stared at the floor, glowering. "Then the guards started telling us to keep it down, but why should we? We weren't fighting—we were having a laugh is all. When we wouldn't stop, they started getting rough, so people started fighting back. That's when all hell broke loose. The president sent Domers down here and threatened to cut off our ventilation system. People got scared, grabbed their kids, and ran home. They put us on lockdown."

"I'm sorry for everything," Jack said. "I really am."

"A bourge is apologizing to *us*?" Raine asked, his tone incredulous.

"I don't like to be lumped in with the likes of Holt. He's a tyrant. For what it's worth, I was marrying Leisel to gain control of the Dome by becoming president. There are a lot of people who don't like the way things are under his government. Unlike President Holt, we don't think you're very lucky down here at all. Things need to change."

Reyes put on an expression of mock surprise. "You mean things should change for the better in the Pit? Isn't that the same crap your fiancée fed Sunny? And look how much better off she is for it."

Music filled the room, heralding President Holt's announcement. A collective groan went through the crowd, but for the first time in my life, I was interested in what Holt had to say. By now he knew we had escaped.

"I bid you a good morning." The president began his address in his usual tight-lipped manner. "The events of the past twenty-four hours have affected us all. My daughter's wedding, which the entire Dome was anticipating with great excitement and happiness, has been the target of two malicious people intent on destroying the very fabric of our society. Jack Kenner, my daughter's estranged fiancé, presented himself to me — and to every one of you — as a man who held great promise as the next president. I believe I speak on behalf of us all when I say my daughter's marriage to him was supposed to be the very symbol of hope, progress, and success for the future of our society.

"Only her wedding day did not turn out to be the beginning of a bright future beside the man she loved. Instead, she was traumatized!" The president's voice rose to a yell and his face turned red. I overheard a few people taking bets on when spit would fly out of his mouth. "Jack Kenner is a traitor! He tried to lead my Leisel down a path that would end in the *destruction* of our society, but she said *no* to him. My daughter is *faithful* to her people. She held the good of the people above her own love for her fiancé and above her own personal happiness, and *that* is why Jack Kenner inflicted pain and humiliation on her!" Holt was beginning to look a little crazed, and the spit was beginning to fly. I heard someone behind me being congratulated on winning the bet.

The president paused, trying to get himself under control. Then he looked directly into the camera. "Jack Kenner is a criminal, and he has escaped, with his new wife in tow. I want them found and brought before the tribunal to answer for their crimes of treason."

His words caught the attention of the entire room. Everyone was sitting up and staring at the television with shocked expressions on their faces. A murmur went through the crowd, and I wanted to sink lower in my chair, but knew it would only draw attention to me. I glanced over at Jack, and his wide-eyed expression told me to stay calm.

"We have already made a preliminary search with no luck in finding them," President Holt continued. "Therefore I appeal to all of you. Anyone with information leading to their arrest will be rewarded with four hundred credits. And anyone found hiding them will be considered a sympathizer to traitors and punished according to our laws. Death."

The Presidential Seal flashed up on the screen, signalling the end of the address.

"Well, that's it then," Jack said, leaning forward to rest his elbows on the table.

I knew he was right. It was just a matter of time before someone recognized us and collected the reward. The reward was enough to ensure an urchin would never be homeless, even if he lost his job. I looked around the table. I didn't think Reyes wanted to collect the reward, but maybe one of his friends?

"What do you mean *'That's it'*?" Reyes asked. "She's a hero down here—no one's going to turn her in." The murmuring among the crowd was getting louder, and Reyes had to raise his voice to be heard above it. I was getting concerned someone would overhear him.

"Reyes, he's right, that's a huge reward. I won't blame anyone who takes advantage of it," I said, resting my hand on his arm to quiet him.

"I'll blame them!" Suddenly he was on his feet, climbing up on his chair. I couldn't believe he was doing it with Jack and me sitting right there. He might as well just turn us in himself.

"*Everyone! Listen to me!*" he yelled above the din of the crowd. The guards stepped forward in response to Reyes's yelling, but the room started to quiet down. In the distance I could hear noise coming from the levels above and below us.

Now that he had the room's attention, he lowered his voice, but only slightly. "Sunny O'Donnell took on the president and his darling little daughter when *no one else* has ever had the guts to do it! The bourge treat us worse than their livestock! Our food is their leftovers!" He kicked his food container off the table, sending it skidding across the floor. "Our lives are devoted to making *their* lives better, and what do we get for it? They kill us for being late, they kill us for not having a job, and they kill us for turning thirty-five!"

He paused and looked around the room. All eyes were on him. A guard was speaking into his communicator. He was probably looking for backup.

"Yesterday, for the first time, we saw the bourge humiliated. We saw what pain does to *them*. And that pain was inflicted on them by *one of us*. Sunny O'Donnell is not a traitor! She's a goddamn *hero*! And anyone who turns her in to the bourge for that measly offer of four hundred credits will have *me* to deal with!" Reyes pounded his first into his palm.

Someone started shouting "Sunny O'Donnell" over and over, creating a chorus that went up among the crowd. People began to stand, throwing their fists in the air. I couldn't believe what was happening. How could they see me as a hero? Leisel was the one who humiliated me, not the other way around. She used me to frame Jack as a traitor, and I went along with her plan. I wasn't a hero — I was a naïve and stupid girl who was duped by a master manipulator.

Jack stood and joined the crowd, putting his fist in the air calling out my name. He was looking at me with that wide-eyed expression again, willing me to do something. Then I realized I was the only one in the room still seated and not shouting out my name. I stood and put my fist in the air too, yelling "Sunny O'Donnell." I felt so stupid. I knew we would be put on lockdown again.

Just as the thought entered my mind, armed guards came rushing into the room. I saw someone at the front of the room get the butt of a gun against the side of his face, knocking him to the floor. Another guard pointed his gun at the ceiling and pulled the trigger, and a loud bang reverberated through the room. I lowered my fist and gave everyone at our table a look that said, "Stop!" I did not want to be the cause of anyone being shot or hurt. Under my angry glare, Reyes stepped down off the chair and lowered his fist.

"Lockdown," I said for Jack's benefit.

"It won't be for long," he said.

"How would you know that?" Reyes asked.

"Because you were on lockdown all day yesterday. They need you to cook, clean, serve, work the mines and do all the things you do. When you don't do them, life in the Dome comes to a halt. We'll be off lockdown by lunch."

As I listened to Jack, something inside me clicked, and I looked at him with new eyes. All along I had only thought of him as the famous bridegroom—as the man who would become president one day. But now I was seeing him in a whole new light. I flashed back to him at the wedding, dressed in the military uniform of a high-ranking officer. I remembered his comments about lockdowns to Bron—about how they were used to divide us. And he thought he knew when lockdown would be over.

It occurred to me that Jack possessed very valuable insight into the bourge and how they ran the Pit... insight that could come in handy if someone wanted to start a revolt.

CHAPTER THIRTEEN

W e all hung back at our table as long as we could before we had to start moving toward the door.

"Take that with you," I said to Jack, pointing to his breakfast. No one in the Pit would ever leave food behind. His full container would sit on the table like a beacon.

I stood beside Reyes as we shuffled out the door with the rest of the crowd. His hand searched for mine, and I willingly accepted it. I felt guilty for getting mad at him earlier and gave him an apologetic look, to which he responded with a sad one. We both knew we could never go back to the way we were. Our future together had disappeared the minute I agreed to be Leisel's victim.

"I was hoping to see Summer, too," I said. "I wonder why she wasn't at breakfast."

Reyes drew his brows together, and his expression became closed off. "She's been eating breakfast somewhere else the past few days."

"What does that mean?" I asked even though I was pretty sure I knew what it meant; Summer hadn't been sent home early from that bachelor party. Someone upstairs had claimed her for himself.

"You know exactly what it means," Reyes said accusingly. "I've only talked to her once since the night you two left for the party, and that's when she told me about you two meeting Leisel Holt. I've seen her a few times since, but she doesn't look at me. She doesn't look at anyone. She just keeps her eyes on the floor."

I knew why Summer kept her head down; she was ashamed. I never understood why girls who were taken as mistresses by the bourge felt ashamed and embarrassed. It wasn't their fault. And the thought of my best friend—the happiest person I've ever known— being used by one of those pompous old men at the party sickened me with disgust.

When we came to the stairs, Reyes dropped my hand to encircle my waist with his arms. I knew he didn't want to let me go, and maybe if I weren't so consumed right now with hatred for the bourge, I would feel the same way.

"Stay safe," he whispered and then kissed me. Reyes dropped his arms from my waist and turned to Jack. "You touch her, and I'll kill you."

Jack stared back at him, seemingly unfazed by the threat. I really didn't want Reyes to create another scene, so I ignored him and joined the flow of traffic on the stairs. Jack followed me. There were armed guards positioned along the staircase who made it their job to keep everyone moving as quickly as possible. It didn't take very long for us to get back to the apartment that was an exact replica of where I grew up, and yet was so unfamiliar.

"I have to take this off," I said as soon as we entered the apartment. Thoughts of Summer and my dad were weighing me down enough without the bulletproof vest adding to it.

Jack lifted up one of my arms to examine the bruises Reyes gave me. "Your boyfriend's a really nice guy."

I jerked my arm out of his hand. "It's none of your business."

"You're right. And that's the only reason he has any teeth left."

I ignored him and went into the bedroom, shutting the door behind me in an attempt to get a few moments alone. I wasn't sure if I wanted to cry or be sick. Summer was always the brightest light in this dark Pit, and it tore me apart inside to think of her being abused. I was worried about my dad, too. There was no way for me to find out if he was safe or not.

I just wanted to kill someone — anyone — to make the madness stop.

I stripped down to the vest, undid the straps, flipped it over my head, and let it fall to the floor with a thud. The weight off my shoulders and chest was a relief. I put Jack's t-shirt back on, and it hung from my skinny frame.

A loud banging on the door invaded the small apartment. I knew it would be a guard to perform the routine check-in. Reluctantly, I left the sanctity of the room and went out to answer it. I was surprised to find Jack stripped down to his waist doing sit-ups on the floor.

"What are you doing?" I asked.

"I'm a little stressed out," he said between deep breaths, "and exercise always relaxes me."

He jumped up off the floor and came to the door with me. I opened it. The guard held out the scanner, eyeing the two of us with a smirk on his face. My shirt was askew, and Jack was half naked and breathing hard. Not hard to tell what the guard thought we had been doing. We both scanned in, and the guard continued to the next house.

"Want to try?" Jack asked, sitting back down on the floor.

"Why not?" It might help me work off the anger I was feeling about Summer's predicament.

I lay down beside Jack on the floor and fell into sync with him. I had never done sit-ups before, but it seemed easy. I still wasn't sure how it would ease my stress, though.

Jack rolled over onto his stomach. "Try this." Balancing with one leg tucked over the other, he began to push himself up and down using his arms. "Push-ups."

I rolled over and did the same. Up, down. Up, down. This felt like a better exercise than the sit-ups. At least I could feel some of the tension in my neck and shoulders turn into fatigue. Jack counted under his breath. We were at thirty.

My breathing was heavier, too. I was starting to sweat. "How many of these are we doing?"

"Fifty. I don't want to push you too hard on the first time."

"Don't worry about me."

After another moment he said "fifty" and stopped. I had only counted thirty-six but stopped, too.

"You're right, it did help to relax me." I rolled my shoulders, enjoying the feel of my weakened muscles, but I still had murderous energy flowing through me. "What's next?"

He shrugged. "I don't know. I don't have any equipment down here. Usually I lift weights, run the track, swim, that kind of thing."

"I know! Teach me to fight—like you fought the guards at your apartment."

"That's actually a good idea. You need to learn self-defense with that boyfriend of yours."

"I don't think that's funny."

"It wasn't meant to be," he said, and pushed a small table out of our way. "We'll start with T'ai Chi, an exercise that teaches martial arts through repetition. Just do what I do."

He stood up straight and slowly brought his hands up to chest height, crossed them, then stretched out his right hand as he extended his right leg. He curled his right leg, bringing his knee waist high, and then set it down. Then he repeated everything with his left side. Each action was very controlled and flowed into the next. He was going slowly so it was easy for me to follow.

"Seems more like a dance," I said. "I was hoping for something faster paced and a little more violent."

No sooner had I spoken than Jack sped up his movements. His leg came up and his foot snapped at my chest, stopping just inches from making contact. Less than a second later, the back of his hand stopped just half an inch from my nose.

He smiled. "Like that?"

"Like that."

"You need to learn the exercises before you can control them. Try again?"

I nodded.

We went back into the first stance he'd shown me, and he repeated all the actions. Our hands were always moving, stretching one way, and then recoiling and stretching another. Our legs were constantly in motion. We squatted one minute then moved one leg up and balanced on the other leg.

"So how long have you and Reyes been together?"

"Why do you want to know that?" My relationship with Reyes was none of his business.

"Just trying to make conversation." He shrugged. "Okay, I'm wondering what he whispered to you that made you so upset."

"He told me that Summer is being used by those ugly old men I saw at your bachelor party."

"Oh." He stopped and looked at me. "I'm really sorry, Sunny."

"Are you?" My anger came bubbling up to the surface again. I decided that killing someone actually would be a good release of all these emotions I had pent up. "How about we try out these moves you've been teaching me?"

I tried to strike out at him as fast as he had struck out at me earlier, but he easily blocked my punch. I raised my leg to kick him, but he stepped out of the way. I momentarily lost my balance, but recovered quickly and threw the heel of my left hand toward his face. Knowing he would block that strike, I had my right hand ready to catch him off guard. But he just grabbed both my wrists and somehow spun me around, pinning my arms to my sides.

"Had enough?" he asked.

I raised my leg and brought it down to stomp hard on his foot. This time I did surprise him, and he let go of me. I whirled around to face him, but he was already in a defensive stance. I took a step forward, he took one back. I sped up my movements and so did he. I threw my right hand in his direction and followed through with my body to put more power behind my strike. Jack stepped backward, but didn't see the chair behind him and tripped and fell. I was already in motion when he went down, so instead of my strike making contact, I ended up on top of him on the floor. I tried to jump up, but he wrapped his arms around my waist and held me there.

"You catch on quick!" he said, smiling. "Who knew sparring could be this much fun?"

"Let me up!" I tried to get out of the hold he had on me, but he was too strong.

Despite my anger, I was very aware that my entire body was pressed against his. Our faces were only inches away from each other. His smile remained as I struggled against his hold on me, his blue eyes never leaving mine. I put my hands on his chest to push away from him and was surprised at how warm and smooth his naked chest felt. I breathed in his scent, a combination of soap and sweat, and my heart beat faster. I wasn't sure if I wanted to kiss him or punch him.

"Let. Me. Go!"

"Not until you tell me why you're trying to kill me."

"Because it's your fault! *You* were supposed to sign her up with some old guy who was going to fall asleep, and then she would be sent home."

Deep down I knew that ultimately Leisel had betrayed Summer, not Jack. But it made me furious that he didn't think enough of Summer to make sure the plan was followed through. And I was angry with myself for letting Leisel manipulate me so easily.

The smile finally left Jack's lips, and his expression became more serious. Our eyes locked for what seemed an eternity, neither one of us saying anything to the other. My hands remained on his chest, and I could feel his heart beating strongly just below my fingertips.

Finally, Jack said, "I did sign her up with Forbes, but I should've done more for her. I'm sorry."

He continued to hold me against him for a moment, long enough for me to see the sincerity in his eyes, and then he relaxed his arms around my waist. I jumped up, relieved to put distance between us.

"Apology accepted." I said it tersely, as if my words were a lie. Despite my mixed feelings, it wouldn't do me any good to hold a grudge against him.

"If I let you beat me up, will you feel better?" he asked, brightly.

I almost screamed. *Let* me beat him up? But I realized that's exactly what I wanted. I needed to release all the hatred inside of me before it ate me alive.

Jack stood up and righted the chair. "Look, I'm frustrated, angry, and feeling helpless, too. I don't know if Holt has my family locked up or not. I can guarantee he's already gathering evidence of treason against me so he can legally execute me. And I'm living down here in the Pit where—what do you call us? Borks?—are hated. But I'm hoping that you and I can at least be friends and help each other survive." He raked a hand through his hair, and it came away black from the coal. "I am really sorry about Summer. If there was any way I could help her, I would."

Once again I was seeing another side of him. I guess I had never really thought of Jack Kenner as a person before, only as a famous bourge I frequently saw on television. But he stood before me, half naked and apologetic, struggling with his own fears for his family.

Maybe Jack and I could be friends.

"Bork?" I asked. "We call you bourge. But I think I like bork better. It rhymes with dork." I gave him a sheepish grin. "A truce?"

"That would be nice, because I have a feeling it's going to get rough down here."

"What do you mean?"

"I mean you. You heard Reyes and his friends— you're a hero. The one thing people needed down here was a victory and you gave them one. I know you think Leisel humiliated you, but that's not what they saw. They saw an urchin taking down a bourge and putting her in her place." Jack looked at me as if waiting for my reaction, but I was still trying to make sense of how I went from being a victim to a hero. My brain hadn't accepted that information yet.

"That's not all they saw," I said. "They think they saw a love story between you and me. They believed what Leisel said."

"I know. And it would seem our love story has sparked a hell of a response from everyone down here."

He took a deep breath and dragged his hand through his hair again. "I'm reminded of a saying I was taught at the military academy. It went, 'Red sky at night, sailor's delight. But red sky in the morning, sailors take warning.' It was used to predict the weather. A red sunset meant clear skies, but a red sunrise meant a coming storm. I can't help thinking your mom should've named you Sunrise, because there's a storm on its way, Sunny, and you're at the center of it."

I gave him a look. "A storm? Seriously, Jack?"

He laughed. "That was just my corny way of saying there's a war brewing. You didn't start it, but you seem to be the catalyst for it."

"I think something's brewing too, but I'm not sure about a full-blown war." I shook my head. "You think no one's ever thought of that down here? Believe me, we would have started one a long time ago if we weren't condemned to living in a death trap. But the minute we make any noise, they threaten to lock the doors and shut off our ventilation. How long do you think we'd have before we ran out of oxygen or the entire Pit filled with gas from the mines? Our salvation won't come until we can leave the Dome. But I think a revolt is possible. We could push back a little to let the bourge know we've had enough just like we did when they tried to lower the age of the Cull to thirty."

Jack rubbed the back of his neck. "I don't know. The military reports I've read—during my short career— suggest that unrest in the Pit has escalated over the past few years. President Holt included the Pit in the wedding celebrations as an attempt to pacify everyone down here. You know, include them in the wedding and make them feel like one of us. Unfortunately, his own prejudices prevented him from treating you as anything more than slaves. I'm betting he thought the extra bread with dinner was a huge gift for people so undeserving."

I gave a snort of understanding. "And he never stopped to think that the bread was a slap in the face considering all the food on display in the Dome."

"Exactly — it's a mistake that Holt is going to repeat over and over again because he doesn't know what he did wrong. Life has never been good down here, but it's worked. It's worked because despite how people feel about their president, they still believe their leader is rational, sane, and knows best how to run the Dome. But the Holts have always been tyrants, and this one is particularly bad. Damien is insane. He's cut back your rations and increased your workloads, and he's also given free license to the guards and supervisors down here to keep you in line any way they choose. People are getting scared and desperate, and they're finally losing faith in their leader."

Jack was making a lot of sense. I had felt the tension he was talking about in my own life. We really weren't being given enough food to have the energy to perform our jobs, especially the miners, which only incited the wrath of our supervisors. There were more guards now too, restricting whatever freedoms we had enjoyed in the past. Yet despite how bad life had become, the thought of war inside the Dome was scary.

"War is a bad idea. The president holds all the power and we have none," I said. I sat down heavily. Things were looking bleak.

"I think the ball is already rolling, Sunny." He sat in the chair across from me. "There's nothing you can do to stop it."

"Then maybe we could try to control it. You have a military background, and you seem to know an awful lot about how the bourge run things down here. When you go to work in the mines, share your knowledge with everyone. Teach them to fight, like you're teaching me. Give them what they need to defend themselves."

He shook his head. "It would never work."

"You can't know that unless you try."

"The only way I can teach them to fight is to expose who I am. Do you honestly think the miners are going to tolerate *me* pretending to be one of them? No one down here is going to accept me."

"Reyes already knows who you are. He can help you."

"*Reyes?* If he didn't already have anger management issues, he certainly does now that I've married his girlfriend! He isn't going to help me. In fact, he's probably the first one in line to kill me."

A loud alarm rang out in the hallway, and Jack put his hands over his ears to block out the sound.

"The lockdown is over. You were right."

I retrieved Jack's t-shirt off the floor and threw it to him. I grabbed my hat and put it on.

"Forgetting something?" he asked. I look around not sure what he meant. "The vest. Put it back on."

"Right."

I went into the bedroom and put it on. It felt heavier for some reason. I pulled my t-shirt over it and then put my hat on. I was back to being Autumn Jones.

"I know where the laundry room is, do you know where you're going?" I asked as I came back into the living room.

"Two miles down into the bowels of the Dome."

"At the end of the work day, we'll meet back here, okay?" I held the door open for him.

"Yeah, provided we make it through the day."

People were pouring out of their apartments and heading in all directions, going to their places of work. We joined the flow and headed for the stairs. As we reached them, Jack gently took my arm and turned me towards him.

"Be careful. I don't want to get stuck down here alone."

"You, too."

We both knew it might be the last time we ever saw each other.

Chapter Fourteen

I watched Jack walk down the stairs until I couldn't see him anymore. I hoped Reyes and his friends would reconcile themselves to him. Reyes never actually said how he felt about Jack's presence down there, but judging by the murderous glares he was giving him, I was going to go with hate. I should have talked to Reyes about him when I had the chance.

As I climbed the stairs to the second-level laundry room, my anxiety at coming closer to the main floor of the Dome grew. All I had to do was climb just one more level, and I would be standing right in front of the well-guarded reception area to the Dome. I wondered how long it would take for someone to recognize me. Would they shoot me on the spot? Or take me back to Holt to be dealt with? I think I preferred to be shot on sight.

I hated to admit it, but I was feeling vulnerable being separated from Jack. He was my partner in crime. If I were going to be caught and dragged back to his apartment to await my sentencing, I wanted it to be with him. As selfish as it may be, I didn't want to die alone.

I approached the laundry room and saw people coming and going with carts full of laundry. I came as soon as the lockdown ended, so I wasn't sure how I could be late. Being late would not be a great way to start my job here. Tentatively, I entered the hot room and looked for someone in charge.

"Over here," said someone sitting behind a desk as they motioned toward me.

At first I wasn't sure if the person was a man or a woman, but on closer inspection, I saw she had breasts. She was stocky and had a shadow of facial hair above her lip. A sign on her desk read "Supervisor Madi," a female name.

"You must be Autumn Jones. I got a message this morning telling me to expect you. About time I got extra help around here. I'm Supervisor Madi, and you'll scan in with me personally every morning."

She held out the scanner to me, and I breathed a sigh of relief that I wasn't in trouble for being late. I waved my hand in front of the scanner. It beeped, and the green light flickered on. I hoped Jack was having the same luck.

"Come with me," Supervisor Madi said, getting up from behind her desk to lead me through the laundry room. It was bustling with activity, and I tried not to get in anyone's way. There were clothes and linens everywhere, and I had to watch where I stepped.

We approached an older woman. "Di, got one for you to train. Her name's Autumn Jones," Supervisor Madi said and then left us without any further introductions.

Di looked up from her work and gave me a warm smile. I instantly liked her kind face and tired eyes. Her black hair was caught up in a bun, but a few strands had come loose, and she brushed them away from her eyes. She looked to be in her thirties.

"Am I glad to see you! We sure can use the extra help." She extended her hand to me, and I took it. She clasped both her hands around mine and gave me a tight squeeze. "I'm Di. Actually, my name is Diamond. My father worked in the diamond mines and thought the rocks were pretty, so he named me after them." She laughed. "I can't stand the name, so I shortened it to Di. I don't mind Di."

"I know what you mean." The words tumbled out before I knew what I was saying.

"Why? Autumn's a pretty enough name. What would you shorten that to?"

I shrugged. "Forget it. I'm just nervous." I would have to be more careful in the future. I was no longer Sunset O'Donnell. That name would get me killed.

"Well, it's not a glamorous job in here. All kinds of things end up on clothes, like people getting sick or losing control of their bowels — that one's always fun." She rolled her eyes. "And it all comes down here to be washed. Just be careful with the sorting. You don't want to get that stuff on your hands — you'd be sick before you know it. I sort the clothes by whites, colors, and darks and then make a special pile for the really soiled clothes. Those ones have to be washed by hand first." Di paused to look around and then said in a conspiratorial voice, "They get sent over to Crystal to get washed, and I don't mind at all. She's a stuck up little thing because she has a good singing voice. Not that anyone down here would know. She only sings for the bourge." I was glad she mentioned it. Crystal might just be the type to turn me in and collect the credits.

"Where would you like me to start?"

"I like your attitude, Autumn — ready to dig right in to work. Why don't I keep you with me today, and we'll go through everything together. I'll teach you to sort and how to use the washing machines and dryers. There's a folding station over there, too, but that takes a while to master. The bourge like their things folded just so. Here, you can start with this cart." Di led me to where the carts were lined up. "All the bins with dirty laundry are here, and they'll stack up all day long. The bins are numbered according to where they came from, like this one." She pulled a cart out to examine. She pointed to the number on the side — 5499114. "The five means it's from the fifth level, the four is the section number on that level, the nine nine means its personal laundry as opposed to dining room or something, and the one one four means the laundry came from apartments one through fourteen. We've got a boy working here who runs the carts up and down from the Dome."

I took the cart and wheeled it to a table beside where Di was working. I was a little hesitant to just dive right into the laundry considering what Di had told me I might find in there. I gave the cart a sniff, but didn't smell anything foul. Di was shaking her head at me and laughing. I didn't need to get into trouble on my first day, so I took a deep breath, plunged my hand into the clothes and piled them up on the table. I tried to sort them like she showed me, but Di corrected me a few times. I didn't know there was a difference between lighter dark shades and darker light shades.

"Might seem a bit picky, but if you put something red in with light colors, then everything might come out with a red tinge to it. And you can bet a couple days' credits and a beating to boot that you'll be paying for that!" Di said.

"Supervisor Madi seems very strict." I hoped she didn't think I was being too forward, but I needed to know what I was dealing with.

Di stopped what she was doing and looked directly into my eyes. "And don't you ever think otherwise. That woman is one letter away from being crazier than the president. There's something wrong with her." Di tapped the side of her head. She picked up a shirt and examined it for stains. "And make sure you only ever work with one cart at a time too. The last one who mixed up the carts was thrashed until she was bloody."

That made laundry a whole lot more complicated. If being recognized wasn't enough stress for me, now I had to worry about being beaten to a pulp if I made a mistake. I had heard about supervisors like Madi, and it didn't take much to provoke them.

"All sorted?" Di checked over my work. I was glad she was there to teach me. "Let's take the load of darks." She gathered the clothes up in her arms and walked over to a machine. "Put them in like this." She took each piece of clothing and shook it out before putting it in the washing machine. "They wash up better when they're separated like that and if anything is mixed up in the clothing it will fall out. You don't need a pen exploding ink into your wash—you'll pay for that, too." With all the clothes now in the washer, she shut the door and showed me where to put the detergent. She pressed a few buttons, and the washer started. "Now let's see how you do with the next load. I'll just watch this time."

I did the next load exactly how Di had shown me. It was a mundane task, yet it needed my full attention or my mistake would be Madi's pleasure. I had difficulty focusing when my entire life had been turned upside down. My dad's welfare weighed heavily on my mind, and I was anxious to see him, but there was nothing I could do about it right now. I needed to focus and keep myself out of trouble so I would be able to see him later.

I turned my attention back to the task at hand. I added the detergent to the washer like I'd been shown and then pressed a button. Di corrected me. Then I needed to go back to the table for the third load. Doing laundry was a foreign task, and I suddenly missed the familiar ease of the kitchen. If I had never been drafted to work at Jack's bachelor party, then Summer and I would be working in the kitchen right now, probably peeling carrots or potatoes. That was a mundane task, too, but since I'd done it with my best friend all day, I'd enjoyed it.

I wondered what Summer was doing. Was she working in the kitchen? Or was she up in the Dome with someone she didn't want to be with? I tried to put that torturous thought out of my head.

I gathered up the last load and went to the next available washing machine. I shook out each piece the way I'd been shown, and my thoughts wandered to Jack. The memory of how much I enjoyed the feel of his naked skin beneath my hand made me blush. I worried about him in the coal mine because he had a quality that set him apart down here. He carried himself with a confidence that the average urchin lacked.

Di stopped me in the middle of getting another cart. "Don't mix up your carts, Autumn."

"All my loads are in the wash. I thought I would start sorting a new one."

"Never work with two carts at one time. You'll get the clothes mixed up, and they'll never find their way back to their owner. Keep track of what you have on the go right now. Your first washer will end in about ten minutes, and then you'll need to sort them again since the clothes don't dry at the same temperatures or for the same amount of time."

My head was going to explode. Who knew laundry was this complicated? For the third time that day I told myself to concentrate and put everything else out of my mind. I couldn't afford to make any mistakes.

I went over to the washer that was about to end and watched the clothes spin around. It reminded me of my little training session with Jack this morning. I wished I could fight like him. He could move so fast. I wondered if he would do as I asked him and show the miners how to fight. If he could pass even a few of his skills on to them, it might give them a chance against abusive guards. The washer stopped, and I opened the door.

"Let's have a look," Di said. She started taking the clothes out one by one and shook them again. "Now, see how the pants have a crease down the middle? You're better off leaving them damp and running an iron over them. The iron will dry them. These ones can go in the dryer," she said as she shook each item out again before putting it in the dryer. "Fewer wrinkles to contend with." I paid close attention to what she was showing me. My life really did depend on getting it right.

A young boy interrupted us. "Miss Di, do you have anything for me?" He had a fat lip and seemed to be holding back tears. He looked younger than twelve, but he couldn't be. Twelve is the earliest age you could be assigned a job, although I'm sure the bourge would like to make it younger. More workers would mean more production.

"Well, there's my handsome little Kai." Di gave the boy a hug. "Kai, this is Autumn. She just started working here today."

"Hello," I said. He gave me a weak smile.

"Where have you been?" Di asked him gently.

"Supervisor Madi had me take carts up to the main floor. She said they were getting real mad up there because they haven't had clean clothes in two days."

"Madi give you that?" Di examined his lip.

"Yes, ma'am. I was late. The stairs were just so crowded after lockdown, and it's a long way up here from the eighth level." A tear spilled from the corner of his eye. I remembered the first time I was struck by a supervisor and how awful it had been. I felt sorry for him, but I knew he would get used to it.

"You get docked, too?" she asked.

He nodded. "Half a day's credits. And since we only get half a day because of the lockdown, I'm not getting anything today."

"Don't you worry. You're still living with your parents, and they can take care of you for a few years yet." Di kissed the top of the boy's head and gave him a bone-crushing hug. "I've got a couple of carts for you right over here, and by now there's probably a few more for you to bring down. Come see me when you're all done."

I watched the boy take the carts and make his way out of the laundry room. He cringed slightly when he walked by Supervisor Madi. Di made tut-tutting noises beside me.

"A sweet little boy like that and she just hauls off and punches him in the mouth. It's not right, Autumn." Di shook her head. "There are days when I'm happy that I'm not long for this world. I turned thirty-five this year. I'll be on the next Cull, and I say good riddance to this place."

I was getting the impression that life in the laundry room was more hellish than anything else. "How long have you worked here?"

"Most of my life. It wasn't always a bad place, but the past few years the supervisors have been getting meaner. This one is the meanest. Like most people working here, I'd like to find a job somewhere else, but if Madi ever found out anyone was looking for a new job, she'd beat her to death. It makes a supervisor look bad to the higher ups when too many workers want to leave."

"So you're saying I better get comfortable here because I'm not going anywhere else."

"Not unless you come up with an airtight plan to get out of here." Di cocked an eyebrow at me, which made her statement more of a question. Why would she wonder if I had a plan to escape? Did she recognize me? No, she couldn't have. She would've reported me right away.

"Then you better show me how to iron these pants because I have no other place to go." I put the pants on the ironing board.

Di gave me a thoughtful look, then stepped forward and tested the iron. "The iron gets really hot if you set it too high, and it will burn the clothes. That's why I like to iron when the clothes are still damp—less chance of damaging them." She showed me how to lay the pants on the board and began to run the iron over the material quickly, never stopping in one place. A washing machine buzzed behind us. "That'll be your second load. We need to get it out now because someone will be waiting for the machine."

We left the pants and went back to the washing machine. Di told me to sort everything out myself, and she just watched to make sure I did it right. I made a few mistakes, but she corrected me, and I took note for the next time. I ended up with two more items to iron.

We went back to the ironing board, and she let me finish the pants. She was showing me how to iron a shirt when my third machine buzzed. I went and got the clothes and sorted them, finding a few more items to iron. When I finished that task, I went back to the ironing board. Di was still with me, showing me how to do everything. I still wasn't finished with my ironing when the first dryer signalled the load was done.

"Now we go to the folding station. This will take a bit of time to learn," Di said.

I was feeling uncomfortable with the amount of multitasking I had to do. I still had ironing waiting to be finished, two more loads in the dryer, and now a load to be folded. The carts were stacking up too. Di took out a small board from under the counter, placed it on the back of a t-shirt, and began to fold the shirt around the board. When she was finished, she slipped the board out of the folded t-shirt and flipped the t-shirt upright. It came out perfect. Then it was my turn to try. I wasn't nearly as fast or as good. I tried again.

"You'll need to master this quickly," Di said, looking in the direction of Supervisor Madi.

I understood. I tried harder. "There. How's that?" I presented my folded t-shirt.

"Not bad," Di said after she made a few adjustments. "Try again with this one." She handed me another shirt. I was feeling under pressure with all the work I had piling up. I was afraid of losing track and missing something. I folded the shirt as I'd been shown. "Better," she said.

It took me approximately fifteen minutes to fold the entire load. I was still very aware I had ironing and another load in the dryer that was about to finish, but I went back to the ironing board and did what I could until the dryer signalled it was done. I left to go and fold it. Di was now at her station getting some of her own work done. I realized I had taken up quite a bit of her time.

I was halfway through folding my third load of laundry when the *bong bongs* sounded, indicating the end of the workday. With the lockdown this morning, we only had half a workday, although it felt like I'd put in a full day.

"You'll need to finish up before you go because Kai is waiting to take the last of the carts upstairs. We'll have a busy day tomorrow trying to catch up. Lockdowns might seem like a peaceful break while they're happening, but the work keeps piling up, and we have to stay on top of it." Di sighed.

I tried to hurry my folding, but it didn't work. I just wasn't that adept, so I made myself slow down. Working late wasn't part of my plan for this evening. I was really anxious to find my father and Summer to make sure they were both okay. Jack would be waiting for me too, and most likely worried when I didn't get back on time.

"Autumn, you need to concentrate or you'll never finish," Di said in a firm voice. She took the shirt from my hands and positioned the board in the center of the back. "Like this." She showed me in slow motion. I tried again with the next shirt, pushing aside the panic rising up inside me.

Eventually the laundry was folded, and I could get back to the ironing. Again, I found it slow going, but I had to get it right. Di helped me every step of the way, even though I knew she was frustrated with me. I was truly grateful for her patience and kindness.

I noticed Kai standing beside the last of the carts. With a flush of guilt, I realized I had made him late. And he wasn't even making any credits this afternoon.

"Done!" Di exclaimed when I finished the last of the ironing. "Now, put the clothes in the proper cart. I know Kai wants to get home and eat something."

Di showed me how to stack the clothes into the cart while Kai stood by patiently. I couldn't believe how complicated laundry was. I had a new appreciation for my old job in the kitchen.

"I'm sorry I'm so late, Kai. I'll try to be faster tomorrow."

"That's okay, Miss Autumn. We always end up working late after a lockdown." Kai took the remaining two carts and headed for the door.

"Now we can scan out. I'll see you tomorrow," Di said.

Supervisor Madi was waiting for us with the scanner in her hands.

"I expect tomorrow you'll pick up the pace." Madi glared at me. "I don't like having to stay here late waiting for a couple of urchins to finish their work."

"Yes, ma'am." I waved my hand across the scanner.

It felt good to get out of the heat in the laundry room. I went in the direction of the stairs, pulling the visor of my hat lower. Few people were left in the hallways. I must have been over a half hour late getting off work. I quickened my stride and joined the few people on the stairs.

Then I saw Summer.

CHAPTER FIFTEEN

S ummer looked directly at me, and I could tell by her
expression that she recognized me right away. She
looked terrified and dropped her gaze, refusing to look
my way. I resisted the impulse to run down the stairs
to meet her and instead waited for her to come up to
me. Something must have been wrong because she had
never ignored me before.

She gave me a sidelong glance when as she reached
the fourth level and walked down the hall away from
me. I waited a moment then walked after her. I tried
not to get too close in case someone was watching. She
ducked into the common bath, and I waited a moment
before following her.

"Sunny, what are you doing in the Pit?" Summer
asked the instant I stepped into the room.

"Looking for you." I went to her and wrapped my arms around her. "The whole reason I escaped was so I could see you, Dad, and Reyes."

She took a step away from me. "Are you crazy? They'll kill you if they find you!"

"They're going to kill me anyway. At least now it's on my terms. What happened to you? Why are you still going up to the Dome?"

"You know why, Sunny. Don't make me say it." She sounded defeated.

"But Jack told me he signed you up with some old guy who would fall asleep and you'd be sent home after the party. Why didn't that happen?"

"Oh, it's *Jack* now, is it? Not Mr. Kenner or Mr. Almost President?" Summer really wasn't acting like herself. Her voice was laced with bitterness.

"I want to know what happened to you."

"Leisel Holt happened to me. Jack may have signed me up with a deadbeat, but Miss Holt signed me up to be with her father!"

I stared at her dumbfounded. That was just wrong on so many levels. I couldn't even begin to imagine old President Holt sexually. It was disgusting. And the fact that his daughter signed up a girl for him... "Leisel is the most evil person I've ever met!" Hatred for her consumed me.

"I've been at the Holt residence every night since the bachelor party. The only reason I get to come home during the day is that Mr. President, as he told me to call him when he gives me permission to speak, allows me to go to work in the kitchen every day. He feels that all urchins should be earning their keep. Imagine! Like I'm not earning my keep being his sex slave all night long. It's revolting!" She shuddered. "And if that's not enough, I have Leisel talking to me about you. Between acting like the heart-broken jilted bride in front of her father, she's interrogating me to see if I've seen you and your husband down here."

"So she didn't tell her father that you and I are friends?" I was afraid for Summer, but as long as Holt didn't know she meant something to me there was no reason for Summer to be drawn into my predicament.

"How could she? Leisel can't tell him she knows who I am without admitting she knows who you are. Although given time, I'm sure she'll come up with some story. She's conniving, that one."

"So Leisel told you what she did to Jack and me?"

"Every single detail. She's quite proud of herself. And you should know she and her guard are lovers. He and some of his friends are watching me down here to see if I lead them to you."

"That's why you didn't want to talk to me in the hallway. I'm so sorry I got you dragged into all of this. I've really made a mess of everything. If I could rewind the past few days, I'd do things so much differently. I'd just take getting fired and damn the consequences." I hugged her again.

"Stop it! Just stop apologizing!" She gripped me by my shoulders. "We didn't ask to have bad things happen to us. Our only mistake was being born on the wrong side of the Dome." She dropped her hands from my shoulders and looked at me sadly. "I've got to go. Being late with President Holt is not an option."

I didn't want her to go back to Holt, and in a desperate attempt to save her I grabbed her hand to stop her from leaving. My mind frantically tried to come up with a hiding place for her—in the apartment with Jack and me? Or a cave in the bowels of the coalmines?

"Sunny. I have to go," she said softly. We both knew there wasn't a way out of this for either one of us.

"Be careful, Summer." My words sounded hollow and ineffectual even to my ears.

"You're the one who needs to be careful. Holt is turning the Dome upside down looking for you two. The only reason he hasn't done a thorough search in the Pit yet is because it hasn't occurred to him that Jack Kenner would find refuge down here. But he'll figure it out soon enough. He won't stop until he finds you."

"Jack got us new chips —"

Summer held her hand up to stop me.

"Don't tell me. If I know anything about you, Leisel will find a way of getting the information out of me." She pulled me toward her and hugged me tightly. "You've always been my best friend and you always will be. I love you, Sunny." I felt the tears roll down her face. I knew what she was doing, and it was too much to bear.

"Don't you say goodbye to me, Summer! Holt is not going to win. We'll see each other again."

"Sure we will. Just do me a favor and stay hidden." She gave me a sad smile and kissed my cheek. Then she was gone out the door.

It was insufferable to think I would never see her again. I couldn't imagine what my life would be like without her. Her strength, her ability to take a bad situation and turn it into an adventure enriched my life so much. But my effervescent friend was gone. The same monster that wanted me dead had enslaved her. There was no bright side to this adventure.

I rubbed the tears off my cheeks and left the bathroom. A guard stood at the far end of the hall, but he was oblivious to me. I headed back to the stairs and descended the two flights to our apartment.

"Jack?" I called out when I entered the apartment. There was no answer. "Jack?" I called out a little louder, but still there was no answer. A nervous flutter started in the pit of my stomach as my mind raced to the conclusion that he had been captured. I ran into the bedroom and found him on the mattress, flat on his back and covered in coal dust. He was snoring faintly, and I breathed a sigh of relief.

"Jack, wake up." I sat down on the bed beside him. He didn't even stir. "Jack." I gently shook his arm. With lightning reflexes, his hand came up and wrapped around my throat. For an instant I felt him starting to squeeze. "Jack!" I choked out. He dropped his hand.

"Don't sneak up on me like that!" he snapped. I could tell he still wasn't quite awake.

"They'll stop serving dinner soon." I stood up and massaged my neck, making a mental note to be more careful around him.

He rubbed his eyes to force them open. "I can't decide what I need more—sleep or food."

"Food. You can sleep again later, but food is only served three times a day. Miss a meal, and it will be a long time before the next one."

"Hey, were you crying?"

"I just saw Summer."

"Oh. Look, if you want to beat me up again, then I'll let you know right now I'm too tired to fend you off. Just go ahead and punch me." He threw his arms wide open on the bed to give me clear access to his stomach.

"Maybe after dinner. She told me she's with President Holt. Leisel signed her up to be with her father after the bachelor party."

Jack sat straight up in bed and gave me a look of surprise. He was fully awake now.

"Your friend Summer is within Leisel's reach?"

I nodded.

"Then she's got to be part of Leisel's plan. What angle could she be using with her?"

I hadn't thought about it that way, but I was beginning to learn that everything Leisel did had a motive behind it.

"She set up Summer with the president the night of the bachelor party, but she couldn't have known then that we would escape and go into hiding."

"You're right. Summer was part of her plan that night. How?"

The realization hit me. "Probably as insurance to make sure I did what she wanted! She threatened to tell on Summer for stealing food if I didn't go along with her plan. If the threat hadn't been enough to convince me, she probably would have paraded Summer out in front of me and threatened to do worse. Leisel found my weakness."

"And now that we've escaped, she's keeping Summer close. Does Holt know that you and Summer are friends?"

I shook my head.

"Leisel can't tell him without implicating herself. Summer says she's playing the brokenhearted victim in front of her father."

"A little handicap like that isn't going to slow her down. Are you sure that you and Summer weren't seen talking today?"

"We didn't speak to each other in public—we met in the bathroom and no one else was in there. Summer's aware she's being watched—Leisel has her boyfriend following her. Oh, and she said that Holt hasn't thought to look for you here in the Pit."

"Why not?"

"She said it hadn't occurred to him that you would hide down here."

"So his own prejudices are preventing him from making good decisions again."

I gave him a curious look. I wasn't sure I was following.

"Holt would never be caught dead down here, and he thinks I'm every bit as prejudiced as he is. See, I told you he'd keep repeating his mistakes. At least it gives us a bit more time." He gave me a weak smile. We both knew that eventually we would be caught and killed.

"Then let's use the time we have left. Did you think about what I asked you? About teaching the miners how to defend themselves?"

"You're asking me to do the impossible. First of all, Reyes is never going to trust me, so his friends never will either. Second, there is no place away from the eyes of the guards to teach them. Third, it took me years to learn martial arts, and I have maybe a few days at best before I'm caught."

"So now I know why your family still hasn't won against the Holts," I said, almost to myself.

Jack gave me a blank stare.

"You talk yourself out of every good plan. Sometimes you just need a starting point." I found it frustrating to want to *do* something to help my own people, but being told I couldn't. If Jack didn't want to help, I would find another way. "Never mind. Let's go to dinner before there isn't any left."

"Sunny," Jack began, but I walked out of the apartment. I was almost to the sixth level when he caught up. "That wasn't fair," he said when he came up beside me.

"I don't want to talk about it anymore." I didn't need him to convince me my plan was a bad idea. I had already made up my mind. If people saw me as a hero, then I needed to live up to the title. I wanted my death at the hands of the president to at least inspire change.

At the risk of missing dinner, I turned toward my father's apartment. If he was still in bed, perhaps I could convince him to come and eat with us. I found Bron in her usual spot.

"Sunny..." she said and her expression was sympathetic. "I wanted to come and see you right away, but there were Domers down here."

"What is it?" I knew something bad had happened to my father.

"They took him. I tried to intervene, but there was nothing I could do."

"They took him?" I repeated stupidly. I'd seen her form the words and I'd heard them, but my brain refused to accept the information.

"I'm so sorry. I wish I could have done something."

"Are there still Domers down here?" Jack asked.

"No. They left with her father."

I turned on Jack. "Where did they take him? You of all people would know where they would take him. Tell me!"

"Sunny, I don't know —"

"Tell me!" I yelled.

But he didn't tell me. He just looked at me with a defeated expression, and I wasn't ready to be defeated.

In only a few months my entire life had been shattered beyond recognition. The only anchor I'd had left in my life was my dad still living in our family home where I grew up. He couldn't be gone.

"Tell me!" I yelled again.

But he just shook his head, and my anger flared. I was sure he knew where they took him, and I would do anything to get that information out of him. I pummelled my fists against his chest, but he grabbed my wrists, preventing me from doing much damage.

"Sunny."

I didn't want to hear his lies. "*You tell me!*"

"I'm going to take her home," he said to Bron over my head.

"This is my home! And I'm not going anywhere with *you*!"

I tried to break away from his hold on my wrists, but he pulled me down the hall with him. I wasn't ready to leave my home yet. I needed to see for myself that Dad wasn't in there. Maybe Bron had made a mistake. I pulled against his hold, but he just tightened his grip.

"Let me go! I need to go back and see. Maybe he's still in bed, and Bron just didn't see him," I sobbed.

Jack pulled me to him by my wrists and looked into my eyes. "He's gone, Sunny. They have him."

I didn't want him to tell me that. I didn't want to believe it. But somewhere deep down inside, I knew the truth. Bron said Domers took him. Domers didn't come down here to kick people out of their homes. There was only one reason they would come for my father. Me.

I couldn't have stopped the flood of tears that came pouring out even if I'd had the strength to try. I had been so naïve to trust Leisel. I thought she had been worth the risk of helping, and yet it had cost me far more than I ever could have imagined. Just thinking of her set every fibre of my being tingling with hatred, and it sapped the rest of my strength. I felt my legs give out from under me, and Jack let go of my wrists to catch me.

"I'm going to take you home."

"No. I don't want to go."

"What the hell are you doing to her?" Reyes yelled from down the hall.

I lifted my head from Jack's shoulder and looked up to see Reyes bearing down on us. He looked like he was ready to kill Jack. I pushed away from him, hoping my legs would hold me up. They did.

"Reyes, it's not what it looks like."

But Reyes didn't listen. He headed straight for Jack. "I told you not to touch her," he ground out between clenched teeth. He pushed Jack hard, making him back up a few steps.

"He wasn't touching me like that!"

Reyes was taking another run at him, and I put my hand on his arm and stopped him. I saw Jack getting ready to spring at him. I knew what damage Jack could do to Reyes, and I silently pleaded with him to leave Reyes alone. I saw Jack relax.

"Then what the hell was he doing?" Reyes looked at me for the first time. "You're crying." He gave Jack another accusatory glare.

"Can we go somewhere and talk?" I asked Reyes calmly.

He turned back to me and gave me a nod. I slipped my hand into his and walked down the hall with him. I hadn't been alone with Reyes since the night I was drafted to work at the bachelor party, and I owed him so much.

"They took my father," I said when we'd found a place to be alone.

"I heard. It's always big news when Domers come into the Pit. You know I'm still here for you."

He looked into my eyes and brushed away my tears. I looked back into his dark eyes. When he wasn't angry or upset, he had kind and loving eyes. I always thought they were his best feature. He brought his lips to mine, and we kissed. The kiss was gentle at first, but then he became more aggressive. He backed me up against the wall, and his hands started searching under my t-shirt.

"Stop!" I said, breaking away from his lips.

"I don't want to stop this time." He kissed my neck while his hands continued their search despite my struggles. "What are you wearing?"

"God, Reyes, this is not the time!" I pushed hard against his arms, trying to free myself from him.

"It's never the right time, Sunny." He dropped his hands from me and took a step back. "I don't understand.

We've been together so long! If you loved me you would want to."

"For god's sake, Reyes! I just found out that my father's been taken into custody. I don't know if he's being tortured or already dead." I was astonished by his complete lack of sympathy.

"And I might lose you." Despair laced his voice.

Now I understood his desperation to make love to me, even though it wouldn't help either one of us. In fact, it would just make things more difficult. Not only was I a felon on the run, I was legally married now. "Oh, Reyes," I said softly. "I'm sorry I did this to you. I'm sorry we can't be together."

"We can still be together. You don't have to live with that bourge."

"But I don't have anywhere else to go and neither does he."

"Who cares if he has somewhere to go? Get rid of him, and I'll move in with you."

I tried to figure out what he was asking of me. Why was he bringing this up now, just when I was trying to deal with the news of my father? Didn't Reyes know that my life was a mess? Why was he trying to complicate it even more?

"You know what you're asking is impossible," I said, shaking my head. "The first time we had to scan in during a lockdown, we'd be caught and arrested."

"Or maybe you just don't want to get rid of him."

"What?"

"Maybe your marriage to him wasn't an accident. Maybe it happened exactly like the president's daughter said!" He took another step away from me.

"No. It happened exactly the way I told you. I didn't lie. I'm not in love with Jack, but that doesn't mean I want to see him hurt. Right now, our new identities are the only thing keeping us safe." As I said the words a little voice inside my head started laughing at me. Safe for how long? I wondered if I was going crazy. How could Reyes demand a future with me when I could be dead tomorrow? Didn't he know my life was as good as over?

"I don't know what to do," he said in frustration.

"Neither do I." We looked at each other for a moment, knowing we had reached an impasse. Finally I broke the silence. "It's going to be lights out soon. I need to get back."

"Think about what I asked."

I smiled sadly and gave him one last kiss before I made my way back to the apartment. I could think about it all I wanted, but nothing was ever going to change.

CHAPTER SIXTEEN

J ack was doing sit-ups when I walked into the apartment. I had hoped he would be asleep since I didn't really feel like talking. It was as if my life had become surreal, and I was nothing more than an apparition walking through it. Although being so disconnected from my feelings wasn't an entirely unpleasant experience.

Jack stopped exercising when I walked in and jumped to his feet. "I was worried about you," he said a bit awkwardly.

"There was no need. I was with Reyes."

"That's one of the reasons why I was worried."

I raised my eyebrows. "He wouldn't hurt me."

"Really?"

I glared at him.

"You were very upset."

"Was I? I can't imagine why. I mean it's not like my dad was just taken prisoner, or that my best friend is being used by a monster or that I'm on the run from being executed... Oh wait! I am." I ripped off my hat and threw it on the table.

He spread his arms wide. "You can take your frustrations out on me."

For some reason, my thoughts wandered to Reyes and his insistent groping a few minutes earlier. It had all gone so badly with him. I knew despite everything that had happened that he still wanted me, but I didn't think I had anything left to give. My heart was too full of murderous desire.

"In my mood, I might just do some real damage." I flopped down into a chair. "Tell me now, Jack. Where do you think they would take him?"

"He's probably being questioned about you. About us."

"Would they torture him?" I asked even though I wasn't sure I wanted to know the answer.

"Maybe. I don't know for sure. It depends on what he tells them right away."

I could tell he was being honest with me, but I felt there was something he wasn't telling me.

"Will they send him back? When they're done questioning him, will they send him back here?"

He looked at me for a few moments before he answered, as if weighing his answer. "Probably not." His expression was pained.

I leaned forward, resting my elbows on my knees and my face in my hands, and tried to absorb this information. Yet somehow my mind couldn't accept it. I dragged my hands down my face and looked at him. "What will happen to him?" I wanted to know everything no matter how much it tore me up inside.

Jack looked uncomfortable. "I don't know for sure. Maybe he'll be Culled early."

"Culled early." I rolled the thought around in my head. "There's no such thing as being Culled *early*. Fifteen years ago when your people tried to lower the age of the Cull to thirty, we rebelled and the age was kept at thirty-five. So you see, I know there's no such thing as being Culled *early*. If my father is killed now, it's called murder."

"I'm sorry. Just tell me what I can do for you. I'll do it."

"There's nothing you can do. There's nothing I can do. The bourge will win like always."

"So you're giving up?"

"What else can I do? They've taken away everyone I ever loved. My mother and father are gone, my best friend is gone, and pretty soon you and I will both be gone. We can't win. The odds were always stacked against us." The lights went out, leaving us in darkness. "See? They even tell us when it's time to go to bed. Good night, Jack."

"I'll take the chair."

"No, it's my turn tonight." I made my tone intentionally dismissive.

He hesitated a moment. "Good night, Sunny."

I watched him stumble his way to the bedroom, knocking things over as he went, and marvelled at how completely blind he was in the dark.

I hunkered down in the chair even though I was sure I was never going to get to sleep. My head was pounding and my stomach upset. I tried to sort through the mess that was my life, but my brain refused to cooperate. Instead, I found myself thinking about when Summer and I were kids in school and all we had to worry about was getting our homework done. Somehow, I managed to drift off to sleep wrapped up in the memory.

The *bong bongs* ringing out startled me awake. It felt like I had just closed my eyes. I pushed myself up on my elbows and looked around the bedroom. My bulletproof vest was on the floor beside the bed. I was confused because I was sure I went to sleep in the chair.

I heard Jack moving around in the other room. Although I would have preferred to lie down and pull the blanket over my head, I forced myself out of bed and got dressed. Jack was at the sink splashing cold water on his face when I went into the next room.

"I thought I was supposed to take the chair last night."

"I missed the chair. It's comfortable." I could tell he was lying.

"No, it's not. And you look exhausted."

"You could use some cold water on your face, too."

I realized I must look a mess. My eyes felt hot and swollen from crying so I took his advice. The cold really did feel good even though it was a waste of our water ration.

"Thanks for taking my vest off me last night." Getting the weight off for a few hours was good, but being half naked in front of Jack was not so good.

Jack turned a little red. "It was pitch black. I didn't see anything. But I know how much you hate wearing it."

"I do hate wearing it. It's a constant reminder of what my life's become."

"Ready to go to breakfast?" he asked, his voice falsely bright.

"I'm not hungry this morning."

"Oh, yes you are. Come on." He threw my hat at me, and I caught it. "Food will make you feel better."

I wondered why he was being so nice to me. I figured it was because I was ready to give up and if I did, we would both end up being caught. His survival was inextricably linked to my own. I didn't feel like I owed him anything, but I didn't have any desire to see him dead either, so I put my hat on and followed him out the door.

He headed down to the sixth-floor common room for breakfast. I wasn't sure if I wanted to go or not. Reyes would probably be there, hoping for an answer from me, and there was only one answer I could give him. I knew it wasn't going to be what he wanted to hear.

The lineup for breakfast was still short at this early hour. I looked around the room and almost sighed with relief when I didn't see Reyes. Maybe if we ate fast enough, I could get out of here before he showed up.

"Sorry to see your boyfriend's not here yet," Jack said once we were seated.

I opened my food container and felt a wave of nausea.

"Eat it," Jack said. He must have seen my expression.

I took a spoonful and forced it down. "Summer's not here either."

"You miss her don't you?"

"Very much." The food was getting easier to eat and my stomach was feeling better. I finished the container and downed my glass of water. Jack was finished, too. "I guess we should head to work."

"You don't want to wait and see Reyes?"

I shrugged. "I'll see him tonight."

He raised his eyebrows, but didn't push for an answer.

We walked silently together to the stairs. He surprised me when he gently took my arm and pulled me toward him and kissed the top of my head. "Stay safe," he said and then began his descent into the mines. I stared after him, wondering at his act of affection.

When he was out of my sight, I made my way up to the second floor. Crystal was already there, waiting patiently for the room to be unlocked. When she saw me coming, she quickly turned her attention to the floor. Obviously, she didn't want to socialize, which was fine by me. I didn't want to either. So we stood together in an awkward silence. She gave me a sidelong glance every once and a while. I probably looked awful.

Supervisor Madi sneered when she arrived. "I see we have another early bird." Perhaps being early wasn't a good thing.

She unlocked the door, and I went to follow her in, but she let the door fall back and it almost slammed in my face. I caught it by one hand before it did.

"You didn't think she was going to hold the door open for you?" Crystal asked.

"I'll know better next time."

As I walked into the laundry room, I realized that getting here early wasn't such a good idea. Di wasn't here yet, and I still needed pointers on the finer details of doing laundry. I scanned in and went over to the carts of dirty laundry already queued and waiting to be done. I took the first one, returned to the station I had worked at the day before, and started sorting clothes. I was almost done when Di walked in.

"Good morning, Crystal. Good morning, Autumn," she called out to both of us. Crystal ignored her as she had the day before.

"Good morning, Di," I said.

"Oh, someone had a hard night last night," she said when she saw my swollen eyes. "Lover upstairs?"

Crystal perked up and paid attention to our conversation.

"A lover upstairs?" I asked.

"Are you somebody's mistress? Did he treat you badly?"

Now I understood what she meant. She wanted to know if I was in the same position as Summer was with the president. "No, nothing like that. I just had bad news last night."

"Someone pass away?"

"My father." I thought if I gave her an answer she would stop asking questions.

She put a hand on my shoulder. "I'm sorry to hear that."

I didn't want her sympathy. It made me want to cry again. "I hope I've done this right," I said, gesturing to the piles in front of me.

She looked over my work and changed a few things in the pile. "You really need to pay close attention to the darks and lights. You put dark clothes in with light and it will ruin them."

"Thanks for the advice. I really do appreciate it."

Di left me to go and do her own work. The morning seemed to pass by quickly. I managed to get two carts full of laundry done by the time lunch was brought in. The laundry room seemed infinitely hotter that day. Then I remembered that the day before the room had been closed for half the day due to the lockdown. It really was hotter in there. The bulletproof vest didn't let my skin breathe, and with every minute it felt like it was getting heavier. I wasn't sure how long I could stand it.

I retrieved my food and water rations and sat on the floor to eat, thankful to get off my feet. My water was cold and refreshing, and it was all I could do not to guzzle it. Di sat across from me, looking at me curiously.

"It's hot in here," I said.

"You can have the rest of mine. I'm not that thirsty."

I wavered for a moment, not sure if it was polite of me to take her up on the offer, but I was so hot that I accepted gratefully. Drinking it and dumping it over my head to cool me off were almost equally appealing. I drank it, thinking the latter would get me into trouble.

"You don't look so good," Di said. "You're really hot, aren't you?"

"I guess I'm not used to the heat."

"Where did you work before?"

Her question caught me off guard. I didn't have an answer ready. I couldn't say the kitchen because she would want to know why I would leave such a plum job. And it was hot in the kitchen too, so I would be used to working in the heat. I had to think of something else.

"Sewers." That seemed like a good lie. It was cold and smelly there and perfectly reasonable that anyone would look for a job somewhere else.

She wrinkled her nose. "That's a nasty job."

"Back to work!" Supervisor Madi called out. It had only been twenty minutes since we sat down. When I worked in the kitchen we were given a half hour for lunch.

"She's a slave driver," Di said as she hoisted herself off the floor and walked over to return her empty food container. I followed her and put my own away.

My full stomach combined with the heat of the room was making me sleepy. I became slow and clumsy and kept dropping things on the floor.

"What the hell is wrong with you, Jones?" Madi said, coming to stand threateningly close to me.

"I'm sorry, Supervisor. It won't happen again." I retrieved a shirt from the floor.

"Be thankful it's dirty clothes hitting the floor. You don't want to know what's going to happen to you if they're clean!"

She stood there watching my every move, her hands balled into fists just waiting for me to drop something. I didn't give her the satisfaction. Eventually someone else caught her attention, and she left me to stomp to the back of the room. I heard her scream at another worker and looked up in time to see Madi strike the girl. Blood streamed out of the girl's nose.

I quickly looked away when I saw Madi scanning the room to see who else she could challenge. If only I had the courage, I would gladly confront her, but like everyone else here, I was too afraid. Some hero I was turning out to be.

Di gave me a stern look. I tried to jolt my befuddled brain into an alert state, but it was difficult. I had a sudden urge to run away and hide in the mineshaft like Summer and I used to do when we were kids. Sometimes we'd stayed in there for hours talking about everything and nothing. Life was so much simpler back then.

I managed to get all the clothes into the washer without dropping any, although the real challenge was going to be when I had to take the clean clothes out and get them dried and folded. I forced myself to be more methodical, concentrating on every detail, and somehow managed to get through the rest of the day without dropping anything else. But it took me forever. When the *bong bongs* heralded the end of the working day, I still had clothes to fold. I didn't scan out until twenty minutes later.

"Jones," Supervisor Madi said when I came up to scan out. "I don't care what you're upset about in your life, when you're here in my laundry room you pay attention to what you're doing. I can't say I like you very much. Hopefully, you can change my mind about that."

"Yes, ma'am."

I wasn't sure if I could oblige her, though. After today, I didn't like me very much either.

CHAPTER SEVENTEEN

J ack was asleep in the chair when I got back to the apartment. I shut the door behind me as quietly as I could, but he awoke. He looked drained. The circles under his eyes were every bit as dark as the coal smudged through his hair.

"You had to work late again?" he asked.

"I guess that's the way of the laundry room. Ready to go for dinner?"

He nodded groggily and put on his hat. I could tell he didn't really want to go. He was exhausted and needed to sleep.

I headed toward the sixth-floor common room. Not that I really wanted to see Reyes, but he would wonder why I had disappeared if I didn't talk to him. I didn't want him to come looking for me and create a scene on the floor where we lived. It was better to let him down closer to his own home and far from ours.

The common room was already quite full when we joined the line for food. Reyes was there with Raine and Mica. Although Raine and Mica were both married, I rarely saw them out with their wives. They were always hanging around Reyes.

There was an empty seat next to Reyes, and he patted it when he saw me in line. I headed toward him once we received our food rations, and Jack followed mutely behind. I would talk to Reyes privately once we were done eating.

"So is he going to follow you everywhere now?" Reyes asked.

Jack was midway to sitting down and stood back up. "I don't mind sitting at another table." He turned to leave.

"Stop it, Reyes! Jack, sit down."

Jack hesitated a moment, then returned to his seat.

"You can't expect me to hang out with this bourge and like it," Reyes said.

"Yeah, your boy got his butt kicked again today," Raine said, looking at Jack.

Again? I gave Jack a confused look. He was too good of a fighter to get his butt kicked. "You didn't tell me anything," I said to him.

"You can't blame the guards, the way he walks around down there like he owns the place," Reyes said, never taking his eyes off Jack.

I knew what he meant; Jack reeked of authority. He had a confident demeanor about him that wasn't common in the Pit. It was bound to get him into trouble with the guards. But I still couldn't imagine Jack putting up with someone beating him.

"What happened?" I asked Jack.

"We'll talk about it later," he said.

Reyes snickered. "The guards like picking on him. He backs down pretty fast. Not so big down here in the Pit, are ya?"

Raine and Mica laughed, too.

I was suddenly overcome with pity for Jack. "Reyes, that's enough! You're behaving like a child."

"What? I'm the bad guy here?" Reyes turned to look at me. I had never seen him look at me that way before. Was it anger? Hatred? "The president wants to kill you because of that bourge, and I poke a little fun at him and I'm the bad guy?"

"He isn't the bad guy either. The president wants me dead because of a decision I made, so don't blame him for this." I was startled to hear myself say all that. But I believed every word.

I was done blaming the bourge and Jack for the mess I made of my life. What I did was foolhardy and stupid, and it was the reason the people I loved most in life were in danger. It was time to stop feeling sorry for myself and start dealing with the consequences of my own actions. And I knew Jack could be a good ally. He could help everyone down here and make a difference.

"Give him a chance. He can help us get organized and push back against the bourge. He knows how they work, and he can anticipate their decisions. He can teach you all how to fight. How to defend yourselves." I looked from Reyes to Raine and Mica.

They all burst out laughing. Jack rolled his eyes.

"The way he cowers in front of the guards and you think *he* can teach *us* how to fight?" Reyes laughed in disgust. "Why are you defending this guy? Why are you living with him?!"

"Reyes, we'll talk about this later," I said in a low voice. I should have known his temper would get the better of him. I should have known he would make a scene.

"We don't need to talk about it later. I see your answer written all over your face," he said bitterly. "You know, Sunny, I waited four long years for you to marry me. I put up with your excuses when you kept postponing our marriage. I even stood by you when you chose to be a plaything at this idiot's bachelor party instead of coming to me for help. And then you went and married him! And I'm supposed to be the sympathetic one in all of this. I'm supposed to understand that you married him to save Summer... to save the entire Pit. And up until now, I think I've been very tolerant. But I will not sit here while you stand by his side instead of by mine." With that, Reyes scraped his chair back from the table and stomped out of the room.

I looked around the table. Mica and Raine stared at me while Jack pretended to be interested in his stew.

"He's just hurt, Sunny," Raine said.

Mica gave me a deadly glare and made a show of pushing himself away from the table to follow Reyes. A few seconds later, Raine left, too.

"That went well," Jack said when we were alone.

"Don't."

I could feel a headache coming on. I rubbed my temples, trying to hold it at bay. I was stunned Reyes felt that way. He made it sound like I had taken him for granted all these years. He obviously didn't understand me. But then again, he had always wanted me to be someone I wasn't.

I was vaguely aware of a shift of mood in the room. The dinner hour was done, and the evening entertainment was starting. Someone dragged a stool in front of the room and started singing. Other people joined in. I used to love staying here after dinner with my parents to hear the songs and listen to the stories. But I hadn't been here since my mother was Culled. Now my father was gone, too. There was no enjoyment left in it for me.

I wasn't sure how long I sat there with my head in my hands, but I remembered Jack was still sitting with me. I looked across the table at him. He seemed to be enjoying the song. It was an old one about how we came to be in the Pit. I used to love this song when I was little because there were a few verses only the children sang. The song was a bittersweet one about how we were saved, only to be cast down into slavery. Jack had his chair turned completely around to watch the singers, so

I couldn't see his face. I waited until it was done before I suggested we leave.

"Ready to go?" I thought I saw him rub his eyes before he turned back to me. His lashes were still wet. "Are you okay?"

"The song was... moving." He stood up and walked toward the door. I followed him.

"How about you? Are you okay?" he asked, once we were back on the stairs headed for the fourth level.

"Yeah." Lying was easier.

"You want to beat me up again?"

"Sure." It might just be the thing I needed right now.

As soon as we entered our apartment, I went directly into the bedroom and took off the vest. It felt so good to get the weight off my shoulders and chest. It had almost been the death of me in the laundry room. Jack was lounging in a chair when I returned to the living room.

"So, you and Reyes have been engaged for four years."

I ignored him and went to the sink to get a glass of water.

"How old are you?" he asked after a moment.

"Seventeen."

"Seventeen? I married a teenager?" He sounded shocked. "Wait a minute, are you telling me that you and Reyes got engaged when you were only thirteen?"

"Yes. What's so strange about that?"

"I'm twenty and that's a young age in the Dome to get married. Usually people wait until they're about twenty-five."

"Well, when you face certain death at thirty-five, you speed up your life a little bit."

"You're right. That was thoughtless of me." He had the decency to look ashamed. "Now I really deserve that butt kicking you want to give me. Let's warm up with a few push-ups." He fell to the floor and starting doing push-ups.

I joined him. Working out the other night really had helped ease some of my anger.

"Speaking of getting your butt kicked, what happened today?"

He shrugged it off. "Just like they said."

"I've seen you fight, Jack. I can't imagine you cowered."

"And what do you think would've happened if I grabbed the guard's gun and shoved it down his throat?"

I thought about it for a moment. Not that I wouldn't want to see a guard eat a gun, but he was right. All the guards would've been on him. "I see your point. You were right about Reyes and his friends, too. They're not going to cooperate. Maybe we can find someone else who wants to learn your skills."

I had decided I didn't want to give up on my plan to help change things. After all the hardship I had brought on my father and Summer, I owed it to them to try to make things right. I didn't want to fail.

Jack stood up and went into his T'ai Chi stance. I followed. He began the fluid movements and I tried to keep up, but he seemed to be going a lot faster tonight.

"So you want to start stopping people in the hall and ask them if they want to join the rebellion?" Jack asked, his tone light.

"Well, it sounds stupid when you say it like that."

"Alright, we're all warmed up now." Jack faced me in a defensive stance. "Take your best shot."

"I don't feel like it anymore."

"Come on." He flicked a hand out at me, stopping inches from my face. "Pretend I'm Reyes. You must be mad at him."

I threw the heel of my hand toward his face, which he blocked easily. I followed with a roundhouse kick at his stomach. He pushed me away.

"That's weak, Sunny," he said. "Come on. The other night you just about ripped my head off when you were mad about Summer."

I had been really mad about Summer. Even the thought of her now in the clutches of that crazy president was making me angry. He had my father, too. My anger snuck out of the place where I thought I'd had it tucked safely away and gripped me again.

I threw a punch as hard as I could at Jack, then another. He blocked them both, but I kept coming at him. First with my right leg followed swiftly by my left. He threw a right punch at me, but I pulled my head back and he missed. I instinctively knew he was going to follow with his left fist, and I ducked. He missed again. He was smiling at me. I came at him to wipe the smile off his face, but he turned, and I missed. He grabbed me from behind.

"I see the boyfriend isn't the key to getting you mad. Your best friend is," he whispered in my ear.

I drove my elbow as hard as I could into his stomach. As soon as I made contact, I heard his breath forced out of him. I realized I might have hit him too hard.

"I'm sorry!" I turned around to see if he was okay. He was bent over, holding his stomach. "Jack, are you hurt?"

"I'll be fine," he choked out.

I felt a little helpless watching him struggle to get his breath back. He finally straightened up and gently touched a couple of his ribs.

"Nothing broken." He limped off to sit in a chair. "Maybe I should have told you the first rule of sparring before I started teaching you. You don't actually hurt your partner."

"Sorry. I guess I let my frustrations get the better of me."

"I don't suppose there's a hot shower in here?" he asked, even though he must have known the answer.

"No." I laughed at the thought. "But I can take you to the common bath."

He got up from the chair. "Take me."

I found a couple of towels and a bar of soap in a cupboard. "We only have about forty-five minutes left before lights out. We need to be back by then."

We left the apartment and headed toward the bathroom. I wouldn't be surprised if Jack changed his mind when he saw where he had to bathe. It wasn't anything like the private hot shower in his apartment. We reached the bathroom, and I was silently relieved to see that the water had been changed recently. It wasn't bad at all.

"It's freezing!" Jack exclaimed when he put his hand in the water. "I'm not getting in there."

"You don't actually get in. Soak your towel in the water and wash off that way. You can dry with mine. You go first." I headed for the door.

"Wait. We're supposed to be married. Isn't it going to look weird if we're taking turns in here?"

"I'm not watching you have a bath. I'm only prepared to take the pretend marriage thing so far."

He gave me a wry look. "We'll just turn our backs on each other. It will save time, and we can get back before lights out."

"I don't know. It seems a little... intimate." But there was a guard on duty within view of the bathroom, and he might wonder why we were taking turns.

"I promise I won't peek," Jack said, but I wasn't convinced. "Hey, I'm taking a big risk here, too. You know how many girls would love to see *the* Jack Kenner naked?"

That made me smile. A week ago, that was probably true. "I can't believe I'm going to do this. Turn around."

We both turned our backs on each other. I stripped as fast as I could so I wouldn't have time to change my mind. I heard his clothes drop to the floor. An image of my hands on his naked chest came back to me, and a feeling of excitement began to grow in the pit of my stomach. If I turned around right now we would both be naked and only inches apart. A warm sensation spread through me at the thought, and my chest tightened, making it difficult to breathe. I wanted to banish the thoughts from my mind. I didn't want to think of Jack in that way.

I dunked one of the towels into the water and scrubbed my arms. The water was freezing and made me shiver, but at least now I could blame my heavy breathing on that. And I was grateful that the cold water was helping to douse the heat that seemed to be consuming me. I finished washing, and then rinsed the towel. I stuck it out behind my back and passed it to him.

"That was quick," he said. I heard the water splashing behind me then Jack sucked his breath in. "Oh my god, it's cold!"

I dried off and put on my clothes. I waited for him to finish and get dressed before I knelt down to wash my hair.

"Not so bad," Jack said, but I could tell he was lying.

He dipped his head in the water, ran the bar of soap through his hair, and then rinsed. I was still working on my long hair. A lot of coal was coming out, darkening the water. I felt a little guilty considering the water had just been changed. Finished, I wrapped the towel around my head to hide my red hair until I could reapply the coal.

"Ready?" he asked when I stood up. I nodded. We made our way back to the apartment.

"Even though it was freezing, it feels good to be clean," Jack said when we were back in the apartment.

"I like the cold. It's refreshing." Maybe I would have to have a bath every night if my body was going to continue to respond to Jack like that.

I crossed the room, hung up the towels, and took the hairbrush out of the drawer. I pulled it through my long tresses, working out the tangles. I would have to wait until it was dry to reapply the coal. I put the brush away when I was finished and turned around to find Jack flopped in a chair observing me.

"What?" I asked.

"Nothing." He looked away. But there was something about the way he was looking at me...

"Did you peek?" I asked.

"Sunny," Jack shook his head, but a smile tugged at the corners of his mouth and his cheeks turned pink. "Of course I peeked. I'm a guy."

I threw one of the towels at him. He caught it in mid-air, laughing.

"Jerk," I said, trying to look serious, but the whole thing was ridiculous. I knew I never should have trusted him.

The lights went out, and my eyes quickly adjusted. Jack opened his eyes as wide as he could and looked around the room. I could tell he couldn't see a thing.

"I'll take the chair tonight," I said. "You really need to get some sleep."

"I'm comfortable right where I am."

"It's not fair that you have to have the chair every night."

"How about tomorrow you take the chair. Okay?"

I knew that even if I did get him to go to the bed, he would only put me in it and take the chair once I was asleep. "Thank you, Jack. Good night."

He yawned. "Good night."

I found my way to the bed. I slipped off my pants and crawled under the blanket, grateful to have time alone to think. Now that my initial shock at Reyes had worn off, I could think a little more clearly. If I was going to be honest with myself, I was more embarrassed to be told off by him in front of everyone than I was hurt by anything he had to say.

I had known Reyes forever. We were in the same class in the sixth-floor common room and often played together during lunch breaks. At the age of twelve, we finished school and joined the workforce like everyone else in the Pit. Almost a year went by before I noticed him again. He had gotten a lot taller and more muscular from his work in the mines. And he noticed me too. Our attraction grew quickly and within a few months of reconnecting, we swore a betrothal to each other.

I tried to remember how I felt four years ago when we met again. I remembered thinking how handsome he was, how tall and strong. A lot of other girls wanted him too, but he picked me and that made me feel special. I liked being out in public with him — socializing with our friends. But I couldn't remember even one time that I responded to Reyes physically the way I was responding to Jack. Whenever Reyes had tried to make love to me, the only feeling he stirred in me was fear. If I was to be honest with myself, I hated the way his hands groped at me, pressuring me to do something I didn't want to do. Yet with Jack... just thinking about him made me ache.

Deep down, I knew the only reason I had stayed with Reyes was because we both needed a partner in order to qualify for an apartment. That was the main reason everyone in the Pit eventually married. If I had not accidentally married Jack, then I would have married Reyes after the next Cull. Maybe in time I would have come to enjoy his touch.

It took a long time to fall asleep, but just before I did, I heard Jack softly snoring in the other room. He was my last thought.

CHAPTER EIGHTEEN

Reluctantly, I brushed away the mists of sleep. I felt a glimmer of happiness that morning, and I think it was because I had a nice dream. I'd like to go back to that happy place and forget my reality. Forget the chaos that had become my life. But I had to go to work. I rolled out of bed, put my pants on, and went into the living room. Jack was still sitting in the chair looking exhausted.

"I'd ask how you slept, but..." I trailed off. He probably didn't need me telling him he looked like hell.

"I probably look worse than I feel. I managed to get quite a bit of sleep last night," he said. I was pretty sure he was lying.

"You have to take the bed tonight." If he allowed himself to get too tired, he would start making mistakes in his work and get himself beaten.

Despite the dark circles under his eyes, he did look more handsome than usual this morning. I didn't want to stare, but his eyes were closing and he seemed to be going back to sleep. Then I figured it out. He didn't have the coal in his hair. It was back to its natural light sandy color. His facial hair was thicker too, and it gave him a rugged look. The t-shirt he was wearing was dirty and torn from working in the mines, and where it had ripped, the skin on his hard, muscled torso peeked out. He didn't look anything like the Jack Kenner I first met upstairs in the Dome. He still had the darker skin of the average bourge. My mother told me they were darker because of the special lighting they had in the Dome. But any resemblance to other bourge stopped there. He was more handsome, if that was possible.

I continued my inspection, my eyes following the curves of his muscular arms and back up to his face. I liked the way his black eyelashes framed his blue eyes... blue eyes that were staring straight back at me. I almost jumped when I realized he'd caught me looking at him.

"I was just looking at your hair... I need to darken it." I felt a tell-tale blush creep across my face. He smirked as he closed his eyes again. "And you'll need to get a razor soon. You're beard is coming in blonde and using coal on it will look obvious."

"How do I get a razor?"

"We need to make enough credits to buy one for you."

"How long will that take?"

"Probably longer than we have down here."

I retrieved the coal from the cupboard and rubbed it through the strands of his hair, thinking how surreal this act was. If anyone had told me a week ago that I would be living with Jack Kenner and sharing my secret for dark hair, I would have laughed. Yet here I was enjoying the feeling of his soft, wavy hair between my fingers.

He had fallen back to sleep, for which I was grateful. Maybe when he woke up he would think he had been dreaming when he caught me checking him out. I let him sleep while I darkened my own hair and put my vest back on.

"Jack, time to wake up." I shook his shoulder gently.

He woke up with a start at my touch. I remembered that the first time I had to wake him he'd gone for my throat. This time I stood behind him just in case. He took a few seconds to orient himself.

"Did you see where I put my hat?" he asked groggily.

I picked it up from the table and handed it to him. He got up and followed me out of the apartment.

"I don't suppose you have any caffeinated or energy drinks down here?" Jack asked me on the way to breakfast.

"We have water and occasionally hot tea." I had never heard of an energy drink. Maybe it was like the protein shake he had given me up in the Dome. I remembered it helped combat the effects of the wine.

"Then I'll pray for tea," he said, rubbing his eyes.

I saw the look of surprise on Jack's face when I didn't head down to the sixth level common room, but he didn't question me. The only person down there to see now was Reyes, and he had made it clear he didn't want to see me anymore.

We joined the queue to receive our rations. Jack asked for tea but got water. I spotted an empty table for two and headed toward it. I was happy not to have to share a table with anyone else. Jack sat down and scanned the room, stopping to look at someone in particular.

"She looks familiar," he said with a puzzled look on his face.

I followed the direction of his gaze. "That's Crystal. I work with her in laundry."

She was sitting with two people I assumed were her parents. She cast a glance in our direction, and I could tell she recognized me. Then she saw Jack. I was sure I saw a look of surprise on her face before she dropped her gaze.

"How do you know her?"

"I don't know. She just seems really familiar." Jack turned his attention to his breakfast. "Oh, stew again. What a surprise."

He took a mouthful and I could tell he was forcing it down. I opened my container and did the same.

I was concerned about Crystal. If she'd recognized Jack, we could be in a lot of trouble. I remembered Di didn't seem to think she was trustworthy.

"I'm sorry things didn't work out so well with Reyes," Jack said. I wasn't sure if he was just trying to make conversation or if he really cared.

"I'll get over it."

"To be honest, I'm surprised at how well you're taking it."

I watched Crystal get up and leave with her parents. "Are you done?" I asked, trying to eyeball his container. It looked empty.

"In a hurry?"

"I think I better get a head start on work today. The laundry room is backed up because of the lockdowns, and I don't want to have to work late again tonight." I lied — what I really wanted to do was get to work early again and have a conversation with Crystal.

"Guess I'll get a head start on chiselling out some coal." He stood up, and I followed. We walked down the hall together to the stairs. "Be careful," he said and kissed the top of my head. It was the second time he had done that, and I liked it. I hoped it was becoming a habit.

I watched him until he was gone from sight and then scrambled up the stairs as quickly as I could. Traffic wasn't too heavy yet so it didn't take me long to climb the two levels to the laundry room. As I hoped, Crystal was there waiting for the laundry room to open.

"Good morning," I said cheerfully.

She gave me a nervous smile and then turned to stare at the closed doors. "Supervisor Madi isn't here yet?"

"No," she said almost under her breath. She turned her attention back to the doors.

"So how long have you been working in laundry?"

"A couple of years."

"Do you like it?"

"It's a job."

A deep bruise on her forearm peeked out just below her t-shirt sleeve. She saw where I was looking and tried to pull the shirt down over it. It reminded me of the bruises Reyes left on my arms when he grabbed me the other day.

"That looks like it hurts."

"Mind your own business," she snapped.

"Sorry. I didn't mean to pry." I wondered why she was so touchy about it.

Supervisor Madi came up behind us, cutting off any more conversation. Crystal turned her back to me, making it clear she was here to work, not socialize.

"Scan in," Madi said as she unlocked the doors.

Crystal got to the scanner first then almost ran to her workstation. I waved my hand over the scanner and went in search of the laundry carts. I took the first one and went to my usual station to start sorting the clothes.

Di greeted me with a smile. "Well, you're in bright and early again today. Morning, Crystal," she called over her shoulder. Crystal mumbled something in response. "Looks like you have things in hand," Di said when she saw my sorting job.

"I could always use an expert opinion, though," I said, hoping she would check over my work.

"Let's see." She rummaged through the clothes, a look of satisfaction on her face. "Not bad. I'd put this in with this pile, though. And that should be hand washed." She pulled a dark grey shirt out and placed it in another pile, and then put a dress off on its own. "Good job." She left to select a cart for herself.

I gathered up one pile of clothes and took it to a machine. Lots of people were arriving to work, and the laundry room was getting busy already. I knew once the machines and irons were going full tilt, the room would become unbearably hot again. I added the detergent to the machine and pressed the button. I repeated my steps with the next two piles until my entire cart of clothes was in the washing machines. The only item of clothing left to do was the dress. Crystal did the hand washing, and I was glad for an excuse to talk to her again.

I went over to her. "Di told me this should be hand washed."

"Just put it there." She motioned to the empty counter next to the sink.

"I was hoping you could show me how to wash it myself." That would allow me more time to talk with her.

"That's my job. You don't need to know how to do it."

"I know, but if Supervisor Madi ever asked me to do it, then I sure would appreciate knowing how to do it properly."

She gave me a sidelong glance. She knew as well as I did that if I was ever assigned a job to do and did it poorly, Madi would beat me.

"Just this once. So pay attention," she said. "Feel the temperature of the water." I stuck my hand in the sink. The water was freezing cold. "Colors will run in warm, so it has to be cold. Then you use this kind of detergent."

She pulled out a small bottle and poured a very little bit into the cold water. "Make a few suds like this. Then put the dress in the water and start squeezing it gently."

"Can I try?" She stood aside and let me wash the dress. Within seconds my hands ached from the freezing water. "How do you do this all day long?"

She shrugged. "You get used to it. So I've never seen you in our common room before."

"I'm new on the fourth level. I just got married, and my husband and I were assigned an apartment there." It wasn't a complete lie.

"Was that your husband with you this morning?" She eyed me to see my reaction.

"Yes. Handsome, isn't he?" I was almost certain she knew something.

"I didn't notice." I could tell by her expression she was closing me out again.

"Di tells me you like to sing."

"*Like* to sing? Di should mind her own business." Crystal shot a sneering look over at Di. "The dress is done. Wring it out and hang it."

I wondered what I had said to make her angry.

Madi was bearing down on us. "What are you doing over here, Jones?" I heard her say "Jones," and she was looking at me. Then I remembered *I* was Jones. Autumn Jones.

"I asked Crystal to show me how to hand wash. I thought if I knew how then I could help out if she ever got too busy."

Madi kept coming at me, raised her hand, and struck me across the head. Stars appeared in my vision and for a moment I thought I was going to black out, but then the stars faded and I could see Madi's angry face again.

"You think you can run this place better than me?"

I shook my head. Di had warned me about Madi, but I had no idea she was this quick to anger.

"I knew I didn't like you any more than I liked her," Madi said, jerking her thumb toward Crystal. "Get back to your station and do your own work unless I tell you otherwise! Do you hear me?"

"Yes, ma'am." Every fibre of my being wanted to lash back at her, but I knew it was a fight I couldn't win. I dropped the dress back in the water and returned to my station.

"Crystal, you know better!" Madi yelled. I heard her strike Crystal, and I cringed. "Do your own damn work!"

I watched Madi go back to her desk and plop down into her chair. I felt awful about getting Crystal into trouble. Judging by the bruise on her arm, it looked like she had enough trouble lately.

"I told you before, you mind yourself around Madi," Di whispered to me from her station. "I've seen that woman thrash a worker to death."

I knew now that Di wasn't exaggerating. I should have listened to her before. I put my head down, determined to stick to my own work. From then on, I wouldn't even risk asking Di for help. If I messed up, then at least I would only implicate myself. My head pounded from the force of her blow.

I managed to finish two full carts of laundry before our lunch was brought in. Madi gave us only fifteen minutes to eat today, probably because of my stupid move with Crystal, but I was grateful to have even that short time to drink some water. Di graciously shared her ration with me again, too. The room was unbearably hot.

The lunch break was over almost before it began. I returned to work and managed to do two more carts of laundry before the *bong bongs* rang out. I still had clothes to fold. I glanced in Crystal's direction to see if she was done, but she had a few things to finish up, too. Since I owed her an apology, I slowed my pace to match hers, so we would be done at the same time. I scanned out right behind her.

"I'm so sorry about today, Crystal," I said as we left the laundry room. She ignored me and continued down the stairs. "It won't happen again. I promise."

She stopped and looked at me. "What happened today isn't your fault. Madi will find any excuse to beat a worker. She likes it."

She continued down the stairs, and I followed behind her.

"I'm still sorry I provoked her." We reached the fourth floor, and she turned in the same direction as my apartment. "You live this way too?"

She nodded. "Hey, isn't that your husband?" she asked, pointing in the direction of my apartment.

My heart leaped into my throat when I saw Jack sitting on the ground holding his head in his hands, flanked by Raine and Mica. I broke into a run.

"What happened?" I picked up Jack's head and looked into his eyes. It looked like he was trying to focus on me. "Ja—Ben, can you hear me?" I hoped I corrected my mistake before Crystal heard me. She stopped to regard us for a moment, a hint of concern on her face, but continued on her way down the hall.

Mica laughed. "Your boy here thought it would be fun to take on a few guards."

"Yeah, Ben decided to clock one of the guards in the head, and that's when all hell broke loose. Three guards came at him all at once, and he flattened all three in less than a minute. Then two more came at him, and he just about had them put down when another guard came up behind him. That guard butted him in the back of the head with his rifle."

I probed the back of his head for any bumps. I found a big one. "What were you thinking?"

"I never saw anyone fight like that," Raine said, smiling at Jack. "Maybe I'll let him teach me some moves if he still wants to. That is, if he doesn't die of a brain haemorrhage tonight."

"There's a bunch of other guys interested too. That was the coolest thing I ever saw," Mica said.

"Can you help me get him inside?" I waved my hand over the scanner and opened the door. Jack was able to stand up on his own, but Raine and Mica stayed on either side of him just in case he fell over. He didn't look beaten up, just that huge bump on the back of his head. He made his way into the bedroom and flopped down on the bed.

"You better see about getting some ice for him," Raine said before he left.

"Reyes didn't come with you?" I wasn't sure why I asked because I didn't even care. It just seemed strange to have Raine and Mica around without Reyes.

"Reyes was impressed by your boy, too. He just didn't want to admit it. Give him some time," Raine said.

I nodded. "Thanks for bringing him."

I was grateful they didn't just leave Jack down there on his own. I returned to the bedroom to see how bad his injury was.

"Jack, can you hear me?" I took his face in both my hands and tried to force him to look at me.

"I'm fine. Just a little out of focus." He shook his head as if that would clear his vision.

"No, you're not fine. What were you thinking? You don't hit the guards back!"

"I'm just so fed up." His voice sounded tired. "But I guess on the bright side, I'm still alive and a bunch of guys are interested in joining your rebellion."

"What?"

"Didn't you hear them? They want me to teach them how to fight."

"You didn't deliberately pick a fight to impress Reyes and his friends, did you?"

"It wasn't the reason I started the fight, but once I got going I realized I had their attention. I counted all the guards, but it's really dark down there, and I missed one."

"You could've been killed. What you did was dangerous."

"Did you think starting a rebellion wasn't going to be dangerous? I teach a couple of guys a few moves and the most they'll get out of it is what I got today or probably worse. If you want things to change down here, you need to teach an army how to fight. And if I'm not willing to take the risk of fighting back, don't expect them to listen to anything you want me to tell them. You have to lead by example, and now I have their attention."

The last time Jack had spoken to me like that was in his apartment before the wedding, back when he was about to become the president-in-waiting. He was using the same authoritative, matter-of-fact tone. I didn't like this Jack, even though I knew he was right. And what he was proposing—raising an army—was a far bigger plan than anything I ever had in mind. I just wanted the violence to stop. I wanted every person down there capable of fighting back every time a guard or supervisor raised his hand to strike. I wanted to empower them.

"I have to get some ice." I turned to leave.

"Sunny," Jack said softly. I stopped at the bedroom door. "I'm sorry. That was harsh."

"No. It was right," I said, and left the apartment.

CHAPTER NINETEEN

I decided to go down to the sixth level to get the ice because I was more at home there. I knew the people working behind the counter would give it to me with no questions asked, although I really didn't want to run into Reyes. He would probably start another argument, and I didn't need that tonight.

I was beginning to understand now what Jack had been trying to tell me all along. Arming a few people with the skills to defend themselves was only going to get them killed. Jack's injury was proof enough that the guards weren't going to put up with an insolent urchin. But I didn't see how we could raise an army and stay hidden from Holt as well.

Most people had eaten by then, and the line-up for food was short. I looked around to see if Summer was there. She wasn't. Reyes was there, though, so I kept my head down.

"I need some ice," I said when it was my turn. Ice wasn't a usual commodity in the Pit, but it was available for emergencies.

"What do you need it for?" asked the woman behind the counter.

"My husband may have a concussion. I need ice for the swelling." I hoped I looked pathetic enough for her to take pity on me.

She narrowed her eyes, studying me. "Your husband the one that laid six guards on their backs in the mine today?"

I nodded.

"Then I'll come personally to have a look at him for you."

"It's okay. I just need the ice. He seems fine." Alarms were going off inside my head. If anyone examined Jack closely they would probably recognize him. He wasn't hurt badly enough to take that chance. She ignored me and started rummaging through her things behind the counter to put a bag together.

"You two eat yet?"

"Really, all I want is the ice."

She continued as if I'd never spoken, placing two containers of food into her bag. "I have almost fifteen years of medical training behind me so I can tell you if it's a concussion or not." She came around from behind the counter and headed for the door. I had to run to catch up to her. "Might be I can't do anything for him, but at least I should be able to tell if it's serious or not. Which way?" she asked when we reached the hall.

"My husband's really uncomfortable around strangers. Please, if you could just give me some ice." I realized I should never have sought out help. I was putting us in too much danger of being caught.

"I know who you are," the woman said in a voice so low only I would hear. "And I know who the man is you're trying to protect. Now I don't have much of a soft spot for the bourge, but when I hear a man kicked the snot out of six guards because they were pickin' on a little kid, well I don't mind helping out at all."

All I could do was stare at her in shock. My first instinct was to deny everything she said, but by the look on her face, my denials would fall on deaf ears.

"How do you know?" I asked.

"You think you grew up in the Pit without anyone ever noticing you? It's hard not to notice a girl of your height who likes to put coal in her hair. That hat you wear isn't hiding anything." She laughed.

I started climbing the stairs. "Does everyone know?" All this time I thought we had everyone fooled.

"Anyone who knew you before probably knows you now, too. Not to mention just about everyone down here watched your wedding. You're a famous couple."

I left the stairs at the second level and went in the direction of our apartment. I still wasn't sure about this. I didn't have to go to our apartment and give our location away. I could still mislead her. But Jack did need the ice, and it seemed like this was the only way to get it for him. I guessed she could've turned us in any time but she hadn't, so I decided to take the risk, went to our apartment, and let her in.

She nodded toward the bedroom.

"Is he in there?"

"Yes." I followed behind her.

Jack must have heard her voice because he was trying to stand when we went into the bedroom. He leaned against the wall to steady himself.

"Woozy, are you?" the woman asked.

"Who is this?"

"Just sit back down on the bed before you fall over and hurt yourself," the woman said in a tone not to be argued with. Jack shot me a questioning look, but all I could do was shrug. He sat back down. "My name's Dawn Reed. I already told your wife I have fifteen years of medical training. I'm not educated like the doctors you have upstairs, but I've managed to keep a few people alive in my day." Jack was still staring at me, and his eyes widened at her admission.

"I'm sure my wife exaggerated my condition. She worries about me like that. I'm fine," he said brushing her hands away from him.

Dawn persisted, though, intent on feeling his head for any wounds. She found the bump on his head. "Oh, that's a good one. You'll definitely need some ice on it to take down the swelling." She rummaged through her bag and came up with a small flashlight. "Let's take a look at your eyes." She bent his head back. He tried to jerk away, but it was too late. "Wow, those eyes are bluer in person than they are on television. How have you been hiding them down here?"

"She knows, Jack," I said.

"And you brought her here anyway?"

"She can turn us in whether she knows where we're living or not."

"She's right," Dawn said. "A lot of people have figured out who you are. But no one is going to turn you in. Sunny is a hero down here, and as long as you're with her, you're safe, too… I think."

"You're saying the minute I'm not with her…"

"No one down here likes a bourge, and you're high up on the food chain. I mean, you were pretty close to becoming president yourself, weren't you?" She said it like it was a bad thing. "But if she says you're okay, then we'll let you stay down here. And it didn't hurt that you helped that kid today in the mines either. No one's ever taken on the guards before. Well, at least not six at once."

"So, you're not going to turn me in?"

"Isn't that what I've been saying? Now let me have a look at those gorgeous blue eyes of yours. Don't get to see those too often in the Pit!" But Jack didn't offer his eyes up for inspection.

"Jack, it can't hurt. Just let her have a look," I said. I was rewarded with an angry glare, but he finally submitted.

Dawn held open one of his eyelids and flashed the light at it a few times. She repeated the process with his other eye. "When you stood up earlier, were you dizzy or just off balance?"

"Dizzy."

"Any ringing in your ears?"

"No."

"Bad taste in your mouth?"

"No."

"Can you touch your right index finger to your nose?" she asked. He did it. "Can you touch your left index finger to your nose?" He did but made it obvious he felt like an idiot.

Dawn took a pin out of her bag and began to prick down his left arm. Jack kept jerking his arm away from her, and she seemed satisfied with his reaction. Then she tried his right arm. She began to take his pulse. "Is your vision okay?"

"It is now."

"But it was blurry earlier?"

"I had a little trouble focusing."

"His heart rate is okay," she said. "With dizziness and blurred vision he might have a mild concussion, but I don't think it's anything too serious. He's got all the feeling in his arms." She pulled out a bag of ice and handed it to me. "Put this over the bump on his head, and keep it there as long as he can stand it. The cold will bring the swelling down. I don't want him going to sleep right away, but if he makes it through the next few hours without any vomiting or delirium of any kind then let him sleep. He vomits or acts crazy, you come get me."

Dawn wrote down her apartment number on the sixth level. Then she remembered the containers of food she brought for us and put them on the table.

"Thank you," I said awkwardly. "Thank you for everything — for the advice and for keeping our secret."

I wasn't sure what to say to her. I felt vulnerable with this stranger who knew our identities. All I could do was hope she was trustworthy. I walked her to the door and watched her leave.

I threw my hat on the table and took off my heavy vest once she was gone. I filled two glasses with water and then decided to use some of our water ration for washing. Jack wouldn't be able to get to the bath tonight, and I knew how much he liked to be clean. I filled a basin with water and quickly washed myself. When I went back into the bedroom, Jack was already asleep.

"Wake up," I said, coming to sit on the bed. I laid the bag of ice on the back of his head.

"That's cold! I'm tired and my head is pounding. I just want to sleep."

"I brought you some water and a towel. I'll give you a few minutes to wash up then I'll come back and sit with you."

I went back out into the living room until he called out that he was done. When I returned to the bedroom, he was lying face down on the bed with his shirt off and already asleep.

"You heard her," I said loudly. "You have to stay awake for a few hours." I pushed him farther onto the bed to make room for myself, put one of the pillows against the wall, and leaned back on it. Jack propped himself up on his elbows and gave me an inquisitive look.

"What? If I'm going to be here keeping you awake, I'm going to be comfortable." I held the glass out to him. "Water?"

He drained the glass and passed it back. I opened one of the containers of food and took a bite. "It's still warm. Do you want some?"

He wrinkled his nose at the smell. "Is it still grey?"

"Yes it is."

"Maybe later." He laid his head back down, and I put the ice on it.

"So you didn't tell me there was a kid involved today. What happened?"

"I'll tell you as soon as you tell me how you got that bruise on the side of your head," he said without looking up at me.

I touched my head and realized there was a tender spot just above my eye. Madi must have been wearing a ring. I didn't feel comfortable talking about it with Jack. He beat up six guards in order to help a kid, and I just stood by and watched Crystal get hit. Knowing that I was the reason Madi had struck her didn't help my guilt or humiliation.

"My supervisor is a bit of a hot head." I hoped to leave it at that.

"Then keep your head down at your job, and don't do anything to provoke her."

"Supervisors like her don't need to be provoked. She was born mean. Now it's your turn. What happened?"

"A guard started pushing a twelve-year-old kid around because he wasn't doing something right, and I told him to back off. Another guard came over and started pushing me around. That's when I lost my temper. I mean, what the hell is a twelve-year-old kid doing working in the mines? He should be in school."

"Down here, you're an adult at twelve and have to find a job. Freeloaders aren't tolerated. Those are the rules you bourge force on us. We have no choice."

"I understand why the witch doctor lumped me in with them, but I would hope by now you would know better."

I knew that Jack had a good heart, but he was still a bourge. He was used to being in charge. He hated our food and missed having hot showers every day. Although I admired him for wanting to help us in the Pit, it didn't make him one of us. But I would never say any of this to him. I could only imagine what it must be like to be hunted by your own people and barely tolerated by mine.

"So tell me what it was like growing up as Jack Kenner," I said.

"I just want to go to sleep, Sunny." I could tell his head was hurting him a lot.

"Put your head in my lap."

He hesitated a moment, then laid his head in my lap. I held the ice against his bump and used my other hand to run through his hair, gently massaging his scalp and the back of his neck. My mother had always done this for me whenever I had a headache.

"That feels nice," he said. He wrapped an arm around the top of my legs and snuggled his head into me. I thought that felt nice, too.

"Now tell me your life story—and don't back out of it. You have to stay awake so you might as well entertain me."

"What do you want to know?"

"Tell me about your parents, school, friends, girlfriends… anything."

"I don't really have parents. My mother gave birth to two pawns in her little game of chess with the Holts. My brother and I didn't grow up as sons. We grew up as Liberty soldiers."

"You have a brother?" I asked, surprised. I thought I knew that, but it still sounded foreign to me. In the Pit, no one had siblings.

"Yeah. His name is Ted. He's a couple of years younger than me—about your age. He's in his last year at the military academy. That is, if Holt doesn't have him locked up with my parents."

I felt a flush of guilt at that. Jack must have been going through his own personal hell, yet he was in the Pit helping me through mine. "I'm sorry about your family."

"They're fine for now. Until I'm tried by the tribunal and found guilty of treason, they can't accuse anyone of being a sympathizer. The Families would never put up with that."

"The Families?"

"The ten most powerful Families in the Dome, which includes the Kenners. The Holts, Wests, Powells and Forbes have made a powerful alliance, but the other six Families are still influential enough to keep those four a little more honest."

"Okay, so what's left? School, friends, and girlfriends."

"I went to school at the military academy like all the other privileged kids. You may ask yourself why there's a military academy inside a Dome that doesn't have any immediate enemies. The reason is that the Holts come from a military background and they like to keep up the family tradition. Your turn. Where did you go to school?"

"The sixth-floor common room every day from the age of five right up until I was twelve, just like all the other urchins; best friend Summer Nazeem; boyfriend you already met; favourite subject was nature and science. Your turn."

"I won't ask if you had any other boyfriends since you and Reyes got engaged when you were two." He snickered, obviously thinking this quip was funny. I chuckled halfheartedly and pulled his hair.

"Ow!" He rubbed his head. "Best friend my brother Ted; girlfriend in my senior year, although I had to break up with her in order to pursue Leisel; favourite subject history."

I resumed massaging his scalp and felt him relax into my lap.

"History? You went to a military academy to learn to fight like a ninja, but history was your favourite subject?"

"History is important. Look how the Holts revised history in order to get everyone in the Dome to accept their despotic government. If the truth had been revealed two hundred and eighty-three years ago, we might not be in the mess we're in right now."

"Despotic?" I asked, feeling stupid. Politics wasn't a subject taught in the common room.

"Holt is a dictator. A tyrant. You can even look at the history of the Pit. Your own people revere Benjamin Reyes. I mean everyone down here is named Benjamin or Reyes."

"Because he led everyone from the Valley to the Dome. He saved us from the nuclear holocaust."

"He was also the one who signed the treaty that turned you into slaves. How come no one remembers him for that?"

As I mulled that over, my hands came to a rest. Jack nudged them, reminding me that I was supposed to be giving him a massage. My fingers started moving again.

"It's not that we didn't know Benjamin Reyes signed the treaty, it's just that we prefer to remember him for the good he did. From what you told me about Holt, he concealed the truth."

"I'm just saying history can be changed in different ways. It can be revised or it can be forgotten. But if we forget the mistakes we made in the past, we're doomed to repeat them. That's why I believe so much in Liberty, my family's organization. We're keepers of the truth."

My fingers trailed down to his neck, and he sighed appreciatively.

"What does Liberty do exactly?" I was genuinely curious.

"Liberty was founded on the evidence left behind by Vice President Kenner. It's the true history of the Dome, not the false one the Holts feed everyone. Our organization is about sharing the truth with anyone who's interested. We have several thousand members now. We look for ways to take away the president's power without endangering the entire Dome."

"You mean like marrying his daughter and becoming president yourself?"

"And trying to find out the codes to the nuclear warheads. If we had those, Holt would lose his hold over the Dome and we would find out where everyone's loyalties really lie."

"So you think there are a lot of people who support Holt because they're afraid of him?" I asked, surprised. Although just about everyone in the Pit hated the president, we supported him because we had no choice. It never occurred to me there would be a lot of bourge in the same position.

"Yes, I do. The man is insane."

"Do you think a lot more people would support Liberty if they thought the organization stood a chance of taking Holt's power?" My interest was growing. If Liberty already had a few thousand members and there were more people in the Dome who might join... Add to that the population of the Pit and we could have our army. The bigger question was whether or not Liberty would accept the Pit into their organization.

My hands had stopped what they were doing again, and Jack wriggled his shoulders. I resumed gently squeezing his muscles, coaxing them to relax.

"You seem to be going somewhere with your questions. What are you really asking me?" His arms tightened around my legs, and he snuggled into my lap.

"I'm just trying to make sense of it all. You told me that Liberty was about restoring democracy, which you described as a type of government where the people get to pick their leaders, right?"

"That's right. If Liberty ever does succeed in taking control away from the Holts, and democracy is restored, then there would be an election."

"And would the people in the Pit be included in that election? Would we be considered equals under your democracy?"

I felt him tense up for a moment, my question obviously giving him pause. "I assume so," he said slowly.

"I just find it curious that all of the members of Liberty are from the Dome. Didn't anyone ever think to ask us? I mean, there are roughly five thousand people down here, and we all hate the president."

Jack didn't respond immediately. I thought maybe I had pushed him too far. I didn't want to alienate him. After all, I was hoping he could help everyone down here organize themselves into a rebellion.

"Do you believe in fate, Sunny?" he asked after a while.

"I don't know. I never really thought about it. Why?" I was relieved that he didn't sound mad.

"I was brought up to believe that my main purpose in life was to get rid of our dictator and restore equality and freedom back to the people. My mother was convinced that the best chance we had was through my marriage. And here I am married to you... the girl who just found a way to raise an army."

"Except we're not really married."

"I think everyone inside this Dome would disagree with you. They watched us get married on television—the urchin girl who married the bourge and humiliated the president in the process. That's when your rebellion started," he said thoughtfully. He sat up, stopping to wince at the pain in his head for a moment, and then leaned back against the wall beside me. "All the clues are there—holding you up as a hero, starting riots over you, knowing both of us are down here but they protect us. You're valuable to them. They're looking for you to lead."

"I disagree. I'm not a leader. I don't know the first thing about organizing a rebellion. That's why I'm asking you for your help. You have the training, you know the bourge and how they work, and you even have Liberty with thousands of members."

"So I'll repeat my question: do you believe in fate? Because together we might actually stand a chance of pulling this off."

Now I understood what he was saying. Our marriage could form an alliance.

CHAPTER TWENTY

I woke up early and found the place next to me in bed was empty. I felt the heaviness of disappointment. After he had fallen asleep last night, I decided to stay in case there were any side effects from his concussion. Or at least that what's I convinced myself I was doing. But truthfully it had just felt so good to have the warmth of his body against me as I fell asleep. Now the bed seemed cold and empty.

I heard movement and heavy breathing from the living room.

"Really, Jack?" I called. "You're working out now? You must be feeling better."

"Want to join me? You have time before work."

I reached for my glass of water from the night before and finished it. I might as well get up and join him. The exercise made me feel better. I pushed myself out of bed and went into the living room. I could see his shadow in front of the two chairs in the room. I walked around the chairs and lay down next to him.

"How do you do that?" he asked.

"Do what?"

"See in the dark. I almost killed myself getting out here."

"It's not completely dark."

He was doing sit-ups, and I fell into rhythm beside him. We did about fifty of those and then flipped over for push-ups.

"I missed our sparring session last night," I said.

"Get home on time tonight, and I'll let you try to beat me again." I could almost hear the smile on his face.

"One of these days I will beat you."

"There's no doubt in my mind that's true."

"I don't see why we have to wait until tonight. Why not now?"

"Because I can't see in the dark."

"Then you'll learn a new skill, too. Come on. How many bourge know how to fight in the dark?"

He stood. "All right." He swung his arms wide around him, testing to see if he was within touching distance of anything. I stood up and threw a punch at his face, stopping an inch from his nose. He reached up and batted my hand away, but he was too slow to block my blow. "Well, this is going to be one sided," he said wryly.

I smiled with satisfaction. "It does help level the playing field."

I brought my leg up into a side kick and again he was too slow to ward me off. I followed through with a punch to his torso, then a kick to his other side. He almost blocked my last kick.

"Why aren't you trying to hit me back?" I asked.

"Because I can't see you and I don't want to actually hit you. But I like this. I heard your foot come off the floor and had to gauge where it would hit in order to block it."

The lights came on then, and the *bong bongs* tolled the start of another workday. I saw that Jack still had his shirt off and was covered in sweat. Without warning he came at me. I raised my arm to ward off any blow he might throw at me, but he grabbed my arm and brought it behind my back, pinning it to one spot.

"You're pretty good when the lights are on." We were only inches apart, and his blue eyes twinkled.

"I know." He laughed and released me. "I thought we could go down to the sixth level for breakfast this morning."

"I don't want to run into Reyes."

He raised an eyebrow at my statement, but didn't address it. "I want to see Bron. It's okay. I can go down on my own."

"Why do you want to see Bron?"

"I kind of have a plan, and I need to see if it's going to work out."

"Are you going to share your plan with me? I thought we were in this together."

"We had a good talk last night, Sunny, and it made me think. If my family is locked up right now, then I can take control of Liberty. Bron can help me with that. I also want to know how many Liberty members are guards down here. I don't know why I didn't think of it before. I guess I was too busy feeling like a fugitive."

"You mean you might have members down here?" This was huge news.

"That's exactly what I mean."

"How do you take control? How fast can it happen?"

"I don't know. I'm on the run from Holt, so it's a long shot that Liberty will accept me as head. It's an even longer shot that they'll accept an alliance with the Pit, but if everyone is as loyal to me as Bron seems to be, then I might have a chance."

"Ok, I'm coming with you." I was about to put my hat on and walk out the door when I realized I still needed to color his hair. "I forgot about the coal."

I retrieved the coal from the cupboard and turned to find Jack already sitting in the chair waiting. He was just as anxious as I was to see where this might go. I darkened his hair as quickly as I could without making a mess.

"Your vest," he said.

I ran into the bedroom and put it on under my t-shirt. Finally ready, we left the apartment. We found Bron in her usual spot.

"Good morning, Bron," Jack said. She looked pleased to see him.

"How are you, Sunny?" Bron asked, concern in her voice.

"Have you heard anything about my dad?" I asked.

She shook her head, but the look of pain that flickered across her features was unmistakable.

"We were hoping to talk to you about something. Is this a safe spot?" Jack asked.

I raised an eyebrow at Jack. He wasn't wasting any time getting to the point.

"It's safe at the moment. The other guards on this level are opening up the common room right now."

"Have my parents sent out any messages from Liberty since the wedding?"

Bron looked from Jack to me and back again. She motioned us to a quiet corner in the hallway. It gave us more privacy.

"No one has heard from them. Word is the president has them under house arrest. I'm terribly sorry," Bron said.

"Then I'm going to assume control of Liberty. Is there access to the mainframe down here?" He took his tablet out of his back pocket. "I haven't been able to get a signal."

"There's no reception down here. Too much rock."

"How do the cameras work then? How do you communicate with the other guards?"

"The cameras and televisions are all hardwired to the mainframe. I communicate with the other guards down here using this." She unclipped a small appliance from her belt. "It's like a walkie-talkie. It only has a short range."

"Then I need to ask you a big favor. Can you help get my messages out to Liberty? I assume you have access to the mainframe when you're in the Dome?"

A huge smile crossed her face. "Yes, sir. But I'll need your verification codes to make it legitimate." She unhooked her communicator from her belt and handed it to Jack.

"I can trust you with this, right?"

"Yes, sir," she said proudly.

Jack took her communicator, typed in the information, and handed it back to her. "How many other guards down here belong to Liberty?"

"I'd say about a hundred, give or take a few."

My eyes opened wide at her admission. There were guards in the Pit *on our side*?

"Are they all as dedicated as you?"

"The ones I know are, but I can't vouch for the others. I think anyone who belongs to Liberty must be dedicated."

"Are they supportive of the people down here in the Pit?"

"I'm not sure I follow, sir."

Jack shot me an apologetic look. "Do the Liberty guards on duty down here hate the urchins or like them?"

Bron looked taken aback by his question. She looked at me, maybe to see my reaction to his statement. But I always assumed the guards hated us. Finding out some of them liked us was a revelation for me.

"Anybody who believes in Liberty also believes in equality," Bron said, her voice indignant. "Life down here is far from equal. We do what we can to help the people in the Pit."

"Would you join with them? If there was a revolt, whose side would you be on?"

"The right side." Jack looked pleased with her answer.

"I want to join the Pit with Liberty and start training an army — would you support that?"

"Absolutely," she said without hesitation. "Most of the people I know would feel the same way."

"That's what I'm counting on. We'll need a place to meet and start training. Are the common rooms the only places with cameras?"

Bron nodded.

"If a camera was broken, how long would it take to be replaced?"

"The last time one was broken it took two months to get a new one replicated."

"Let's get the camera in the fourth-floor common room broken. Once our numbers start to grow we may need more rooms, but we'll do it strategically."

"Why not the sixth level?" I asked. "I know more people there."

"Which is why we should stay away from it. They'll expect you to return home," Jack said.

"He's right. They've already done a preliminary search here, and a camera being knocked out on this level might raise suspicion," Bron said. "I should tell you that we do expect a more thorough search of the Pit within the next day or two."

Jack thought for a minute. "Can we arrange for Liberty guards to conduct the search down here?"

"I don't know. Domers are carrying out the searches, not us. I don't personally know any of them."

"May I see your communicator again?" She handed it to him. He typed a lengthy message out and gave it back to her. "Please send that after you've sent the first message."

"Yes, sir."

"Can I have you arrange for the fourth-floor common room to be secure by tonight? Camera gone and only Liberty guards on duty in there?"

"I'll make sure it happens. And might I suggest, sir, after your unfortunate episode yesterday in the mines, that I assign Liberty guards down there as well? There are rumours that the guards you took out yesterday might have it in for you."

"That's not a bad idea, Bron. If there are only Liberty guards in the mine, that would give us another place to train. Start phasing them in and let me know when it's all friendlies down there." Jack shook her hand. "You've been extremely helpful."

"I'm honored to be a part of this, sir. It's been a long time coming. Is there anything else I can do?"

"Actually, there is. Sunny and I could use a change of clothes — is there any way that's possible?"

"I'll see to it."

I was amazed by her willingness to help. Bron had always been the kindest guard I had ever known, but I still had no idea how she felt about things in the Pit. I had always assumed she was just a kind bourge, but still a bourge. This conversation had been an eye-opener.

"Thank you again, Bron," I said.

Jack and I left and made our way to the sixth level common room for breakfast.

"What were all those messages you were typing into her communicator?" I asked.

"Encrypted messages for Liberty members. I announced I was taking over Liberty, we were joining with the Pit, and I needed some Domers down here on our side." He shrugged. "Either I just started raising an army or I just gave away our location. We'll see what happens."

"That's really great, Jack." I shot him a dry look. He was smiling.

The common room was full when we arrived. It occurred to me that that morning might be the last time I came there to eat since we were securing the fourth-level room for training. I looked around for Summer and was disappointed to see her parents sitting alone. If she were here, she would be eating with them.

My eyes fell on Reyes, Mica, and Raine sitting together and they noticed us too, but Reyes turned his head away from me. It was fine with me if he wanted to be that way. Jack and I picked up our food and water and found a table in the corner where we could sit alone together. I deliberately sat with my back to Reyes.

"You should talk to him," Jack said when we sat down. "Make peace."

"I don't have anything to say to him." I opened my container and began to eat.

"Really? After four years of being together you have nothing to say?"

"He hates me. He's not going to listen to me." Absentmindedly, I looked around the room, and my heart almost leaped into my throat when I saw her walk in. "It's Summer!"

She didn't look like my happy Summer. She looked tired and worn out. I noticed a bruise on her upper arm and wondered who gave it to her. Holt? I still couldn't imagine my best friend in the clutches of that monster.

"Put your head down!" Jack barked at me.

"What?" I did as he asked because I heard the urgency in his voice.

"The man who walked in behind her is Desmond — Leisel's guard. He's watching her."

I snuck a peek in the direction of the door and saw him. He wasn't dressed in his Domer uniform, but he still looked out of place. He was too clean-cut and well-dressed. I remembered that Summer told me Leisel was having her followed.

"They're looking for us," I said.

"I know. I'm going to try to block his view."

Jack casually got up and pulled his chair next to mine, which strategically put his back toward Desmond. Desmond cast a glance our way, his attention caught by Jack's movement, but quickly returned to watching Summer. Then Jack surprised me when he put his hand under my chin and tilted my face toward his and kissed me on the lips.

"What are you doing?" I tried to ignore the thrill that went through me at the touch of his lips on mine.

"We're just a young married couple madly in love sharing breakfast, okay?" he whispered. "We can keep our heads close together and out of view of him." He laced his fingers through mine, and I marvelled at how soft and warm his skin felt.

I looked into his blue eyes. "This isn't going to help calm Reyes down." My voice had a low, husky quality I'd never heard before. I cleared my throat.

"Do you have a clear view of Desmond behind me?" To anyone else in the room who cared to look our way, Jack probably looked like a lover showering his wife with compliments.

"He's watching Summer. He barely noticed us." I was surprised by how breathless my voice sounded. My eyes wandered down to his lips, and I wanted him to kiss me again.

He looked down at my container. "Don't forget to eat."

Eating was a good idea. It gave me an excuse to unlace my fingers from his and get my emotions under control.

"I wish I knew what Summer looks like," Jack said, leaning forward to whisper the words in my ear. He kept his head nuzzled to the side of my neck for a moment. I was pretty sure he was scanning the room behind me. His warm breath was sending shivers down my spine. I needed him to stop, but wished he wouldn't.

"She's hard to miss. She's beautiful."

"There's a pretty girl who just sat down with an older couple."

Jack stopped nuzzling my neck and concentrated on eating his breakfast. I was glad he put some space between us. The effect he was having on my senses was unnerving.

"Her parents are sitting in the back corner. She probably sat with them."

With our faces safely turned away from Desmond, we ate our breakfast. I could still see him if I peeked over Jack's shoulder. He remained by the door. The few people I could see in the room were nervous in his presence. They knew he didn't belong. I emptied my container of stew and sipped my water.

"She's leaving now," Jack said.

Summer came into my view then and was looking our way. I made eye contact with her, and she looked a little startled when she recognized me. Her eyes widened for just an instant and then she put her head down and continued walking toward the door. But it was enough to make Desmond suspicious, because now he was looking in our direction. My face was in full view, and I needed to hide it. Without hesitation, I leaned forward and pressed my lips to Jack, wrapping my arms around his neck.

My kiss caught him off guard at first, but soon his hands were travelling up my back pressing me closer to him. At his touch, I felt the fluttering of desire rising up threatening to cut off my breath. My breathing became a little laboured and my heart pounded. He must have known I wanted him. I blushed, pulling slightly away to put some distance between us. I needed to focus on the crisis at hand. Desmond.

"Is he looking this way?" Jack asked against my lips.

"Yes."

I narrowed my eyes to slits so I could observe Desmond inconspicuously. A bolt of panic went through me when I saw him looking right at us. He started walking in our direction. If he pulled Jack's head back and saw his blue eyes, he would know for sure he had found his target. Somewhere behind me I heard a chair being scraped roughly across the floor. Then Reyes came into my line of vision as he stomped from the room, nearly knocking Desmond over.

"Hey, Summer, wait up," he called out.

Desmond did an about face and followed Reyes. I watched them go until they left the room.

"That was close," I said.

"You can let go now, Sunny," Jack said, gently pulling at my hands. I became conscious of the fact that I was clutching his t-shirt.

I let go of his shirt. "Sorry. That was a little intense." The heat of my blush still radiated from my cheeks. Jack gazed at me thoughtfully, a smile playing around his mouth. He was making me feel even more self-conscious. Should I try to explain the kiss?

"I saw Reyes staring at us. I'm surprised you don't have two holes burned into the back of your head," Jack said.

I hadn't been thinking about him when I kissed Jack. Now I wondered what it had cost Reyes. I felt ashamed.

"He looked upset when he left," I said.

"I'm sorry he had to see that. Talk to him later. Try to explain you had to do it because of Desmond."

My eyes flew to Jack's face when he said that. Was he being sarcastic? I decided to ignore his remark and my reaction to his kiss. Talking about feelings would only make things awkward between us.

"He's not going to listen, and I don't blame him." I really did feel like an awful person. After all Reyes and I had been to each other, I just hurt him. If I were him, I'd hate me too.

"Don't be so hard on yourself. You did what you had to do to stay alive." Then he picked up my hand and kissed it. "And on the upside, I enjoyed it. Thank you." He gave me a wicked smile.

I could feel a blush creeping across my face again and snatched my hand away from his. I had never deliberately kissed anyone like that before, and it had felt exhilarating.

CHAPTER TWENTY-ONE

As usual, Crystal was waiting at the laundry room doors. As I came up beside her, I noticed the bruise on her upper arm again, and it made me think of the bruise on Summer's arm. I wondered if Crystal was being used by a bourge, too.

"Good morning," I said cheerfully.

"How is your husband?"

Something in the way she said "husband" made me question again if she recognized Jack. "He had a headache last night, but he's fine today. Thanks for asking."

"I didn't see the two of you at breakfast this morning. I thought maybe he was in trouble."

"In trouble?" That was an odd word to use.

"With his head injury. When I didn't see you at breakfast, I thought maybe it was serious."

"Luckily it wasn't serious at all."

"Six guards. I wonder where he learned to fight like that."

My inner alarm was starting to go off. I was almost positive she knew Jack's identity, but before I could question her any more, Madi made her presence known.

"Well, what do we have here?" Madi asked. "Are you two conspiring on how to run the laundry room again?"

"No, ma'am," Crystal and I said in unison.

I looked down at the floor and hoped Crystal did the same. Madi unlocked the door and went through. We mutely followed, heading toward the scanner.

"I don't want any crap from either one of you today. You both hear me?" Madi yelled.

"Yes, ma'am," Crystal said. I echoed her.

Crystal and I went to our respective stations. I took a cart full of laundry as I went and pulled it along to the table. I was halfway through sorting when Di came in.

"Good morning, all!" Di said to Crystal and me. Crystal ignored her.

"Good morning, Di," I said.

"So you're making a habit of coming in early like Crystal. You're going to make me look bad!"

I was trying to think of a witty response when my hand wrapped around something cold, wet, and sticky. I smelled the vomit before I actually saw it. I felt my gag reflex working and tried not to get sick. Madi would be all over me for that. I pulled a man's pair of pants out of the cart, and the vomit was the same color as the blackberry wine Leisel had fed me. The pants were probably ruined. I wondered if Madi was going to blame me.

"Oh dear," Di said when she saw it. "What a mess. I told you there are some pretty disgusting things lurking in those carts. Give it to Crystal."

I remembered that Di told me she took pleasure in giving Crystal the really soiled clothing because she thought Crystal was stuck up. But I think I knew Crystal better. She wasn't stuck up. She kept to herself because she was humiliated by what the bourge were doing to her. She was misunderstood, and it wasn't fair.

I picked up the pants and walked toward Crystal's workstation. She looked a little apprehensive when she saw me coming her way. I held up the soiled pants so she could see my visit was legitimate.

"Thanks," she said sarcastically when she saw the vomit. "You can wash your hands before you go." She stepped away from the sink to give me access.

I turned on the tap and reached for the bar of soap.

"Are you kidding me?" Madi screamed at us. "Are you two going to act up again today?"

I saw Madi raise her hand to strike Crystal and with reflexes I didn't even know I had, I stepped in front of Crystal and took the hit myself.

Madi's eyes widened in surprise. "What the hell?" she exclaimed.

"I'm sorry, Supervisor Madi," I said, holding up my hands to ward off any more blows. "We weren't up to anything. I have laundry that needs to be cleaned by hand." I reached over and picked up the vomit-soaked pants and held them up for her inspection. "I was just washing my hands so I didn't get vomit on anything else in the laundry."

Madi gagged and covered her mouth with her hand. "That's disgusting!" She turned and walked away.

"Thanks," Crystal whispered.

"It was my fault." I quickly washed my hands and returned to my station.

I finished sorting the clothes, knowing Madi was watching every move I made. A few times she came over to inspect my work and then went to inspect Crystal's. Di had told me that Madi wasn't right in the head, and I understood exactly what she meant then. Madi was cruising for a fight. She was looking for any excuse, and I knew it was only a matter of time before I did something that provoked her. I just wasn't that experienced at laundry.

I managed to get through the morning without further incident, but when the lunch *bong bongs* rang out, Madi informed Crystal and me that we had to work through the break. The food I could go without, but I was so thirsty. The heat of the laundry room with the vest on was unbearable. Di tried to slip me her water ration, but I refused to take it. Madi would want to know who had given me the water if I got caught. I wouldn't do that to Di.

I was feeling dizzy toward the end of the day, but I forced myself to focus on my work. Madi gave Crystal a hard time when she accidentally splashed water on the floor, but I didn't think she hit her hard enough to leave a bruise. I was folding my second-to- last dryer full of clothes when I saw Kai coming toward me. The swelling in his lip had gone down, although he still had a scab where it had split.

"It's almost the end of the day, Miss Autumn. It's best not to start another cart," he said kindly.

"Thanks, Kai. I'll try to take my time with this one and see if I can draw it out."

I cast a well-concealed glance at Madi. She wasn't looking at me for a change so I slowed my pace. All I could think about was getting water and taking the vest off. It was getting hard to breathe and stars exploded across my vision from time to time. When the *bong bongs* finally sounded, I was folding my last load and stacking them in the bin for Kai to take. I was relieved to see Crystal was finished, too. I didn't want to scan out and leave her alone with our supervisor.

"Well, look at that. The two conspirators arrive at the same time and leave at the same time," Madi said.

Neither Crystal nor I said anything back to her. We just scanned out and left, hoping Madi wasn't going to follow us. I was relieved when she didn't.

"Are you all right, Autumn? You don't look very good," Crystal said.

"I just need water. I'm so hot right now." The stairwell looked dimmer than usual and the stars across my vision were coming more frequently. I needed to get the vest off, but I couldn't tell Crystal that. "I'm sorry about everything. I should never have asked you to show me how to do the hand washing. Madi is never going to let it go."

"You're new in the laundry room. You didn't know what she's like."

We walked together in silence until we came to my apartment and I said good night. As soon as the door was shut, I took my hat off, whipped my t-shirt over my head, and almost ripped the vest off my body. With the weight off my chest, I sucked in a huge breath and let it out before I ran to the faucet. I stuck my head under the stream and started gulping. I heard the apartment door open and knew Jack was home. Somewhere in the back of my mind I realized I had stripped down to my bra, but I didn't care at that moment.

"Sunny?" Jack said. Then he was right beside me. "What happened?" I couldn't answer him. I was too dizzy. "My god, you're burning up."

He picked me up and sat me in a chair, then returned to the kitchen and soaked a towel. After wringing out the excess water, he wrapped the wet towel around my shoulders. It immediately started bringing down my body temperature.

"Put your head down between your legs."

He went back to the sink to get me a glass of water. I drank it all.

"Feeling better?" He squatted down in front of me and brushed my hair away from my face. "Not again," he said, touching the bruise under my eye. "You have to get out of there."

I shook my head. "I can't. Madi isn't the type of supervisor to let her workers walk away. Besides, I'm not exactly in the position to go looking for another job."

"I'm afraid she's going to kill you if you stay. Maybe you need a few Liberty guards in the laundry room."

I almost laughed. "What's that going to do?" Was Jack really that naive about the way things worked down here? "A guard would never interfere with a supervisor disciplining her workers. And if a guard ever did, Madi would have him transferred out of there."

Jack raised my face and made a closer inspection of my bruise. I could only imagine how awful I must look. I still had the bruise over my other eye from the day before.

"I don't want you to work there anymore," he said in a tight voice. I could tell by the determined set to his jaw that he thought his statement brooked no argument.

"Maybe it's time for you to grow up, Jack. This is life in the Pit. You think this is the first time I've been beaten? Do you know what it did to my parents every time I came home with a new bruise or a cracked rib? Or how I felt when I saw them beaten and broken? We live with that threat every day." Jack dropped his hand away from my face and stood up. I could tell he didn't want to hear what I was saying. "At least I know what to expect from Madi. She gets mad and she hits. It could be worse. My last supervisor sent me upstairs to be a sex toy at your bachelor party. I'd rather take what Madi's doling out."

Jack blinked quickly a few times before he turned his back on me. He raked a hand through his hair before he picked up his hat and put it back on. "Are you okay now?" His voice was strained.

"Yes."

Without another word, he left the apartment. I didn't expect that reaction from him. Perhaps I had been too honest. He didn't need to know that I had been beaten before. It wasn't really something we talked about down here anyway. Being beaten was always a humiliating experience. Everyone walked around with bruises, but no one ever said anything about them.

I raised my head upright, checking to see if I was still dizzy. Thankfully, the world stayed in balance. A canvas bag sitting just inside the door caught my attention, and tentatively I stood up. There was a slight rush to my head, but then it was gone. I retrieved the bag and sat back down. It was full of clean clothes, and a razor and a communicator. Bron had come through for Jack.

The sink was still filled with cool water, and I decided not to waste it. I stripped naked and bathed right there in the kitchen. I was taking a huge risk—Jack could return any minute—but given how mad he was when he left, I figured it would take him a while to calm down. I dried off and rummaged through the canvas bag for a clean outfit. The clothes were a lot better quality than I was used to. In fact, they were a lot better quality than anyone in the Pit was used to. I hoped they wouldn't make us stand out.

I hung up my wet towel and was about to drain the water when I thought better of it. I could wash my hair tonight before bed. Maybe Jack's habits were wearing off on me.

I was putting the soap away when I heard the door open. I turned to see Jack looking at me from the doorway. He had a strange look on his face.

"I'm sorry about what I said earlier. I didn't mean to be cruel," I said.

"Where did you get those clothes?"

"Bron must have brought them. She brought you a razor and a communicator, too," I pointed to the bag. "There's some water here if you want to wash."

"They're really..." he stammered. "They fit you a lot better than my clothes did."

"These are my size. Your clothes weren't."

"Are you going to be able to fit your vest under that t-shirt?"

I moaned. "Oh, that stupid vest! I forgot to put it back on. Do you think anyone would really notice?" I wanted to stop wearing it. It was going to be the death of me in that laundry room.

"Yes, people will definitely notice. Go put it on, and we'll go for dinner. Bron came through on securing the common room too. It's going to happen tonight."

"Tonight for sure?" I asked, a little shocked. He nodded as he took his dirty t-shirt off and walked to the sink. It struck me that we were getting pretty comfortable around each other. "I'll give you some privacy."

I went into the bedroom and closed the door, glad for the opportunity to lie down for a few minutes. The heat exhaustion I'd suffered that day had really made me tired. And I had forgotten about tonight. A nervous flutter began in the pit of my stomach. How were we going to broach the subject of a rebellion with everyone? Would they laugh at us? Run us out of the Pit?

I was starting to drift asleep when Jack knocked on the bedroom door. "Ready," he said.

I got up, put the offensive vest on and went out into the other room. He was dressed in snug-fitting jeans and a black t-shirt. He looked good. Really good. I was suddenly conscious of how stupid I looked in my vest.

My stomach started making noises, and I quickly put my hand across my abdomen to stifle it. It sounded so loud in the quiet of the apartment.

"Let me guess. You weren't allowed to eat today either," Jack said wryly.

"It happens." I put my hat on and headed out the door before we got into another argument.

The common room was already bustling with the dinner-hour rush, and the line-up was long. It was a lot more crowded than our room on the sixth level. The line moved quickly, though, and we didn't have long before our turn came to receive rations. We went in search of a place to sit and saw Raine and Mica motioning for us to join them. At first I was surprised to see them on this level then guessed they must be there for Jack's training session. I was surprised to see Raine's wife with him. I rarely saw her anymore.

"Who is that woman with them?" Jack whispered as we made our way to their table.

"That's Raine's wife."

"I didn't know he was married."

"It's good to see you, Flo," I said to Raine's wife as I sat down. Her real name was Flower, but like me she preferred the shortened form. She gave me a weak smile and went back to vacantly staring around the room. Jack secretly gave me a curious look, and I subtly gave him my best "tell you later" look.

"Everything is set?" Raine asked as we sat down.

"I'm told it is," Jack said. He looked up at the broken camera and scanned the faces of the guards in the room. All of them seemed to be looking back at him.

I felt a nervous flutter again, but ignored it and concentrated on my food. I didn't join the conversation until my container was empty. My thoughts were preoccupied with how I was going to appease Madi tomorrow to ensure I received at least water for lunch.

"How do we get started?" I asked Jack. "Does everyone here know about it?"

"I put the word out in the mine today." Jack looked around the room. "I recognize some of the people I talked to."

"Yeah, Jack's a legend down there already, and not just because he flattened eight guards but because he got away with it. I mean, we all expected he would be in a lot of trouble, but the guards are leaving him alone. I think they're too embarrassed because they got their butt kicked by just one urchin!" Raine said, laughing.

I smirked when I heard the guard count was up to eight now. But Raine did bring up a good point about the guards leaving Jack alone. I wondered if Liberty guards had taken over the mine already and that's why he was safe.

"I thought a lot more would show," Mica said, looking around.

I noticed there was one person missing. "Reyes didn't come." I knew why.

"I'd stay out of his way if I were you," Mica said.

"No offence or anything, but what was that this morning? You were all over him. It ripped the heart out of Reyes," Raine said.

The weight of my guilt suddenly seemed heavier than the bulletproof vest I was wearing. How could I have done that to Reyes? He deserved so much better.

"It wasn't her fault," Jack said. "One of Leisel's guards followed Summer into the room, and we did it to hide our faces."

"Oh," Mica said in mock understanding. "Maybe next time you can just pull your hats down lower or something. It would be kinder."

Mica had always been Reyes's most loyal friend. I knew it must be difficult for him to watch Reyes in pain because of me. He probably hated me, too.

Jack was studying the people in the room. There was no more line-up for food and the servers behind the counter were packing up to leave. Many people who had finished eating, particularly those with a small child in tow, were leaving as well. The room was no longer as crowded as it had been at dinner. I could tell by the expression on Jack's face that he wasn't pleased.

Bron walked in. I didn't expect to see her here tonight. She was always on the sixth-floor.

"I guess it's now or never," Jack said.

He nodded to Bron, and she sent two of the guards to close the door. Jack got up and went to the front of the room. This was the time of the evening in the common room where people had a chance to sing or tell stories, so Jack's presence at the front of the room wasn't unusual. Everyone stopped talking and looked at him expectantly.

"I've never been up here before so I guess I'll start by introducing myself. I'm Ben Jones," he said.

A murmur went through the room acknowledging him. Some said welcome.

"Some of you may know me, but for those of you who don't, I'm the guy who had a bit of scuffle with the guards in the mines yesterday."

Someone called out, "You kicked their butts, brother!"

Jack laughed. "Yeah, I kicked a few butts. Some of you asked me how I was able to do that, so here I am. Anyone wanting to ask me questions or learn to throw a punch, now's the time."

I felt so nervous for Jack; he wasn't just risking exposure, he was risking rejection. I held my breath waiting for someone to volunteer to go up and be the first to learn from him. No one seemed to be coming forward, though. I shot Raine and Mica a pleading look, but they didn't want to be the first to go up either. So I stood up and walked to the front of the room to stand beside him. He looked at me with relief in his eyes.

"I see my wife is volunteering to be my first victim tonight!"

A laugh rippled through the crowd.

Just then the door burst open, and Reyes walked into the room. He regarded Jack and me with disgust and then looked around at the expectant crowd of people sitting in their seats watching us. "Don't listen to anything this filthy bourge has to say," he said loudly. "He's Jack Kenner!"

CHAPTER TWENTY-TWO

"Reyes, what the hell are you doing?" I yelled. Anxious chatter filled the room and all eyes were on us.

"What I should've done a long time ago. Bourge don't belong in the Pit!"

I could almost feel his rage. "Do you know what you've just done?"

"Sunny, your face. Where did you get those bruises? Did *he* give them to you?" Reyes balled his hands into fists and set out after Jack.

"*Stop!*" I screamed.

Behind Reyes I saw two guards step forward, but Jack must have motioned them off because they stepped back.

"Go," Jack told me.

I stayed rooted to the spot. I couldn't just let this happen. I had to stop it. But Jack stepped in front of me, cutting me off from Reyes. He raised his arm and blocked the punch Reyes threw at him. Jack waited for his next move and blocked that too. Reyes came at him harder, and Jack had to back up a few steps. I finally moved out of the way. This was out of my control.

Reyes kept coming at Jack, and Jack kept blocking his punches. At one point they ended up in the crowd, and people scattered to get out of their way. I noticed that Jack never once threw a punch at Reyes, only defended himself against the rage Reyes inflicted on him. Reyes was getting frustrated that his strikes were having no effect. I could tell he was tiring too. I felt so horrible, so guilty. What had I done to him? The fight came to an end when an exhausted Reyes desperately dove toward Jack to take him down, but Jack easily stepped out of his way and Reyes crashed into an empty chair, breaking it.

"Got it out of your system yet?" Jack asked.

"You're an idiot, Kenner!" Reyes said, picking himself up from the floor. He stared at the guards. "Maybe you didn't hear me when I said this is *Jack Kenner!*" He pointed to Jack. The guards looked blankly at Reyes.

"Sorry, Reyes, they're on my side," Jack said.

The crowd became very nervous when they heard that. Everyone started talking at once. Jack was still wearing his hat, and he took it off then. While the coal still darkened his light hair, there was no mistaking his blue eyes.

"That's right. I am Jack Kenner. And for the record, I didn't give Sunny those bruises, although I'd like to have words with the person who did." He gave me a fond look.

I smiled back at him. My respect for him was growing. He could have really hurt Reyes if he had wanted to, but he hadn't.

"Is that bourge down here with you, O'Donnell?" someone from the crowd asked.

I stepped out from the corner and walked over to Jack. "He is."

"How come the guards are on his side?" someone else asked.

Strong agreement rose up among the room. They eyed the guards suspiciously.

"You may find this hard to believe, but there are people in the Dome who are on your side. People who want to see things change down here," Jack said.

"On *our* side?" someone shouted out at him in disgust. "I'm thirty-two years old, and not once in my life have I ever seen anyone from the Dome down here fighting for us!"

People started agreeing, their voices growing louder.

"And since when are guards here to *help* us?" someone else shouted out. "More likely they're here to shoot us in case we do something they don't like!"

I could feel the crowd starting to turn on us. The more questions they asked, the more nervous they became. They were talking themselves right into a riot. Everyone had been through too many years of abuse from the bourge to suddenly start trusting one that had almost been president himself.

"If you don't trust him, trust me," I said loudly. Not many people looked in my direction because they were too caught up in their own fears. Jack gave me a defeated look, but if we gave up now I knew the only thing we would have achieved tonight was exposing our identities. In a desperate attempt to get their attention, I stood up on a chair and whistled as loud as I could. Most people stopped talking and looked at me. *"Trust me!"* I shouted as loud as I could. The room finally became quiet. I stood on the chair looking at their expectant faces, knowing that whatever I said could change the course of life in the Pit forever.

"The bruises on my face came from my supervisor." I pulled back my hair to show everyone. "And last month a different supervisor ordered a guard to beat me when I was too slow at my job. I got a few cracked ribs from that one. You might wonder why I was slow at my job, knowing that I would probably be beaten for it. The answer is that I was sad. Sad because my mother had to join the Cull last spring." Even now my tears were quick to spring up when I talked of her. "How many people here have lost someone to the Cull?" Everyone in the room raised their hand. "How many people here have been beaten?" Every hand remained in the air. "And how many of you are fed up?" At this, even the people sitting down stood up to raise their hands higher.

"I am one of you. I have the scars to prove it. I've suffered the beatings, I've lost my mother, my best friend is a plaything for the bourge, and now they have my father. I didn't marry a bourge to escape the Pit. I married Jack Kenner because he said he wanted to change things for the better down here. He told me about Liberty, an organization with a few thousand members who all want the same thing — to see President Holt replaced with a government that will give us all equal rights. A government we can be a part of."

I looked at the crowd as I said this and saw their shocked expressions. Although there had been uprisings in the Pit before, no one had ever suggested getting rid of the president. It was a new idea. It was a dangerous idea.

"You want us to join some bourge organization to get rid of the bourge?" someone asked. "Something doesn't make sense here."

"It makes sense if you stop thinking of Jack and these guards as bourge. They're members of Liberty, and they're here to join with us."

"I'm not joining some bourge organization!" someone called out and was met with a round of approval.

"Then let's make our own organization. Liberty and the Pit will join and become the Alliance," I said. "They have skills they can teach us, and we have power in numbers."

"I know about his skills," a man said, looking at Jack. "I'm David Chavez, and I work with you in the mine. I saw what you did for that kid. The guards were going to beat him, and you stopped them... and I didn't lift a damn finger to help." His eyes were bright with tears. A few other men in the crowd hung their heads in shame. "My wife's about to have a baby, and all I've been able to think about is what if it was my kid? When the guards want to beat my child, will I stand there and do nothing again? If I have a daughter, will I stand by and watch her taken upstairs to be used by the men in the Dome?" He shook his head in disgust, and the tears rolled freely down his cheeks. "I want better for my kid. I'll join you."

The crowd was silent while David spoke. He had touched a nerve in everyone. Several men came forward to stand beside him, nodding their approval. The only sound that could be heard in the room was the sobs of a very pregnant woman. I assumed she was his wife.

"What if it backfires? What if we can't win?" asked a faceless voice from the crowd.

Someone else stood up and answered, "Then would we be any worse off than we already are? I don't have much time left before I'm Culled, but I'd like to make my last months in this world count. I'm in."

One man voiced everyone's worst fear: "If we make the bourge mad, they could cut off our ventilation system and kill us all!"

"You would have to make them pretty mad before they went to that extreme," Jack said. He waited to see the crowd's reaction before he continued. "I know the bourge put you down, call you urchins, tell you you're less than them and that you're lucky to be in the Dome safe from the nuclear fallout. The truth is that you are important to them. Without you, the Dome wouldn't be able to function. You mine the coal, you run the sewage treatment, you do their laundry, their cleaning, prepare their food. Don't ever underestimate your value to them."

"But they have all the power, and we have none. Look around this room. There's maybe fifty or sixty people here and you think we can take on the Dome?" someone said.

"You're right. We need more numbers. The more of us there are, the more powerful we become. But tonight is a start."

"I know everyone is scared," I said. "And no one is suggesting the small group of people in this room rush upstairs and try to throw the president out. We need to convince more people to join us. We need to start training. We need to come up with a strategy."

"We can start training tonight," Jack said. He motioned to Bron to come and stand beside him. "This is Bron. Those of you from the sixth level might recognize her. She's taking a big risk being here tonight, but she came to show her support and to help with the training."

"I guess it won't hurt to learn how to defend ourselves," someone mumbled.

More people stepped forward. Everyone seemed eager to learn how to fight.

I saw Reyes standing with Raine and Mica, staring at me as if I had gone mad. As I returned his stare, he gave me a disgusted look and stomped out of the room. I hopped down from the chair

"I need to talk to him," I told Jack and ran after Reyes.

"Reyes," I called out, but he kept going. "Reyes, please stop." A Liberty guard was standing outside the door of the common room, and he respectfully turned his head in the other direction.

"Later, Sunny," Reyes said, throwing a hand up in the air to wave me off.

"I don't think I have a later, Reyes. In fact, someone could be turning me in as we speak. Thank you for exposing us." That stopped him.

"I wanted to expose Kenner, not you. I want him gone so I can have you back. But after watching you in there — standing up on a chair preaching to everyone — I don't even know who you are anymore."

"I haven't changed. I'm the same person I've always been. Why can't you see that?"

A familiar frustration came boiling to the surface, and I wondered how many times and how many different ways we could have this same conversation. He was always trying to change me and I was always unwilling to change.

"You know, after I said those things to you the other day I wanted to take them all back," Reyes said, his eyes bright with unshed tears. "A part of me hoped that you would come and find me and try to make things right between us, but when you didn't, I knew I had to be the one. I don't know where you live, so I waited to see you in the common room the next day but you never showed up. I was so happy to see you this morning, but then you walked right by me and started kissing that bourge." A tear fell from his eye, and I knew in that instant how deeply I had hurt him.

"Please know that I didn't do it to hurt you. One of Leisel's guards was following Summer, so we pretended to kiss to hide our faces." But even now, just remembering that kiss, I felt a warm sensation spread through me. None of Reyes's kisses had ever affected me like that.

"So you're not in love with him?"

A stab of guilt went through me when I saw the hope in his eyes. He thought I was here to make amends. He thought we could still be together.

"All those things you said to me the other day — about me constantly making excuses and always choosing other people over you — were all true." A lump formed at the base of my throat, but I fought back the tears. "You always wanted me to be someone I wasn't. You always wanted me to be with you, to let you protect me, to be the girl who hung on your every word. I'm not that girl, Reyes. I kept thinking that maybe I could be that girl once we were married, but whenever our wedding date crept closer, I realized I wasn't ready to stop being myself yet." I felt tears roll down my face. Saying goodbye was hard even though it was for the best. "The person you saw tonight in that room is me, Reyes. I haven't changed. Why can't you see that our relationship has been like trying to fit together two pieces of a puzzle that don't belong; we can try as hard as we want, but we'll never fit."

"So you *never* loved me?"

"Of course I loved you," I said, wiping the tear from his cheek. "I just couldn't be the person you wanted."

He took my hand away from his face and dropped it.

"I can't believe I wasted so much of my life on you." He turned around and walked away.

I let him go, knowing I deserved his hatred. I had led him to believe we would spend the rest of our lives together instead of being honest with him and myself. It was my fault he was hurting. I knew I should feel guilty, so I tried to ignore the elation bubbling up inside me at the realization I was finally free of him. I had so many other things in my life to worry about, and our dead-end relationship didn't need to be one of them. Reyes would survive this.

I went back into the common room and was pleasantly surprised to see a training session in full swing. Raine and Mica had remained, despite Reyes's angry exit. Jack saw me and raised his eyebrows. I guessed he was asking me if Reyes was coming back in, so I shook my head. He turned his attention back to the people he was working with.

"If you can't disarm your opponent, then use his weapon against him," Jack said to the whole room. "Like this." He motioned for a guard to join him. The guard stood with his rifle pointed at Jack. In one swift movement, Jack grabbed the barrel of the rifle and struck at the guard's face with it. He didn't hit the guard, but the force of the attack made the guard back up a few steps, which left him off balance. Jack seized the rifle and kicked the guard in the stomach, knocking him flat on his back, and in one final movement had the rifle pointed at the guard. Everyone clapped. Jack offered his hand to the guard to help him up. He instructed the guards to work with the people standing at the front of the room and then came over to me.

"Everything okay?" he asked.

"You mean besides the fact that everyone in this room knows who we are?"

"When he gets mad he makes it count, doesn't he?"

"He always had a temper." I didn't want to talk about Reyes. I needed to close the door on that relationship. "So do I get to learn how to do this? I missed our session last night."

"Sure. Let me get a gun, and you can try and take it from me."

Jack went to the guard by the door and asked to borrow his rifle. I studied the people currently engaged with trying to get the guns away from the three guards working with them. No one was having much success. I saw how clumsy their movements were.

"Ready," Jack said.

He stood with both hands on the gun. I replayed in my mind how he had taken the gun away from the guard a few minutes earlier. I attempted it, but Jack was too quick, and I ended up on the floor. I jumped up and came at him again hoping to catch him off guard, but he easily pushed me away. I stepped back and thought about it. It occurred to me that as long as the barrel of the gun wasn't pointed at me, he couldn't shoot me. So I needed to get around the barrel and close enough to engage him in hand-to-hand combat. If I could do that, he would need to let go of the gun to fend me off.

I went at him as fast as I could, and when I saw the nose of the gun come up, I pushed it down and used it to give me balance. I raised my leg and kicked him in his side. His grip on the gun loosened for a second, and I grabbed it with both hands while swinging my leg in a backward arc that brought me behind him. I brought the gun up under his throat and held it there. I heard people clapping and looked up to see them staring at me.

"You do catch on quickly," Jack said, smiling.

I loosened my grip on the rifle, and he lowered it. "Am I scaring you, Jack?"

Suddenly Jack's hands were on me, and he threw me over his hip. I hit the floor with an ungraceful flop.

"A little bit." He stepped away and left me to pick myself up. "It's going to be lights out soon so we should wrap it up," he said to the room.

"Can we try again tomorrow?" Raine asked.

Jack looked around the room to see if anyone else was interested. Most people wanted to come back. Jack asked the guards, and they agreed as well.

"You were amazing tonight," Jack said once we were alone. "You blew me away."

"I guess it went well."

"You were great, but we only had maybe fifty people in that room, not nearly enough to take on the few hundred guards that patrol down here. I told you before, power comes with numbers, and we don't have numbers."

"I don't think we stand much of a chance anyway. I expect someone in that room will gladly turn us in for the four hundred credits Holt is offering."

When we arrived at our apartment, I scanned my hand across the lock and went in.

"I know. I think that too." Jack shut the door behind him. Then he picked up one of the chairs and put it under the doorknob. I gave him an inquisitive look. "At least it will give us a little notice if someone comes."

"I've always known we'll be caught eventually, but now that it might be real, I'm scared."

I didn't want to die now that I had found a reason to live. I wanted to see this rebellion through and free Summer from Holt; have the chance to find my father if he was still alive; help liberate the Pit from centuries of slavery. I wanted time to finish what we started.

"You're scared?" he asked in surprise. "I can't believe the girl who stood up on a chair and convinced an entire room to start a rebellion is scared."

"And you're not?"

"Terrified. Hey, what was wrong with Raine's wife? She seemed a little out of it."

"Women get that way after they're sterilized."

"After they're what?"

"Sterilized." He had an odd look on his face. "You must know about the Sterilization Program. Your government came up with it ten years ago. If a couple doesn't qualify to have a child, the woman is sterilized and whatever they inject her with makes her go… blank. The injection changes a woman. She's not as… full of life as she used to be."

Jack was staring at me with a horrified look on his face when the lights went out, leaving us in darkness. Maybe he didn't know about that program.

"We should get some sleep," I said.

"I'll take the chair."

"No. We shared last night, we can do it again tonight." Considering the way I responded to his kiss this morning, it probably wasn't a good idea. But we both needed a decent sleep. Jack was exhausted from sleeping in the chair, and I couldn't afford to be tired and sloppy with Madi as my supervisor.

"Are you sure?"

"Yeah. Just stay on your on side of the bed." But I didn't really mean it. I walked toward the bedroom.

"That bed isn't big enough to have sides." He stumbled after me, knocking a chair over.

"You really can't see, can you?"

"And you're surprised? It's pitch black in here."

I took him by the hand and guided him toward the bedroom. He took off his t-shirt and flopped down on the bed. Since he was blind in the dark, I stripped off my vest and put my t-shirt back on before I climbed in.

"It's not pitch black in here. The guards use nightlights, and it leaks into the apartment."

He opened his eyes as wide as he could and looked around the room. "I guess you have to born in the Pit to find light where there isn't any."

I rolled that thought over in my mind and realized just how true it was.

CHAPTER TWENTY-THREE

It felt like I had just drifted to sleep when the sound of the *bong bongs* invaded my dreams. I had barely slept all night because I kept imagining that guards were going to come crashing through the door at any moment and take us into custody. I tried to close my mind off to the annoying sound. I didn't want to wake up. For some reason, I felt warm and safe, and I wasn't ready to let go of that feeling. I wrapped my arms around my pillow to pull it tight under my head, but my pillow was hard and wouldn't scrunch up. Then I realized that the sound of a beating heart was playing under my ear. The shock of what I was doing brought me fully awake. I was snuggling Jack.

"Oh my god, I am so sorry!" I flew into a sitting position. Jack was wide awake and smiling at me... or maybe he was laughing. It was hard to tell.

"I don't mind."

"I was asleep. I didn't know what I was doing." I rolled off the bed and stood up. "I'm so embarrassed."

"There's no reason to be embarrassed." Jack got out of bed, too. He stood close to me and brushed a lock of hair away from my face. "It's not your fault. I'm just a hard guy to resist." Laughter lit up his face.

I rolled my eyes at him and left the bedroom. I went to the faucet and splashed cold water on my blushing face. Jack's habits really were rubbing off on me. Just a few weeks ago it would never have occurred to me to waste water like this.

"Well, we made it through the night," Jack said. Our imminent capture was probably weighing heavily on his mind too.

"I barely slept at all."

"Oh, I think you got a few good hours." Jack gave me a wicked smile before he ducked his head toward the sink and splashed water on his face.

I dropped the towel next to him and went into the bedroom to put my vest back on. It felt heavier every time I wore it.

"You can't wear that again today. It almost killed you yesterday."

"I can't show up to work ten pounds lighter either," I snapped. "I'll just have to stay on Madi's good side so I can get my water ration." Although I knew that was easier said than done. She was cruising for a fight.

We put our hats on and left the apartment. "You're not in a very good mood today."

"I can't imagine why. My life is so fantastic."

He was right, though. My mood was particularly bad. Not only was I feeling vulnerable with my identity exposed, I wasn't altogether happy that not many people had showed up the night before. All the hope I convinced myself of seemed to have been dashed with a bad night's sleep. And the only thing I had to look forward to was going to work in a room that was hotter than Hades under the glare of a sadistic supervisor. I was exhausted.

Jack put his arm around me and pulled me closer to him as we walked toward the common room. I stiffened at his touch at first, but decided to let him do it. We looked like any other married couple on their way to breakfast. I put my arm around his waist.

"Try to remember we have people down here on our side now," he said in a low voice. "Even if someone wants to turn us in for the credits, it will probably be Liberty guards who come looking for us."

I cocked an eyebrow at him. "You mean Alliance guards?" He gave me a wry smile. "I wish I could feel as confident as you do." Maybe it was the lack of sleep the night before, but I really couldn't shake this feeling of doom.

It was still early, and there wasn't a big line-up to get into the common room. A guard stood by the door as usual.

"Good morning, sir. Ma'am," he said as we walked through the door.

Jack bid him good morning, but I was too shocked to speak. No one had ever called me "ma'am" before, let alone a guard.

"Why did he call me that?" I whispered.

"He's trained to show respect to his leaders."

"But I'm not his leader."

The woman serving the food greeted us with a huge smile. She grabbed one of my hands with both of hers and held it warmly for a moment. "You're doing a good thing," she said. She gave Jack a smile too before she passed us our containers of food, water, and cups of hot tea. "A treat this morning."

"Hot tea? What's going on?" I said to Jack once we were seated.

"You're a hero to your people, Sunny. They want to do nice things for you."

"But I haven't done anything to deserve the title."

I wasn't a hero. I had been a naïve girl who had fallen for Leisel's lies and was on the run from her father. I suddenly felt bad for keeping that truth to myself so everyone would think I was someone I was not.

"Sure you have. Stop being so hard on yourself."

I gulped my breakfast down and drank my water. I wasn't sure if I was going to get a lunch break today or not, so my meal was especially important to me.

The room was starting to fill up, and it surprised me every time someone walked by and greeted us. Some people I recognized from the night before, others I didn't. It concerned me that so many people knew who we were.

"Drink the tea. It lowers body temperature, which you could use in that hot laundry room," Jack said.

"Really?" I wasn't sure if he was serious or not, but I drank the tea anyway.

I absentmindedly watched Crystal leave the room. The day before I would have run to catch up with her and try to find out what she knew about Jack, but there was no longer any doubt in my mind she knew who we both were. I wondered if she would tell Madi.

"Sunny?" Jack said.

"What?"

Jack gave me a puzzled look. "Are you okay?"

"I'm fine. Just preoccupied. I guess now that everyone knows who we are I'm feeling vulnerable. I don't know how you're not feeling that way, too."

"I am feeling that way. I'm just better at ignoring it. I take comfort in the fact that we have guards down here on our side. I know you still don't trust them, though, and I understand." He picked up my hands from the table, held them in his, and looked at me with his intense blue eyes. "I'll do everything in my power to keep you safe." I appreciated his reassurances, but I just didn't believe them. He was every bit as powerless as I was.

"I better get to work. I'm usually there waiting for Madi, and I don't want to disappoint her this morning!" I tried to sound cheerful. I really did need to shake off the melancholy mood.

Jack and I stood up at the same time. He slung his arm around my shoulders and squeezed me against him as we walked through the door and out into the hall. I knew he was just trying to show his support and put me in a better mood.

"Be careful at work. Drink water today," he said then kissed the top of my head and started the climb down the stairs toward the coal mine. I watched him go until he was out of sight.

I walked the few flights up to the laundry room. Crystal was already there, as I knew she would be.

"Good morning, Sunny."

I stopped dead in my tracks and gave her a blank look.

"Don't look so surprised. Everyone knows who you are now. Although, I figured it out the first time I saw you with Jack Kenner."

So I had been right. She had recognized him. "How do you know Jack?" There was no point in keeping secrets now.

"I sing at all the presidential parties and dinners. In fact, it's the only time I'm allowed to sing. I used to see Jack there all the time when he was engaged to Leisel. As much as I hate the bourge, Jack was hard to miss. I was supposed to sing at their wedding reception."

I tried to imagine him at a stuffy party as Leisel's fiancé but couldn't. The Jack I knew didn't fit the image of presidential heir. And the thought made me a little mad. I didn't want to think of him as a bourge, particularly one who had a relationship with the president's daughter. Yet he must have fit in at those parties.

"What was he like up there?" I asked hesitantly, not sure I really wanted to know.

"I never talked to him personally, but he always seemed polite to everyone. I did notice that whenever they brought girls up from the Pit for their parties, he never touched them. That is, until he left with you the night of his bachelor party."

"You were there? At the bachelor party?" I asked in surprise.

Crystal nodded. "I was serving the head table. I belong to Malcolm West, one of the president's closest advisors."

"You *belong* to Malcolm West?" She nodded again. I wasn't really sure how it worked between a bourge and someone he claimed as his own. "Just like my friend belongs to Holt," I mused out loud.

"You know Summer?"

I raised my eyebrows in surprise. It never occurred to me that she would know Summer, too. "Yes. But don't tell anyone she knows me!" I was horrified that I had just divulged that information. "If Holt ever knew she was my friend, he'd use her to get to me."

"I promise I won't say anything. I feel sorry for your friend. The president is really crazy, and he seems obsessed with her. Don't get me wrong, I hate being touched by Malcolm, but at least he's not insane like Holt. There's no way out for her."

"What do you mean there's no way out for her?"

"President Holt has killed every mistress he's ever had. He's fanatical about keeping the bloodlines clean — you know, bourge and urchins. As soon as he convinces himself she's pregnant, he'll kill her."

"What?" In my utter shock and disbelief, I couldn't even process the information she'd just given me. "Convinces himself? You mean she doesn't even need to be pregnant?"

"None of the girls he's killed has ever been pregnant. Rumour has it he's not capable of having children. And if the rumours are true, Leisel's mother took an urchin lover and Holt killed her for it, but kept the baby as his own."

"Is Summer in any danger yet?"

"No. It usually takes a year or two before he turns on his mistress. It depends how long he stays obsessed with her."

President Holt was a bigger monster than I had ever imagined. The rebellion became that much more important to me in that moment. I had to find a way to get Summer away from him before he turned.

"Do you see Summer a lot?"

"At least once a week Holt and Malcolm have dinner together in the president's suites. I sit in the corner with my guitar and sing quietly, while Summer serves them. I'll probably see her tonight. It's the president's birthday, and Leisel is having a small dinner party for him."

"If you talk to her, can you tell her I think about her all the time? That I miss her horribly?"

"We don't get much of a chance to talk." A sad, scared look came over Crystal's face. "When the president and Malcolm are alone, they talk, and… well… Summer and I *hear* things. Things we shouldn't hear."

"Like what?" Crystal looked scared and I wanted to know why.

"Forget it. I shouldn't have brought it up. I would be killed if I ever repeated what I heard." Crystal shook her head. "Is it true you and Jack are organizing a rebellion?"

"Yes, but it's hard to start a rebellion with only fifty people. Not enough people are interested."

"They're interested. They're just scared."

"About the things you've heard," I began, but Madi walked around the corner, and I cut off my words.

"Conspiring again? Don't let me interrupt," Madi said sarcastically. She unlocked the door and walked into the laundry room, letting the door slam in our faces.

I tried not to let Madi irritate me, but already my hand was itching to slap her across the face. It was going to be a long day in my current mood. I scanned in and went to my workstation.

I was feeling better about Crystal now that we had talked. I thought someone in the Dome was using her, but it still surprised me to learn that she knew Summer. I felt closer to Crystal now. I understood her better.

I took a cart full of dirty laundry and started sorting it. I tried to shut everything else from my mind and concentrate only on the clothes. I didn't want a repeat of the day before. I needed water in order to work in this hell.

"Good morning, *Autumn*," Di said cheerfully as she came to stand beside me. I guess she knew that wasn't my real name, too.

"Good morning, Di."

"News travels fast around here."

"So I see. Are you going to turn me in?" I almost didn't care at this point. At least they would put me in a cool apartment with running water so I wouldn't die of heat exhaustion.

"Don't you worry." Di patted my hand. "Anyone down here that turns you in is asking for a slow and painful death. We all agree about that!"

"Hey, Di," Madi yelled as she walked toward us. "No reason for you to help Jones any more. If she doesn't know how to do her job yet, I'll beat it into her by the end of the day."

Di took off. Our supervisor came to stand behind me. "You know how to be a good worker, right, Jones?" she said in a threatening voice.

"Yes, Supervisor Madi." How long could I put up with this woman?

She slapped the back of my head then walked over to Crystal's station and watched her in a menacing way. I saw the threatening look she gave Crystal before she went back to her desk. Supervisor Madi was a problem that just wouldn't go away.

I finished sorting my cart and took each load to a machine for washing. I had a small pile of hand washing that I was afraid to give Crystal. Any contact with her might provoke Madi in the mood she was in, but I didn't want to give it to Di either, in case she was discovered doing my job. I swallowed my fear, picked up the few articles of clothing and started walking toward Crystal. I saw Madi look at me, her brows drawing together in anger. I held up the clothes for her to see.

"Supervisor Madi, may I take these to Crystal to be hand washed?" I asked as respectfully as I could. Madi gave me a reluctant nod.

I put the clothes on the counter beside Crystal and retreated quickly back to my table. My first wash was done, and I sorted it. I spent the rest of the morning painfully conscious of Madi's stares but managed to finish two carts of laundry before lunch. I was already hot and knew I needed the water badly. I prayed Madi wasn't going to prevent me from having it again.

I was grateful when I was given water and food. I drained the glass right away, worried that Madi might change her mind and take it from me. I was halfway through my stew when I noticed Di staring at me.

"Have mine, too," she said, offering me her water.

"No. You need it. It would only provoke Madi if she saw you give it to me anyway."

Madi's head came up, and she looked at us when she heard Di and me chatting. I put my head down and finished my lunch.

"Back to work!" Madi yelled before the lunch break was over.

Di groaned as she got back on her feet. I hadn't seen Kai off in the corner by himself. He walked over to us with a sweet smile on his face.

"Is that cart finished, Miss Autumn?" he asked

"Yes, it is, Kai. Thank you." I returned his smile. He was the first person I talked with that day that didn't make it clear he knew I was Sunny O'Donnell.

The afternoon got hotter and hotter, and I tried to think of other things besides my need for cold water. Madi kept cruising between Crystal and me, trying to find fault with our work. Crystal had a lot of hand washing and ironing to do. She was having trouble keeping up, and it didn't go unnoticed by Madi.

As the day wore on, I could tell Crystal was getting anxious. She hurried through her work, which made her sloppy. Water splashed over the sink a few times, and Madi screamed at her to be more careful. The *bong bongs* sounded, and Crystal still had a lot of work to do. I saw her look of panic. Then I remembered she told me she had to be upstairs for the president's birthday dinner.

"You have to finish, Crystal. Those shirts and dresses still need to be pressed. They came down here with specific instructions to be done in time for this evening," Madi said.

I wished I could go over and volunteer to finish Crystal's work, but I knew that would send Madi over the edge. Crystal was doing her best to finish, but Madi was standing over her watching her every move. Tears were starting to fall from Crystal's eyes. She was in an impossible predicament. She had to finish pressing the clothes for the people who were attending the president's party, even though she had to be at the party herself. She couldn't leave this job, and she couldn't be late for that one.

"Cry one more time on that shirt, and I'll make you wash it again!" Madi yelled.

Everyone had left for the day, save for myself, Di, and Kai. I could tell Crystal was about to break. I felt my own anxiety rise as I watched her in distress. The more Madi screamed at her, the harder Crystal cried and the more I cringed.

Then Madi struck her. Hard.

Crystal fell to the floor, and I watched, as if in slow motion, as Madi pulled her leg back and kicked Crystal in the stomach.

Something inside me snapped.

"Go home, Kai," I said in a low voice.

I strode toward Madi, picking up speed as I went. I had to stop her.

She saw me coming and turned her attention to me. I thought I saw a smile on her face, and I was gladly going to wipe it off for her. As I closed the distance between us, she pulled her right arm back to throw a punch at me. I easily ducked it and brought my right fist into her stomach. As she doubled over, I snapped my knee into her face. I moved like Jack had taught me, allowing one move to create the next. I grabbed her by the hair, pulled her face up, and slammed her back against the table. I didn't see her reach back and pick up an iron, but I saw it when she swung it at my head. I stepped back, and the iron missed me by less than an inch. The distance between us gave Madi an opportunity to punch me in the stomach. I felt the impact, but not as much as I could have. The vest I was wearing gave me an advantage. She pulled her hand back in pain, and I smiled. I brought my leg up and kicked her back against the table.

I came at her fast, but she recovered quickly and was ready for me. She bent down and came at me full on, grabbing me around my waist and pushing me backwards. I hit the floor hard, and she came down on top of me. She was heavier than I'd expected, and I struggled against her weight. To win this fight I would have to get her off of me. I rolled on to my side to throw her off, but I couldn't get enough force behind the movement to budge her. Madi held my arms down at my sides. I was pinned.

"Now I got you, bitch," she said sitting up on top of me.

She let go of my arms to use her fists against me and as soon as she did, I punched her, catching her at the base of her throat. Her eyes widened as both her hands went to her throat. She gasped for air. She rolled off of me onto the floor, and I got up as fast as I could, getting ready for her next attack. But none came. She flopped around on the floor looking for a breath that never came to her.

Madi was dying.

I had killed her.

CHAPTER TWENTY-FOUR

I watched in utter shock as Madi struggled to hold onto life. She obviously couldn't breathe, and I didn't know how to help. A heated numbness flushed through my entire body as the shock of what I had done penetrated my brain. I became aware of Crystal and Di staring at me. Sweat was dripping from my face, and I felt a little dizzy.

I stepped up to the sink and stuck my head under the faucet. I let the cold water run over the back of my neck before I turned my mouth to the stream and gulped. Finished, I leaned against the sink for a moment, trying to collect my scrambled thoughts.

I turned around to face them. "I didn't mean to hurt her that much!"

Di picked up a sheet and threw it over Madi's spastic body. Crystal and I both gave her a strange look.

"What? I don't want to watch that mean old thing die." Di shuddered. "And she got what she deserved if you ask me. Well done, Sunny."

"Maybe you shouldn't put the sheet over her until she's dead," I said.

"You take the sheet off if you want to," Di said, shaking with revulsion.

Within seconds, Madi's body became still, although none of us moved for a long time.

"Do you think she's dead now?" Crystal asked.

"Yes," I said.

I wasn't sure how I felt about killing someone. A jolt of panic went through me, but then I remembered how hateful Madi was, and it went away. I knew I would be in a lot of trouble for killing a supervisor, but I was already wanted for execution. Life really wasn't going to get any worse for me.

"What are we going to do now?" Crystal asked.

"You're going to get upstairs before you're late for the president's party," I said. I would deal with the body.

"But I can't just leave you with this mess. It's because of me that you —" Crystal began, but I cut her off.

"This is not because of you. This is because she was a mean and hateful woman who was spoiling for a fight. And I gave her one." I wouldn't let Madi's death make us feel guilty. Di was right. She got what she deserved.

"Where did you learn to fight like that?" Crystal asked.

"Jack taught me." Fighting was the last thing I wanted to talk about right now.

"Is that what the two of you are teaching everyone in the common room?"

When Crystal mentioned it, I remembered I was supposed to be in the common room right then having dinner with Jack. After that we would train with whoever stayed behind to learn. Now I wasn't sure I could make it there on time.

"It's not just about self-defense. It's about uniting everyone to work together for a better future. Unfortunately, fifty people in a common room learning a few good moves aren't going to change anything. We need everyone to make it work." I knew I sounded preachy, but I didn't care.

"Well, you can sign me up," Di said brightly.

Crystal was looking at the lump under the sheet that used to be Madi. "After tonight, I'm a believer. No matter what, you and Jack have to succeed. You're our only hope."

Tears streamed down her face. Was she crying for Madi or for something else? Then I remembered she said she had heard things. Things she wasn't supposed to hear. Did she know something the rest of us didn't? I wanted to talk to her, but she was going to be late if she didn't leave now, and I had a mess to clean up.

"You better get yourself upstairs," I said.

"You're a good person, Sunny O'Donnell. Don't ever forget that." Crystal hugged me and then left.

"You want to check her or should I?" Di asked. I raised my eyebrows. "To see if she's dead or not."

"I will." Though I was pretty sure she was. I pulled back the sheet and nearly ran away screaming when I saw Madi's eyes open wide and staring vacantly at me. I forced myself to check her pulse. There was none. "She's dead."

"Well, that's it then. What will we do with the body?"

"I'll get rid of it. I don't want you to get involved any more than you are."

"I hated that woman from the day I met her. I don't mind helping to get rid of her."

"Look, I have nothing to lose here. I'm already wanted for execution. But you're free. Don't get involved in this."

"Free?" Di sounded surprised. "There's not one person living down here who is *free*. 'Cull' is just another word for execution, and I'm due in less than a year. So stop being self-righteous and learn to accept help when it's offered."

I hadn't expected that response from Di. She had always seemed so... tolerant of her situation. It surprised me that she might be fed up and angry, too.

"Okay. Help me get her in one of the laundry carts. Are you able to finish Crystal's work and get it upstairs? I really don't need anyone nosing around here tonight."

"I can do that."

I retrieved a cart full of dirty laundry and wheeled it alongside Madi's body. I took out some of the clothes and motioned for Di to grab her arms while I picked up her legs. We hoisted her into the cart.

"Where are you going to dump her?" Di asked.

"Probably best I don't say. That way when they find the body you can look genuinely surprised." I put the pile of dirty clothes on top of her and made sure no parts were showing. "I'll be back as soon as I can to help you finish the ironing."

"Best hurry up before she gets stiff in there or you'll have a time getting her out." I didn't respond. The thought was gross enough.

I rolled the cart out of the laundry room and checked the halls to make sure they were clear. There was one guard lounging against the wall, and I would have to walk past him to get to the mineshaft. I pulled my hat down over my eyes and strode purposefully past him.

"What do you have there?" he asked with mild interest. Was he one of Liberty's guards?

"Laundry." I looked back at the room I just came from with the big "Laundry Room" sign over the door.

"Oh, yeah." He waved me on.

I was grateful he didn't ask me where I was going. There was no reason to take a laundry cart down this hall.

I continued on, rounding a corner, which took me out of view of the guard. Thankfully there were no more guards to be seen. Almost everyone in the Pit would be in the common rooms having dinner, so it was the time of evening the guards took a break, which was lucky for me.

I pulled open the door to the mineshaft and held it with my hip as I pushed the cart through. I gently closed the door behind me, trying not to make any noise, and stood for a moment to let my eyes adjust to the darkness. Once I was able to see the edge clearly, I wheeled the cart closer. I thought about sending the whole thing over, but realized that would be a mistake. I might have a chance of getting away with this if I made it look like Madi had fallen down the shaft.

I dug all the clothes out of the cart and piled them by the door. Then I turned the cart on its side and tipped it until I felt the body slide out. It was difficult work. Madi was a large person. The drop to the bottom was just slightly over two miles so it took nearly a minute before I heard a distant *thud*. I put the clothes back in the cart and left the shaft.

The same guard was standing there when I returned. He gave me a questioning look when he saw I still had the cart full of clothes.

"I took the wrong cart," I said.

Di was almost finished with the ironing when I got back. She was obviously experienced at it because she was a lot faster than either Crystal or me. I started loading a cart with the freshly laundered clothes.

"No problems?" Di asked.

"There's a guard outside. You might want to mumble something about doing it yourself if you want it done right."

Di finished the last shirt and put it on top of the pile.

"Don't come back here when you're finished. If anyone asks why you're bringing the laundry, you just say we're short staffed after hours and you worked late to help out. I'm going to leave and not come back until tomorrow morning. In the morning, we'll all just stand outside waiting for Madi like we always do. Okay?"

"Got it," Di said. She sucked in a deep breath, scanned out and wheeled the cart through the doors.

I tidied up the mess Madi and I had made when we were fighting and scanned out, too. I made my way to the fourth-level common room, which was thankfully in the opposite direction of the guard I had passed earlier. There was another guard standing by the door outside of the common room.

"Good evening, ma'am," he said as he opened the door. I didn't think I was ever going to get used to being treated that way. I thanked him awkwardly and walked through the door.

The training session was already in full swing. Three guards stood with their rifles gripped in their hands while people lined up to take their turn disarming them. I noticed with disappointment that there weren't as many people as the night before. Jack was correcting someone when he looked up and saw me come into the room. He shot me a questioning look, but I had no answer for him.

He went back to his task, and I took the opportunity to sit down. I think it was the first time I rested all day.

The shock of what I had just done was starting to set in. My hands were beginning to shake, so I tucked them under my legs to try and still them. Then my legs started shaking. Emotionally, I didn't really feel anything at all, so I was angry that my body would betray me like that. Jack motioned for me to come over and help. Would my legs support me? I wasn't sure. I shook my head. Jack would have to do this on his own.

The training session seemed to take forever, but finally Jack said it was time to wrap up. Everyone thanked him and filed out of the room. I stood up to leave, although I still wasn't sure my legs would work. I took a few steps, ignoring the weakness in my knees.

"Where were you?" Jack asked in a low voice. "I've been going out of my mind! I sent a guard to look for you."

"Was that an Alliance guard outside of the laundry room?"

"Is that where you've been? Working late? Was Madi on you again?"

"Can we talk about this at home?" My lack of sleep last night and current trauma of having just killed someone was starting to crash in on me.

Jack put his hand at the small of my back and steered me toward the door. "You're shaking." He gave me a sidelong glance, but didn't ask any more questions until we were safely inside our apartment.

"What happened?" he asked as soon as he shut the door.

I sat down heavily in the chair. "I killed her." There was no sense keeping it from Jack. He just stood staring at me, not saying a word. Maybe he didn't hear me. "I killed Madi."

"You mean you killed her for real? She's dead?" I could tell by his shocked expression that he didn't believe me.

"I didn't mean to kill her. She was beating Crystal, and I knew she was going to kill her... and I just snapped. I went after her, and we got into a fight. She had me pinned on the floor at one point, but as soon as she let go of my arms, I punched her. I got her here." I pointed to the base of my neck.

"You *throat punched* her? Didn't you know you could kill someone that way?"

"Well, I do now!"

He gave me an apologetic look and sat down in the chair across from me. "What did you do with the body?" he asked. I could almost see his mind trying to work out a plan to cover it up.

"I put her in a laundry cart, wheeled her to the mineshaft, and threw her body down the shaft. There was one guard who saw me with the cart. I'm hoping he was the one you sent to look for me."

"He didn't see the body, though?"

"No. She was covered up with dirty clothes."

"What about any mess in the laundry room? Any blood?"

"No blood, and I picked up anything we knocked over during our fight."

"I'm impressed, Sunny. It sounds like you covered your tracks well."

"I feel like I just made a mess of everything. My life was already complicated enough without adding murder to the list."

"Defending yourself against a crazy person isn't murder. It's self-defense."

The lights went out and left us in darkness. I was exhausted, but I didn't want to go to sleep. My numbed brain was still processing the events of the evening. Jack stood up and held his hand out to me. I knew he couldn't find his way to the bedroom in the dark, so I took his hand and led him there. He crawled onto the bed, and I took the heavy vest off before I laid down myself. He surprised me when he pulled me into the crook of his arm. I pulled back, but he firmly put my head on his shoulder.

"I'm not looking for anything, Sunny. I just think we could both use the human contact tonight. And besides, we both know you're going to be all over me again as soon as you fall asleep." He laughed softly.

I couldn't help but laugh, too. He was probably right. And after the day I'd had, it did feel good to be pressed against the length of him and feel his arms holding me.

"There weren't as many people there tonight," I said.

"Some left when they saw you weren't there. I almost cancelled the whole thing to go look for you myself. But

I knew if I did that I would never get the few back that were interested in being there. You don't know how worried I was." His arm tightened around me, hugging me closer.

"Did you think Holt caught me?"

"That was one scenario I imagined. I also thought maybe you suffered heat stroke and died. Or your supervisor was beating you to within an inch of your life. I can honestly say it never crossed my mind you killed her and dumped her body." He started shaking with laughter

"It's not funny." I playfully hit him in the chest. He caught my hand in his and held it.

"I don't know how this rebellion of yours is going to work if we don't get more people involved," Jack said, his voice serious.

"It doesn't matter anymore. Our time here is running out. I guess it was a stupid idea."

"It's not a stupid idea. We'll find a way to make it work."

As he talked, the rhythmic sound of his deep voice hypnotised me. I let go of all my fears and allowed myself to feel secure in his arms. Sleep took me almost instantly.

CHAPTER TWENTY-FIVE

I bolted awake, my heart pounding, an image of Madi still burned into my mind. I'd dreamed that she wasn't dead when I dumped her and that she was climbing back up the mineshaft looking for me. Now that I was awake, the dream seemed ridiculous. She was very dead when I sent her down there.

I was all over Jack again, just as he had predicted. My legs were entwined with his and my arm was sprawled across his chest. He was snoring softly, so I gently eased myself away from him and got out of bed. My stomach was protesting the fact that I'd missed dinner last night. I padded into the kitchen and drank a glass of water to fill the emptiness.

I was wide awake now and knew there was little chance of getting back to sleep. The back of my neck was tight with stress, and my head ached. I decided to exercise. It always eased my stress whenever I worked out with Jack.

"Sunny?" Jack called from the bedroom.

"You'll be happy to know I'm working out. You've taught me well, Jack," I said between deep breaths.

He stumbled his way into the living room, stubbing his toe on one of the chairs. When he was done cursing, he joined me on the floor. "You couldn't sleep?"

"Bad dreams."

"You shouldn't let it bother you. I bet a lot of people in the laundry room will be happy today when she doesn't show up."

"It doesn't bother me that Madi is dead. It bothers me that I killed her."

"And yet you want to start a rebellion. People always get killed when there's a struggle for power. No one's going to miss a supervisor like Madi. They won't blame you for killing her. They'll respect you."

"People aren't going to know I killed her."

"I thought there were other people in the room when it happened?"

"Di and Crystal were, but they won't say anything."

"Maybe not to a guard, but they'll talk."

The *bong bongs* rang out, and the lights clicked on. Jack had taken off his t-shirt, and there was a film of sweat on his muscular torso. I averted my eyes since I found the sight a little too appealing. I got up and filled the sink with cold water.

"I'll give you some privacy if you want to get washed. But don't drain the water," Jack said as he left the room.

I bathed as quickly as I could, fearing he would come in while I was naked, but he remained a gentleman. Then we exchanged rooms, and I found more clean clothes in the bag Bron had brought us. I put the hated vest on and went back out when Jack was done.

The line for breakfast was already getting long by the time we got to the common room. People greeted us cheerfully when we joined the queue. It shocked me that Jack and I had become so well known in such a short span of time. Just the day before I had been a stressed-out ball of nerves waiting for Domers to come and take us away at gunpoint and hand us over to President Holt. Today I was being addressed as ma'am by the guards and had complete strangers wanting to shake my hand. It all felt so foreign, but it did help me to feel more confident that no one would turn us in.

Jack and I collected our rations and found a seat alone together. Despite my nervousness at the thought of returning to the scene of the crime, I was starving.

"You want mine, too?" Jack asked when he saw me gulping down my breakfast.

"No, thank you." I was embarrassed at eating so fast. I was getting far too comfortable around him.

I looked around the room and saw Crystal get up and head for the door. She was leaving for work already. She walked with her head down, hiding her face behind the curtain of her long hair.

"Are you going to be okay this morning?"

"I have to be."

We pushed our chairs back and left the room, heading for our respective jobs. I tried to squelch the nervousness in my stomach, but it wouldn't go away. Jack reached for my hand and held it as we walked along the hall to the stairs. I was grateful for his support. He kissed the top of my head before he left, as had become his habit. I watched him walk down the stairs until I couldn't see him anymore, as had become mine. I climbed the few levels to the laundry room.

Crystal was already there, standing in front of the doors looking a little lost. The bruising on her face was worse today. One of her eyes was almost swollen shut. She had a hand protectively wrapped around her side where Madi had kicked her.

"I'm not sure what to do," Crystal whispered when I walked up to her.

"Just stay here as if we're waiting for her. That's what we do every morning."

"Okay. By the way, I saw your friend last night."

"Summer?"

Crystal nodded.

"You didn't tell her what I did, did you?" I didn't want Summer to know. I was worried about what she would think of me.

"No. I'm not going to tell anybody what *we* did. I just told her what you wanted me to tell her. She says she misses you, too. She also said that the president is getting really upset because you and Jack haven't been found yet. He had a complete door-to-door search done in the Dome and didn't find any sign of you. He's finally beginning to think that maybe you're hiding down here."

"I'm surprised he hasn't looked here yet. I mean, what is it that makes him think we wouldn't come here?"

"Because he still thinks of Jack as one of them. As much as the Holts hate the Kenners, their family still belongs to their elite group. None of them would ever be caught dead in the Pit, so they assume neither would Jack."

"They must know I would come home, though." Could Holt really be that blinded by his own prejudices?

"Don't forget, Leisel told her father that Jack married you for love, and he believes that every good wife follows her husband. It's never occurred to him that Jack would follow you. But he's come up empty looking for you two in the Dome."

"How much time do you think we have left?" I knew I should be grateful for the amount of time we'd already had, but it still made me anxious to know that my death was getting closer.

"I don't know. Last night I overheard the president tell Mr. Forbes to put together a search team for the Pit. You might have a day or two at the most. Sunny, can I ask you a personal question?"

I nodded.

"How did you and Jack end up married?"

"Leisel tricked us into it so she could discredit Jack. But don't tell. Everyone thinks our marriage is a big love story."

"You mean it isn't a love story?" Crystal looked confused. "I see the way Jack looks at you. He never looked at Leisel like that."

Her confession surprised me. I didn't really think Jack was attracted to me. "No, we're not together like that." I shook my head. "Like every bourge I've ever met, he likes the finer things in life, and I'm... well, I'm just me. An urchin."

"I think you're wrong—on both counts."

The conversation made me uncomfortable. "So things went okay at the party last night?"

"Mr. West was really angry when I showed up with a black eye. He likes me to look pretty when I sing at public events. He demanded to know who gave it to me, so I told him truthfully. He talked about sending his own guards down here to have a word with Madi. I'm sorry. I should've lied. I didn't expect him to take any action."

I put a comforting hand on her shoulder. "You had to tell the truth. If you lied, then you would be implicating someone who didn't deserve punishment." She nodded. "Just remember, if they do show up, act like you know nothing. We came to work this morning and Madi didn't."

"Oh good!" Di said, startling us. "It's just the two of you here. I had an epiphany last night." She marched right past us and into the laundry room.

Crystal and I looked at each other in confusion before we scrambled to follow her.

"Anyone here?" Di called out to the empty room. No one answered. "You know, I think I would've messed my pants if someone answered back." She laughed nervously. "I was thinking last night if we keep this place running ourselves, it might be quite a while before they notice Madi is missing."

I gave it some thought. We didn't have many options. "It might work."

Madi's scanner was still sitting on the desk, so we scanned in. As we did, a few more workers came into the room and lined up behind us. No one seemed to notice Madi wasn't at her desk. Crystal went to the sink, and I claimed a cart of dirty laundry and started my day. Di did the same. A few minutes later, Kai came in. I could tell by the look on his face that he wondered where Madi was. I held my breath for a moment waiting for him to ask, but he didn't question it. He scanned in and went to see Di.

"There are some carts over there for you to take up," Di said. "Drop those off and pick up the dirty ones for us to work on today."

Kai did as she told him. We worked for a few hours before a pair of Domers came strolling into the room. I assumed they were the ones being sent by West on Crystal's behalf.

"We're looking for Supervisor Madi," one of them called out to the room at large. No one said anything.

"I expect to be answered." Both guards raised their firearms.

"We haven't seen our supervisor all morning," Di said.

"Who let you in this morning?"

"The place was already open when I got here. Guess she had somewhere else to be."

"Any chance you know where that might be?" the other Domer asked.

"No, sir," Di said.

"Does anyone here know?" he called out to the room again.

I watched the confused expressions on everyone's faces and mimicked them. The guards went back to Madi's desk, rummaged through her things, and checked her calendar. One of them picked up her communicator and gave the other guard a puzzled look. Guards and supervisors were supposed to have their communicators with them at all times. I had forgotten about that. The guard holding the device typed a message into it. They were probably letting Madi know she was wanted for questioning. I was relieved when they left.

I had some hand washing to give to Crystal and made my way over to the sink.

"Do you think those were West's guards?" I asked.

"Probably. I don't know for sure."

I still felt sorry for Crystal. As bad as my situation was, at least I had some freedom. But she was a slave every single minute of her life. During the day, she worked here under the supervision of a malicious woman, and at night she belonged to a man old enough to be her grandfather. I knew that if I had not met Leisel on that fateful night, I might have ended up just like Crystal and Summer. I think I preferred my death sentence.

"How long have you... belonged to West?"

"Two years."

I remembered she'd told me she was fourteen years old. "You were only twelve when you were sent upstairs?" Even I could hear the revulsion in my voice, and I felt bad for making my feelings so clear.

"I know." She hung her head in embarrassment.

"I didn't mean it the way it sounded, Crystal. I know it's not your fault. Was Madi the one who sent you up there the first time?"

Crystal nodded.

"Then I'm glad I killed her. The Pit is a better place without her in it." For a moment my guilt at having killed Madi morphed into a sense of justice, and I relished the feeling.

"The Pit is a better place with you in it, Sunny. I'm going to do *everything* I can to help you and Jack." Tears rolled down Crystal's cheeks. "Someone needs to save us and you're the first person who's ever stepped up."

"Crystal, you said something last night —" I started to say, but she cut me off.

"People need to know what I know! And you need to get them ready."

"Crystal, you're scaring me. Just *tell* me what you know." I tried not to sound frustrated, but I was. She kept hinting at something, and I wanted to know what it was.

Just then the *bong bongs* announced the beginning of the lunch break. Workers came in with the food and water cart and set up in their usual spot near Madi's desk. Everyone stopped working and lined up to get their rations.

"We need to finish this conversation!" I told Crystal as we joined the queue.

"Finish what conversation?" Di asked as she came to stand behind me in the line.

I shrugged. "Nothing important."

"Those guards that were here today looked official. Any idea where they came from?" Di asked.

"We think Mr. West sent them because of Crystal's eye. She didn't look very pretty singing for the bourge last night. They want to have a word with Madi."

"Malcolm West?" Di seemed shocked.

I nodded. "Crystal's owner."

Di gave Crystal a look of understanding. "I owe you a big apology. I had you pegged all wrong, sweetie."

"Most people do," Crystal said, her tone defiant.

"Well, I expect they'll be back when they don't hear from her," Di said.

"I think you're right," I said.

We halted our conversation as we collected our food and water and then returned to our stations to eat. The laundry room was every bit as hot as it always was, and I was relieved Madi wasn't there to stop me from drinking water. I gulped the liquid down, and felt the moisture quench my parched tongue and throat. If I hadn't been worried about the guards coming back, I would have been tempted to take off my vest and hat and let my skin breathe.

"Madi's not here today. You can go to Crystal's sink any time you want," Di said.

"I hadn't thought of that." There were definitely perks to not having a supervisor around.

"What is it you're wearing that makes you so hot?"

"Believe it or not, it's a bulletproof vest." I laughed. "It puts weight on my frame and makes me look less like Sunny O'Donnell."

"Well, down here Sunny O'Donnell is a hero. You might want to start looking like yourself again. I told a few people how you saved Crystal last night. I hope you don't mind."

"Di, you weren't supposed to tell anyone!" Now the news would be all over, just as Jack predicted it would be.

"Why not? It's about time someone stood up to the Madis of the Pit. That woman was a mean, nasty piece of work. Good riddance, I say."

"But *I* killed her," I whispered. Was I the only one who understood the gravity of that act?

Someone announced the lunch break was over. We all returned our empty containers to the cart and went back to work. It nagged at me that Di had told people about my actions. Heroes weren't murderers, so what would people think of me now? I hoped it wouldn't impact the plan Jack and I were trying to implement. If people thought badly of me, maybe they would stop showing up.

The day was almost over when the doors burst open, and the two Domers that had been there earlier marched in unannounced.

"Has anyone seen Supervisor Madi today?" one of them demanded.

"No sir. She hasn't been in today," Di said.

"When was the last time anyone saw her?"

"Last night," I said. If anyone was going to be questioned, it should be me.

The guard came closer to me. "At what time?"

"About six-thirty. We finished late last night." At least that was the truth.

"Was she here when you left for the day?"

"Yes." The lie made me a little nervous.

"Were you the last one to leave?"

"We both were," Di said.

"I'll need both your names."

"My name is Diamond Murphy," she said.

He looked at me expectantly. There was no way out of this. I cleared my throat. "Autumn Jones."

The guard recorded our names on his communicator and then left without any further questions. Now they had my false name. How long before they figured out Autumn Jones was an imposter?

I spent the rest of the afternoon nervously looking over my shoulder at the doors, but no more guards came bursting through. A few times I went to Crystal's sink to get a drink and put cold water on the back of my neck. I hoped no one else in the laundry room noticed, but the cool, refreshing liquid was too tempting to ignore. Madi's absence was turning out to be a luxury.

For the first time since I came to work in the laundry room, I wasn't struggling to finish my cart at the end of the workday. It was all done. Crystal and Di were finished, too. Maybe things did run smoother without a supervisor.

"I'll be seeing you tonight," Di said as we walked out the door. "I'm going to bring my lazy husband with me."

"I'll see you tonight then," I said.

She walked away, leaving Crystal and me alone.

"I wish I could see you tonight, too," I said to her.

"I'll see what I can do." She gave a brilliant smile and hugged me.

Then she was gone, running down the stairs without waiting to walk with me.

CHAPTER TWENTY-SIX

T he apartment was empty when I arrived, and I took the opportunity to get out of my vest for a while. I could feel the heat from the laundry room radiating off my skin. I wet one of the towels and put it on the back of my neck. It felt refreshingly cool. I splashed cold water on my face, and soon my body temperature came down. I put my t-shirt back on just before Jack came through the door.

"I was worried about you today. How did it go?" he asked.

"A couple of Domers came looking for Madi, and I talked to them."

"Guards from the Dome?" He looked confused. "Why were they there?"

"Crystal's owner didn't like her having a black eye and wanted to talk to the person who gave it to her. They asked when I had seen her last, and I told them truthfully. They wanted my name."

"And you gave them Autumn Jones, right?"

I responded with a sarcastic look. He ignored it.

"That was unexpected," he said. I'm hoping your alias checks out okay. I didn't have a lot of time in that storage room."

He sat down heavily in the chair. I could tell he was thinking hard about the information he had made up on Autumn and Ben Jones.

"And you were right this morning about people talking. Di said she told a few people about what happened last night."

"I know. It was the main topic of conversation in the mines today. You're inspiring a lot of people! Today was a good day. We finally have only Liberty guards in our section, so we were able to do some training. A lot more people have joined us."

"Di said she and her husband were coming, so I managed to find two more people to join." I made a face.

"Wow, two people. You *were* busy." Any sarcasm he had meant to be included in his tone was softened by the fond smile he gave me. "Speaking of tonight, I'm starving. I'm even looking forward to eating that grey muck you call dinner."

At his reference to our food, I was reminded of my conversation with Crystal that morning, and an image of Jack at presidential parties floated into my head. He really did prefer the finer things that only the Dome could offer. I couldn't imagine him ever being attracted to an urchin like me.

"You're such a bourge," I said almost under my breath.

"What was that comment for?" He seemed taken aback.

"Nothing." I went into the bedroom and put the vest back on. "Ready."

Jack was already standing by the door waiting for me. We left together and headed for the common room. He didn't hold my hand or put his arm around me this time. I wondered if my comment had made him angry.

Even though it was early, the room was already packed. The guard at the door greeted us in his usual manner, and we queued up with everyone else. We collected our food and went in search of a table. David Chavez was there with his wife and asked us to join them.

"I'm not sure if you've met my wife, Terra," he said.

"Pleased to meet you," Jack said, extending his hand to her. She took it.

"I'm Sunny," I said, taking the seat next to her.

"I know." She smiled.

I gestured at her large round tummy. "How far along are you?"

"I'm due any day. And the little one is getting heavy, so he can come out any time!"

"You're hoping for a boy?" I asked with mild interest. I wasn't sure why anyone would want to bring a baby into this Pit, but I kept that to myself.

"A boy would be... easier. I was never sent upstairs, but..." She trailed off, looking from me to Jack.

I understood what she meant. I looked at Jack to see his reaction, and noted he was looking uncomfortable.

"Though I'm glad it worked out for the two of you," she said in a rush. "It's just that your love story is very rare."

If only she knew the truth, I thought to myself.

"Don't be so sure that girls have it rougher than boys," a man said as he pulled up a chair and joined us. "They killed my son a few years ago. He got a job working in the sewers, but it made him so sick to his stomach that he couldn't keep up with the workload. They beat him more times than I could say before they killed him. He was only twelve years old. I hope they all rot in hell." His tone was bitter, his cheeks wet with tears.

The woman at the table next to us pushed her chair back and gave the man a sympathetic pat on the back. "I lost my husband five years ago when the guards beat him to a pulp," she said. "He was working the diamond mines and accidently broke three picks in one day. As if that's a good enough reason to kill a man!" She shook her head. "I've remarried now." She turned to look at the man she was sitting with. "I had to remarry if I wanted a place to live. No offence to you, lover," she said to the man fondly.

Someone put a hand on my shoulder, and I looked up to see an unfamiliar face.

"I heard how you handled that supervisor," the woman said. "God bless you."

Jack flashed me his best "I told you so" smile, and I gave my best sardonic smile back. He looked smug.

"It's about time something was being done," the man who'd joined us said, tears still glistening in his eyes.

"We all have scars," a woman behind me said. Her voice was familiar. I turned to find Summer's parents standing there. "Right now my baby is in the hands of that monster we call a president."

"Mrs. Nazeem!" I said, jumping up to hug the woman. "I miss Summer, too."

"I know you do. You've always been a good friend to her." She hugged me back.

"I'd do anything to help her. You know that."

"You are doing something, Sunset," she said. She took off my hat and let my hair fall around my shoulders. "Who knew the little girl who was always trying to hide her beautiful hair would one day be the person to lead us? Your mother would be so proud."

I blushed at the compliment but knew she couldn't be more wrong. I wasn't the leader in all of this. Jack was.

Before I could respond, I heard a commotion at the door and turned to see Crystal coming into the room carrying a guitar. Her eye was still badly swollen and starting to turn black. She had a sad smile on her face as she grabbed a chair and went to the front of the room.

People were pouring into the room behind her until it became so crowded it was standing room only, and yet more people remained out in the hallway, standing on tiptoes to get a glimpse of her. I felt Jack's hand at the small of my back as he came to stand beside me. He had a puzzled expression on his face.

Crystal raised her voice to be heard throughout the room. "Hi, I'm Crystal."

A few cheers went up.

"Now I know her!" Jack whispered in my ear. "She's Malcolm West's mistress. She's a really good singer."

"I know."

Crystal propped a leg up on the chair and rested her guitar on it. She strummed a few chords. "Like most of you, my life down here hasn't been all that great. I've lost people I loved. I've been used in ways I never imagined possible. And I've been beaten." She pointed to her swollen face. A few people wiped tears from their eyes. "Yet I wake up every morning, willingly go to work for a woman who beats me, and allow myself to be the lover of a man I detest. And not once have I ever done anything about it." Her voice was getting husky, and she stopped to clear her throat. I could feel the tears welling up in my own eyes.

"I recently had the privilege of meeting someone very special. Someone who showed me that taking control of my own life was in my hands—*not theirs*! She showed me that if life is ever going to get better for us, then we're the ones who need to change," she shouted. "And she and her husband are trying to show you the way, too. So I wrote a song for them. I wrote this song for us all."

The entire room was silent as she began to strum her guitar. It was a slow, haunting melody that spoke to the heart.

> *Nothing's ever been right down here*
> *We live and die under the rule of fear*
> *Into slavery we are bound*
> *Then they beat us down*
>
> *They sentenced us to live in a rock*
> *And if we cry they put us under lock*
> *They promise us one day we'll see the sun*
> *But when we finally get one, she's on the run*

The chords she strummed became faster, louder, and she sang out with a powerful voice.

> *So rise up, rise up*
> *It's time to make a choice*
> *Everyone here has a voice*
> *It's time you learned how to use it*
>
> *Unite! Unite!*
> *They're here to help us fight*
> *If we turn our back on them*
> *Then we're all condemned*

Her strumming became slower then, more haunting.

> *You probably didn't know*
> *But I overheard it said*
> *The Pit they want to blow*
> *And soon we'll all be dead*
>
> *Don't forget they promised us the sun*
> *And now that we have one, she's on the run*
> *If we keep believing their lies*
> *We might as well say our goodbyes*

Crystal was strumming hard and fast on her guitar. The entire room was rocking with the emotion of her music. She stood up on the chair, letting her music fill the room. She sang out again.

> *So rise up, rise up*
> *It's time to make a choice*
> *Everyone here has a voice*
> *It's time you learn how to use it*
>
> *In a world full of wrong*
> *They're the only thing that's right*
> *It's time to make a stand*
> *It's time to unite!*
>
> *Rise up! Rise up!*

She strummed one last chord with flourish and raised one arm in the air. The crowd went wild. Everyone was cheering and clapping. Not one eye in the room was dry. Jack gazed down at me, his dark eyelashes glistening with tears.

"She's a hell of a songwriter, too," he said.

I nodded, too choked up to speak.

Crystal took a bow, jumped off the chair, and started walking for the door. I didn't want her to leave before I could talk to her. I pushed my way through the crowd and caught her just before she left.

I touched her arm. "Crystal!"

"Sunny! Did you like it?"

"*Like* it? It was the most beautiful song I ever heard." I wiped the tears from my eyes. "Thank you."

My weak "thank you" didn't even come close to expressing the emotion her song had evoked in me. I didn't know how to convey my appreciation in the aftermath of her beautiful music.

"You inspired it," Crystal said. "You stood up for me when no one else ever did. You're standing up for us all, and I love you for it. But I have to go now. I don't have much time."

She gave me a sad smile, kissed my cheek, and went out the door. The crowd parted to let her through and then followed her. There was an exodus of people out of the common room as others joined her entourage.

I wondered where they were all going.

CHAPTER TWENTY-SEVEN

When the crowd following Crystal had left, I returned to the room to look for Jack. Despite the number of people that followed Crystal, a large crowd remained in the room, anxious for the evening's training session to begin. I found Jack with a group of people gathered around him, sharing their life stories. Many people were still wiping the tears from their eyes. They spoke of beatings, killings, and rebellions. A group of younger people behind me was singing Crystal's song.

Jack put his arm around me and pulled me close enough for him to whisper in my ear. "It's happening."

I nodded. I knew what he meant; Crystal was uniting the Pit. I should have been happy. That was what I wanted. But my mind was still on Crystal. Why was everyone following her, and why did she say she didn't have much time? I spotted her parents sitting alone at a corner table in the back of the room. Her mother was sobbing uncontrollably. I excused myself and went to talk to them.

"Hi, I'm Sunny, a friend of your daughter." My introduction seemed a little silly considering the song Crystal had just sung. "I wanted to say that Crystal is a beautiful singer. Her song really touched a lot of people."

"Forgive my wife," Crystal's father said. "She's very upset right now."

"I can tell. I wonder if there's anything I can do to help?"

"You've helped enough!" Crystal's mother spat at me.

"I'm sorry?" I was taken aback by her anger.

"Crystal knows what she's doing," her father said through his tears. "I have to trust in that."

"I think you need to tell me what's going on."

"Mr. West has forbidden her to sing down here. She's only allowed to sing at his request," her father said.

"But the camera is broken in this room. He'll never know she sang here."

"But they aren't broken in the other common rooms. She's going to every level to sing her song so everyone will hear it. She already sang on the first three levels. It's just a matter of time before someone upstairs hears her," he said, his voice laced with despair.

Now I understood why everyone was following her and why she said she didn't have much time. If West had heard about her song, then he probably already had Domers on their way down to get her. People in the Pit had been beaten to death for lesser crimes. We needed to help her. Without another word I ran to Jack.

"We have to help Crystal!" I said, pulling on his arm.

"What's going on?"

"Her parents just told me that West has forbidden her to sing without his permission and she's going to every level. We have to smash the other cameras!"

I ran out the door and down the hall with Jack on my heels.

"Wait!" he said when we reached the stairs. He reached into his back pocket and pulled out the communicator that Bron had given him. He made sure he was on the right frequency to reach the Alliance guards and sent out the order to break the cameras from the fifth level down to the eighth. Five guards confirmed receipt of the order.

"It's done," he said.

I turned to go down the stairs. "I want to make sure."

I heard Jack's exasperated sigh, but he followed me anyway. We passed the fifth and sixth levels and kept going until we were almost to the seventh level, but the number of people on the stairs was too thick to get through.

"We'll just have to trust that our guards got to the rooms," Jack said.

I heard the clatter of footsteps racing down the stairs behind me and turned to see a small army of Domers marching toward us. They were armed.

"Clear the way!" one of them shouted.

Jack grabbed me, pushed me against the stone wall, and used his body to block me from the guards.

"You don't have your hat on, and your hair is almost back to its normal color. They'll recognize you in a second."

"But we have to help her!"

"You're my first priority. When the guards pass by us, we go back up."

"No!" I wouldn't abandon her.

"Clear the way!" the guards were yelling.

But there were too many people on the stairs to clear the way for them. One of the guards unhooked something from his belt and held it high.

"Clear the way or we use the gas!" His voice boomed through the stairs.

"Dammit!" Jack said under his breath.

Cries of fear rose up, and the crowd started slowly moving forward as the people farther down left the stairs. Jack and I were caught between levels and had no place to go but down. Going back up would take us right into the path of the guards. He kept me in front of him, hiding me from their view. When we reached the seventh level, we stepped off the stairs and joined the hordes of people there. I expected the guards would pass us by, but two remained on our level while the others kept going down.

"Crowd control," Jack said. "We're stuck here until they leave."

After several minutes passed, we heard a scuffle on the stairs as the guards came back up from the eighth level dragging Crystal with them. We were close enough to the stairs for me to see her. I didn't see any new bruises on her face, so I hoped that they hadn't hurt her. She saw me standing among the crowd and gave me a huge smile.

"Rise up!" she yelled to the crowd. They responded with a cheer, raising their fists high in the air.

I wrenched free of Jack's grasp. "I can't just stand here and watch this happen!"

I pushed my way through the crowd, intent on saving her. I wasn't sure how I was going to do that, but I couldn't just let her be dragged away. I was vaguely aware of the crowd getting louder, their cries getting angrier, and then people started moving forward. Everyone wanted to save Crystal. I had almost reached the stairs, but then I was being crushed in the surge of angry people. I felt hands grab me from behind and knew Jack had caught up to me. I tried to kick him to make him let me go, but he pushed me up against a wall and pinned me there. I was dumbfounded when he ripped off his t-shirt, balled it up, and pressed it against my face. I tried to pull it away, but he kept a firm hand on it. A shot rang out and something landed not too far from us. A few seconds later tear gas filled the hall.

Jack's eyes started tearing up right away. I tried to give him the t-shirt he had pressed against my face, but he wouldn't take it. Instead he rearranged it to cover my eyes, too. I was blind, but I could hear the chaos going on around me. Jack was gasping for air. I pulled at the shirt to get it off my eyes, and it shifted enough for me to peek out. I watched in horror as Jack fell to his hands and knees in a fit of coughing. I had to get him out of there.

The alarms rang out, signalling a lockdown. In a few minutes there would be more guards down there, forcing us into our homes. I pulled at one of his arms, urging him to get up. My eyes were beginning to sting, and I put the t-shirt back over my face. I would be no good to him if I became incapacitated too.

Jack managed to stand up. I seized him by the wrist and started making my way through the mob. Every time I peeked up from the t-shirt, my eyes stung. The stairs weren't far from us, but it seemed to take forever to get there. When we finally made it, the stairs were littered with people dealing with the effects of the gas. I was appalled at the sight, but one thought kept me going past everyone: Jack couldn't breathe. I stepped over people, pulling him behind me. My eyes were beginning to sting more, and breathing was becoming difficult. I was coughing too, and it slowed our progress. But I didn't stop moving. I could hear Jack wheezing behind me.

We made it to the fifth level, and the air up there was clear. I took his t-shirt away from my face to make better time. The stairs were still thick with traffic, but it was moving steadily. I could hear the arrival of the extra guards. We were almost to the fourth level. I pushed through the crowd and nearly lost my hold on Jack's arm. His eyes were still closed and tearing badly. I looked around and saw other people in the same shape, trying to find their way home.

We reached our level before we met the guards on the stairs. Instead of going straight to our apartment, I ran to the bathroom. He needed to rinse the gas out of his eyes. There were a few other people already there with the same idea, but they made room at the stone tub for Jack. His eyes were still closed against the sting, but as soon as he felt the water, he madly splashed it in his eyes. He dunked his entire head under, scrubbing at his hair and the back of his neck. When he came up for air, his eyes were open.

"Come here," he said, pulling me down to kneel beside him. His voice was deep and hoarse.

I splashed the water in my own face. My eyes weren't as bad as Jack's, but they were still stinging quite a bit. The water felt cool and relieving.

"All the way," he said roughly, plunging my head into the freezing water. He pushed all of my hair in as well and splashed water along the back of my neck. I came up gasping for air when he finally let go of me.

"What did you do that for?" I asked.

"You have to get the gas off your skin and hair." Then he looked at everyone in the room. "When you get home, strip your clothes off and wash them."

More people staggered into the bathroom, and Jack and I left to make room for them. The halls were still thick with people, most of them moaning and crying. Guards yelled, telling everyone to get to their homes. But most people were too desperate to get to water and relieve their stinging eyes.

As soon as we walked into our apartment, Jack unzipped his jeans and almost tore them off his body. He ran to the sink and filled it with water. A rash covered his back. I grabbed one of the towels off the rack, soaked it, and started rinsing his back. His sharp intake of breath told me it hurt. I realized he must have taken a good dose of the gas when he was blocking me.

"Thank you for saving me," I said.

Jack smiled and was about to say something when he went into a fit of coughing. My eyes were beginning to sting again, and I wiped at the tears, which only made them worse. I opened the cupboard door to get him a glass for water but could barely see. My eyes were starting to roll up in the back of my head. I wiped at them again, but that made them even worse.

"Stop rubbing your eyes. It's on your hands," Jack said, gripping my wrists and wrenching my hands away from my face. He bent his head close to my t-shirt and his eyes started tearing again. "It's all over your clothes."

He grasped the collar of my shirt in both hands, ripped the front of it open, and let it fall to the floor. I still had the vest on so it hadn't soaked through to my skin, but the outer shell of the vest would have to be washed. I took it off, careful not to drag it across my face.

"Now the pants," Jack said impatiently.

I unzipped them and took them off. Once I was down to my underwear, Jack let me rinse my eyes and face. I was conscious of the fact that we were using a lot of our water ration. I prayed we didn't run out. He gathered up our clothes and put them outside the door of the apartment and then came back to wash his hands. While he was at the sink with his back to me, I picked up the wet towel and gently dabbed his red skin.

"Does it hurt?" I asked.

"A little. It's just a mild chemical burn, so it should be gone by tomorrow. The canister must have gone off right behind me."

"It did. I watched it hit the floor. I didn't think tear gas was this bad."

"Tear gas has been used so much down here that no one is afraid of it anymore, so they changed the formula to make it more... effective."

I remembered that he'd already had his t-shirt over my face before they had even released the canister. "How did you know they were going to use the gas?"

"Because it's the order I would've given if I was in charge."

"You do have insight." Once again I was confused over whether or not I liked this side of Jack.

He turned his head to look over his shoulder at me, a scowl on his face. "Just because I was trained by them doesn't mean I'm like them. And I think my insight has been valuable."

"It has been valuable. I'm sorry." I finished wiping his back with the wet towel. "Better?"

He nodded. "Thank you." He turned around to face me. "Tonight was just the first battle. There will be more."

"Crystal was amazing. Her song really brought everyone together." Goose bumps rose up on my skin when I thought of her song... and when I thought of the inner strength it must have taken for her to defy West and do what she thought was right.

"Every battle has its heroes, and she was definitely the hero tonight. No matter what happens, always remember she knew exactly what she was doing."

"What does that mean?"

"Hopefully nothing."

We locked eyes for a moment while I pondered if I should challenge him to tell me what he was really thinking. But did I want to know? Maybe it was best to wait and see what would happen rather than torture myself with my imagination.

Jack's eyes wandered down the length of my body, and I became conscious of the fact that we were both standing there in just our underwear.

"I better get dressed. The guards will be here soon for us to scan in. We're still under a lockdown." I headed for the bedroom.

"Sunny?" I turned to look at him. "It took a lot of conviction and belief in your own people for you to put on that wedding dress. You knew the risk you were taking when you did it. You and Crystal are more alike than you know."

I didn't respond to him, but kept going on into the bedroom. I didn't believe what Jack was saying. Leisel had intimidated me into doing something stupid. It was nothing like Crystal's act of heroism.

I dug through the bag of clothes Bron had brought us and found an outfit. It felt good to have the heavy vest off my shoulders, so I decided not to put it on again. It was unlikely a guard would recognize me on a routine scan in.

"Your turn," I said as I came back in the living room.

Jack was just coming back into the living room pulling a t-shirt over his head when there was a sharp knock at the door. That would be the guard.

"Your hair!" Jack said.

I looked for my hat then remembered it was still on the table in the common room. "I left my hat behind."

"Use the towel."

I took the dry towel off the rack and wrapped it around my head. Jack put on his hat, but the ends of his light brown hair were still visible. There was nothing we could do about it now. I opened the door.

"Good evening, sir. Ma'am." The guard greeted us with a smile. "Could you scan in, please?"

I breathed a sigh of relief that it was an Alliance guard. We waved our hands across the scanner.

"Was anybody seriously hurt tonight?" Jack asked.

"A few people with asthma had a difficult time, but one of our guards had an inhaler so we were able to save them. The ones with chemical burns were taken to the baths."

As I stood there with the door open, I could hear the faint sounds of distant singing. I cocked my head to one side, trying to hear. "What is that?"

Jack and the guard became quiet, listening too. The singing became louder. Doors opened up and down the hall as people stepped out of their apartments, defying the lockdown order. I stepped out too, looking in wonder at all the people who raised their voices and sang Crystal's song. I was vaguely aware of Jack coming to stand next to me. He wove his fingers through mine as we stood and listened to a Pit united.

"This is bigger than I ever imagined. We need to come up with a plan."

He was right. The time had come to make our plan of attack.

CHAPTER TWENTY-EIGHT

Nightmares plagued me every time I closed my eyes. The vision I had seen earlier of people littering the stairs, gasping for breath, turned into a bloodbath in my dreams. Instead of gas raining down on them, I saw bullets. My mind kept replaying the image of Crystal being dragged away by the guards, but instead of shouting, "Rise up," she shouted, "The Pit they want to blow and soon we'll all be dead!" Then the guards turned around and gave me an evil smile and their faces turned into Madi. She was dragging Crystal away to beat her to death.

Somewhere through the haze of my dreams, a sensation of warmth and heaviness engulfed me and the nightmares disappeared. Did someone put my vest on me? I felt bulletproof. I turned toward the warmth and tried to get closer to it. It felt hard and muscular. It felt like the only good thing I had left in my life.

I opened my eyes and found myself lying face-to-face with Jack, his arms wrapped around me. His eyes were opened, but I didn't think he could see me. He was blind when the lights were out.

I raised my hand and stroked his face; he captured my hand and kissed my palm. His touch was so gentle that I wanted to feel it on my lips. I leaned forward and tentatively pressed my mouth against his. I wasn't sure if he wanted me to kiss him, but his lips moved gently against mine. He ran his fingers up my arm and into my hair, leaving a trail of tingling goose bumps in their wake. I wanted to know what his skin felt like, too. Shyly, I moved my hand away from his face, running it down his shoulder and onto his side, coming to stop at his hip. I heard his sharp intake of breath, and an ache started somewhere deep inside me. His kiss became hungrier, searching for something deeper, and I realized where this was going.

Despite my body's response to his touch, my mind was screaming "no." We came from two different worlds, and our accidental marriage didn't change that. I had to remind myself that not long ago I would only ever have shared a bed with Jack Kenner if he had chosen me from a group of urchin girls and ordered me to do it.

"No!" I pulled away with such force that I ended up rolling out of bed.

"Sunny?" Jack raised himself up on an elbow and peered into the dark. I was pretty sure he couldn't see me.

"I'm sorry. I shouldn't have done that."

He lay back on the bed and dragged both his hands through his hair. "Don't be sorry. I was out of line. I misread your intentions." His breathing was ragged.

"I'm going to get some water." I didn't want to get into a blame game. I was the one who started it. I pushed myself up off the floor and went in the direction of the living room.

"Sunny?" Jack's voice stopped me at the door.

"Yes?"

"You don't still think of us as bourge and urchin, do you?"

"Honestly?" I drew in an unsteady breath. "Sometimes I do."

"I want you to know that I don't. I never did."

I didn't know what to say, so I just left and went into the kitchen. I poured a glass of water and drank it all. I was hoping the coolness of the liquid would help douse the fire that had started inside me, but it gave me little relief.

I sat down on one of the chairs, not wanting to return to the bedroom. I was afraid if I did I would finish what I started with him. He had kissed me back, so I knew he wanted me, too. I tried to imagine a world where our relationship could actually work, but I couldn't. Jack had been born aristocratic, and I had not.

Why had I never felt this way with Reyes? Kissing him had always been a comfortable and familiar thing to do that never left me wanting more. If only I had felt a fraction for Reyes of what I was feeling for Jack, I would have married him years ago and my life would be simpler right now.

I needed to stop thinking about Jack because the temptation was too strong. Not that I knew what making love to someone was like, but the emotions he stirred inside me made me want to explore that option more. Even the short time I spent in his arms helped me forget all the tragedy going on around me. It had felt good, but I also needed it to feel right.

I deliberately turned my thoughts away from Jack and concentrated on the nightmares instead. When I thought about my vision of Crystal being dragged away by the guards who turned into Madi, I remembered the words she had been singing: "The Pit they want to blow and soon we'll all be dead!" But it wasn't just in my dream she had sung those words. They were part of her song. How did that refrain go? Did she say, "I overheard it said?" Is this what she had overheard Holt and West talk about? It didn't make sense, though. If they blew up the Pit, the Dome would go with it. Why would they plan to kill themselves?

The lights came on, and the *bong bongs* sounded. Lockdown was over. No guards had bothered us through the night to scan in, so I assumed it must have been Alliance guards on this level. I remembered the guard had said he would drop my hat off if he found it. I got up, checked the door, and was happy to see it there.

Jack came into the living room just as I was shutting the door.

"Morning," he said uncomfortably.

"Good morning." I wasn't sure what to say to him.

"You didn't come back to bed. You must be tired." He looked sheepish.

"I thought we could both use a little space."

"Look, I know things are difficult between you and Reyes right now and I promised you that I wouldn't get in your way. I just want you to know what happened last night will stay between us. He won't find out."

He was obviously uncomfortable with all of this. I regretted kissing him. Things were going to get awkward between us.

"Don't worry about it. Reyes and I aren't together anymore."

His head snapped up, and he looked stunned. "What? Why didn't you tell me?"

I shrugged. "I don't know. I didn't think it was relevant."

"You didn't think it was *relevant?*" He put both hands up to his face and covered his eyes for a moment. I wondered what he was so upset about.

"We've been busy with the Alliance... and Madi... and Crystal... My breakup with Reyes seemed so small compared to everything else."

Jack dropped his hands away from his face and looked at me. He wore a pained expression. "I understand — life is complicated. It's just... well, *both* of us are under a lot of pressure and stress right now... and we're living together... and... I'm interested in what's going on in your life."

I knew he was trying to tell me something, yet he had said nothing. I wasn't sure how to respond. "I didn't think you would be interested considering everything else that was going on in our lives."

"Wouldn't you be interested if I had a girlfriend?"

His question caught me off guard. The mere thought made me feel threatened, and I couldn't help but be surprised by this knowledge. I was attracted to Jack, which I had always admitted to myself, but when did I develop feelings for him?

"Yes," I said.

He gave me a satisfied smile.

"I'm sorry. I should have been more honest with you. And I really don't want things to get awkward between us." I didn't know what I would do without him.

Jack closed the distance between us in two strides. He brought his hand up to brush a lock of my hair away from my face.

"It won't be awkward as long as we're honest with each other."

I thought he was going to kiss me, and I held his gaze. I wasn't going to run away this time. But he just searched my eyes, looking for something in them. I couldn't stand the distance between our mouths. With a will of their own, my arms came up around his neck and pulled his head toward mine. I had spent most of the night trying to forget the feel of him, and then it was all I could think about. So much had gone wrong in my life, and yet standing there within the circle of his embrace was the only thing that was right. As my lips met his, I breathed in his scent and tasted his mouth and welcomed the warmth and aching that spread through me like fire. I wanted Jack more than I had ever wanted anyone in my life.

"Sunny," he breathed, barely pulling his mouth away from mine.

"Ssshhh." There was no need for words right now. I didn't want reminders of anything. I just wanted him.

"Are you sure?"

"Yes."

He wrapped his arms tighter around my waist and picked me up off the floor. Instinctively, I wrapped my legs around his waist. I wanted to be connected to him with every fibre of my being. I wanted to touch and be touched. I was vaguely aware that he was walking back to the bedroom, so I wasn't surprised when he sat down on the bed, bringing my clinging body with him. As he lay back on the bed, my hair fell down around our faces. He let his fingers run up the length of my back, and I shivered in response to his electric touch. I felt his hands tangle in my hair, pulling my face closer to his.

My desire for him increased to a pitch I never thought possible. With feverish urgency, I sat up and started fumbling with the button on his jeans. I tried not to get frustrated when it wouldn't give way under my hands. It was taking forever, and I didn't want to spoil the mood. Jack gave me a curious look, and I looked away, not wanting to meet his eyes.

"Sunny?"

I could feel heat creep into my cheeks and hoped that my blush wasn't obvious. He probably thought I was an inexperienced little girl, which was exactly what I was. I just didn't want him to know it. But it was so obvious... how could I avoid being found out?

"I'm sorry. I've never done this before."

"What?" Jack looked confused.

"I've never... you know."

It must have been obvious, so why was he making me say it? I put more effort into my task, hoping to free the button of his jeans before time robbed me of all spontaneity. But his hand stopped mine.

"You've never made love before?" he asked gently.

"No."

He raised himself up from the bed with me still straddling his lap. He was looking at me differently now. The want and lust I saw a few seconds ago had been replaced with something else. In my heart of hearts, I knew he was going to tell me I was nothing but a child and I didn't know the first thing about pleasing a man.

"We can't do this," he said, staring directly into my eyes.

A lump began to form in my throat, and I fought it back. I had cried over so many things in my life, and I refused to let this be another one. I disengaged myself from his touch and stood up. He gave me a confused look.

"That's fine." My embarrassment was overwhelming.

"What the hell!" Before I could leave the room, he grabbed my arm and spun me around to face him. "You're on, and then just like *that* you're off?"

"You just made it clear that you don't want me." I hoped I kept any emotion out of my voice.

"Don't want you? You're all I've ever thought about since before I even married you! You're the first thing I think about when I wake up in the morning and the last thing I think about before I go to sleep every night. You're the most amazing, brave, beautiful woman I have ever met, and I've been going out of my mind wanting you." Jack's voice was raw with emotion. He reached a hand toward me, and I took it. I could see the honesty in his face. I knew he was struggling just as much as I was. I took a step toward him, and he held out his other hand to me. I laced my fingers with his. "But despite how much I want you, I won't let your first time be in a heated rush before we have to get to work. You deserve so much better than that."

I almost laughed. Was that all he was worried about? We could both be caught and executed today and the only thing I would regret was that I never knew him in the way I wanted to know him right now. I stepped closer and kissed him again.

"I want you too, Jack," I said against his mouth.

He breathed deeply, pulling me closer against him. "You can show me how much tonight, when we have hours to spend wrapped up in each other, okay?" His eyes darkened with the desire I knew he felt. My heart skipped a beat and my longing for him quickened.

"I spent a lot of time last night talking myself out of making love to you. Now that you've talked me back into it, it doesn't seem fair that you're not following through."

"Consider it payback for last night." He smiled, and kissed me again. "Come on. Let's go to breakfast before it's over."

I tried to bring myself back to the moment, but it was difficult. I suddenly didn't want to leave our apartment. I wondered what it would cost us if we just didn't show up for work today. If we just stayed there and explored each other instead.

"We still have to do our hair," I said, bringing myself back into reality. I went to the cupboard, took the piece of coal and ran it through my hair, then went to Jack to do his hair. "I was thinking about Crystal last night. I've been thinking about her song. I can't get it out of my head."

"You mean the part about blowing up the Pit?"

"Yes! I had nightmares about those lyrics. When I woke up I couldn't tell if I had dreamed them or if she really said them."

"She said them. I just don't know what it means. I don't doubt the president would set off the warheads if he thought he was going to lose control of the Dome, but a few riots don't add up to losing control."

"She didn't say blow up the Dome, she said *the Pit*. And it's not just that line that bothers me. She sang 'I overheard it said... the Pit they want to blow and soon we'll all be dead.' A few days ago she told me that she overhears things when Malcolm West has dinner with the president. She wouldn't tell me what exactly. She said she would be killed if she ever told anyone."

"And yet she sang it to the entire Pit? That would definitely get her killed. None of it makes sense."

I finished Jack's hair and put the coal away. My stomach was growling now, and I realized we were really late for breakfast.

"Your vest," Jack said. It seemed he had to remind me every morning.

I used one of the towels to make sure all the gas was off of the shell before I put it back on. I hated the heavy feel of it and wondered if there would ever come a day when I didn't have to wear it.

"Ready," I said putting my hat on and joining him at the door.

Jack started to open the door and then closed it again. He looked at me thoughtfully for a moment.

"Sunny, I know you think that with everything that's going on our personal lives aren't important... but I feel differently. The only thing keeping me together is being here with you at the end of every day."

I was surprised to hear him say that. But since he had said it, I knew exactly what he meant. He had become my source of strength. And living there in that apartment with him had become home.

"Me too."

He opened the door and held out his hand for mine. I took it, lacing my fingers between his. As we walked down the hall together toward the common room, I felt stronger than I ever had in my life.

CHAPTER TWENTY-NINE

The mood in the common room was sombre. It looked like most people had had a sleepless night. All conversation was about Crystal. Everyone was outraged that she had been dragged away simply for singing a song. I realized all along I had been hoping to see her there—silently praying that Malcolm West had just given her a slap on the hand and returned her to her parents.

"She's not here," Jack said, as if reading my thoughts.

"No, and I don't see her parents either."

David Chavez waved us to his table once we had collected our rations. He was sitting with a large group of people, his wife beside him.

"I hope you avoided the tear gas last night," I said to Terra.

"David took me home as soon as we realized Domers were coming down into the Pit. We were safe," she said, hugging her round tummy.

"It was barbaric," said a man sitting at the table. "They sent a small army of guards to drag that little girl away, and for what? Just because she was singing a song!"

"And we're not supposed to get upset about that?" someone else chimed in. "Of course we were mad. What did they expect?"

"They did expect it. That's why they sent so many guards to get her," Jack said.

All eyes at the table turned toward him, disgust written on many of their faces. I knew without a doubt that in the aftermath of what happened to Crystal, they were seeing Jack as a bourge again.

"Hate him if you want, but he does have valuable insight into the way the bourge work," I said. "We would be smart to listen to him."

"I agree with Sunny. He's done right by us so far," David said. "If it wasn't for him, there wouldn't be an Alliance."

"All right." One man at the table turned to Jack. "What do you know about it?" Malice laced his voice.

"I know that they underestimated your reaction when they took Crystal into custody, otherwise they would have sent more guards," Jack said. "Next time they will."

"Has anyone seen her today?" the woman on the other side of me asked. We all shook our heads. "Then they still have her... or they've killed her."

"They wouldn't kill her just for singing a song, would they?" I asked Jack, not sure I wanted to hear the answer.

"That song had enough impact to spark a riot, and I think we all know she wasn't just singing a song. She was urging all of you to go to war. That's treason."

Jack's words didn't surprise me, but I still didn't want to hear them. People were exchanging worried looks, and some were slamming their fists on the table in frustration.

Raine joined our table. Mica was standing behind him. "We need to save her then," Raine said. "She put herself on the line for all of us. We owe it to her."

"I agree," I said.

A murmur of approval went through the crowd. People who had been sitting elsewhere were now gravitating toward our table.

"We'll need a plan," Jack said. "First of all, we have to find out where she is. Does anyone know for sure if she came home last night or not?"

A young girl about Crystal's age spoke up. "I checked in on her this morning. She wasn't there. Her parents are devastated."

Jack nodded, acknowledging the girl. "Then we need to find out where they're holding her. I'll coordinate the Alliance guards to track down that information. Tonight we'll come up with a plan and get her back."

A man sitting at the table raised his hand. "I'll help!"

Soon there was a chorus of people wanting to help rescue Crystal. Seeing everyone come together — standing up for each other — was every bit as powerful as Crystal's song. I knew she would be happy to know the impact her music had had.

"Until then, let's not give them a reason to send any more Domers down here," Jack said. "Anyone starts a riot again and we'll be back on lockdown. We'll meet back here right after work."

"Everyone okay with a bourge calling the shots on this?" a woman from the crowd asked.

"I think it's time we started trusting him," someone else said.

I was relieved when I heard the crowd agree, even if most were reluctant.

"Thank you," Jack said. He pushed his chair back and stood up. Everyone followed suit. We all needed to get to work on time. I joined the queue of people filing out of the room, and Jack fell into step beside me.

"They still don't trust me."

"You have to see yourself through their eyes. It wasn't long ago we watched interviews with you and Leisel talking about the future of the Dome. One minute you're the presidential heir, the next you're promising to help them revolt against the current president. People are bound to question your loyalties."

"If they don't trust me, this rescue operation could go bad quickly."

"Not if it's just you and me doing the rescuing." Jack raised his eyebrow at me in question. "The fewer people involved, the better off we'll be."

"You're probably right," he said thoughtfully. When we came to the stairs he pulled me closer to him. I expected the mandatory kiss on my head, but it never came. I tilted my head back to look at him. "You trust me, don't you?" he asked.

"Yes, I trust you. And they're starting to trust you too. Don't give up."

"Don't worry, I'll never give up. I owe everyone down here at least that much." Before I could ask him what he meant, he pulled me against him and gave me a long kiss. He released me reluctantly. I watched him descend the stairs until he was out of sight, and then made my way up to the laundry room.

A guard was standing outside the door when I arrived. He gave me a nod that was almost imperceptible, and I knew he was an Alliance guard. The laundry room lights were on and the door was unlocked, so I went in. I was surprised to see a woman sitting behind the desk. She didn't look very old—maybe early twenties, which was young for a supervisor. I looked over at Crystal's station, hopeful that she might have made it to work, but there was no one at the sink. I was the first worker there.

The woman behind the desk pointed to the scanner. "Scan in."

I wasn't sure if I should give her a respectful greeting or not. Madi had never been partial to us talking to her unless we had been spoken to first. I had no idea what this woman was going to be like. I decided to err on the side of caution and stayed silent. I waved my hand across the scanner, and it beeped. I felt the familiar moment of relief when I saw the green light.

"Autumn Jones," the woman said thoughtfully. "I'm Supervisor Gina. I'll be working here now."

"Good morning, ma'am."

"What is it you do here?"

"I operate the washers and dryers and sort the clothes, ma'am." I respectfully turned my eyes to the floor. I didn't want to provoke another supervisor.

"We're going to be short-handed today. Do you think you can help out with hand washing?"

"Yes, ma'am."

I tried to hide the alarm I felt when she mentioned hand washing. She obviously knew Crystal wouldn't be in that day. I wondered what else she knew.

"Well, just go about your normal duties, and we'll see how the day progresses." She dismissed me.

I took a cart of dirty laundry on the way to my station and began sorting. A few minutes later, Di arrived. She scanned in and talked to Supervisor Gina. Once our new supervisor dismissed her, Di took a cart of dirty laundry and stopped to greet me on the way to her station.

"Good morning," she said cheerfully, motioning with her eyes at Gina. "So if this one turns out like the last one, we going to kill her too?" Di gave me a wink.

"Keep it down," I whispered. "Hopefully this one isn't like the last one." But if she were, I wouldn't hesitate to get rid of her. Life was so much better without the Madis of the world.

Di looked over at the two guards lounging against a wall talking. "There seem to be a few extra guards on today."

"I think they're with the Alliance. They might be trying to find out information on Crystal."

I saw Gina looking over at us, raising her eyebrows at our whispered chatter. I dropped my eyes to the laundry I was sorting and Di went to her station. More workers began to arrive and scan in. Everyone seemed uneasy with a new supervisor. Little wonder, considering how bad the last one had been.

I put my sorted loads in the washing machines and gathered up the hand washing to take to the sink. I wasn't sure what to do with them, so I decided to play dumb and just set them on the counter like I normally would if Crystal was there. I was walking away when Supervisor Gina stopped me.

"The girl who usually works there won't be in today," she said. "Do you know how to do the hand washing?"

"I've been shown once. I can try."

I returned to the sink and started filling it up with cold water. I remembered how achy my hands and arms had become when Crystal had showed me how to hand wash. I wasn't looking forward to having my hands in cold water all day, but on the bright side, I wouldn't suffer heat exhaustion. Supervisor Gina didn't leave. She stood there watching me. I felt uncomfortable in her presence. She seemed to be studying me.

"You're tall for a girl," she said matter-of-factly and then returned to her desk.

I wondered what she meant by her comment. Was it just an observation? Or did she suspect who I was? I hadn't forgotten about the bounty on my head. I knew supervisors didn't make much, so four hundred credits would be appealing.

My arms and hands were aching by the time I finished washing the few clothes I had. Di came over with a bundle, but offered to do her own when she saw how much pain I was in. I thanked her and let her. I didn't know how Crystal managed to do that all day.

As my first washer stopped, I sorted the clothes between hang-to-dry and spin dry. I was conscious of Gina frequently glancing up from her computer to look at me. I wondered why. I cast a sly look over at the two Alliance guards in the room. I knew a third one was right outside the door. If Domers did come down here to arrest me, how far would the Alliance guards go to help me? If they challenged the Domers outright, they would expose themselves as traitors and face execution as well. I wasn't sure I wanted that on my conscience.

I kept my head down and did my work, not wanting to draw any attention to myself. I knew there would be no escape from here if they came for me. I was relieved when the end of the workday finally arrived. My work was finished, and I could leave this room, which I now thought of as a trap.

"Be here bright and early again tomorrow, *Autumn*," Gina said as I scanned out.

I know I didn't imagine the emphasis on my name. Now I was positive she suspected that I wasn't Autumn Jones. But if she knew for sure I was Sunny O'Donnell, she would have reported me by now.

"Yes, ma'am," I said.

I opened the door and left the laundry room. I knew I couldn't come back.

CHAPTER THIRTY

I went directly to the common room after work hoping to find Jack there, but he wasn't. His climb up out of the mine was significantly longer than the few levels I had to descend to get there. I noticed Terra sitting alone eating, so I picked up my rations and sat with her.

"Oh, hi!" she said. "I've never seen you here this early before."

"For a change, I didn't have to work late tonight."

"I usually wait and eat with David, but I'm starving!"

A guard came into the room and turned on the television. The official presidential seal appeared on the screen. There hadn't been a speech from the president since he appealed to the people to find Jack and me.

Terra narrowed her eyes. "I wonder what that's all about."

"I don't know."

I wondered what it was all about too. Had Gina reported me? Was this going to be an appeal for someone to hand us over to Holt? Or maybe it was about the riot last night. I doubted it would be about Crystal. Malcolm West would handle her himself. It had to be about either the riot or Jack and me.

Jack came in with a few of the other miners and scanned the room. I waved to him. He nodded toward the screen, looking uneasy.

Terra's husband David was the first to join us, and others came toward our table with their food. A few of us got up and pushed tables together making more room. We were all leery of what the president had to say.

"What were you able to find out about Crystal today?" I asked Jack when he was sitting beside me. Everyone at the table quieted down at my question.

"She's with West in the most heavily guarded wing of the Dome."

"But you have a plan, right?" I asked.

"It's not an easy plan. First I need a couple of Domer uniforms."

A few people laughed out loud. "You're right, that isn't going to be easy," David said. "In fact, it's going to be impossible."

"Maybe not. If Sunny and I disguise ourselves as guards, we can get upstairs into the Dome. Once we're on the main floor, my computer will be back online, and I'll be able to get into the storage room where they keep the uniforms. As Domers, no one will question our presence on the tenth floor."

"Your plan sounds complicated," Raine said. I hadn't noticed him joining the table. My heart jumped a little when I saw Reyes beside him.

"We're here to help," Reyes said curtly, never taking his eyes off my face.

"I'm glad." I didn't want Reyes to be my enemy. I had enough of those.

"Good, because Raine and I plan on going with him to rescue Crystal. You stay here," Reyes said to me. I couldn't believe he was still barking orders at me after all I'd said to him. He would never change.

"Thank you for your concern, Reyes. Jack and I have it covered."

Reyes opened his mouth to respond to me, but Jack cut him off. "We appreciate both of you volunteering to help, but the fewer people involved in this, the better chance we have of succeeding."

He would have continued, but the national anthem began to play, heralding the president's address. The picture of the presidential seal turned into an image of Holt himself. Everyone in the room turned their attention to the screen.

"I bid everyone good evening," the president said in his usual manner. "Yesterday's riot was a most unfortunate event. I am told that no one was hurt or killed, for which I can only thank God. I truly believe that if not for His divine intervention, evil may have triumphed over good. And I know what that evil is! I know Jack Kenner and Sunset O'Donnell are hiding in the Pit. And I know Jack Kenner is spreading his filthy treasonous words and convincing the good people of the Pit to rebel against me. What surprises me is that people are listening to him. We were all appalled to hear Crystal Adams singing words of treason. A sweet, innocent girl corrupted by the words of a traitor!"

An Alliance guard came running into the room and headed straight to Jack.

"Domers in the Pit. Lots of them," he whispered urgently.

"How many?" Jack asked.

"At least twenty per level. They're heavily armed."

"To everyone living in the Pit, I ask you if you think you know Jack Kenner as I do—a conniving manipulator intent on destroying people's lives. Look at how he betrayed my daughter. Now he's using all of you to strike back at me. To cause dissention in our Dome!" Holt paused for a moment, his face reddening with anger. "I will *not tolerate treason!*" he yelled, coming to his feet behind the presidential desk. He pointed directly at the camera. "*You brought this on yourselves for listening to that evil traitor!*"

Jack moaned. "Oh dear God." He grabbed my head and pressed it into his chest. "Don't look," he yelled to everyone in the room.

I pushed my head away from Jack in time to see an image of Crystal. She was blindfolded and standing against a white stone wall. The blindfold was wet with tears and in an almost inaudible whisper I heard her singing her song. Then the unseen guns fired. I watched Crystal's body spasm as each bullet hit her and her body fell to the floor, almost in slow motion, out of sight of the camera.

Someone screamed, and then I realized it was me. Jack was holding either side of my face, looking at me with a wild expression.

"I won't ever let that happen to you! Do you hear me? *They will never do that to you!*" He had to yell above the din of the chaos that had erupted all around us.

I became vaguely aware that everyone in the room was on their feet. Some people were throwing their tables over in a fit of rage. The president's face came back on the screen, but few people were paying attention now. The crowd pulsed with fury.

The president continued his tirade, spittle running down one side of his chin. "Let this be a warning to anyone caught cooperating with Jack Kenner. I do not tolerate traitors, and I will kill every last one of you. I know where you are, Jack Kenner, and I'm coming for you."

I wanted to reach through the screen and beat Holt to death with my bare hands. How could such an evil being exist? How could he take such a sweet girl with the voice of an angel and kill her? He was the epitome of evil, and he had to be stopped.

Domers were coming into the room threatening to use tear gas, but instead of compliance they were met with fists and chairs being broken over their heads.

Jack released me and charged at one of the Domers. I stood up to join the fight, but stopped when I heard a moan somewhere beside me. I looked down to see Terra gripping her stomach. David's chair was empty. She was alone.

"I have to get you out of here," I said.

"When they shot her..." Terra began, but broke down in tears. "When they shot her, the shock was too great."

"I know." Tears streamed from my own eyes. I needed to get myself together.

I took Terra's arm and wrapped it around my neck and helped her stand up. Her pants were soaked. Her water had broken, and she was in labour. The room was in total chaos, and it would be a challenge to get to the door. I stayed close to the wall, putting myself between her and the fighting. A crowd had forced two Domers to the ground and was pummelling them with their fists and feet.

I reached the door and went out into the hall. It was just as chaotic as the room we had left. Terra was gripped by a contraction, and we had to stop. I was getting worried about them using tear gas again and wondered if I should take off my shirt now and put it over Terra's mouth, like Jack had done for me. But it looked like the Domers were losing. Holt had underestimated our reaction.

"Okay," Terra said when the contraction had stopped.

We resumed our trek down the hall, dodging falling bodies and fists that seemed to be flying everywhere.

Ahead of us, a chorus of screams went up, and I knew something was coming our way. I didn't have to wonder for very long. Soldiers were beating their way into the hall, and we were in their path. I looked behind me to find an alternative escape route, but the crowd was beginning to scatter with the approaching army, clogging the hallway.

"Flatten yourself to the wall," I said. We would have to make room for the soldiers and hope they passed us by without incident.

They marched past us followed by a group of Domers. We were almost in the clear when two of the Domers came walking back to us. My heart seemed to stop beating for a moment. Was it too much to wish that they just wanted to help a pregnant woman in distress?

"Give me your hand," one of them demanded. When I failed to follow his order, he took my hand. He waved a scanner across it. "Autumn Jones... aka Sunset O'Donnell. We got you."

My mouth dropped open in shock. How did they know? Then I remembered Gina. She must have reported me. They would have all the information about Autumn Jones, including the floor I lived on. They knew where to come looking for me.

The guards grabbed me by my arms, forcing me to let go of Terra. I gave her a terrified look.

"She needs help. She's in labour," I said.

"That doesn't concern us," one of them said, no trace of emotion in his voice.

I wrenched myself free of his grasp and threw a punch at the Domer in front of me, aiming for his exposed torso. Surprised by my assault, he bent forward as his breath left him with a groan. I was already bringing my knee up when the other guard grabbed me from behind and lifted me off the floor. I kicked my legs wildly in an attempt to get free, but the other guard took a baton from his belt and touched me with it. An electric jolt went through me, making me go limp. The guard holding my arms twisted them behind my back and secured my wrists with cuffs. They forced me down the hall and up the stairs.

There were still a lot of people on the stairs even though soldiers were using their fists and the butts of their rifles to beat them into submission. I heard someone scream my name, but I couldn't identify the source. I didn't think it was Jack. There was a commotion behind me, and a gunshot rang out. My entire body jerked in response to the reverberating sound. How many people would be shot today? How many would die?

They opened the door and marched me out of the Pit. As the door shut behind us, the sounds of gunfire and screaming were replaced with soft music piped in through the speaker system. The Dome was bright, and I had to shut my eyes against the glare. But the guards marched on, and I stumbled blindly with them. They stopped at the reception desk and scanned in.

The big steel door was opened, and we crossed the threshold into the Dome. I peeked out from my narrowed eyelids and looked around the room. It was a stark contrast to the battleground we had just left. A few people were lounging by the fire, drinks in hand and deep in conversation. Another person was curled up on a chair reading a book. All were oblivious to the war being fought right beneath their feet.

The guards dragged me to an elevator and marched me in when the doors opened. One of the guards pressed a button for the tenth floor. That was the presidential floor. Were they taking me straight to Holt? Maybe I wouldn't have to face a firing squad like Crystal. The image of her dying was permanently burned into my brain, and it terrified me. Maybe the president would kill me with his bare hands. I think that would be preferable to everyone watching me be executed.

The elevator doors opened, and they dragged me to the entrance with the Holt family name printed above it. I had been there before when Leisel had invited me to pretend to be her on her wedding day, so I knew this was where the president's living quarters were located. I wondered why they were taking me there instead of the president's office. Silently I prayed Summer wasn't going to be there. She wouldn't be very happy to see me die.

But the guards didn't take me to the president's suites. They stopped in front of Leisel's apartment. I forced my eyes to open wider and looked at their faces through their visors. Then I recognized one of them—Leisel's boyfriend Desmond. Why hadn't I recognized him before? He knocked on the door, and Leisel answered it.

"I brought you a present," he said, taking off his helmet. He gave her a big smile. Leisel almost jumped into his arms, knocking me out of the way.

"Oh, Dezzi, do you know how much I love you?" Leisel exclaimed, kissing him on the mouth.

"You better, considering all the things I do for you." He kissed her back.

"But this is the best thing!" Leisel removed herself from his embrace to take a look at me. "Well, well. The elusive Sunny O'Donnell. Get her inside."

The guards pulled me into the apartment and forced me down into a chair. She walked over to me and pulled the hat off my head. My hair spilled down around my shoulders.

"I recognize this. It's Jack's," she said, looking at the hat. Then she looked at my hair. "Black?" She curled a few strands around her finger and rubbed it. "It's coal! That's ingenious, Sunny. And have you put on weight or..." She felt my shoulders and chest. "You're still wearing that thing." She laughed at the bulletproof vest. "Well, you certainly are a master of disguise. I mean, even on my wedding day you were absolutely brilliant. No one suspected a thing."

She looked at me with laughter in her eyes. I realized she was every bit as deranged as her father. Maybe more.

"What? You have nothing to say for yourself?" she asked.

"What would I have to say to a conniving little bitch like you?"

"You might want to be a little nicer to your captor. I can do whatever I please with you."

"Do what you like. I'm dead anyway."

"Brave words." She laughed. "But if you don't willingly tell me where Jack is, let's just say you'll be begging me to kill you."

"I don't know where he is," I said, truthfully. At that precise moment, I didn't have a clue where Jack Kenner was.

"Really? Do you want to know how I found you?" Despite my disinterested expression, she continued. "I intercepted a tip from someone named Gina who was hoping to collect the reward. She said a tall girl by the name of Autumn Jones was working in laundry. I checked the name and found out Autumn and Benjamin Jones are living on the fourth level. So I sent Desmond to see if Autumn might be Sunny O'Donnell, and here you are. Now I'd like to know where your husband is."

"I don't know what you're talking about."

"I assume Benjamin Jones is Jack Kenner." She scrutinized my face to see my reaction. I averted my eyes from her gaze, afraid they might give away my emotions. "Or maybe you're living with that handsome boyfriend you told me about. What did you say his name was?"

"I didn't," I snapped.

"Oh, touchy subject. Here I thought you've been living happily ever after with Jack, but now I think maybe you weren't." I could almost see the wheels working in her head. "I'm sure Summer knows his name. I'll have a chat with her while I'm at my father's for dinner tonight. So here's the deal. You tell me where Jack is and I'll let your boyfriend live. You don't and I'll have him brought here and shot in the head in front of you."

Crystal's execution replayed in my head again, and hot tears stung my eyes at the thought of Reyes being killed in front of me. I knew she would do it, but there was no way I would tell her where Jack was. My only hope was that Summer wouldn't tell her Reyes's name. Given that Leisel was a master manipulator, I knew my hope was in vain. She could easily trick that information out of Summer.

"Change your mind yet?" Leisel asked. I remained silent. "I *will* get my way, Sunny. I want Jack so I can give my father the matching set. He'll be so proud of me. He might even make me president right there and then." She laughed with glee. "But now I have to meet him for dinner, so I'll be nice and give you a few hours to think about our little deal. When I come back, I'll have your boyfriend's name. The choice will be yours." She turned to Desmond. "Tie her up."

"Do you want me to stay and guard her?"

"Obviously! But stay inside the apartment. You'll arouse suspicion standing around outside."

Leisel watched Desmond tie me to a chair and pulled the rope to make sure it was secure. Then she gave him a passionate kiss and told him again how good he was to her.

I got the impression she was manipulating him, too.

Chapter Thirty-One

Desmond eyed me warily and then turned his back on me. He stripped off the rifle that was slung across his back and unsnapped his belt that held the tear gas canister and knives. He went into the kitchen for a glass of water and then took up residence on the sofa.

"It *seems* like Leisel really loves you," I said.

He glared at me. "Did I tell you to talk?"

"I was just making conversation. I mean, it's going to be a long night sitting here in silence."

"Well, if you want to talk so much, how about you tell me where Kenner is?"

"I really don't know. I've always been honest with Leisel. I don't know why she doesn't trust me now."

"She doesn't trust you because you're protecting Kenner."

"Why would I protect him? He's just another no-good bourge who thinks he's better than everyone else. The only reason I'm married to him is because Leisel tricked me into it."

Desmond narrowed his eyes. "Leisel thinks you two are hiding together."

"If he's down there, then someone else is hiding him." I hoped he would believe my lie.

He eyed the ball cap that sat on the table. "What are you doing with his hat then?"

"I took it from his closet before I left."

"Yeah, and I suppose you're the one who knocked out the guards assigned to his apartment. You're lying."

"Of course he was the one who took out the guards. I told him I would get him down to the Pit if he could get us out of there. And that's what I did. I got him to the Pit and said goodbye. I don't know if he stayed or if he left. But one thing I can tell you, bourge are not welcome down there. It wouldn't surprise me if he's up here somewhere." Lying was coming easier to me.

Desmond studied me for a moment. "I don't trust you."

"You don't trust *me*? You're in love with a woman who betrayed her fiancé and used me to do it. Don't forget, Jack Kenner thought she was in love with him, too."

"What's that supposed to mean?"

I shrugged. "Nothing. It's just that I can't help but think if she could do it to one man..." I let him finish my thought.

"Leisel is in love with me. She trusts me." He was almost yelling.

"I'm sure she does trust you." I forced my voice to stay calm. "You've been very useful to her. Did I say useful? I meant helpful. You've been very helpful."

He slammed his fist down on the arm of the sofa. "I think it's time for you to shut up."

I could tell by how angry he was that I should leave him alone. Now I just hoped the seeds of distrust I had planted would take root. If Desmond stopped working for Leisel, there would be no one to do her dirty work. No one to bother Reyes. The plan was weak, but I couldn't think of another.

After a few minutes of silence, Desmond got up and paced the room. He was obviously deep in thought. I had never manipulated anyone like that before and was surprised at how easy it was. Leisel was a good teacher.

I kept my gaze on the floor, glancing at Desmond every so often. The look of confusion and anger on his face told me that my plan was working. I wasn't sure how much time had passed, but I knew she would be back soon. Of course I had to keep in mind that Leisel really was the master of manipulation and she could easily calm all of his fears and have him wrapped around her finger again.

I nearly jumped when there was a sharp knock at the door. Desmond was immediately alert and went quickly to the door.

"Who is it?" he demanded.

"Leisel sent me to pick up the prisoner," said a male voice from the other side of the door.

Desmond gave me a sharp look. I gave him my best "I told you so" look. Angrily, he pulled open the door and was met by the butt end of a rifle smashing into his face. He dropped to the floor, obviously dazed by the blow. A Domer walked in, letting the door close behind him. I recognized Jack under the visor.

Desmond sprang to his feet and reached for Jack's rifle with both hands. The two men struggled, sending a vase crashing to the floor. The noise was so loud I braced myself for more guards to come running in, but none did. Jack had Desmond backed against a wall and used the rifle like a bar to pin him there. With his visor still on, Jack head-butted Desmond, smacking his head into the wall. A vacant expression came over Desmond's face, and Jack let him drop to the floor.

"Miss me?" Jack asked as he crossed the room and untied my binds.

"How did you find me?"

"I saw them take you. I recognized Leisel's pet." He motioned with his head in the direction of Desmond.

"How did you get in here?"

"Leisel has the cameras jammed again, and I'm beginning to suspect she owns the guards on this level.

SUNSET RISING   415

It explains why they disappear whenever she needs them gone."

"Did you find Terra?"

"She's fine. Or I think she is. She was giving birth when I left to come up here."

"Thank God!" I took a deep breath to steady my nerves. "Leisel will be back any minute."

"Then let's get out of here." Jack returned to Desmond and stripped the uniform off his limp body.

"Leisel is going to go after Reyes."

He handed me Desmond's uniform, and I put it on. It was too big for me, but with a few tucks and the added weight of the bulletproof vest, I could pass.

"What does she want with Reyes?"

"She wanted to know where you were, and I told her we went our separate ways after we escaped. But she knew that Autumn Jones has been living with someone and wanted to know who that someone was. When I wouldn't tell her, she guessed it might be my boyfriend that I told her about when we were drinking wine in your apartment that night."

"Does she know his name? What other information did you give her that night?"

"I didn't give her his name, but she's going to try and weasel it out of Summer. And I don't know what else I told her. I was drunk. I don't remember."

"Yeah, you were pretty drunk." Jack chuckled.

Once I had the uniform looking like it fit, I put the belt with the tear gas and knives around my waist. It was heavy, and I cinched it as tight as I could. It fell off.

"Leave it. Maybe no one will notice," Jack said.

I dropped it on the floor and slung the rifle across my back. The final piece of the uniform was the helmet, and I took a moment to tuck my hair up inside it. Jack opened the door, looked both ways, and then motioned for me to follow him.

It took every bit of my will power not to sprint down the hall and out of view of Leisel's apartment. I breathed a sigh of relief when we made it into the stairwell and closed the door silently behind us.

"We can't go back. She knows where we live," I said.

"I figured as much." He started down the stairs.

"Where are we going?"

"To the Pit."

"What's happening in the Pit right now? Are they still fighting?"

"It's on lockdown, although not many people went willingly to their homes. It's not pretty down there."

"Jack, we can't go back down there. We might start another riot if a guard recognizes us and tries to take us into custody. Everyone's been through enough with Crystal's execution." My voice was hoarse with emotion. I didn't want to start crying now, not while we were trying to escape Leisel. But regret for not coming to Crystal's rescue earlier plagued me. Why did we wait?

Jack stopped suddenly and walked back up the few steps separating us. He pulled me roughly into his arms.

"What happened to Crystal is *not* going to happen to you. I won't let it."

I could plainly see that her execution had affected Jack just as much it had me. If watching her die wasn't horrific enough, we both knew we were doomed to the same fate.

"Jack, you might not be able to stop it." I pulled away just far enough to look into his eyes. "But that doesn't make it your fault. If anything happens, you need to understand this was out of your control." A series of emotions played across his face until he hardened his lips into a straight line.

"I'll do everything I can. As long as we can get back down into the Pit we'll be okay for a few hours. David and Terra are waiting for us."

"We can't put them in that kind of danger."

"It's safe. Even if the guards run a routine check-in during the lockdown, no one is going to come in and search the apartment. There's no reason to."

I hesitated, but had little choice left for a place to hide. I followed him down the ten flights of stairs and out into the main lobby. We walked through the lobby as if we had every right to be there. No one questioned us. When we got to the door, a guard asked us to scan in. Jack kept going right past him, and I kept pace.

"No time. There's an emergency down there," Jack said gruffly and quickened his pace. Domers outranked guards assigned to the Pit and reception duty, so the guard didn't question Jack any further.

We strode through the doors to the Pit and descended the stone stairs. I could hear a distant hum of voices, and as we came closer to the first level, I made out hundreds of voices singing Crystal's song, just as they had the night before. The emotions bubbling up inside me threatened to cut off my breathing, but I fought back the tears and won.

I wished with all my heart I could just go back to our apartment, curl up beside Jack on our bed, and have a good cry. But we didn't have a home anymore. There was nowhere left to run.

As we passed each level, I saw at least three or four Domers still on duty. I guess with everyone singing about rebellion they weren't going to take any chances. I was relieved to see the army gone. I wondered how many people had lost their lives that day. How many more would follow. The fighting was so senseless. All we were asking was to be treated with respect, but they couldn't even grant us that.

Jack left the stairs on the fifth level, and I followed. I didn't see any Domers on this level, just guards from the Pit. Jack raised his visor and nodded to them. They were with the Alliance. He walked a short distance down the hall before he stopped at an apartment and knocked on the door. David opened it and motioned for us to come in. I was surprised to see Bron there, too.

"Are you okay, Sunny? Did she hurt you?" Bron asked as soon as David closed the door.

"No she didn't hurt me. But she might come looking for Reyes. She was going to try and use him to get information out of me. Hopefully, she leaves him alone now that I've escaped, but she might go after him if she thinks he knows where I am."

"We'll keep a close eye on him, although Reyes can look after himself. He's been doing very well in training," Bron said.

"How's Terra? Did she have the baby?"

"She and the baby are fine," David said with a smile. "They're in the bedroom if you want to say hello."

I walked over to the bedroom and peeked in. Terra was lying on the bed gazing down at the sleeping infant beside her. I knocked softly at the door, not wanting to wake the baby.

"Sunny!" Terra whispered excitedly. "I thought I heard your voice. Are you okay?"

"I'm fine. How are you?" I asked, coming into the room.

"I didn't know what to do when they took you. I wanted to help you, but I couldn't even stand up."

"I'm just relieved you didn't end up having the baby in the hallway. Jack told me that David was able to get you home in time."

"David was beside me a few seconds after the Domers took you, and then Jack was running after you. David took me straight home, but with all the fighting, he couldn't find a midwife and ended up helping me

himself. I don't know who was more scared, him or me."
She chuckled.

I looked down at the tiny little bundle. "The baby is
adorable. A little boy?"

"A girl."

"I know you wanted a boy," I said gently, hoping she
wasn't disappointed. But by the misty-eyed look of love
in her eyes, she wasn't.

"I'm going to name her Sunny, so she knows to fight
back if someone doesn't treat her right."

"I'm very flattered, Terra. She's beautiful." I wanted
to tell her that there were prettier names out there than
Sunny, but she seemed quite taken with her choice. And
I really was flattered. "You better get some rest. You
look exhausted."

I gave her a kiss on the cheek and gave the baby one
last look. Terra's eyes were already fluttering shut, so I
quietly left the room and joined the others.

"There were at least a hundred casualties today,
maybe more," Bron was saying when I came into the
room.

"That many?" I asked in shock.

"There were just as many on their side. Only ten
Domers made it out alive. A few guards were killed too,
although none were from the Alliance. The fight was as
good as over once the army showed up," Bron said.

"That was the first time I ever saw soldiers come into
the Pit," I said.

"It is the first time soldiers have ever been sent down here," Jack said. "And the message was loud and clear. This isn't a rebellion anymore. Holt's declared war." He was thoughtful for a moment before he continued. "There was something... orchestrated about it all, though. I understand why he sent Domers down here before the execution, but he had the army ready to go. It doesn't make sense. If Holt publicly executed her as a fear tactic, then obviously the outcome he expected was obedience from the Pit. But he had the army ready to go, which tells me he anticipated a confrontation. Was he deliberately trying to provoke a fight?"

Bron shook her head. "That wouldn't make sense, sir. The Pit is too valuable. A war would destroy it."

"I know. That's why something doesn't feel right," said Jack thoughtfully.

"Crystal's song," I said. "'The Pit they want to blow.'"

David looked stunned. "She did say that in her song. What are they up to?"

"I don't know," Jack said, dragging a hand through his hair. "And I don't know if we have enough time left to find out." He gave me an apologetic look.

I went to him and put my arms around his waist. He pulled me close against him and held me there tightly. We were running out of places to hide and by now Leisel knew Jack had rescued me. She was probably convincing her father to start a door-to-door search for us in the Pit. But I doubted we would be any safer in the Dome. Our chips wouldn't work anymore, and there was no place to hide there anyway. The Dome was only so big.

And then it came to me.

"I know where we can go," I said to Jack. "Outside."

"What?" he asked in disbelief.

"Just hear me out. No one's been out there in almost three hundred years—maybe it's safe. You and I could find out. And if it is safe, then we come back and let everyone out. It solves everything."

"But I know Holt's been sending out drones for years and everything has come back radioactive. It's not safe out there," Jack said.

"Well, I think we know Holt isn't the most trustworthy person in the Dome. What if he's been lying?"

"Why would he lie about that?"

"I don't know. Why does he want to blow up the Pit?"

"It would solve everything," David said. "It's what our people have been praying for since we were first cast down here."

"He's right. We've always known it's our only salvation," I said.

Jack shook his head. "I know I can get us out, Sunny, but I don't think I can get us back in."

"We'll find a way. We always have. Sometimes you just need a starting point."

Jack pulled me back toward him and rested his forehead against mine. I could tell he was struggling with my proposal.

"I don't know if I can watch you die of radiation poisoning any more than I want to see you in front of a firing squad," he whispered to me.

"If it's just me you're worried about, then you should know I'd rather die trying to save my people than waiting here to get a bullet in the head," I whispered back.

I pushed his head back to look in his eyes. They were wet with tears, and I dried them with my fingertips. For once I didn't feel like crying. I knew my decision was right.

"Then we'll go," Jack said.

"Sir, it's suicide," Bron said.

"Staying inside the Dome is suicide," I said. "Maybe outside we have a chance."

"How will you get back in?"

"I don't know, Bron," Jack said. Then he smiled at me. "But what I do know is that every plan Sunny has ever come up with has worked. I don't know how. She never thinks things through. But they work out. If there's a way to get back in, she'll find it. This is just one more adventure she's going to take me on."

"And we should get started on our adventure before we're caught," I said. "Leisel probably has a search party out for us by now."

"I have my computer, and if there's any way I can find a signal out there to let you know what we've found, I'll send you a message," Jack told Bron. Then he looked at David. "In the meantime, you two take control of the Alliance, and keep everyone down here as calm as you can. Continue the training, but no more riots. I don't trust Holt, and he can annihilate everyone in the Pit just by turning off the ventilation system, so don't give him a reason. There are some powerful families in the Dome that will stand up for the Pit, but if everyone is down here cruising for a fight and causing trouble, you'll lose their support. Just keep training and be ready to go in case the news from outside is good."

"I'll try my best," David said. "But everyone here is just so angry. It's going to be hard to keep them under control."

"We'll train harder with them. Let them work out their frustrations that way," Bron said. "How much time should we give you?" she asked Jack.

"I honestly don't know. It could take a day or a week to figure out if we have radiation poisoning or not, then find a way back into the Dome... I guess if you haven't heard from us in a month or two, odds are you won't."

"A month is a long time," David said, looking disheartened.

"Just don't give up hope. Even if you never hear from us again, don't give up," I said.

"We better go," Jack said, nudging me toward the door.

"Take care of yourselves," Bron said, looking a little misty eyed. "Your mom would be proud of you, Sunny."

I gave them both a hug before we slipped out of the apartment and back into the hall. The same guards were on duty, and they nodded in our direction as we passed.

Then we began the climb up the stairs that would lead us to the Dome. I tried not to think about the fact that I might never come back there again. It was the only home I had ever known.

"Hey, are you two on your way to the Dome?" a Domer called out to us as we passed the third level.

A pile of six or seven dead bodies was on the landing beside the stairs. I averted my eyes, sickened by the consequences of this battle.

"Yes, we are," Jack said.

"Can you ask them to send down more help? These guys have been dragging bodies for about two hours now. If there wasn't a lockdown, I'd make the urchins clean up their own damn mess!"

"I'm on it," Jack said, and we continued on our way.

We reached the main level without any further incident. I wasn't sure where we were going, so I blindly followed Jack. A guard waved us toward the scanner as we approached the doors into the Dome. Jack waved his hand across the scanner, and it beeped green. Without much choice, I followed his lead, and my scan worked, too. Leisel must not have flagged my Autumn Jones chip. We went through the doors and back into the Dome.

He went up to the second level, back to the storage room where we had changed our chips before. He gave a sharp knock at the door. No one answered. We went in.

"Maybe this will give us a little more time again," he said, taking the box of chips off the shelf.

"We should have done this before we went down into the Pit. I thought we were going to get caught when we had to scan in."

"I didn't think Leisel would cancel our chips because she's trying to catch us. She'll be waiting for us to scan in somewhere. Now she'll know the last place we scanned in was coming into the Dome. She won't have to do a search in the Pit."

"I hadn't thought of that."

Jack extracted the chip from my hand. I took the Spritze device from him and took his chip out. He picked up a new chip, popped it into his computer, and started tapping away.

"What would you like your name to be?" he asked.

"Crystal." I wanted to be named after a hero.

He took the chip out of his computer and implanted it in my hand. Then he put another chip in. "Who should I be? How about Ted, after my brother." He typed on his computer again, and then it was his turn to get a new chip.

"Crystal Malloy and Ted Anderson. I gave myself a pretty high-ranking last name in case I need to use the power."

"We're not married this time?" I asked, disappointed.

"No, we're Domers this time. Now I just need to get the message out to the Alliance that we're headed outside and Bron and David are in charge."

I waited for Jack to finish sending the message. I was trying not to think about the fact that we were going outside. My stomach was starting to tie itself into little knots.

"Done," Jack said. "Before we go, there's someplace I'd like to take you. I have it all set up if you say yes." He held up his computer.

"But shouldn't we go before we're caught?"

"It's important to me."

I smiled. "Then how can I say no?"

CHAPTER THIRTY-TWO

H e opened the door and we strode out of the storage room, easily blending in to the light traffic in the hallway. I wasn't sure what time it was, but it was getting late. It would soon be lights out in the Pit.

Jack led me through a maze of hallways until we came to another set of doors with two Domers guarding the entrance. He gave them a nod, and we strolled through. This section was different. Most of the doors we passed had windows in them, and I could see what looked like laboratories. A few of the rooms even had caged animals.

"What is this?" I whispered.

"It's the 'bio' part of the Dome."

I only saw a few people in the labs, and they were too engrossed in their work to notice a couple of Domers walking by. At the end of the hall was another set of doors that were also under guard. Jack walked toward the two Domers and waved his hand over the scanner. I did the same.

"Enjoy your evening," one of the Domers said.

Jack pushed open the doors, and we entered a small chamber. We had to scan in one more time, and then the main doors opened.

My breath caught in my throat as we entered. I had never seen anything like it. Hundreds of huge trees loomed up before us, and the ground was covered in thick foliage. I could hear animals and birds everywhere. I took off my helmet to get a better view. The light was a lot brighter than I was used to and I almost put my visor back on, but I wanted to feel the warm, moist air against my skin. My nose was assaulted by scents I had never smelled before. Sweet scents mixed with earthier notes.

"What is it?" I asked in wonder.

"A rainforest," Jack said. He took off his helmet, his eyes never leaving my face.

"Thank you." I never thought I would get to see anything like this in my lifetime.

He smiled. "I thought you might like it. I remember the stack of my nature magazines you went through."

"I knew you were mad about that." I shouldn't have touched them.

"Well, not mad. Annoyed maybe..." He smirked. "Come on. I'll show you around."

"Are all the bourge allowed to come here whenever they want?" He seemed to know his way around, and yet I had never even heard of the place.

"No!" He laughed. "No one other than the scientists and guards are permitted in here. It's too important to the ecosystem of the Dome to allow it to be damaged in any way."

"Why? What is it for?"

"A lot of thought went into building this Dome long before the bombs were ever launched. Because the inside of the Dome is sealed off from the outside world, it needs to make its own atmosphere, which isn't easy. So the scientists who designed it had to think about the earth's own processes and try to duplicate them, right down to the water and carbon cycles in order to create an atmosphere in here. The only way they could do that was to grow nature inside. So they built a rainforest, an ocean, and a boreal forest. There's also a prairie with a freshwater lake that's used to farm meat and grow vegetables. The rainforest produces fruits and vegetables, and the ocean provides fish. There are a lot of animals in here too as a way to restock the earth once we can leave the Dome."

I was amazed. "An ocean, too?" He nodded. "If only Domers and scientists are allowed in here, how did you come to know it so well?"

He patted the computer in his pocket. "Because I know how to get in and out without being caught. Ted and I used to come here all the time and hide in the foliage whenever the guards walked by. We loved this place. I used to fantasize about bringing the girl of my dreams here." He blushed.

"So I take it you never brought Leisel here."

"No! That would have ruined this place for me."

We were strolling along a footpath, but he stopped for a moment and pointed to something in a tree. I looked and saw some type of monkey. It was small and reddish in color.

"I think it's called a tamarind," Jack said. "There are a few monkeys in here that like to throw their poop at you, so stay away from them."

I looked around nervously. "How will I know which ones they are?"

He gave me a confused look. "They'll be the ones throwing poop at you!" I laughed. "Don't worry. I'll protect you if we come across any."

"My hero." I tucked my hand into the crook of his arm. He seemed pleased. "I have noticed that we're the only two guards in here. Where is everyone?"

"After I made our new identities, I scheduled us to guard the rainforest for the night shift. I cancelled the two that were supposed to be here. I assume they'll just get sent home when they show up for work. It's late, so there's no scheduler on duty to check with."

"You always think of everything, don't you?"

"I told you before, that's how every Kenner is raised." He gave me an admonishing expression as if my forgetting that detail was unforgivable. Then he smiled.

"Come on. I want to show you the ocean before the lights go off."

We followed along a well-worn footpath through the forest, taking care not to trample any foliage. There was an occasional rustle in the bushes, which startled me, but I quickly got used to it. I felt like all my senses were coming alive there. I wanted to see, smell, and touch everything.

"Is it just me, or is it getting darker in here?" I asked. My eyes were no longer feeling so light sensitive. Everything seemed dimmer.

"They simulate the sun going down and the moon coming up."

The foliage became less dense as we travelled the path, and I noticed the soil was fading away and being replaced by white sand. The trees weren't as tall, and fruit grew on some of them. We broke out of the forest into a clearing, and there it was. The ocean.

"It's beautiful!" I said breathlessly. I felt strands of my hair lifting away from my face. "Is that wind?"

"The air current is generated when the warm air of the rainforest mixes with the cool water of the ocean," Jack said.

"What kind of fish is in the water?"

"Tons of different fish and coral reefs, which provide the Dome with food. But it's the algae that are the most important feature of the ocean, since it contributes to our oxygen supply. The enclosure itself is made of thick Plexiglas. It's really ingenious when you think about it."

I had never seen an ocean for real — only in books and movies. And this one looked real enough to me. It was massive. Waves lapped against a sandy beach, and crabs popped up out of the sand. Birds flew above, diving occasionally to come up with fish in their beaks. It was the most beautiful place I had ever seen.

As we stood drinking in the beauty of the ocean, a dimmer, bluish light was quickly replacing the bright light of the sun.

"Is that the moon?"

"A fake moon, but beautiful anyway."

"A beautiful ending to a horrible day. Thank you for bringing me here." I gave him a sincere look. "I'm sorry you didn't get the chance to share it with the girl of your dreams."

He smiled at me. "I did. Why do you think it was so important for me to bring you here?"

My heart caught in my throat when I realized he was talking about me. He raised a hand to brush the hair away from my eyes and then cupped my face in his hands. His kiss was slow and gentle, and I wrapped my arms around him, pressing myself against him. But the bulletproof vest prevented us from making any real contact. I cursed it silently.

"You're the most amazing woman I've ever met, Sunny O'Donnell," Jack whispered in my ear. I laughed and pushed away from him in order to see his face.

"You can say that after everything I've dragged you through?" I asked in disbelief. "If it wasn't for me, you would probably be married to Leisel right now and training to be the next president."

"Married to Leisel?" He grimaced. "Way to kill the mood, Sunny." He pushed away from me playfully.

I caught his hand in mine. "Seriously, Jack." I gave him a sobering look. "When I allowed myself to go along with Leisel's plan, I ruined your life. And I need you to know how sorry I am for doing that. You would've been a good president, and all this fighting could have been avoided."

Jacked studied our entwined hands. His brows drew together, and he frowned. "I wouldn't have made a good president. My only agenda was the same as my family's — restore democracy. I didn't have any plans for the Pit." He raised his eyes away from our hands and looked into my eyes. "My whole world was up here, in this Dome, sealed away from the Pit. The most consideration I ever showed the people down there was to advise the president to stop decreasing rations and concentrate more on decreasing the population through stricter controls. Do you believe that?" He shook his head and chuckled bitterly. "For most of us up here, the Pit is just a place where our coal comes from, where our sewage is treated, where our laundry is cleaned."

My heart sank with every word he spoke. Why was he saying those things? The Jack Kenner I had come to know wasn't like that. I dropped his hand. He looked at me apologetically.

"My time down there with you was... a revelation. My view of the Pit — god, my view of the Dome — has changed so much. I'm a better person for having you in my life. Don't ever apologize for that."

"So you never wanted to help us?"

"Not before I met you. You changed me. The Pit changed me. Listening to the children sing in the common room changed me. And Crystal's sacrifice…" He shook his head sadly. "When I was growing up, my parents told me there were monsters down in the Pit. They always threatened to send my brother and me down there if we didn't behave. Their threat always worked because we believed in the monsters. It wasn't until I was living there with you that I found out the monsters were us." He rubbed a hand across his eyes. "I just want to be honest with you, Sunny. You putting on that wedding dress was the best thing that ever happened to me. It was the best thing that ever happened to the Pit. Don't be sorry."

I remembered when Jack had asked me if I believed in fate, and now I saw why. If we had never gotten married things would never have changed in the Pit. I didn't like what he was saying, but I did appreciate his honesty.

He picked up my hand and stroked my palm with his thumb. "Don't hate me."

I looked into his eyes. "I don't hate you. I'm glad you're being honest with me." I didn't want to lose Jack. We needed each other now more than ever. "But if you felt that way about the Pit, why did you come with me? I mean, once we escaped from your apartment you could have found someone to hide you."

"One reason was that I didn't think Holt would look for me there right away, and I was right. And another reason was... I wanted to see where you would take me." He smiled shyly.

I looked at him in surprise. Jack *wanted* to be with me?

"Don't look so shocked. Do you know how hot you looked in that green dress?!"

"That tacky green dress? Ugh!" I closed my eyes at the memory. It was the most hideous thing I had ever worn.

He chuckled at my discomfort. "I didn't say it was a tasteful dress. It left little to the imagination, and I think every man in the room stopped to look at you when you walked in. I was glad to get you out of there. But I didn't really notice you until the next day. You were wearing my bathrobe, all the makeup washed from your face, looking so young, innocent, and beautiful. And then you told me you were willing to risk your own life to save your people. Something inside me just clicked, and I knew I had met the girl of my dreams."

I stroked his face. "That's the most beautiful thing anyone has ever said to me. I wish I could tell you I liked you then, but I didn't. I really wanted to scratch your eyes out at one point."

"I know, and that was part of your allure. Every other woman in the Dome wanted to sleep with the next president, but not you. You wanted to kill me."

I laughed. He was right. "To be honest, I struggled to stay with Reyes when I went home even though I knew

I couldn't offer him a future. I just felt like I owed him. And then when we broke up I felt so… *relieved*. I felt free. And I let myself look at you in a different way."

"So you *do* have feelings for me?" he asked cautiously.

I was happy that we were finally being honest with each other, but I felt self-conscious talking about my feelings so freely. "Of course. I don't go around kissing just anybody, you know."

"And now that you're married, you better not start." Jack pulled me to him and kissed me again. Any awkwardness I had been feeling melted away as his kiss became deeper. I wrapped myself around him, wanting to get closer. Everything about him was suddenly intoxicating.

"Damn vest!" he muttered.

I was about to offer to take the vest off when a hot, piercing pain exploded into my side. I opened my mouth to scream, but nothing came out. I couldn't catch my breath.

Jack looked at me in surprise. "Sunny?"

I heard another bullet whip past our head.

My rifle was still slung across my back, and Jack reached behind me, aimed it, and pulled the trigger. The gun fired, jolting me against him. I heard a thud somewhere behind me. He picked me up and ran for the forest.

"Can you breathe?" he whispered. My breath was starting to return, but I was still gasping. "Where did it hit?" He set me down and pulled at my shirt.

I grabbed his arm and sucked in a breath. "It hit the vest."

Jack nodded. "There's another shooter. Stay out of sight."

I was actually able to breathe, though my back screamed with each breath I took. I ducked my head when I heard another shot.

"We have to move!" Jack whispered, pulling me up with him. He had his rifle in one hand and took aim at the area the shot had come from.

"I'm okay," I said, ignoring the pain.

We moved farther away from the beach and into lusher foliage. I listened intently for any sounds. The animals had become eerily quiet, so it wasn't difficult to hear the twig snapping about twenty feet away from us. I looked in the direction of the sound and clearly saw a Domer moving through the forest with his rifle raised. If only I knew how to use the rifle I carried, I would have shot him. Instead, I tapped Jack on the arm and pointed. He peered into the dark forest and shrugged. I pointed again, not wanting to talk or make any sound. How he could he not see him? Jack looked again, but still didn't see him. The guard was now a scant ten feet from us and still advancing. Jack finally saw him, took aim, and pulled the trigger. The guard dropped.

I heard the doors to the rainforest opening, followed by the sound of footfalls coming into the room. I didn't know if they were here for us, or just responding to all the gunfire. Jack motioned for me to follow him. We stayed low, keeping to the bushes and away from the footpaths. We didn't travel far before we came up against a stone wall.

Farther along the wall I could see the shadow of a doorway. I pulled Jack in that direction, and he shook his head. I pointed to the door. He looked, but I could tell he couldn't see the shadow. I wondered how he could be so blind when the moonlight was so bright in here. I firmly took him by the hand and pulled him toward the door. Reluctantly he followed.

There was a scanning device on the door itself. I was about to wave my hand in front of it when Jack grabbed it and shook his head. He took out his computer and tapped away on the screen, which seemed to take forever. I could hear footsteps getting closer to us. I looked for any figures coming through the darkness, but didn't see anything yet. Finally, the door unlocked.

We went through and silently closed the door behind us. We were in another section of the bio-dome. This section was a lot more open than the rainforest we had just left. There were a few trees and bushes, but no dense foliage to hide in. I could see several corrals with animals in them. Some of the animals were becoming restless with our arrival. I wondered if this was the prairie section Jack had told me about earlier.

We moved into the room, using the corrals as cover. The animals really didn't like our presence. The horses were the first to start whinnying, moving about their enclosure as if to get away from us. I didn't like being here at all.

"Someone there?" a Domer called out. Of course this section would be guarded, too.

Jack grabbed my hand, and we ran from behind the horse enclosure to the cows. They weren't any happier to see us. The guard on duty was alerted and used his communicator to call his partner for backup. I desperately looked around for another door and found one on the opposite side from where we were hiding. I pointed it out to Jack. Not surprisingly, he couldn't see it. I took him by the hand and headed in that direction. With each enclosure we left we had to run and hide behind another one. We were more than halfway across the room when one of the guards saw us. A shot rang out, and we dove behind a pigpen. I heard them running toward us. Jack took out his computer and tapped on the screen.

"Run," he said in a low voice once he had the door unlocked.

We both stood up and made a run for the door. The guards stopped running in order to take aim and shoot at us. We ducked as low as we could, still running at full speed to make it to the door. A bullet whizzed by my head so close I felt my hair move. I resisted the urge to panic and kept going.

I heard more Domers filing into the room, and they shouted for us to stop. We didn't. Jack was the first to reach the door, and he yanked it wide open for me to run through. We shut it quickly, and he reprogrammed the lock.

"That should hold them for a while," he said.

We were standing in some kind of utility room. The door leading out wasn't locked, so we just went through. We were presented with three different hallways to choose from: left, right, or straight ahead. Jack pulled up a map of the Dome on his computer and figured out where we were. He went left, and I followed. We had just reached the end of the hall and were going through a door when I heard the utility room door burst open and guards come pouring out. Jack quickened his pace, and I kept up. He was following the map he had in his palm. I wondered where in the Dome we could run and not be found. We were out of places to hide.

He led me through a maze of hallways and doors, and it seemed to me that this part of the Dome was dirty and smelled bad. We finally turned down a dead-end hall dominated by a huge steel door.

"Where are we?" I whispered, afraid of giving our position away.

"Garbage chute. This is how we get out. It's one way."

Jack began to do his magic on his computer, and I kept glancing nervously over my shoulder, expecting an army of Domers to come crashing down on us at any second. I decided that if that happened, I would make them shoot me right there, right then. I wasn't going to allow my death to be put on display as some kind of fear-mongering tactic by a crazy president.

I breathed a sigh of relief when I heard the garbage chute door open. It didn't open out toward us like the steel doors at the reception area of the Dome. This door retracted into the left side of the doorway. It was the thickest metal door I had ever seen.

"Not the nicest way to leave the Dome, but any other exit we take will set off an alarm," Jack said.

We walked in together. A lot of garbage already filled the room. Most of it was mining debris, but there were barrels of chemical waste, among other things. I was thankful there was nothing organic rotting in here, otherwise the smell would be unbearable. All organics in the Dome were composted and used again. Jack tapped on his computer again, and the huge steel door closed, sealing us inside. It was so dark once the door shut that even I couldn't see. Jack illuminated his computer and used it like a flashlight.

He touched my back, and I flinched in pain. "Ouch!"

"Those vests are good for stopping bullets from ripping through you, but they still leave their mark. You were lucky you were wearing it."

"So this leads outside?" I asked.

Jack nodded.

"Is there air from outside in here now?" I asked hesitantly. I wondered if I was already breathing in toxic air.

"No. I'll show you." Still using the light from his tablet, he took my hand and led me to the back wall. "This is another door reinforced with lead that divides this chamber from an outer one. The floor we're standing on is actually a conveyer belt. When it's activated, this door opens, the garbage from this room is advanced into the next chamber, and the door closes. The weight of the garbage triggers a high-powered air current to turn on, an outer door opens, and the conveyer belt dumps the garbage outside. The air current is used to prevent air from outside coming into the chamber, so it doesn't shut off until the outer door is sealed shut again. Then a ventilator comes on and sucks out any poisonous air that may have come into the room. The ventilator runs for at least twelve hours to ensure there is no radiation before the next load of garbage is moved forward. You can hear the hum of it now."

"So if the ventilator is on, that means garbage has been dumped within the last twelve hours?"

"Yes. It won't activate again until it's done the twelve-hour cycle," Jack said, raking a hand through his hair. I noticed almost all of the coal was gone. "You sure you want to do this?"

"I'm sure." I lied. I was scared to death. Even the thought that I could be breathing poisonous air right then was terrifying to me.

"We're both exhausted. We should try and get some rest. We'll need all our strength soon," Jack said.

He led me to a corner of the dump and pulled me down beside him. I laid my head on his shoulder, positioning myself so nothing touched my bruised back. He wrapped his arms around me and held me against him.

It felt good to rest.

It felt safe in his arms.

CHAPTER THIRTY-THREE

The sound of a door opening and the floor moving startled me awake.

"Jack!" I screamed.

I felt his whole body jerk awake beside me. I tried to stand, but the moving floor was throwing me off balance. I took hold of a nearby barrel and pulled myself up.

"Take my hand!" I said.

He pulled himself up, and then gripped the barrel tight with both hands. The conveyer belt was far from being a smooth ride. It jerked and lurched and threw us both off balance more than once.

We passed through into the next chamber.

"This is it," he yelled over the din of the machinery. "There's no turning back."

He took my arm and tried to hold it. I didn't want to get separated from him so I clutched at his hand.

"Don't let go!" I wanted to be brave, but I could feel the panic rising up.

The conveyor belt took us farther into the next chamber, and the ride got rougher. The barrel we were using for support fell over and rolled on the floor. Without its support, we both lost our balance and fell, too.

"Stay down. I'll crawl to you," Jack yelled, but another barrel came rolling at him, and he had to dive out of the way. We were getting farther apart.

I got to my hands and knees and tried crawling toward him, but the pitching of the floor kept throwing me from side to side. The more we advanced into the next chamber, the more vibration rattled the floor.

I heard the sound of the steel door shutting behind us. In a few seconds we would be completely cut off from the Dome. My whole body started to shake with fear. When the door shut, the floor stopped moving. Jack got up and ran to me.

"Are you hurt?" he asked.

I shook my head. I couldn't find my voice. The terror had stolen it.

The high-powered air current Jack had told me about clicked on, and he held my hands as tight as he could. The force of the current was so strong it pushed us along with the garbage in the direction of the door. The big steel door that led to the outside world started opening up.

Jack and I clung to each other.

"Still think this was a good idea?" he screamed over the hum of the machinery.

I grasped the lapels of his uniform and hung on tightly, but we were sharply torn apart by the conveyor belt jerking back to life. I tried to make my way back to him, but between the conveyor belt and the air current, that was impossible. The doors were halfway open now, and the brilliant light beaming into the room struck me. My eyes rolled up into the back of my head.

The conveyor belt continued to move me forward, but I was blind. I had no idea when I would be dumped out into the waiting world.

I think I screamed for Jack. I didn't even know if he was still in the room or outside already. I heard garbage thud and clunk as it hit the ground, and then I was falling. It must have been only for a second or two, but it felt like an eternity before my body touched down on something. The pain from the bruise on my left side was excruciating, and I bit down on my lip.

I forced my eyes open, but I could only keep them open long enough to catch glimpses of the world around me. I didn't see Jack. I screamed his name again, but the noise from the high-powered fan was too loud for me to hear even my own voice. Did he make it? Was he alive?

"Sunny!" I heard Jack yelling when the doors finally shut and the sound was gone. He was close by.

"I'm here!" I heard him making his way toward me.

"Are you okay?" he asked, feeling my arms and legs. "Did you break anything?"

"I'm fine. I just can't open my eyes. The light is so strong."

"I know. The sun is strong for me, too. Do you believe it? We're seeing the sun!"

"Well, if I could open my eyes I could see it. It feels warm on my skin," I said in wonder.

"I'll get you off this slag heap and into some shade. That might help. Put your hands on my shoulders and follow in my footsteps."

The terrain of the mound was jagged and unstable, and our progress was slow. As we worked our way through the heap, we discovered the sun's rays weren't just bright, they were hot, too. We finally reached the edge of the mound, and I opened my eyes long enough to catch a glimpse below.

I think I saw trees, which didn't make any sense. We were always taught that the nuclear winter had destroyed every bit of life on earth. I opened my eyes again and peeked at the ground. It was a long way down.

"This should be easy for someone who's used to climbing a dark and scary mineshaft," Jack said.

"But I could see in the mineshaft. I'm blind right now."

"I was blind in the shaft, and you made me do it." He tugged at my hands, pulling me closer to the back of him. "Just hang on to me and follow my every move."

I clung to him as we began our descent. The sides of the heap were even more unstable than the top, and every step we took had us sliding a few feet. Then the slag weakened at one point, and we slid a good fifteen feet. I forced my eyes open, bearing the pain of the sun on my eyes. I lost my grip on Jack, and he ended up sliding farther down the mound than I did.

"Just slide down to me," Jack said.

I did as he instructed and found it a lot easier than trying to walk. After that, I opened my eyes more frequently, scared I might miss a step and send myself careening off the man-made hill. It seemed to take forever, but finally we reached the bottom.

"Not far now," Jack said. He took my hand and led me into some trees. "Try opening your eyes."

I did, and the shade provided some relief from the glaring sun, but my eyes were still extremely sensitive.

"Are we in the woods?" I asked in amazement.

"We are." Jack was smiling. "This isn't what I expected at all."

"I thought everything on earth died with the nuclear winter, but… " My voice trailed off as I looked in wonder at the world around me.

Trees taller than I could imagine were bursting with green leaves. I looked up at their canopies through narrowed eyes, trying to tolerate the pain of the bright sun. I caught glimpses of blue sky and white fluffy clouds floating past. A breeze blew against my face, bringing with it the foreign smells of earth and water.

A screech that almost sounded human startled both of us, but when I found the source of the noise I saw a bird sitting in a tree looking at us curiously.

"A bird," I said in astonishment.

Jack offered his hand to me. "Let's go explore."

"First I want to take this uniform off. I'm so hot." We both stripped down to our clothes, and then I turned my back to him and took off the vest.

"That is a nasty bruise," Jack said when he saw my naked back. "Does it hurt to breathe?"

"I'm getting used to it. I don't think I broke any ribs." I let the vest fall. It hit the ground with a thud. "I'll never put that on again." I pulled on my t-shirt.

"I won't argue," he said, letting his eyes rove up and down my body. "At least while we're out here. But when we go back inside, it goes back on."

He gathered up the uniforms and the vest and stashed them in the base of a tree.

I looked back from where we'd come. The huge mound of garbage that had accumulated over the past two hundred and eighty-three years was the only eyesore in what was otherwise paradise. I turned my back on the ugly mound and focused on the beauty of the woods.

"It's amazing! I never thought I would ever see this."

Jack breathed in deeply. "The air is so different out here. It's so much... richer."

I knew what he meant, and it wasn't just the different smells. The air itself was almost inebriating. Breathing it in made me feel more alive, like all of my senses were suddenly put into overdrive.

"Is it just me or can I hear better?" I asked.

"I know what you mean. It's as if my ears just opened up. Sounds are so much sharper out here."

I forced my eyes to open wider and took in the sight around me. Every detail of the forest came into focus: shadowy areas dappled in sunlight, some areas dense while others were open. Then I realized the open area was a path, not unlike the footpaths we had followed in the rainforest.

"Come on," I said to Jack excitedly.

The path was narrow, and we had to walk in single file. I could see depressions in the soil, and I knew I was looking at animal tracks. Animal tracks! Things were living out here. But it didn't make sense. Radiation was toxic, which was the whole reason why we all lived in the safety of the Dome. But this paradise didn't seem like a place that would kill us. It was warm and welcoming.

"I wonder what kind of animals made these tracks," Jack said.

"I don't know, but a few of them are huge." I pointed to one large print that was surrounded by claw marks.

Jack gripped his rifle a little tighter. "Hopefully we don't meet up with it."

"Maybe it's friendly."

He didn't look convinced.

I heard a distant trickling that sounded a lot like running water, and as we followed the path it became louder. We came upon a stream of water rushing past us in a hurry to get to the bottom of the mountain.

"A river!" I exclaimed.

I looked upstream and saw an animal drinking from it. It was a small and gentle- looking creature. I tapped Jack on the shoulder and pointed, not wanting to scare the animal away. He looked in astonishment.

Slowly he moved toward the river's edge, careful not to startle the animal. He bent down, scooped water into his hand, and drank it. "It tastes fine."

I tried some myself. It tasted sweet and refreshing. Better than the water we had in the Pit.

We both stood up, smiling at each other. I threw my arms around him, laughing at our discovery. The earth was fine!

"You know what this means?" I asked, hugging him close.

"We can save them."

"We have to find a way back. We might even be able to get everyone out by tonight!" My mind whirled with the possibility of setting everyone free.

"Slow down," Jack said gently. "Finding a way back in isn't going to be easy. The Dome is a fortress."

"What does that mean?"

"It means the Dome was built to be impenetrable. I told you getting back in was going to be a problem."

"Can't we go back in the way we came out?" But even I knew that was going to be impossible.

"Not even you could climb up against that air current with debris falling down on you." He gave me a dry look. "I have maps of the Dome on my computer, and I'll study them to find a weak point. In the meantime, my military survival training has taught me that our first order of business should be to find food, water, and shelter. Water we've found. Shelter is next."

"Can't we explore first?"

"We can explore while we look for shelter. I don't know what time of day it is, but I don't think it's in sync with the Dome."

We walked along the edge of the meandering river and saw several more animals along its shore. I was surprised by the amount of wildlife there was considering I had been taught to believe everything out here was dead. I couldn't believe we had been living inside the Dome all this time when we could have been out here, free.

"Head down that path," Jack said from behind me. "There are too many animals by the river to make camp here."

I saw a path leading away from the river and followed it. As we walked through the forest, the sound of rushing water became fainter, and once again we could hear birds cawing and whistling at each other. Large rocks jutted out of the ground in places, speckled with bits of foliage growing in their crevices. It looked like something out of a movie.

"Wait," Jack said. Something in the tone of his voice put me on edge. He bent down to examine something on the ground. "Look at this."

I went back to take a look and saw long tracks dug deep into the ground. My eyes followed the length of the track, and I realized it stretched far behind us and far in front of us. It was one long continuous track.

"What are they?" I asked. The tracks didn't belong to an animal.

"They're tire tracks."

Then we heard it—the low hum of a motor coming closer to us. I was about to suggest we hide when something came crashing through the forest and stopped in front of us. It was a man dressed in tattered clothes, his eyes looking at us wildly.

"Don't just stand there!" he screamed. "*RUN!*"

END OF BOOK ONE

A note from the author, S.M. McEachern:

If you enjoyed reading *Sunset Rising*, you may be interested in reading the Satellite Stories I am creating to go along with the series. Satellites are short stories designed to give the reader greater insight into areas of the story that the main character, Sunny, cannot see. They are an accompaniment to the series, but not a necessity. They're just for fun! My first Satellite will be posted on February 1, 2013. For updates, you can follow me on Twitter:

Blog: http://smmceachern.wordpress.com

Twitter: https://twitter.com/smmceachern

Facebook: https://www.facebook.com/S.M.McEachernAuthor

To see what others are saying about *Sunset Rising*, or to leave your own thoughts, please visit *Sunset Rising* on **Goodreads or Amazon**. I always love hearing from readers!

Made in the USA
Charleston, SC
02 May 2016